green and pleasant land.

'I absolutely devoured this book . . . It was **tender, challenging and as warm as it was razor-sharp**'
BETH O'LEARY

'Malik was another of last year's standout discoveries for me . . . this novel constructs a **sublimely witty and touching** story' JONATHAN COE

'This wonderful novel will **make you laugh, make you cry** *and* **leave a mark on you long after you've finished reading it**' SARAH SHAFFI

'This **wise, warm-hearted** novel deserves to be shared by reading groups across the cities and shires'
THE SUNDAY TIMES

'A **gorgeous, fun**ny, smart, uplifting story about seeking unity during tim... ...escribe it to the country' ...HANAN

'Witty, **insightful,** and shot through with pathos . . . for me it's **the standout book of the year**'

ABIR MUKHERJEE

'*This Green and Pleasant Land* is a **clever and thoughtful** novel about identity and belonging . . . **the perfect novel for these Brexit-y times**'

RED

'A **witty meditation** on race politics [and] **what it means to be British . . . Satirical, controversial, knowing and essential**'

VASEEM KHAN

'An inquiry into faith, identity and **the meaning of home**'

GUARDIAN

'Simmers with **tenderness, charm** and **warmth** . . . a gorgeous, **deeply relevant** book that is bound to ruffle a fair few feathers, but the right feathers, and for the right reasons'

CAROLINE O'DONOGHUE

'A **prescient** novel in our uncertain Brexit times'

COSMOPOLITAN

'Overflowing with **warmth, humour** and sharp-eyed observation'

RUTH WARE

'A novel that **touches our capacity for human sympathy** and connection in important ways'

THE TIMES

This
green
and
pleasant
land

Ayisha Malik is a writer and editor, living in South London. She holds a BA in English Literature and a First Class MA in Creative Writing. Her novels *Sofia Khan is Not Obliged* and *The Other Half of Happiness*, starring 'the Muslim Bridget Jones', were met with great critical acclaim, and *Sofia Khan is Not Obliged* was chosen as 2019's Cityread's book. Ayisha was a WHSmith Fresh Talent Pick, shortlisted for the Asian Women of Achievement Award and *Marie Claire's* Future Shapers Awards. Ayisha is also the ghost writer for *The Great British Bake Off* winner, Nadiya Hussain.

🐦 @Ayisha_Malik
www.AyishaMalik.com

This
green *and*
pleasant
land.

ayisha malik

ZAFFRE

First published in Great Britain in 2019
This paperback edition published in 2020 by
ZAFFRE
80-81 Wimpole St, London W1G 9RE

A CIP catalogue record for this book is
available from the British Library.

Paperback ISBN: 978-1-785-76450-9
Hardback ISBN: 978-1-785-76754-8
Trade Paperback ISBN: 978-1-785-76752-4

Also available as an ebook

1 3 5 7 9 10 8 6 4 2

Typeset by Palimpsest Book Production Limited, Falkirk, Stirlingshire

Printed and bound in Great Britain by Clays Ltd, Elcograf S.p.A.

Zaffre is an imprint of Bonnier Books UK
www.bonnierbooks.co.uk

For my babies, Zayyan and Saffah Adam
I hope the house of God lives in your heart
wherever you go

And for my great friend, Clara Nelson, who creates a
community no matter where she is.

. . . would you be able to understand your fellow countrymen if a majority of them – in order to assert their own rights – were one day to dispossess you?

Questionnaire, *Max Frisch*

prologue

SAKEENA HASHAM HAD THE ability to linger in a person's psyche like a vaguely traumatic experience. For sixty-three years she'd been the rare combination of practicality and hopefulness, reality and dreams. Her dreams, unfortunately, hadn't quite worked out. Real life had cast shadows over the rainbows she'd wanted to chase when she first left Rawalpindi, Pakistan, for Birmingham all those years ago.

Now, she was lying in the ultimate shadow of death. She clutched her son, Bilal's, hand with her own slight and withered one, squinting at him before raising her hand to his face.

'Beta,' she said. Her boy was in her home, once more, enclosed within the patterned walls, treading the green carpet she'd had for too many years. 'Maybe grow a beard?' she whispered hopefully.

He took a deep breath, pursed his lips and nodded.

Bilal looked too polished for this place. His wife, Mariam, sitting in the chair in the corner, clearly knew it, the way her sharp eyes darted around, taking in the surroundings. *Well, to hell with her!* What did Mariam know about struggle and sacrifice? What did even Bilal know?

Rukhsana sat on her other side, wiping the tears from her eyes with her dupatta, and Sakeena wished, amongst many other things, that her younger sister wouldn't give way to her tears so often.

'Bilal has forgotten everything I taught him,' whispered Sakeena to Rukhsana. 'Who wears a suit to visit their dying mother?'

Rukhsana burst into sobs.

'You will look after your khala?' said Sakeena to Bilal. 'The way I have looked after her?'

Bilal swallowed hard and glanced at his wife. 'Yes, Ammi. Of course.'

Next was the tricky part, but since when did trickiness bother Sakeena? She was about to give her son the task she knew would bring him back to the most important thing in life: faith. It was ridiculous the way he'd abandoned everything about it when he moved to that absurd village, Babbel's End, eight years ago. He'd been determined to open up an accountancy firm. As if numbers were more important than God. Well, he might be successful now, but still. What a decision! Didn't he think about the significance of living in a place that hinted at the end of something? She was no fatalist but even she had her limits.

She sighed inwardly – Bilal never did think about the important things like symbolism. To think she had cultivated forty years of her life with her son in this multi-coloured city. For *him*! She'd not have him be the only brown face for miles: as conspicuous as he was invisible. And she wasn't illiberal – she'd made sure from the beginning that Bilal had a mix of friends, unlike other children who were encouraged to 'keep to their kind'. No, she made cucumber sandwiches for his white friends and jerk chicken for the black ones. If he'd brought any Chinese or Japanese friends home then she'd have made noodles or sushi, or whatever it was they ate. She had noticed Bilal's cheeks redden at her culturally presumptive ways, but she was his mother – she knew what he needed, even when he didn't.

When her husband had left her in the first year of their marriage she knew she would have to make sense of things on her own; to *understand*. Understanding, her local imam had told her, was the key to everything. Especially the afterlife. Which was puzzling because how could you understand something you'd never experienced?

Sakeena stared at her son with a hint of wonder. 'Who are you?' she asked finally.

Bilal looked stricken and glanced at Mariam again as if *she* would have the answer.

'Ammi,' said Mariam, stepping forward to hold her dying mother in-law's hands. 'He's your son. Remember?'

Sakeena waved at her as if swatting a fly. Then, strad-
dling life and death, Sakeena's vision became clouded by
a black fuzz instead of the light she'd always anticipated.

'Listen to me,' she said urgently.

Bilal's head jerked and she noticed his eyes settle on
her locked cabinet. She found salvation in faith; her son
found it in the medicine cabinet.

'Remember the grave,' she said.

'She's not making sense,' said Bilal, looking at Mariam.

He'd had that look when she'd first dug a grave-shaped
hole in her backyard and then proceeded to lie in it every
night. 'How can you really live if you don't think of dying?'
she had told him then.

She'd steeled herself against the sense of claustrophobia,
imagining the dirt being thrown over her, the inevitability
of leaving things – leaving Bilal – behind, and how in
death nothing would matter but the good she might have
done in her life.

'Ammi,' Bilal had said, looking at her lying in the
ground. 'You could contemplate death without being six
feet under. This isn't method dying.'

Hain? There was no method to dying. But she could
concede that it was the penultimate act. *Understanding.*
It could skip oceans and bloodlines.

'Listen to me,' she said now, bringing herself back to
the present, holding Bilal's hand with all the strength she
could muster. His hand felt so powerful in that moment
she was heartbroken that she would never feel it again.

This was the final hour we were all, one day, heading

towards. Except she was catapulting and, quite frankly, it was making her sick. Namely because no-one was catapulting with her. She felt a pang of regret that she hadn't lived in a way contrary to death.

How had all these years passed her by?

She had so much to say about so many things. Now that it was her last chance, why weren't these thoughts manifesting into words?

She glimpsed the faint outline of what could be a dark figure, looming in the doorway. This wasn't the time to panic. Death was, quite literally, at her door and there was one last job she had as Bilal's mother. She'd even forsake the time it took to say the first *kalima* prayer when dying. Because, yes, death is solitary but life shouldn't be, because Bilal's life wasn't just his own – it was everyone's he came in contact with. If he didn't know who *he* was then how would others *really* know him? *Understand* him?

'What have we done here?' she said.

Bilal leaned forward, a frown creasing his brow. If he would just lean in a little further, she could kiss the high forehead that had always given him a perpetual look of surprise. Sakeena blinked back the shadows only to have her vision hindered by spots of white light. She gripped Bilal's arm, no longer able to see her baby boy properly.

'Who will know and understand that we're meant to make life better for each other?'

'Ammi,' said Bilal. 'It's okay, I'm here. Don't panic.'

His voice broke and she was relieved to see there were tears in his eyes. Perhaps he regretted not coming back home sooner? Maybe he was sorry that their last game of backgammon was probably over three years ago? Perhaps, watching her slip away, he'd understand why she'd chosen to lie in her own grave.

'Build them a mosque, beta. Build them a mosque,' she said.

'Get the doctor, Mariam,' Bilal said. 'Quick.'

Mariam rushed out of the room.

'*Ya Allah*,' came Rukhsana's voice, who muttered prayers under her breath, blowing them over Sakeena.

Bilal looked at his khala, agitated. 'Can't that wait?'

'Show these people our Islam,' Sakeena continued, urgently.

'Sshh,' he urged, tears now falling freely down his face.

She hadn't loved life in the way she'd seen others love it, she had simply made the most of what she had, but in this moment, looking at her son, she didn't want to leave it.

'This isn't the time to shush,' she said, her heart cracking, along with her voice. 'This is the time to *speak*. You must guide yourself to goodness, beta. And everyone around you. Like those Christian missionaries,' she said.

'Missionaries?' he replied, bewildered.

She reached up to Bilal's face, the boy for whom she could forsake saying the *kalima* because she'd die the way she'd lived: doing what was best for him.

'Babbel's End,' she said, unable to hide the contempt from her voice – remembering the village green and rolling hills, the bustling main street with its cobbled pavements and Victorian lamp posts, its two churches (how excessive!), the way the sun would glisten on the water as all those white, white people walked their dogs on the pebbled beach nearby in their wellies and big coats. What kind of people went to the beach in the middle of winter? Then she imagined a minaret, soaring in the midst of all of this, the call to prayer drowning out the noise of all the barking dogs, and the idea brought her that ever elusive sense of contentment (which, to Sakeena's mind, was superior to happiness). She smiled, a tear in her eye, thinking of how sad endings could be but also of the hope you could leave behind.

'Babbel's End . . .' she repeated, harnessing her last breath, 'is your Africa.'

And she was gone.

'*Inna lilla hai wa inna ilayhi raji'un,*' muttered Khala Rukhsana under her breath.

We belong to God and to God we shall return.

〰

So, Bilal was left with his guilt and grief, and the Arabic prayer his mum had been unable to say was on his lips for the first time since he could remember.

〰

Because when something dies, you never know what else is coming to life.

SIX MONTHS LATER . . .

chapter one

'SO, JENNY WILL EMAIL about the latrine in the lay-by, and Pankhurst, you'll keep a tally of the cheese factory lorries driving up and down our roads,' said Shelley Hawking with a deep sigh. 'Make no difference to our village, indeed. Two years they've accosted us with their incessant noise.'

There was a grumble of assent around the village hall. Bilal loosened his Paul Smith tie, undoing the top button of his now-damp white shirt. He looked around to see if there were any more windows they could open. The unusually hot August day, after three days of non-stop rain, was made only more oppressive by the length of the parish council meeting's agenda. It almost made him impatient.

Harry Marsh flicked Bilal's arm with the agenda, which

he'd put to use by fanning himself. 'Armageddon,' he whispered with a grin.

'We've all agreed to Sunny Hill School's bake sale and a participant's fee for each pub quiz to raise more money to fix St Swithun's church bell, yes? We've only £2,376 to go to meet our £10,000 target,' added Shelley briskly.

More assent.

'And we'll promise to adhere to the speed limits on *all* roads?' she said, her eyes settling on Bilal, who looked away, rubbing his chest, his nausea making an appearance. 'Until the next meeting then. Copperthwaite will follow up to confirm everyone's duties.'

George Copperthwaite grunted from the councillors' table, his bald head looking particularly shiny, his Ascot tie (pale grey and maroon today), tucked into a white shirt under his houndstooth jacket. Shelley sat next to him, Jenny Ponsonby on the other side – the presiding council over the community. Jenny's features and manners, Bilal had always observed, were as kempt as her sweat glands – even in the blistering sun she never seemed to need to wipe her brow.

'You'll be put in the stocks next time you go over the speed limit,' said Harry to Bilal as they scraped back their plastic chairs and people began to disperse.

Harry had left London several years ago to bring up his family here in the green and peaceful West Plimpington countryside, and so was in the enviable position of having lived a life big enough to make fun of the village's trivial preoccupations, while ignoring how much he benefited from them.

'It's the new car,' replied Bilal in an excited whisper. They walked on to Skiffle Road, the moon visible before the sun had begun to set. 'Incredible engine.'

'It's a thing of beauty. Meanwhile, the wife thinks we've got a poltergeist.'

Bilal paused. 'Why?'

'The blueberries were moved from the kitchen counter.'

'Right,' replied Bilal.

'I mean, they were right there, *on the counter* – but when we came back home they were in the fridge.'

'Cleaner?'

'She doesn't come on Wednesdays.'

'Hmmm.' Even now, years after moving to the village, the absurdity of its trials didn't cease to surprise Bilal. 'Well, don't tell Mariam or Haaris won't be allowed to come over and play with Sam.'

'Bill,' came Shelley's unmistakable voice.

'And I'm off,' said Harry, jumping into his silver Land Rover.

'Glad I caught up with you,' said Shelley. 'Have you spoken with Richard? I've left him several messages about Tom's bush. I was hoping he'd come to the meeting.'

'Sorry,' said Bilal, shuffling on his feet. His nausea was always heightened by conversation with Shelley. 'Haven't seen him this week. I'll pass on the message if I do.'

Bilal unlocked his car door as Shelley looked at the shiny black Lexus with delicately laced disapproval. Her eyes tended to linger on things – and the activity had lent itself to deeper crows' feet than Shelley would've liked

– a natural by-product of having been a headmistress for thirty years. She pressed her clipboard to her chest.

'You've been very quiet at these meetings lately.'

'Oh . . . well.'

Bilal felt a lump in his throat so unexpected he wondered if he'd swallowed a fly. Shelley paused as people walked past, waving their goodbyes.

'It was hard for me too, when my mother died,' she said quietly.

'Yes. I'm sorry,' said Bilal.

'It was a long time ago now, but I understand. Hers was cancer too . . . just not quite as sudden. It's a horrid thing.'

For a moment they both paused, united in their mutual and timeless grief.

'Thanks,' he said as he got into the car.

He'd have to remind himself to be more gracious about Shelley.

'Drive sensibly,' she added with another one of her looks. 'And careful of that pothole in Rayner's Lane – it is a lot deeper than it looks.'

Bilal started the engine and knew he'd have to go into town for Gaviscon. Shelley was right. Bilal had been quiet. If he were honest he was offended, on death's behalf, at the way life seemed to march on, trampling on thoughts of his dead mother. The way it had only given him a mere few weeks to understand what was going on. That it was the end for her – no going back, no changing things. And now the minutiae of living in the face of mortality had triggered his ulcer. He waved at John Pankhurst, who was passing him in the opposite direction and slowed down, rolling down the window of his grey Fiat.

'My turnips have only gone and got club root,' he said, his mouth barely visible beneath his ever-growing grey moustache.

'Ah, yes, my mum always used lime for that,' replied Bilal.

'That's the one. Thanks, Bill,' said Pankhurst as he drove off.

His mum and her love for gardening . . . When he'd looked at her on the day of her funeral, he'd suddenly felt as if, in life, he had understood nothing at all. For six months now he'd been involved in a desperate attempt to forget the remnants of her death: grief, regret, too much Tupperware and her dying bequest.

Build them a mosque.

Of all the things in the world.

Since her death he'd donated a lot of money to their local mosque in Birmingham. Wasn't that almost the same thing? He'd even sponsored a child in Uganda. It was clear that his mum didn't know what she'd been talking about. Babbel's End was certainly *not* Africa. On a mission or not, Bilal wasn't here to colonise anyone. It would be a dreadful business not to have moved on from that kind of thing. Taking over things, after all, was incredibly impolite. But his mother's dying wish kept coming back to him after every cycle of his own reasoning, beginning again at the point of his guilt.

Bilal focused on the road ahead, his hands gripping the steering wheel in case reality slipped away from him. He drove past the now quiet village green with its post office, Mr J's Bookshop – owned by Jenny's husband, James – and Babbel's Bric-a-Brac, which sold everything from old maps and atlases to compositions of wax flowers in glass domes. He glanced at the Life Art gallery, which always struck him as ironic, given there was never much life in there. Rounding the corner past the eighteenth-century coaching inn, The Pig and the Ox, with its multi-coloured flower baskets hanging outside, he followed Coowood Lane (past Tom's overgrown bush), and sped up as he met the A-road. It was the tall pine trees that lined the route, blocking the light and leading on to the wide road that made Babbel's End feel like the type of place you discovered in the back of a magical cupboard: other-worldly but of the world, giving it an air of mystery. Though Babbel's End was not waiting to be discovered. It had always been a proud introvert.

It was a twenty-minute drive into Titchester. Under the fluorescent lights of the only Spar in town he loaded his basket with the necessary stomach medication, along with paracetemol and superglue for Haaris's school project. Bilal picked up some sugar-free biscuits for Mariam and looked at them for a moment. In the grand scheme of things would it really matter if, for once, his wife decided to have normal, sugar-laden biscuits? An anxiety opened up in his chest, filtering into his stomach, as he thought about her ex-husband, Saif, who was suddenly so interested in being a proper father to Haaris. Bilal took a deep breath, took an Ativan out of his pocket and swallowed it without water. If the spirit that had lived inside his mum had disappeared, then who was to say that what existed on the outside couldn't vanish too? Was the pain in his chest, the nausea, real? Was he sick? Or was it just a figment of his imagination? Each crisis seemed to balloon with every product that he scanned at the self-service checkout.

Bilal got back into his car and sped home, weary of his own company. He opened the front door to see Mariam in black leggings and a white vest-top, walking down the stairs with her laptop.

'Sorry,' he said, raising the bag and walking in, shoes clicking against the walnut flooring. 'Had to go into town.'

Mariam walked into the second living room and set her laptop on the table, taking a seat on their plush ivory sofa.

'What were you doing?' he asked.

'Hmm? Nothing,' she replied, avoiding his gaze.

He decided there was no use asking any further questions. 'Got your sugar-free biscuits.'

'Oh, thanks. I'd run out.'

'I know.'

He bent down and kissed her on the head.

'How was the meeting?' she asked.

He gave her the details as she looked at him now and again, distracted by the laptop's screen.

'Are you working?' he asked.

'That's why I'm sitting at my laptop.'

'Haaris asleep?'

He watched Mariam's eyes flicker to the clock on her laptop screen. *No, he's sitting at the table with us*, he imagined her thinking.

'Right,' replied Bilal to her absent words.

Mariam's eyebrows were knit in concentration as she must've been poring over her every word, ready to file her story about the village spring clean, or whatever her latest topic was for the *West Plimpington Gazette*. Bilal was no stranger to the feeling of discomfort, but it was only exacerbated when he watched his wife work. He took personal responsibility for Mariam moving from reporting local government corruption in Birmingham to writing notes on a badger cull in Babbel's End, and other freelance jobs that weren't challenging his wife's intellect. Fulfilment – and the lack of it – for his family was just another thing on his conscience.

After ten years of marriage, Mariam had changed very little. She was petite, her straight, silky hair was still short enough to not give her any pause to style it. He used to love running his fingers through it. It was all part and parcel of her no-nonsense demeanour, complemented by the perpetual crease in her brow. To some it might've looked severe but to Bilal it was inquisitive: ready to question rather than judge because of the sympathetic way her eyelids drooped. But then who could account for perception? In all three of Bilal's prior relationships there weren't many emotional conversations he was subjected to which weren't followed by a trip to his local pharmacy. But his wife was the epitome of self-sufficiency, just like his mother had been. Except his mother would also sing in the kitchen, hear an old Bollywood song and make her son dance with her. Khala Rukhsana would look on and laugh at them, shaking her head, and then toddle off to the kitchen to make them all snacks, which she'd end up eating herself. Bilal was overcome with the kind of desperate fondness for his mum that one could only feel for someone they'd never see again. It was swiftly followed by an overwhelming feeling of his mediocrity as a son. His mother had been an extraordinary woman, trapped in an ordinary life. What Bilal hadn't bargained for was the way in which his wife's self-sufficiency had lately given way to his own feeling of redundancy. A feeling that had bubbled to the surface, along with her ex.

He slapped his legs and got up, refusing to give in to paranoia. Mariam's eyes continued to flicker over the laptop screen.

'Tea?' he asked.

'No, thanks.'

He cleared his throat. 'It's muggy out.'

Mariam sighed and leaned back on the sofa. 'Do you want to have a conversation?'

He looked at her.

'Because we can have one and get it over with so I can finish my piece, or you can wait until I'm done and then tell me whatever you'd like to tell me.'

Bilal was just about to venture into explaining these feelings – the inconsequence of it all – when the phone rang.

'Hello?' he said into the receiver.

There was a lot of noise in the background. The uniquely loud Punjabi kind.

'Hello?' he repeated.

'Haan! Beta!'

He moved the phone away from his ear.

'Beta?'

'Yes, hello?'

'Bilal, beta?'

'Yes, this is he.'

'Who?'

'Bilal.'

More hubbub in the background.

'*Aho*. Bilal, *hega*,' shouted the lady on the phone, ostensibly, to another lady.

'Who is this?'

'Auntie Shagufta.'

Oh, God.

'Ah, Auntie.'

'You remember me then? Hmmm?'

'Of course.'

She was the one with the borderline blonde hair, not the one with the walking stick.

'*Of course*, beta? You have forgotten how to speak Punjabi?'

She laughed. So did Bilal, albeit nervously.

'No, no, Auntie. Well, yes. It seems I have.'

'Hain?'

'Yes, Auntie, I've forgotten.'

He looked around to see Mariam mouthing: 'who is it?'

He put his hand over the speaker. 'Auntie Shagufta.'

Mariam took a deep breath.

'Your Khala Rukhsana has taken a very bad fall, beta. Very bad.'

'Oh, gosh. Is she okay? What happened?'

Auntie Shagufta cleared her throat. 'Beta, we cannot look after her every day, na. Not like this. You must come and take her and keep her for a while.'

Mariam walked up to Bilal, folding her arms and looking up at him with her signature scrutiny.

A woman in the background spoke in Punjabi: 'Tell him she cannot walk properly. She cannot move. She has very bad kismet.'

'She has bad kismet,' Auntie Shagufta related.

Bilal wasn't sure what his khala's poor kismet had to do with him. Mariam took the phone. It was just as well; Mariam always seemed to have more answers than Bilal. Though probably because she often raised the questions.

'Salam, Auntie. What happened? Oh, God. Poor thing. How is she?'

Mariam slipped into speaking Punjabi far too easily for a woman who looked so *un-Punjabi*. Bilal felt proud of his wife. She was a woman of layers and she made him more interesting as a result of it.

'*Acha,*' she said. '*Aho.*'

Mariam glanced at Bilal, still speaking in Punjabi. 'She'd be so lonely here. We're hardly home.'

She made a face, as if she couldn't think of a better

excuse, and for a moment they were united in their desperation to keep Khala Rukhsana away. Bilal tried to assuage his annoyance. He was sure he loved his khala in a blood-is-important kind of way, but she'd ambled on the periphery of his childhood memories – a woman his mum had to take into account when making decisions rather than helping towards them.

'*Acha?*' said Mariam, still looking at Bilal. 'But . . . hmm. Yes. No, it's just that . . . right. Okay. I understand.'

She put the phone down.

'What happened?' he said.

'It's as if we pushed Khala down the stairs ourselves.'

'Well?'

'There was nothing for it,' replied Mariam, folding her arms.

'Oh, God.'

'I know,' Mariam said, getting back to her laptop. 'We'll have to manage somehow. She'll probably end up staying a few weeks—'

'Weeks!'

Mariam looked him steadily in the eye. 'Maybe this way you'll stop feeling guilty about not actually looking after her—'

'I look after her,' interjected Bilal.

'I don't think a monthly stipend is what your mum had in mind.'

Of course he'd asked Khala Rukhsana to come and stay with them after his mum's funeral, but when she refused, he didn't ask twice – that would be badgering, surely?

'There were a lot of things my mum had in mind,' he said.

'That's true.'

'A *mosque*,' he said finally. 'Can you imagine what the neighbours would say?' he mumbled. 'I drove five miles over the speed limit and Shelley's been on to me like a hawk. True to her name.'

Mariam paused. 'As a social experiment it'd be pretty interesting, though.'

'This is the problem with all religious people,' said Bilal. 'They're so obsessive.'

His mum's request somehow felt preachy, manipulative, clinging on to him like burned plastic on skin. There should be a legal ban on deathbed requests. But then the memory of her singing and dancing came to him. There was no understanding some people.

'You can't say she didn't have ambitions for you,' replied Mariam. 'The height of success for my mum was me marrying the man she told me to when I was eighteen. Now look at me, divorced and re-married to a man who can't even speak Punjabi.'

'Why can't they all just speak English? They did choose to come here.'

Mariam gave him a small smile and shook her head. 'Tory.'

'I'm just not quite myself in Punjabi,' added Bilal.

'Well, *exactly*.' She looked at him pointedly. 'Anyway, since my mum's dead too, you needn't worry about it.'

Mariam's bluntness still made Bilal flinch.

'Spoken to your dad lately?' he asked.

'No. He's too busy shagging his third wife, probably. I lose count. After every trip to Pakistan he brings back a new one.'

'You know what I say?'

'Yes, yes,' replied Mariam. '"At least he stuck around to watch you grow up."'

'It's true.'

Bilal sat down opposite her on the ivory egg chair. Maybe the perpetual crease in Mariam's brow wasn't her being inquisitive (or judgemental), maybe it was just a product of her childhood – her fatalistic mum and wayward dad, etching their life's mistakes on her face.

'The thing is,' he finally said, 'I feel that Mum was right.'

'About my dad being a no-hope philanderer?'

'No. Well, that too unfortunately,' he replied, as Mariam gave a small laugh. Bilal smiled. 'But I mean, about *life*.'

Mariam creased her brows again.

'When we . . . ' he cleared his throat. 'You know . . . *die*. What will we have left behind?'

He thought of his dying mother on her bed, the deep-set wrinkles in her skin, the hazy blue around her pupils – he was becoming too familiar with this ache in his heart.

'What did Mum leave behind?'

Mariam looked at Bilal for a moment then down at her laptop again. 'Khala Rukhsana, that's what. If she's coming then I'll need to get the cleaner in to sort the room before I drive into town . . . Oh, since you're going to Birmingham, we can stock up on halal meat. Saves me driving an hour for it. She does eat meat, doesn't she? Does she prefer chicken or lamb? You should call her and arrange a time to collect her tomorrow.'

'Tomorrow?'

'When else?' said Mariam. 'That's the problem with you – by the time you've thought things through and decided to actually do them, someone's either over it, or dead.'

He bristled.

'Sorry,' she said. 'You know what I mean.'

He wasn't entirely sure he did.

That night Bilal went to bed and waited for his sleeping pills to kick in, so he didn't hear Mariam come into the room. If he'd been awake he'd have felt her gently kiss his forehead, whispering 'sorry' in his ear. The way she so often did when she knew he couldn't hear.

chapter two

BILAL DROVE THROUGH THE familiar urban streets of Selly Oak, Birmingham, past the park where he got into his first fist fight (he lost), behind Cherry Oak school where he tried to smoke a cigarette (he threw up), and saw there was now a Homebase in the place where he had his first kiss with a girl (she threw up – on account of being drunk, not Bilal, or so he liked to tell himself). He glanced at a group of students walking into Frankie & Benny's, people swimming in and out of Sainsbury's, some girls and boys on the corner of Dartmouth Road, smoking, as several men in their *jubbas* walked past on their way to Jalalabad Mosque. The place was peppered with multi-culturalism – headscarves and skull caps, short skirts and African print dresses – Birmingham's red brick walls and grey roads were graffitied with colour and recollections. Except no matter how much Bilal tried to tell himself that this was the place where memory should meet nostalgia, he couldn't help but instead feel that it met a very familiar nausea.

'Call Mariam,' he said into his phone.

'Hi,' she answered. 'Traffic?'

'No, almost there.'

'Ha, triple word score.' There was a smile in her voice as she spoke to Haaris.

'Playing Scrabble?' he asked. 'Got all the shopping done?'

'Yep,' she replied.

Bilal stopped at the traffic lights, observing a woman in white trousers and a bright pink vest-top with large golden hoop earrings. The murky clouds and humidity seemed to press upon the people outside, damp patches on their clothes, sweat on their sullen brows. Bins were overflowing with empty Coke cans and rubbish, the streets littered with plastic bags and glass bottles. Though a new green patch with children on swings and a slide was a hopeful sight.

'God, this place,' he said to Mariam. 'Do you ever miss it?'

There was a pause. 'Yes. Sometimes. No, *gumbit* is not a word.'

'What? Yes, it is,' exclaimed Haaris in the background.

'Oh?' said Bilal.

'It's where we grew up,' Mariam replied. 'See? I told you. It's *gambit*.'

'Hmm.'

'Your wife thinks she can beat me just because I'm a kid,' came Haaris's voice.

'Well,' said Bilal. 'Have fun.'

'You too. Don't forget the halal meat.'

And without pausing, Mariam put the phone down.

'Call Vaseem,' said Bilal.

'Bro! You here yet?'

'Almost. Where are you?' asked Bilal.

'Something came up, isn't it. Some *panchod* drove into the back of my car. Can't make it today. Why d'you never visit? Anyway, take Auntie R and make her better, yeah. Oh, *teri maa di . . .* '

Before Vaseem Bhai could finish the Punjabi expletive of the *your mum* variety, he hung up. Despite having spent most of his childhood in a headlock with Vaseem Bhai, he often managed to allay Bilal's anxieties. They weren't family by blood, but his and Bilal's mum had been friends since they arrived in the UK in 1982 and there was nothing like feelings thrown up by diaspora to bond people.

Bilal tapped his fingers on the steering wheel. He'd have liked to call Mariam again but he knew she'd only ask why. Every now and then, when he thought about the people in his life, they seemed so far removed that he felt untethered. His mum's words would echo in his head: 'We belong to no-one, and no-one belongs to us.'

'Don't I belong to you?' he'd asked her when he was only eight years old and heard her say it for the first time. She'd tucked his hair behind his ear, kissed his forehead and hugged him tight so that he was enveloped in sweet musk mingled with the smell of fried onions.

'No, my beta. We only belong to God,' she had said.

'The light's fucking green,' someone shouted as they beeped their car horn at him.

Bilal waved his sorry to the man, who stuck his finger up at him. Soon enough he pulled up in front of what used to be his mum's two-bedroom house and knocked on the door. A robust woman with honey-blonde hair appeared.

'Auntie Shagufta,' he said.

The hot pink of her lipstick in the midst of Birmingham's faded bricks and mortar took him aback.

She looked over her shoulder and shouted, 'He's here!' so loud he started.

Now that his mum was gone, he covered the cost of Khala Rukhsana living in the familiar home with its unfamiliar air, and paid Auntie Shagufta across the street to look after her. After thirty-four years of being in the country, Khala never had got the hang of shopping alone or the transport system. She had flown almost five-thousand miles from Rawalpindi, only to confine herself to within a two-mile radius of their home in Birmingham. And she had seemed content with it, no matter how much his mum urged her otherwise.

'Your khala's like a tortoise always in its shell,' his mum had once whispered to him.

'They always win the race,' he'd replied, itching his head as he considered his next backgammon move.

'*Le*,' she said. 'How can you win a race you've never entered?'

The only thing Khala Rukhsana raced towards was praying. What exactly she prayed for he never knew.

He walked into the brown carpeted hallway, feeling too big for the space. Had the passage always been so narrow? Or had present life – in his light and modern detached home in Babbel's End – detached him from his past one? Bilal noticed the corners of the busy wallpaper had curled.

'I keep telling Rukhsana to replace the paper, beta,' said Auntie Shagufta, shaking her head. 'Paint the walls – wallpaper is so old-style – but she always says she is old and alone and doesn't need fancy things.'

Bilal gave a weak smile and made a mental note to get an estimate from a decorator. He noticed small cracks in the ceiling, the faux-crystal and brass chandelier dusty from neglect. His mum would not have been pleased.

'Salam,' he said, entering the living room to see his khala laid on what looked like a gurney placed in the middle. 'What . . . what are you doing there?'

Auntie Gulfashan, Vaseem Bhai's mum, looked up at him from the sofa.

'My nephew has come,' replied Khala.

She looked so absurd on the gurney, her bulk barely supported by it, he felt embarrassed for her. A faded brown leather suitcase and another navy hand trolley were resting against the wall. The helpless look on Khala Rukhsana's face irritated Bilal, so naturally he moved forward and took her hand.

'Can you move?'

'Yes, I'm fine. It was a silly fall coming down the stairs. We've always had such narrow steps. Shagufta shouldn't have called you.'

She gripped her gold necklace. It had been given to her as a wedding present from her late husband and Bilal was sure she'd never taken it off. He then noticed a whistle also strung around Khala's neck.

'In case she needs help,' explained Auntie Gulfashan.

He assumed she was referring to the whistle, but he never could tell with these aunts.

'You've lost weight,' Auntie Gulfashan continued, putting her hand over his head as he bent down. 'Is Mariam not feeding you?'

'Have I?' He was still distracted by the gurney. 'Why are you on a gurney?'

'We call it the journey gurney,' said Auntie Gulfashan.

'Sorry?'

'*Journey gurney,*' Auntie Shagufta interjected, beaming. 'Every time someone is ill or takes a fall, they get the gurney. Your Auntie Gulfashan thought of the name. She's the clever one.'

'Right,' replied Bilal. 'Well, are we ready to go?'

Auntie Gulfashan squinted at Bilal, her chiffon dupatta draped over her grey, set curls, her glasses dangling on a chain around her neck, walking stick by her side. For a moment Bilal felt sorry for Uncle Gulfashan (so-named on account of their marital power structure).

Khala Rukhsana tried to get up. She winced with a move

here, changing direction there. Bilal went to help her, feeling her doughy arms in his grip.

'No, no, beta. You must stay for lunch,' said Auntie Shagufta. She went out and came back with a glass of juice. 'I cancelled a lunch with *Ambreen Beghum*. O-ho, you know the one who's running to be an MP?'

'Ah,' he said, taking the juice and remembering that Auntie Shagufta had always been quite taken by politics – she had canvassed in the last election with his mum, who'd always been a persuasive canvassing buddy. The whole thing made Auntie Shagufta an optimist, at least.

He looked at the dark pink guava, brimming with sugar and e-numbers, wishing he'd brought Gaviscon with him. Mariam would've made an excuse and said no to it. Bilal had never been good with excuses.

'Thank you.'

'I have missed you, beta,' said Khala Rukhsana as he took a seat between Auntie Shagufta and Auntie Gulfashan.

A tortoise always in her shell. The genuine warmth in her tone brought an unexpected sense of guilt. Maybe it was because if he closed his eyes it could be his mum speaking – they had such similar voices.

'Excuse me,' he said, pretending he needed the bathroom.

Instead, Bilal walked out into the garden.

The flower beds were now bare, save for a few stalks and weeds, white pots dotted around with nothing but earth in them, and the fence that his mum had painted red was chipped and worn. What did Khala do all day?

Why hadn't she told him that the house needed work? How could she be so indifferent to life? He would've ripped out the weeds if he hadn't seen what he'd come out for. The heat clung to Bilal as he undid the top button of his shirt, letting out a small laugh at the huge hole by the flower bed that used to bloom with roses.

He looked into the depth of the earth where his mum used to lie. What was he hoping to find? His mother looking up at him from her makeshift grave? Bilal looked over his shoulder to check if any of the aunts were watching. He took the stepladder his mum would use to climb in and out of the grave, easing it into the ground before he climbed down and looked around the enclosed space. Even in the summer heat it felt damp and cool, the world carrying on over his head. It took a steely sense of logic to prevent him from climbing right back out. Empty or not, a grave was a grave.

When his mum had first told him what she was going to do, he'd laughed. It had to be a joke. There was eccentric and then there was unhinged.

'I thought I'd brought you up better than that, Bilal.'

'But—'

Before he could finish his sentence she'd already stood up from the kitchen table and made her way outside.

'Who exactly is brought up to understand a person digging their own grave? It's mad,' he'd called after her, following her into the garden.

Back then forget-me-nots and daffodils still blossomed on one side, turnips and rosemary grew in the pots. The garden had been small but alive with his mum's handiwork. And here was another lasting example – only this was more gloom than bloom.

'What on earth has brought this on?'

His mum had looked at him, disappointed, as if he were just another prosaic product of material living.

'Bilal, everyone is mad, some people just hide it better. You should never trust those people.'

He stared at her as she shovelled earth to one side, the strength in her arms surprising him.

'No, Ammi. Not everyone,' Bilal insisted. 'Khala. She's many things, but she's not *mad*.'

Never had his mum's eccentricity felt so trying. Sakeena laughed and leaned on the shovel, her face not yet lined with wrinkles around her mouth, her red dupatta flapping in the breeze, her figure poised as if she was ready to conquer the land.

'Rukhsana is the maddest,' Sakeena exclaimed. 'She can't even forget the man she was married to for only a week before he died. *One week*,' Sakeena repeated. 'He wasn't even good-looking. Your *abba* was a *haramzaada*, but at least he was handsome.'

Bilal always balked when his mum swore. She'd begun digging again as Bilal marched back into the house and into Khala Rukhsana's room, informing her of her sister's mental unravelling. Rukhsana had shaken her head fondly.

'Beta, since when did your ammi ever do anything that was normal?' she'd said.

Khala was sitting on a wooden chair, Qur'an in hand.

There was no use asking her about rational behaviour.

Now he was standing in the same spot his mum had laid night after night.

'Beta!' came Auntie Shagufta's voice. 'What are you doing?'

'Nothing,' Bilal said, scrambling up the stepladder and brushing down his trousers. 'Just wondering if I should get rid of . . . *this*.'

'Oh no, beta. Your khala likes to rest here and look at it.'

Bilal imagined Khala Rukhsana sitting by the grave, alone.

In that moment he understood how sometimes spaces could connect a person to another, even when time couldn't.

⁓

Rukhsana glanced at Bilal as he drove them out of the city and south west, towards his home. He'd always been kind-looking and she felt proud of the man her sister's little boy had become: tall, maybe too thin, his hairline receding a little, but with the air of someone like that man in the *hadith* – sayings and stories of the prophet's time – who went to heaven for picking up the skin of a banana in case someone slipped. Still, people whispered about Bilal moving so far away (not even a halal butcher close by) from his single mother and widowed aunt. If she'd had a son she wondered what he'd have looked like. Rukhsana recalled the stoutness of her late husband,

Jahangir, his rugged face and thick brows. Perhaps it was just as well those genes were laid to rest, along with his body. He had been as kind a husband as he had been brief. Sometimes she'd think about her wedding night and the lightness with which his rough hands had touched her. She had kept her eyes closed the whole time, embarrassed to look at the man who was doing things to her she'd never imagined. She blushed even now to remember how her body had reacted, as if she was free-falling all the way to that end. Next time, she had thought as he'd kissed the top of her head and left the house to go to work, I will open my eyes. I will touch him, too. She would have to speak to her sister about it. But Sakeena was all the way in England and it wouldn't be right to ask her, not when her own husband had left her and little Bilal. Rukhsana had been mortified to think of her sister having shared such moments with a man, only to be abandoned by him. She would write Sakeena a long letter, leaving out details of her happiness. She had, after all, a lifetime of it ahead of her.

Then her husband had died.

'Good time to visit,' said Bilal now in broken Punjabi.

Rukhsana looked out of the window, shifting the pillow supporting her back and aching hip. She'd been so preoccupied with the thoughts in her head, she'd missed what was going on outside it. Bilal had turned off the busy A-road into a road lined with pine trees, the sun dappling the ground with its rays.

'If you peek through there, you can see the small church

– St Swithun's. The bell's broken. We're raising money to get it fixed.'

'Beta, you go to church?' asked Rukhsana, alarmed.

'Oh no. But it's important, you know. To the village. There's a bigger church too, but on the other side,' said Bilal.

A fearful fascination took hold of Rukhsana as she leaned forward, whispering *alhamdolila* on a loop. She was now staring at high grey, stone walls. What was behind them, she wondered. Enclosed spaces reminded her too much of her sister's grave, which led to thoughts of isolation. And, naturally, death. There was just no escaping it. Rukhsana shuddered. The road seemed to last for ever. If Sakeena were here she'd know exactly what Rukhsana was thinking, would have made a joke and Rukhsana would've laughed. How would she ever get used to life without her older sister? Just as Rukhsana began to feel the beginnings of motion sickness to complement her grief, they drove up a hill and the view opened up to land bathed in a sunlight that intensified the shades of green and yellow.

'*Subhanallah,*' she whispered.

Bilal smiled. 'Not quite Birmingham, is it?'

It hadn't occurred to Rukhsana that the country could be anything different from Birmingham, though Sakeena had tried to describe the village to her.

'How green it is,' she said.

Bilal smiled at the insertion of 'green' in English in the otherwise Punjabi sentence. 'If you wait just a little while

. . . ah, there.' He pointed. 'That's Hayward Beach. Can you see?'

She sighed with a smile at the misty outline of the sea beyond the rolling hills. To think just a few minutes ago she was thinking of Sakeena's grave. But then she had always known that on the other side of the grave lies heaven. Or hell, depending on your life's deeds.

The few times Sakeena had visited Bilal, Rukhsana had decided to stay in the confines of their home. The breaking of her routine too often led her to break into a rash. She felt harassed by new things. Maybe that's why she was so adept at recounting old feelings. Ever since her husband had died she'd told herself that her emotional capacities were worn, and now, years later, her sister's death reinforced the truth of it. What's more, Rukhsana was going to be a burden to her nephew. What a way to live: to constantly be the responsibility of another.

'Your ammi never liked it. "Too quiet," she said. "Too many white faces."' Rukhsana stared out of the window. 'I said you live in a white person's land – what colour should their face be?'

'That was Ammi: always liking the idea of something,' Bilal replied in English.

'Hain?'

'Nothing.'

'I like to leave the house and not know who I will meet,' Sakeena had said the first time she returned home after a trip to Babbel's End. She stitched the golden buttons on the cuffs of Mrs Patel's hot pink kameez. Sakeena had started off sewing bits and pieces as favours for people, until she realised she was good enough to make money from it. 'In that village everyone knows each other and everyone looks the same.'

Rukhsana had shook her head fondly, unpicking another customer's trouser hem. 'You only see the same faces here as well.'

'Oh, *nahin*, Rukhsana,' she'd replied. 'That's because you're not looking for anything new. I tell you, if I look for something new here, I can find it.'

Rukhsana would do the laundry, dust the coffee table, organise kitchen cupboards, help with sewing (she was quite talented herself). Cooking and cleaning for Sakeena was the only way she could thank her for having saved her life. Actions being handy when the appropriate words failed. Rukhsana had now lost the impetus to do all those things, purpose having died with her sister.

Bilal drove into what seemed to be a cluster of life after that vast expanse of green land.

'This is the heart of the village,' he said.

Apparently a few shops and a post office was enough to give something heart. There were a few people going about their business, some cars parked up.

'*Bas*?' she asked.

'That's it,' Bilal repeated.

In only seconds they'd passed it and were on a windy lane where Bilal stopped in a lay-by to let a car go by. The person waved at him.

'You know him?' asked Khala.

'No.'

People were obviously politer in villages. Bilal slowed down at a white signpost with arrows pointing in different directions as he took a left. There was a woman herding sheep through a gate in a walled field on one side, several cows chewing on grass on another. Rukhsana wanted to ask Bilal to pause. She could barely take in one image before being faced with the next. They passed a large yellow house, decked with hanging baskets in full bloom, and it was a good few yards before the next house. Each had its own garden path, leading to their front doors. Some houses were yellow-painted with thatched roofs; others white-washed and wooden-beamed; black-framed windows and bottle-green doors; ivy sprawling over red bricks; lavender and daisies growing in beautiful excess.

'Here we are,' said Bilal.

Rukhsana watched as they pulled into the drive of a tall, white-washed, detached house with pointed wooden beams. She counted eight windows, each flanked with their own pair of wooden shutters. Another black car was parked out front, with those big wheels. Rukhsana didn't like her chances of getting her leg up into that.

'Oh, God,' Bilal muttered as he opened Rukhsana's car door. A skinny, tall old lady was marching towards them, with two dogs barking and bouncing behind her. Rukhsana was caught between fearing the unruly animals and admiration for how full of energy a woman with so much grey hair could be.

'Hallo! Have visitors, do we, Bill?'

The dogs came charging towards Rukhsana as she shuffled back into the car. Dogs were smelly and their saliva made you unclean. Her prayers wouldn't be accepted and the fewer the barriers to God's grace, the better.

'Juno! Rusty! Down!'

The woman smiled as she dragged the dogs away, saying things that Rukhsana couldn't understand. Bilal pointed at Rukhsana, shielding his eyes from the sun, as the old lady smiled again, the dogs sitting back on their haunches, their tongues lolling out. The old woman grabbed Rukhsana's hand and shook it so hard she thought it would trigger her arthritis.

'You. Are. Welcome. Here. I'm *Margaret.*'

Bilal spoke too fast. The old lady – Margrit? – made sympathetic faces and then attempted to speak to Rukhsana again. Her heart beat faster as she tried to make sense of the words, but the blood rushed to her ears and she tried so hard to understand that she missed it all.

Bilal put his hands in his pockets and said in Punjabi: 'She said she's really happy you're here.'

'But she doesn't know me,' said Rukhsana, puzzled.

Margrit was now looking at Rukhsana's green and purple printed shalwar kameez. She spoke to Bilal, smiled so widely Rukhsana wondered at her having a facial spasm, and then walked away, taking her dogs with her.

'How old is she?' asked Rukhsana.

'In her mid-seventies, probably.'

'*Subhanallah.*'

How come Margrit walked without limping? Maybe it

was the food that white people ate? Maybe her kismet was really good. The air smelt of freshly cut grass with a faint scent of manure. Margrit kept a farm! So much energy. Rukhsana looked around and saw the next house was a hundred yards or so away and set back from the road. It was taller than Bilal's, older and much bigger, with two statues of dogs on pillars either side of a grand black gate.

'That's Margaret's house,' said Bilal.

How exposed it all was. How unprotected she felt by the open skies and miles and miles of green land. She began to repeat her *Allah hu Akbars* as she grabbed her necklace – remembering God was the only thing that comforted her soul. She turned to Bilal as a ripple of dread ran through her veins.

Bilal smiled. 'Home sweet home.'

chapter three

AFTER HAVING CALLED THE cleaner, done the shopping, cooked dinner, played a game of Scrabble with Haaris and dropped him at his friend Sam's house, Mariam had pattered up the stairs. The latest article Jenny wanted for the *West Plimpington Gazzette* could wait. She hadn't missed a deadline in the past five years, after all. Writing for the district's paper was a mindless enough task, and coupled easily with her other freelancing, which prevented Mariam from considering too often where her ambition had gone. She clutched her laptop as she walked into the study, sat on the floor and opened up a new internet tab. She typed in 'Adalrik Muller', trying to calm her breathing as she scrolled down the screen, searching for the clip for forgiveness.

'Where is it?' she muttered before she found it, beneath *Holding on to Hatred*.

Bilal and Khala Rukhsana would be a few more hours yet but she peered over the window ledge, just in case, before clicking 'play'.

To forgive is to not just react, but sometimes to do nothing at all. To ignore those who live in a state of unconsciousness is to have your own consciousness fully in the present.

She drank in the words, each philosophical insight dispelling her anxiety. Psychology – pseudo or otherwise – had done wonders for the tightness that lived in Mariam's chest.

Every situation in life can be a test; when one is challenged one is forced to give deeper of themselves – without it we'd remain superficial. We can protect ourselves in the cocoons we make for ourselves, but can we sustain that in the real world?

The world, however, remained disjointed. Mariam put her head in her hands as the video ended. After some time – knowing she shouldn't – she took the step ladder into her walk-in wardrobe to rummage for the box she knew she'd stored at the top at the back of the cupboard, where Bilal would never look. In it was a plain, black lever arch file, which looked like it might contain admin documents, rather than the pieces of Mariam's life before it broke. Opening the box, she saw a photo of her wedding day with her first husband, Saif. There he was, typically light-skinned, tall and handsome, setting her up for a typical heartbreak. The black moustache should've put her off

– no good could come of something that glossy – but she'd liked him despite it. Had she really ever smiled that easily? Some of her college friends in Birmingham had laughed at her – the English Literature geek, marrying someone from Pakistan. He'd have an accent! Did they even *read* in Pakistan? But, according to her mum, he was a good boy from a good family.

'Goodness is subjective, Mum,' eighteen-year-old Mariam had replied with a sigh, bent over her desk, writing a critical analysis of Tennyson's 'The Charge of the Light Brigade'.

'You should grab these *opportunities* when they come.' Her mum wagged her knobbly finger.

Despite twenty disgruntled years with Mariam's dad, her mum hadn't understood that opportunity didn't just come in the form of a marriage proposal. It never seemed to strike her mother when he shouted for her to get him his dinner, nor when he – upon occasion – would hit her, that life might offer something more than self-sacrifice. Mariam had agreed to the marriage in order to avoid one of her dad's violent episodes. Plus, her essay was due the following day.

So, during the summer holidays, she had travelled with her parents to Pakistan with indifference. And she'd ended up in love. Saif and she had bonded over their mutual love for George Eliot, and argued over Austen and the Brontës.

'Austen was the master of irony,' exclaimed Mariam, laughing.

He'd leaned in so she could feel his breath on her neck.

'But the Brontës were the masters of passion,' he'd whispered. 'That's better than irony . . . no?'

Her preconceptions had been muddied by her friends and washed away by Saif's love for her favourite classics. She was in awe, which was only amplified by him reading Urdu poetry to her.

It was the age of furtive glances, looking at the ground when he paid a compliment, holding hands when no-one was watching. Mariam had never had a boyfriend, being too shy and quiet to attract attention, so the way he ran his fingers through her hair was nothing short of euphoria. If love was falling, she had fallen. And so, she thought, had he.

Now, she rifled through six weeks' worth of faded love letters about feelings that brimmed and the life they'd lead together.

Sitting in her five-bedroom house, Mariam re-read some of the letters, cringing that she had once believed that six weeks was long enough to know you wanted to marry someone. Truthfully, she'd known after six days, but she had contempt enough for herself not to dwell on that.

These things happen, people had said, back in Birmingham. *He got his passport and left.* But Mariam knew there had been kindness, there had to have been love, it just obviously wasn't enough for him to also stop loving the woman he'd left behind in Pakistan. Was the way he'd looked at Mariam a reflection of something he'd really felt? It hadn't occurred to her then that the love *she* had felt might have simply been respite from her parents' mutual hatred. She sighed. Why was she still going over all this, even now? Because Saif was back. And it was all she could do to stop herself from asking: *what did it mean?*

When she had said yes to marrying Bilal ten years ago, it was because she'd believed that things endure only when they have no replacement. A mutual friend had introduced them and their more considered approach to one another was cemented by the discovery of the shared emotional issues their respective mums (and in Mariam's case, dad) had gifted them. Then Mariam's mum died and Bilal had helped her carry the weight of her regrets.

'You can only regret things you think you could've changed. Your mum was always going to be . . . well, you know,' he had said, sitting on the sofa.

Haaris had been asleep in the room next door. Mariam and her toddler had lived in a one-bedroom flat, next to the chicken shop on Cooksey Road in Small Heath. The place had reeked of fried chicken and disappointment.

'You can regret things you can't change, too,' she'd replied. 'It's just a bit more depressing.'

She thought she'd seen the flicker of a smile, though she hardly knew why. He'd shifted closer and held her face in his hand as he said: 'I'm going to try and change what this is. Are you okay with that?'

Signposting intention might not have seemed romantic, but it gave Mariam a sense of control over her choices, which she'd hitherto never experienced. When he kissed her it had felt like the beginning of a new way of life.

Except now Saif was back, wanting to be a bigger part of Haaris's life, finally, and those memories of him sprawled into the avenues of her mind. They invaded her thoughts as she scoped out a new writing brief. They hammered in her chest when she ran, resurfaced unexpectedly – usually when she felt reasonably happy – they caught in her throat. A leaden and unyielding love. No matter how hard she tried, she wasn't able to control her nostalgia, even though it was for a time that she knew didn't actually exist. Some part of her had repackaged it, selling her a memory that disguised itself as fact.

'Who we are is just a set of stories we tell ourselves,' she said to herself.

Some Sufi teachings had been handy in her search for self-actualisation, but they hadn't fully done the trick. Sometimes she'd take out the prayer mat and say her supplications, which could be soothing.

Suddenly Mariam heard a car pull up outside. She rushed to store everything back in its place as Bilal's voice came from downstairs. Clearing the laptop's history – she prided herself on being meticulous – she took a deep breath, then walked down the soft, carpeted stairs to see Khala Rukhsana staring up at her. The shalwar kameez reminded Mariam of her mum. Her dad always told her to stop being so primitive – to wear trousers and burn those stupid shalwar kameezes. If Mariam had still lived in Birmingham, she'd wear them in front of her dad, just to irritate him. There wasn't much call for them in Babbel's End.

'Salamalaikum, Khala,' she said.

Mariam liked to avoid physical contact, but acquiesced that this wasn't always possible. She steeled herself, ready to be enveloped in Khala Rukhsana's pillowy arms.

'Beti,' said Khala.

Her own mother had never held her this closely and her lack of experience with it rendered Mariam motionless. She extricated herself from Khala and couldn't help but notice that her arms, along with the rest of her body, were decidedly fleshier than when she last saw her. A person could never gain ten pounds without going down in Mariam's estimation. It was impossible to deny that people who let themselves go had actually let go of life. She helped Khala on to the sofa, giving her a stool to rest her feet on, which Khala insisted she didn't need. Bilal went to put her bags in the downstairs guest room before going into the kitchen, where Mariam was making tea.

'We saved her from the coven,' he said.

'That bad?'

'The good, the bad and the obscure,' Bilal replied. 'I'm just glad we're home so you can speak to her in Punjabi. Where's Haaris?'

'Gone to Sam's. Making the most of the summer holidays.'

'Ah.'

'This morning he told me he wants to be a philosopher,' said Mariam.

'Where'd he get that from?'

'He Wiki'd Aristotle. He's quite taken by him.'

Bilal laughed and leaned against the granite kitchen

island, folding his arms. Mariam wondered at her emotional capacity for misdirection: her current husband's love for her first husband's son only increased the potency of her first affection. But she liked the way Bilal's laughter loosened the seams of his tightly knit personality. Perhaps she should try to laugh more often. Habit *could* become character. She gave it a shot.

'Are you all right?' asked Bilal as Mariam coughed at the saliva that went down the wrong way.

'Yes, it's just funny, isn't it?' she replied, recovering from failure. 'Haaris and Aristotle.'

'He doesn't get that from his father, does he?' Bilal said.

Mariam measured hot milk into three mugs before pouring water from the hot water dispenser.

'Who knows.'

He probably did. She let the teabags brew, getting out a tray and biscuits.

'He's coming next week to collect him?' asked Bilal.

Mariam felt irriation again. Why did he always have to ask questions with the most obvious answers? Were they so bereft of conversation? Was *he* so bereft of originality?

'As agreed,' replied Mariam.

'Hmmm. Making changes.'

'So it seems.'

Mariam tried to measure her breath as they walked through to Khala Rukhsana surveying the living room with its exposed stone wall and low-hanging chrome chandelier.

'Beautiful home you have, beta,' she said.

Mariam wished she could make room for sympathy for

Khala, that her presence didn't already oppress her. She must try to be a better person.

'I'll show you around when you've rested,' replied Mariam, hoping her smile seemed genuine. But a sudden paranoia that Bilal would find her letters took hold.

'Excuse me,' she said.

She went to make sure she'd hidden the box well enough. As she left she heard Khala say, 'Look at the world you've built here.'

Mariam had to be patient and remember that each feeling, each situation had its time – that next time she wouldn't choke on her own laughter. That even sadness couldn't last for ever.

⁓

Mariam awoke with a start past four in the morning, the space next to her empty. Bilal had probably just gone downstairs to get a glass of water or a sleeping pill, but after last night, the way he'd looked at Khala Rukhsana as she spoke about his mum, the quiet way he went to bed, Mariam decided to check on him. She crept down the stairs, peeking into both living rooms before going into the kitchen to see the floodlights on in the garden. She wrapped her silk dressing gown tighter around her and opened the garden door.

Her husband, sleeves rolled up, knee-deep in soil was digging a hole in the ground.

'*What* are you doing?'

Bilal swivelled around, shovel in hand, floodlights catching his eye like a deer in headlights.

'Oh,' he sighed with relief. 'You gave me a heart attack.'

'It's past four in the morning,' said Mariam, walking down the manicured lawn, past the Koi pond, and looking over at him, his eyes level to her chest.

'I couldn't sleep.'

'So you're digging a hole?'

Bilal leaned on the shovel and looked up at her. 'I . . . it's . . .'

'Oh, God,' said Mariam. 'It's not?'

'I just wanted to see,' replied Bilal.

Mariam scrunched up her face, stepping closer to the hole in question. 'All because you saw her grave?' This was concerning. 'It isn't normal, you know.'

He looked at his handiwork, almost halfway complete. A pile of dirt was heaped between their rose bush and apple tree.

'That's not the point,' he said, wiping the sweat off his brow.

A light breeze travelled through the fresh night air as Mariam bent down, hair tumbling over her face, and grabbed the shovel from him. 'Why are you doing this?'

She glanced around, wondering if their neighbours could see, surprised that she cared.

'Because,' he replied, taking the shovel back.

The muscles in his forearms tightened with each dig as Mariam watched him, focused and resolute. His grey pyjama bottoms were tucked into his socks above his trainers.

'What exactly are you going to get from this?' she asked. 'Can you put that down for a second? You're being . . . '

'What?'

'*Eccentric.*'

The accusation hung between them. Bilal hesitated.

'No,' he said, finally. 'I'm trying to understand.'

'Beta, what is happening?'

This time both Mariam and Bilal turned to see Khala Rukhsana's figure at the door. 'I got up to pray and wanted some water,' she called out. 'Why are you in the ground?'

She winced as she stepped into the garden, rosary beads in hand, and hobbled towards them. By the time she reached them she seemed to have understood something and was already nodding. '*Acha*, your ammi.'

'See?' said Bilal to Mariam. 'She gets it.'

'With any luck it'll rain and wash the whole thing away,' added Mariam, looking up at the sky, which promised no such thing.

This possibility seemed to have only occurred to Bilal. He pushed himself out of the hole, went into the shed and came out with a piece of white tarp.

'This is big enough, isn't it?' he asked, unfolding and assessing it before jumping back into the grave.

Mariam looked at him, wondering if this was it: if he had finally lost his senses.

'The neighbours will think you're burying someone,' said Mariam.

He paused to consider this. 'No-one can see our garden from here.'

'Margaret?' said Mariam.

'She doesn't count.'

He continued to dig as Mariam and Khala could do nothing but stare. What the hell had got into him?

Bilal paused and looked at Khala Rukhsana. 'I never really got why she did it.'

Khala gave him a sad smile, her eyes glistening with tears, which possibly alarmed Mariam more than the grave.

'Peace,' she finally said.

Mariam understood the mechanics of grief, the need for solitude, the way in which the brain and heart could flit between memory and feeling, with nothing but despair in between. There was nothing to do but wade through the cacophony of emotion while loved ones bore witness to it. But for a surprising moment Bilal looked like the type of man who was in *control* of things. Then he stopped and scratched the inside of his elbow.

'Think my rash is playing up,' he added. 'I'll go and get the hydrocortisone.'

Mariam sighed. Life was nothing but an ongoing illusion. Bilal left her and Khala as Mariam looked into the ground, imagining her own dead body lying there, and shuddered. Yes, it was eccentric, but then she wondered if the experience might do something for Bilal. Wasn't it better to dig through the pain rather than sit still and be encased by it? She, after all, understood: *to detach and reflect was to promote self-awareness, recognise the patterns of our life's decisions so we never repeat mistakes.* Unless the first mistake was ongoing . . . She caught Khala Rukhsana looking at her as Bilal came back out.

'Are you honestly going to carry on with this?' she asked him.

She needn't have bothered; he was already piling up more dirt as she spoke.

'I've wasted enough time,' he said.

Something was shifting. It made Mariam distinctly awkward.

'Well, some of us want to lie in our beds, not graves,' said Mariam.

As she and Khala Rukhsana walked back into the house, Mariam knew Saif would never have thought of such a thing. She wasn't sure if she liked him more or less for it.

⁓

Lying in the grave was always going to be uncomfortable. Anything to do with death generally is. It wasn't helped by the conversation Bilal had had earlier with Mariam about her ex-husband. Bilal believed he'd taken on the role of stepfather rather well, but now he was in danger of being usurped. The less Mariam spoke about Saif, the more Bilal worried; the potency of emotions tended to grow when unvoiced. He shuffled to adjust the towels he'd finally placed underneath him to keep his clothes from getting dirty.

The pink haze of dawn was breaking as he took a deep breath. When he'd awoken in the middle of the night the notion of digging the grave came to him as a fact. He'd put on his long johns – out of habit rather than necessity – under his pyjamas, tucked them into his socks, wore his trainers and walked into the garden to cure his thoughts of eternal damnation. The earth was dry but even so, with the effort of all the digging, he'd decided the grave didn't need to be six feet, like his mum's had been. Less than half of that would probably do. He had a vague paranoia that it might only lead to half an understanding, but the sweat on his brow and emerging blisters on his hands helped him get over that.

As he now lay, eyes closed, in the womb of the earth, he remembered the woman who gave birth to him. The idea of a coffin stifled him, and he wondered whether there was something liberating in the Islamic tradition of simply being wrapped in a white sheet. He opened his eyes and considered the soul. The science of organisms didn't explain the way his mum would laugh, or why she'd break into song; why she was determined never to marry again. The answer didn't lie in her flesh and bones or the neurons in her brain. There was nothing predictable or pre-determined about the way she had lived. Where had it all gone?

The laughter.

The song.

The soul.

'Ammi, ammi, ammi.'

'See?' he imagined her saying. There she was, standing at the edge of his makeshift grave against the breaking dawn, in her sandals and bright red socks. Her sense of style never quite matched her natural beauty. 'I told you. How can you live properly if you don't think about death?'

A tear slid down Bilal's temple and he shook his head, his scalp rubbing against the soft towel as he detected the faint scurry of spiders. His mother never could do things like normal mums. The way she'd say hello to his non-white friends in their parents' mother tongue; the way other Pakistani mums looked at her as if she was trying too hard to be *angraiz*. Well, it was England, why shouldn't she be *English*? Except he'd think of how his English friends would smile at her – uncomfortable, pitying – when she said, 'I'll just have tipple,' as she filled her glass with Fanta. Now that Bilal was older, wiser, he was embarrassed of his embarrassment.

He closed his eyes again and an image came to him.

He's taking off his shoes outside a door and he walks into a large room with a carpet of red and beige prayer mats. White pillars stand tall and Arabic prayers are painted in black around the walls, the dome of the ceiling carved with more script. He does his ablutions and the sound of the muezzin's call to prayer reverberates in the room before Bilal begins to pray. Mariam and Haaris are by his side. Maybe even Khala.

Growing up, he'd never enjoyed visits to the mosque in Birmingham, but here, now, in Babbel's End, that image felt *right* . . .

Just then he heard the faint rumble of some kind of motor.

He wondered if it was thunder but the sky was coloured with strokes of bright orange and tufts of pink as the rumble drew closer. The noise broke through his spiritual barrier and roared into the garden, the automatic light flooding the garden as he sat up. The engine shut off.

He looked up to see a figure with a shock of wild, curly hair towering over his resting place. The light bathed her in an angelic hue, which was disconcerting.

'Extraordinary,' she said. 'Dug yourself a bit of a hole there.'

'Margaret?' he replied.

She rested both hands on her hips, her pearl necklace swinging back and forth and her dungarees splattered with mud. The noise had been Margaret's quad bike roaring through the stone archway that led on to her farmland at the back of the house. Bilal knew he should've had a gate built into it, but he hadn't wanted to appear rude. He stretched his legs out in front of him and cleared his throat.

'What are you doing here? It's the crack of dawn,' he said.

'I should ask you the same question.'

As a woman well into her seventies, Margaret had managed to retain the quality of child-like wonder, which very often led her, uninvited, into other people's homes.

Bilal hesitated. How was he meant to explain this? *Oh, you know, just decided to dig my own grave since that's what my mum used to do and I wanted to* . . . What did he want to do?

'I fell,' he said.

'Yes, but what did you fall into?'

That's what he'd have liked to know.

'My grave,' he replied.

Margaret straightened up and showed her overlapping front teeth in a broad smile.

'Excellent.'

When the Hashams had moved to Babbel's End Margaret had especially worn the paisley pashmina she got from Lucknow during her travels around India. She had entered their home and taken her shoes off.

'*Assalam-o-Alaikum*,' Margaret had said, glancing at Mariam's disappointingly English brogues.

'*Walaikum*,' Mariam had replied with a polite, rather than amused, smile.

Mariam's footwear, Bilal had learnt through Jenny, had been an acute disappointment to Margaret. The height of cultural experience came only when his mum had visited once or twice. She was the type of woman Margaret would have liked to have lived next to.

'It's always the interesting ones that die first,' Margaret had said.

But here was a happy turn of events for her: Bilal digging his own grave. Did she think it was some sort of mid-life ritual specific to their branch of Islam? In all her education about world religions perhaps Margaret thought there was a bit where people pretended to be dead?

'Well, young man,' she said, offering him her hand. 'It's time to rise from the ashes.'

~

'So? How was it?' asked Mariam as Bilal walked into the bedroom.

'You're awake.'

'Yes.'

'Margaret interrupted me,' said Bilal.

'On her quad bike?'

'Hmm.'

'Thought I heard it.'

'We really should get a gate built into that archway,' said Bilal, taking off his pyjama bottoms.

'You always said you liked that it opened up to the farm,' replied Mariam, glancing at his long johns. Bilal thought he detected her sigh as he sat on the edge of the bed.

It was the openness of the land he loved. The gravelled path that led to the farmhouse where Margaret had employed a troubled local kid to do odd jobs over the weekends to keep him busy; the cows that supplied the dairy for the cheese factory; the chickens and hens that clucked about.

'I suppose I did.' He stared at the carpet. 'You know, there's a strange serenity to lying in the grave. When Margaret's not barging in on her quad bike.'

'You're six-feet under, Bilal. Of course it's serene.'

'More like three feet, really.'

The idea of building the mosque was burgeoning within him and he thought he might burst. So, he decided he'd put the kettle on.

'Tea?' he asked.

'At five-forty-five in the morning? Aren't you tired?' she asked.

Yes. Trying to make sense of life after death and the sheer willpower it takes to root yourself to reality was quite tiring.

'Did you pray?' he asked, noticing the prayer mat folded in the corner.

'Hmm.'

Bilal paused before he went into the bathroom, did his ablutions and came out.

'Morning prayer time's over, you know,' said Mariam. 'The sun is well and truly up.'

He laid out the mat anyway and tried to remember the Arabic prayers, but they didn't come to him readily.

'*Subhanakalla humma,*' said Mariam.

She sat up in bed, watching him and guiding him with her words as he bowed his head, prostrated on the floor, repeating these actions until the end.

'Been a while since you've done that,' she said.

'The function of praying is quite interesting, if you think about it,' he said.

There was an orderliness in the five separate prayers at set times, a discipline and dedication that he supposed was worthy of admiration.

'I wonder if death is turning me into a zealot?' he said.

'Time to build that mosque,' Mariam replied with a wry laugh.

This time when he got into bed, Mariam turned to him.

'What do you miss most about your mum?' she asked.

Bilal looked up at the ceiling with its spotlights and thought about it for a moment. 'Playing backgammon. That and never knowing what might come out of her mouth next.'

Mariam gave a soft laugh.

'Yours?' he asked.

It took her so long to reply he thought she'd fallen asleep.

'Nothing,' she replied.

He put his arm around her and kissed her on the head as they fell asleep.

When they went downstairs a few hours later, Haaris and Khala Rukhsana were already at the breakfast table.

'Why's there a hole in the garden?' said Haaris, peering out of the window.

Mariam raised her eyebrows to Bilal, who in turn looked at Khala Rukhsana, though he wasn't sure why.

'It's an experiment,' said Bilal.

Haaris sat at the table with his bowl of Cheerios. 'Explain yourself.'

'Haaris doesn't speak any Punjabi or Urdu?' asked Khala Rukhsana.

'I understand it and can speak it a bit, but my dad's going to teach me it properly,' Haaris replied, playing with his Cheerios. 'He says I talk too much like an *angraiz da puttar.*'

If Mariam bristled, Bilal didn't detect it. What right did Saif have to say anything after years of ignoring his son? He wanted Haaris to tell his dad: I *am* the son of an Englishman. Except Haaris wasn't. He was Saif's son and just because Saif had a passport, it didn't make him English. If asked for details, Bilal might be hazy when it came to describing the exact characteristics of an English person, but he knew a fake one when he saw one.

'I'm going to pop to Richard's,' he said, ruffling Haaris's hair.

Mariam looked at him and he glanced again at Khala.

'I won't be long,' he added.

'Right,' said Mariam.

Khala Rukhsana had been busy counting her rosary beads. She might not have understood English but she could tell when she was being a nuisance. 'I think I'll rest in my room.'

Haaris sprung off his chair to help her stand. 'Do you want some of my Cheerios? Or juice? Do you always wear a whistle around your neck? Your arms are really nice and soft. What cream do you use?'

Mariam laughed as she watched Haaris and Khala. Bilal took the opportunity to grab his car keys and head towards finding some answers.

chapter four

'I'M HAVING TROUBLE WITH this faith thing,' said Bilal
finally, sitting in Reverend Richard Young's front
room.

Richard put his hands in the pockets of his grey jogging
bottoms, his thick – but, largely agreed upon, handsome
– brow raised towards his even thicker salt and pepper
hair.

'Just a casual chat then?'

Bilal noticed how white Richard's T-shirt was.

'Coffee?' added Richard. 'Too early for something
stronger.'

'Just as well. Mariam always gives me that look when
she knows I've had a drink.'

Richard made the coffee as Bilal looked around his
home. It was significantly smaller and cosier than Bilal's

– he only had one living room for starters – and his was one of several houses lined down Petty Street. A humble abode with humble surroundings, offset by a view of St Paul's church from the point of the hill upon which Richard's house rested. While Bilal and Mariam's home was open and bright, Richard's was all brown and red hues, leather-bound volumes stacked on mahogany shelves. The place smelt of books and faith.

Richard came out, handing Bilal his mug of coffee.

'You don't have somewhere to be, do you?' asked Bilal.

'Just going to the hospital to see the Joneses and then to the gym.'

Bilal looked at his friend's broad frame and nodded. 'Keeping those looks in check.'

Richard was too handsome to be a vicar. Too at ease and cool to be someone religious. Bilal thought of the imams he'd grown up around: bearded and severe, never looking his mum in the eye when she spoke to them, as if she might tempt them into sin.

'My face is up here, Bhai Sahib, not on the ground,' she'd once said. The imam didn't have a chance to reply as she grabbed Bilal's hand and stomped off. Bilal heard that nowadays the imams were young, engaged and had a new perspective on things like heaven, hell and the proper length of a man's beard.

'Stop flirting with me, people will get ideas,' said Richard. 'Sunday sermon tomorrow and you know I always come up with my best ones on the treadmill. Not that there'll be more than ten people attending.'

Richard's easy smile seemed to falter as he sat on the sofa opposite Bilal. He looked at his watch.

'Shelley's been looking for you, by the way,' said Bilal. 'You weren't at the meeting last week.'

'I've been meaning to call her.'

'About Tom?' asked Bilal.

'And fixing St Swithun's church bell,' he said with a sigh.

The smaller church, St Swithun's – along with Babbel's End – was so old there was evidence that it had existed as far back as AD 992. These days it was rarely opened, but its bell had rung out every day in times of both world wars and peace, and so the more superstitious village folk were beginning to think a prolonged silence was a bad omen. The less superstitious felt that a break in continuity was as good as a crisis.

'So,' said Richard, leaning forward, his face open and betraying just a hint of a troubled soul. 'Faith?'

'Or lack thereof.' Bilal scratched his head, unsure of where to begin.

'I'd say take your time but I'll need to leave in a half hour. Go ahead.'

Bilal felt himself relax. 'I dug myself a bit of a grave.'

'How so?'

'I mean, I literally dug one last night.'

'Oh,' said Richard. 'I see. Like your mum had?'

Bilal nodded, observing Richard's now furrowed brow.

'I thought you always considered it a bit . . . extreme,' said Richard.

'I did. *It is*. Isn't it?'

'It's unusual. To say the least.' Richard always had been an expert at understatement but he couldn't hide the concern on his face. 'How was it? I mean, what happened in there?'

'Well, Margaret turned up on her quad bike.'

'Naturally. Gerald says he's sure she only keeps the farm because it's an excuse to get on that thing,' said Richard fondly. 'But what possessed you?'

'It was when I went to collect my aunt and I saw the grave my mum had dug.'

Richard cleared his throat. 'It's still there?'

'The house is falling apart but my aunt's managed to keep that intact.'

'And?'

'I stood in it,' Bilal replied.

Richard gripped his coffee mug tighter. 'How did it feel?'

'Odd.'

Richard paused. 'You understand that it's not a real grave? That, essentially, it's just a hole.'

'It's what you make of it, though, isn't it?' said Bilal. 'While I was in there, I wondered . . . '

'What?'

Bilal rubbed the back of his head. 'What's all this for – when that's everyone's ultimate destination?'

Bilal suffered from what his mum had called the affliction of logic – the kind that couldn't make room for an all-engrossing and unverifiable God. His mum's religious intensity had peppered his logic with a faraway idea that maybe God existed, but he couldn't remember a time when he'd felt a compulsion to pray or fast, or do any of the things that Muslims were meant to. Until he got back to his bedroom, after lying in the grave, and stood on the prayer mat. The experience had thrown off his religious apathy. Did he do it to feel connected to God, or his mum? Or something else entirely? Perhaps a part of himself that he hadn't wanted to consider before? Either way it was inconvenient.

'You're asking yourself a question that everyone should stumble upon once in their life.'

'But who has the answer?' asked Bilal.

Richard leaned back, turning his untouched coffee mug around in his hands. 'The inclusive answer would be that no-one knows. We all just die trying to figure it out. But Christian to Muslim – if I may . . . ?'

Bilal waved his hand as if he'd accepted his fate at being labelled a Muslim many years ago.

'It's to serve God and humanity.'

Bilal took a deep breath.

'It all sounds very noble, doesn't it?' continued Richard. 'I don't know many people who care for it. Depending on your definition of serving humanity, of course.'

Bilal paused. 'What did she mean? Asking me to do such a thing?'

'You mean the mosque?' asked Richard.

When Bilal had first told Richard about it, it was as if

he were giving the punchline to a joke. Now Bilal wondered if the joke was on him.

He nodded.

'I don't have that answer,' Richard replied. He put his mug down and his hands up as if in Christian prayer.

'I feel like . . . I think that . . . ' But Bilal wasn't entirely sure how to turn his liquid feelings into solid words. 'What if I *did* build the mosque?'

There! He'd said it out loud.

'Right,' said Richard, sitting up and meeting Bilal's gaze. 'I see.'

'Do you think it's absurd? It must be guilt.'

Bilal waited for Richard to respond.

'It could be,' came the reply.

'It's just . . . it feels like a betrayal. Not to at least try.'

'Betrayal of who?' asked Richard.

Wasn't it obvious that he meant his mum? But as Bilal thought about it, he wondered what else he was betraying.

'She really was extraordinary,' said Bilal. 'I know, everyone thinks that about their mum—'

'You'd be surprised,' interrupted Richard. He paused before he added: 'I'll admit, though, she was a rare combination of earnestness and defiance.'

Bilal recalled the disarming way she had smiled and taken Richard's hand when they first met, shaking it with energy. 'Pleasing to meet you, Mr Richard Vicar Sahib.'

The colour had risen to Bilal's cheeks. 'Ammi, just call him Richard.'

Bilal felt his throat constrict.

He'd always presumed he'd have more time with his mum, but time had its own plans and it rarely filled people in on them.

'She asked me who I am. On her deathbed. For a split second I thought she really didn't recognise me – her own son . . . And I didn't have an answer for her. Do you think I'm mad?'

'I think you're grieving.'

They both fell silent.

'And . . . ?' Bilal asked eventually.

'And that's quite natural.'

'Right.'

'But I'm not sure lying in a makeshift grave is the answer. Not for someone who's just lost a parent. And you know . . . it's best not to be impulsive.'

Impulsive? It'd been six months since she died.

Richard cleared his throat. The ticking of the clock seemed to grow louder.

Bilal tapped a foot on the floor.

After an uncomfortable moment Richard spoke. 'Well, I suppose, Shah Jahan built the Taj Mahal for his wife.'

'Not exactly the same thing,' replied Bilal.

'No.'

Tick tock, tick tock.

Bilal looked at Richard. 'You should get one if you can. A wife, that is.'

Richard gave a small smile and rubbed the back of his neck.

Bilal disguised his earnestness with the hint of a laugh.

'Maybe you're the wrong person to ask about this. A Church of England vicar is hardly going to say, "Yes, of course, build a mosque in our village".'

Richard leaned back. He was one of those people blessed with a twinkle in his eye, so it often seemed that while God lived in his heart, irony was alive in his mind. Except there was no twinkle this time.

'I may be,' replied Richard.

'Oh.'

Richard had helped Bilal and Mariam settle in with Haaris when they were new to Babbel's End. He'd included them in email round-ups and village news, proved to people that the Hashams were not just another pair of rich city-dwellers who'd taken to the idea of living in a peaceful village, of which they never intended to be a part.

'Of course,' said Bilal, looking at his watch. 'I'd better get going. You have your duties.'

Richard looked at him and paused. 'I'll see you at the next pub quiz?'

'Yes.'

'How are Mariam and Haaris?' Richard added, following Bilal to the front door. 'Things okay with his dad?'

'Fine, they're fine. My aunt's come to stay.'

'I'll come over and say my salams.'

Richard always greeted Mariam with a salam, but just then it sounded forced, somehow disingenuous.

Bilal nodded. 'Pop by whenever,' he replied.

He got into his car and pulled out, watching Richard wave goodbye. A despondency took hold of Bilal as he pressed on the accelerator of his Lexus, hurtling back down Petty Street. He caught view of Shelley emptying her bins. Bilal slowed as she signed for him to stop. For a moment Bilal considered ignoring her and driving past, but his bravery failed him at the last minute. As it so often did. He stopped and wound down his window.

'Somewhere urgent to be?' said Shelley, adjusting her floral apron.

'Picking up Haaris from Sam's,' Bilal lied. 'Getting the bins ready?'

'You know what I say: never leave things to the last minute,' she replied. 'You want to be careful. You won't mind me saying that Haaris is no saint but Sam Marsh is . . . ' She paused. Shelley felt it important to give people time to absorb the significance of her words. 'Well . . . his parents aren't exactly disciplinarians.'

Shelley still hadn't got over Sam planting a whoopee cushion under her seat at the village fair. Four years ago.

'You'll mind Tom's bush on your way?' she said, clearly realising Bilal's nod was the only response she was getting out of him today, and pursing her lips.

'It's an outrage,' she said. 'The man listens to no-one.'

Bilal noticed the blue veins protruding from her bony hands, quite at odds with her otherwise ample figure. Her wrists were the size of a child's. How would Shelley feel about a mosque?

'It's a real pain,' replied Bilal, feeling on side with Shelley for once.

Why had Richard paused for so long earlier? What had

gone through his mind when Bilal said that he felt he should try to build this mosque? He'd fail, of course; Bilal knew that, and even Richard knew it, so why the hesitation about the concept? Was a mosque such a social abomination?

'Copperthwaite waited for *fifteen minutes* for that cheese factory lorry to pass because of how overgrown the bush is now. His poodle missed its vet appointment,' continued Shelley.

'Yes, well, I'd better go,' said Bilal. 'Or I'll be late.'

Shelley went back to dutifully realigning her bins.

Driving past the village green, Bilal waved to James, who was adjusting the board outside his bookshop, and he wondered: if he *were* to build a mosque, in all the green downs, where would it be?

chapter five

Dear Tom,

It is in my official capacity as parish council chair-woman, churchwarden and concerned community member that I must insist on the trimming of your bush. It is creating huge problems and has already resulted in Copperthwaite missing Benji's vet's appointment. As an owner of several dogs yourself, you must know the distress this caused him.

I am afraid to tell you that if you do not do something about the bush very soon, my hand will be forced to make an official complaint to the district council. I do not wish your family to undergo any more grief than it has already experienced this past year and yet, *as an elected parish member, I must think of the wider community's needs.*

Yours respectfully,
Shelley Hawking

Driving to Evergreen General Hospital, Richard waved to Tom, who was walking his dogs. Tom – who suffered from the trifecta of age, a bad temper and tragedy – was dressed in his flat cap and red trousers. He looked at Richard, his shoulders hunched, before grinning and sticking up his middle finger.

'Thanks, Tom,' Richard mumbled as he watched him through his rear-view mirror. 'God give you strength,' he added with a tired smile. 'And us too, while He's at it.'

The skies were clear and blue as he drove down Coowood Lane, taking in the big oak tree that stood, majestic, against the bright day. There was a pebbled path through the fields, past the lavender, that led to the green next to St Paul's church, and an image of a minaret dome came to him. He tried to shake it from his mind and instead wished autumn would arrive. The different seasons reminded Richard that there was no such thing as consistency, which was a good thing. Consistency was often apathy's predecessor.

Richard reached Evergreen fifteen minutes later to discover Mrs Jones dabbing her eyes with a handkerchief.

'I'm so sorry I wasn't here,' he said, thinking the worst

had happened and her grandfather had died. The day had started off with far too many failures.

'Oh, no, he's still alive,' she replied, blowing her nose.

'Oh.'

'It's just the waiting, Reverend. He was meant to have gone six weeks ago. I've barely slept three hours every night and the other day I accidentally gave Amy the dog food for her school lunch.'

It was typical – death either came too fast, or not fast enough, and either way there was guilt attached to it. Richard said what he could to reassure Mrs Jones.

'We don't know what we'd have done without you these past few months. Do we, Fred?'

Fred, her husband, seemed to have only just noticed Richard.

'A beacon, that's what you are,' added Mrs Jones, beaming at him through tired eyes.

Richard tried to smother his discomfort by bestowing words of comfort. But as he did so he had a creeping, and then overwhelming feeling that he was a fraud.

To any onlooker he must've appeared to be a kind, strong and thoughtful figure. His curacy in Edinburgh had been followed by two years working with inner-city children because he thought he'd been made for life's grit. Except he'd underestimated the emotional toll of failing to fix people. It was one particular boy – Saleem, aged fourteen – who ended up being stabbed in a gang fight that sent Richard into a depression that was not fitting for a man of faith. Saleem's face, with his light brown eyes and olive complexion, friendly smile and sharp tongue, would still come to Richard in his dreams.

Richard's diminishing faith had led the deacon to send him to Babbel's End fifteen years ago, and it was in this community that Richard began to rediscover a world that wasn't always as hard-edged – its troubles more aligned with his capacity to cope. Yes, to people like the Joneses he was the open-minded vicar who ran marathons in Sudan, went canoeing with underprivileged children, took part in anti-austerity protests (much to the dismay of the village), and yet Bilal's mosque had become a snag in the picture of him that had been woven by the community – maybe even by himself.

Richard left Mrs Jones and sat behind the wheel of his Volkswagen and looked up at the clear, blue sky, scrutinising his intentions. Then he turned on his CD player and closed his eyes, listening to 'Blessed Assurance', the need for which he felt more than usual.

He got to the gym and programmed his forty-five minute run on the treadmill, increasing the incline. For the past fifteen years he had, quite literally, sweated out his Sunday sermons.

What is faith?

Richard wished he'd said something positive to Bilal. The problem was that he couldn't separate the friend from the vicar, like church and state. He wasn't in the habit of lying to people or himself, but the truth was he hadn't liked the mosque idea. Most surprising was his own reflexive emotion, unable to distinguish between his gut reaction and what might just be years of conditioning. After all, it was only recently that the church allowed female and gay priests. Just because one was unaccustomed to something didn't make it unnatural.

'Yo, wassup, Richy-rich?'

A scrawny five-foot-ten teenager in a white vest and black jogging bottoms bopped up to his treadmill. He grasped Richard's hand, before, as usual, ending the hand-shake with a fist bump. The sun shone through the windows on a spray of tiny pimples on Gerald's forehead, which clustered at his shaved hairline. Richard often felt that Gerald's mum must've been an optimist when she named him. A Gerald could never be taken seriously in a street fight or gang. You wouldn't buy drugs from a Gerald. Yet he knew, not three streets over from where Richard lived, people used to.

Gerald's conviction for carrying marijuana had led his mum to march over to Richard's, who had spoken to Margaret, who had then employed Gerald to work in her farmyard on weekends. One more offence, they'd warned him, and he'd get thrown in prison.

'You doin' weights later?'

'Of course. How are you?' Richard asked, watching Gerald closely. 'Getting on at Margaret's?'

'Yeah,' Gerald laughed. 'She's a joker. But like . . . ' Gerald shrugged. 'It's still fucked up, isn't it?'

Richard raised his eyebrows.

'Sorry. But like my nan says – you've got to move on, don't you?'

'Wise woman,' said Richard.

He couldn't help but think that what Gerald had gone through – and not just with Tom's grandson, Teddy – *was* fucked up. *Faith is looking fucked up things in the eye and saying you will still keep that faith.* At least that was a variant of what he told Gerald's nan whenever she came to Richard, half despairing, half resigned about the company Gerald kept.

Gerald eyed Richard appraisingly. 'Looking good. For an old man.' He laughed, revealing a gold tooth.

Richard felt suddenly fond of him, followed by an acute sense of depression that the average Geralds of the world would never make it out of their cyclical poverty. In light of so much inequality, what harm was a mosque? Richard corrected himself – a place where the faithful gathered couldn't be called harmful. Allah or God, it all amounted to the same thing. There was the whole Jesus not being the son of God contention, but who could see eye-to-eye about anything nowadays? And if someone had wanted to build a synagogue, how would he feel about that?

'Meet me afterwards by the weights and we'll see who's old, son,' replied Richard.

Gerald flexed his muscles and beat his chest. 'Yes, *sir!*'

He walked over to his friend, Dan, at the dumbells, who looked as bored by the world as Gerald seemed excited by it. Whereas Gerald fidgeted, jumping from one foot to the other, Dan remained still. Unmoved even by his numerous convictions at the ripe age of seventeen. Richard heard he was still on parole and wondered what might become of him. How could quiet, unassuming Bruce Barnes be the father of an angry boy who carried himself with the assurance of having either too much money or far too good looks. Dan's case was the latter and it was a mercy that he wasn't born with both.

Richard's thoughts wandered towards Anne Lark. They always did whenever he saw Gerald. Sometimes when he was driving too. Now and again when he was making himself a cup of tea, of course. Often when he was talking to a prison warden or inmate during one of his visits. Richard mourned the way Anne's life had been labelled a tragedy since she was abandoned by her mother when still a baby – though she never let that define her.

Until she lost her son, Teddy.

The loss of that bright and thoughtful sixteen-year-old boy reminded Richard of Saleem, and he realised that failure didn't concern itself with geography.

Only this time he didn't think of his own grief – he had to think of Anne's. Despite the fact that they no longer talked and laughed together, despite the fact that this turn in their relationship rattled him still, he would persevere.

The news had come to him, nearly a year ago now, via Shelley, knocking on his door repeatedly.

'Teddy's dead,' she'd said, pale-faced, declaring it out loud as if to herself.

'What? What do you mean?'

'Gerald found him in Daniel's car. The two had left him in there. He said he'd been feeling dizzy and was acting strange.'

'Who had?'

'Teddy.' She looked up at Richard, confused, her mousy, grey hair sticking out underneath her navy cloche hat. She was wringing her gloved hands together. 'They came back and he was unconscious. They said they took him to the hospital as fast as they could but . . . '

'Shelley . . . '

'Anne and Tom are there now.'

Richard had grabbed his coat, jumped in his car and sped towards Evergreen Hospital, leaving Shelley behind. The hills were covered with a frosting of snow, the sky a muted blue.

'It can't be,' he'd said to himself. 'It just can't be.'

When he saw Anne, sitting in the orange chair in the waiting room, he knew it was. She'd looked up at him as if she hardly knew who he was, and when he'd gone to hold her she was limp in his arms.

He would call in on her on his way home today even though she wouldn't want to see him. As for tomorrow, he'd begin his sermon with a reading from Numbers, verse 13. Or perhaps he'd choose something from Revelations? He picked up speed and tried not to think of just how few people would turn up to Sunday service at St Paul's. Richard wasn't fond of feelings of despair, but what did people believe in now?

He noticed Gerald lifting weights, Dan looming over him in his Nike T-shirt with his floppy blond hair, pushing him harder, as Richard's treadmill picked up more pace. His mind flurried. He tried to focus, come up with something profound, when he caught his reflection in the walled mirror. His hair had greyed considerably in the last year, his jawline, for which he'd always been complimented, had begun to sag. He smiled at the glory of God – how each day passes without rupture, until you wake up and don't even recognise yourself in the mirror.

Where does your essence lie but in the actions of your past and present, and what is your body but a betrayal of all of it . . . ?

He felt himself break into a sweat. The treadmill picked up momentum as Richard was encased in his faithful fog.

chapter six

Dearest Shelley Hawking, esteemed leader of our humble village,

I have received your letter and am in admiration of your service to the community, which, I'm sure, is infinitely grateful for your selfless dedication.

Please regard this as my polite but firm refusal of your request. My bush will stay exactly as it is and the issues caused to drivers can be taken up with the Queen for all I care – I can't imagine she has much else to do. Should any of the village folk impinge on my private property, let it be known that though I am old, I'm happy to become acquainted with the process of pressing charges. In fact, it would be a welcome excuse to fill the time I'd otherwise spend trimming my bush.

*If you could excuse me now I must tend to my dogs,
who are, I am pleased to say, in excellent health.*

Your most humble servant,
Tom

If Shelley had loved her beagle, Holly, any less, she
might have accidentally ripped off her fur while stroking
her.

'It's typical,' she exclaimed to her husband of forty
listless years.

'Hmm,' he grunted.

'That man's always thought himself above us all, with
his quips.'

Shelley got up, pausing to let her knees adjust to the
movement, patting the lace throw over the floral sofa
harder than necessary.

'And it's not as if I never tried. But would he have my
help when that Isabelle abandoned her family? Awful
woman. To suggest that I was the reason she left. *Me* and
my so-called *accusations*. I'll tell you, they're only accusations when they're not true.'

Arthur increased the television's volume.

'"Your most humble servant"? It's enough to . . . to . . .
well, just . . . '

She grabbed the letter again, the edges of the paper
crinkling in her sweaty palms. Shelley stalked up to Arthur
and shoved the paper in his face.

'Don't you *see?*'

He skimmed through the words that brought her blood – which usually simmered anyway – to a decided boil.

'*Well?*'

'Well,' he replied, looking at the television screen again. 'The Queen's not going to care about the bush.'

Shelley looked at Arthur – the head of whispy white hair, the dark eyebrows and Roman nose, thinking of the way he had once made the beats of her heart skip to a new tune. Now, here they were: his hand on the remote, watching the races, and hers on her skipped-out heart. The only comfort that Shelley felt in this ocean of disappointment and irritation was that her parents were too dead to say, *I told you so.*

'Of course the Queen won't care, Arthur. That's not the point.'

Holly rested her face on Arthur's lap as he patted her head absentmindedly.

'Then why should you? Oh, come on,' exclaimed Arthur at the horses on the television.

What Shelley had once viewed as charming unflappability, she now recognised as apathy and downright laziness.

'This isn't just about what *I* feel. This is about everyone in the village – all the lives it affects. Society is not made up of just looking after what *you* care about.'

Which reminded her to call Guppy about St Swithun's garden's maintenance.

'Hmm.' Arthur leaned forward as his horse gained speed. 'Yes, that's it, girl.'

Holly whined. Shelley would've done the same if she didn't have more pride.

'Oh, you bugger.' He leaned back and looked at Holly. 'I knew I should've gone with The Colonel. She looked like a winner, didn't she, Hols?'

'Don't you care?' said Shelley.

'Leave Tom be, woman. His family's been through enough.'

'Arthur, I'm not heartless. I know full well what they've been through with Teddy – that's what happens without a father figure, you know. Still, I'll grant you, she was brave for bringing him up after getting herself into trouble.' Shelley pursed her lips. It was a distasteful subject, after all. 'I'm sorry for it, but God knows I've spoken enough about children having too much time on their hands – the devil makes work for those thumbs.'

It had been a case of serious bad luck. Teddy's anxiety medication had reacted with the MDMA he took, which cost him his life, and now the once full life of his mother. How, after all, was Anne ever to overcome the unique grief of losing one's only child?

There had been fervent debate in the village as to whether it had been an 'accident.' It wasn't as if Teddy wasn't perfectly intelligent enough to know his medication's risks and side-effects. People were left to draw their own conclusions, and it suited them this way. Shelley shuddered to think of it. How many times had she warned those children about addiction? She should've given them more detentions, more *direction*. Isn't that what people always needed? Even Gerald and Dan, who had been 'clean', so to speak, had to bear some of the responsibility for what happened to Teddy. Whether it had been intentional or not was beside the point – it didn't change the outcome.

It was Copperthwaite who'd telephoned to tell her, voice trembling, because he'd been at the hospital for an MRI. She'd asked for more detail but, unable to finish another sentence, he'd put the phone down. (Teddy, in Copperthwaite's view, had been the only tolerable teenager in Babbel's End.) Didn't Arthur know that it had shaken Shelley? She had gone to her room and sat on the edge of her bed for a full three minutes, swallowing the lump that had formed in her throat, thinking about that poor Anne and the blows life had dealt her. Shelley had been headmistress to the boys for the majority of their secondary school lives until she'd retired. Teddy's round face, when he was just twelve-years-old, had kept swimming before her. Then she had pulled herself together to do her duty and inform Richard. Shelley was a firm believer that sentiment should never eclipse responsibility.

'But this letter isn't a man grieving – it's . . . it's spiteful.'

Arthur grunted. 'Not like that's new around here.'

'Anne doesn't act like this. She's shut right into herself, and it's a sad thing but sometimes it's as if it was our fault that Teddy killed himself.'

'Shelley,' said Arthur. 'No-one knows for sure if that's what happened.'

His voice was stern, his eyes still fixed on the television. There was no more conversation to be had with this man.

Shelley went to their bedroom, scrutinising the letter and thinking that it would take just one more problem in her life to push her over the edge.

⁓

'Oh, it's you.'

Anne folded her arms, the door closed behind her. Richard had expected as much when he parked outside her house on Whitbury Crescent – one of five houses in a small enclave on the other side of St Paul's church. He made a mental note to himself to fix the wooden gate that scraped the ground. He was no fool – whatever people thought his belief in God made him – he had asked himself if his excess interest in Anne's life was more than holy and he affirmed to himself that it was not. They'd been friends, after all. But conviction was always easier to believe when unchallenged.

'I wanted to see how you were doing,' said Richard.

'At least you're not in your costume,' she replied, casting her eyes over his lack of a white collar.

She had her hair back in a pony tail, as usual, wearing jeans and an open shirt with little birds on it. Anne, tall with a broad frame, seemed impervious in both look and manner. She'd never been a slim girl growing up, and years of being called fat in school hadn't scarred her. She refused to make jokes about her shapely hips, nor had it led to an obsession with her weight. Rather, as she'd shared with him in one of their long chats – before – it taught her how to hold herself in the face of criticism, also helpfully imbuing her with empathy and kindness. It was the spirit of resistance that Richard admired, though sometimes Anne's certainty of self made Richard second-guess himself.

'Thought I'd have more chance of being invited in for tea.'

Anne took a deep breath and opened the door as Richard followed her through the familiar narrow passage. It was a small space, the kitchen visible from the dining area that was also connected to the living room, and the light wasn't brilliant. The kitchen seemed rather too tidy – was she eating properly?

'I just saw Gerald at the gym,' he said.

Anne sat down, hugging her shirt to her. 'How is he?'

'Feels more than he says, I'm pretty sure.'

She looked at her lap. 'I suppose you were preparing for your sermon?'

When he had told her, years ago, that his best sermons came to him when he was on the treadmill, she had laughed and said: 'A spiritual leader, running on the spot?'

'Sometimes we're already where we need to be,' Richard had replied.

'The treadmill seems too much like punishment. What are you atoning for?' She had squinted, mocking him in that playful manner that never seemed to cause anyone offence. 'Open skies and on the road is how any normal person should run.' A small dimple had appeared on her cheek as she smiled.

Richard couldn't remember the last time he had seen Anne smile, but he knew it couldn't have been in the past nine months. It was only now that he appreciated the rarity of fluid conversation – perfect, surprising responses, which activated the better part of his mind. He clasped his hands together and leaned forward.

'My sermons aren't as forthcoming nowadays,' Richard replied.

'Existential crisis?'

'Some sort of crisis.' He paused. 'I don't suppose Tom's relented about this bush business?'

'You'd have to ask him.'

'I saw him on the way to check on Mrs Jones's grand-father.'

'And?'

'He stuck his finger up at me.'

'Well . . . that's my dad.'

'He did it in such a charming way I almost didn't mind.'

Richard thought he saw a hint of a smile.

Tom's particular charm stemmed from his short-lived marriage. His wife, Isabelle, had been a 'free-spirit', as Shelley called her with the raise of an eyebrow. Isabelle's uninhibited laughter, along with her cascading blonde hair and large blue eyes, endeared her both to her students (she and Shelley had taught together their very first year), and their fathers alike. Shelley had been raised on the virtue of inhibition and so she might've suggested, to more than one villager at the time, that Isabelle's coquettish tone, and the touching of a student's father's arm, had rattled and, ultimately, broken a marriage or two. Anne had once told Richard, over tea on a cold winter evening, that Tom – between laying bricks for big houses in which other people would live – would leap to his wife's defence. When Isabelle fell pregnant with Anne, she'd felt the power of her seductions wane. She witnessed Tom's own spirit bind itself to their daughter in the three-bedroom home he had built for his family. This shift in adoration irritated Isabelle. And if there was one emotion she apparently couldn't abide, Anne had said, it was irritation. So, she decided it was time to untie the thread of matrimony and motherhood that kept her tethered to Babbel's End and left a five-line note:

Darling Tom,

I'm sure I still love you, but God, this place is a bore. I'm going to India, though our hearts will always be entwined. I do hope Anne loses that sour look of hers when she grows up. Don't forget to water the daisies.

Love, Bella

Tom had kept that note in a drawer on his bedside table, next to the pills he took for his ailing heart. The letter was worn and thinned, some of the writing barely legible after years of him re-reading it every night. He was a man who had mistaken the eye of a storm for a whirlwind romance.

Tom's foul mood, it was widely acknowledged, had started on the day Isabelle left that note, and it hadn't ceased since. Except with Anne. Tom would cease everything for Anne.

'He doesn't like many people,' said Anne. 'And nowadays people of God are at the top of his list.'

Richard nodded. 'I suppose they would be. We all need someone to be accountable at times like these.'

'As if you'd know anything about "times like these".'

Richard met her gaze and shook his head. 'No. Of course not.'

He knew there was no shortcut out of grief, and you never got to the other side anyway. It had to be felt and then, slowly, a person would learn to manage it so that their life could run side-by-side with it.

'Have you spoken to Mariam lately?' he asked.

Anne paused. 'Not really.'

'Right.'

The vacancy in Anne's gaze bothered Richard. There must be a way to reignite a spark. He'd hoped that Mariam would help somehow along the way. All he knew was that the two friends had quickly drifted apart after Teddy's death.

'I thought she might've told you about . . . ' Richard stopped.

'What?' asked Anne.

His attempts to help were making him indiscreet.

'Oh, nothing.'

And there was Anne's retreat.

'Just Bill's new grave escapade,' he added.

'His what?'

'Not that it's an escapade,' said Richard.

His words were coming out all wrong. He tried to measure them as he gave Anne the details of what some might call Bilal's meltdown.

'An actual grave?' she asked, eyes glinting with curiosity. It was a hopeful sight.

'Well, just a hole in the ground if you think about it but . . . really, I've never heard anything like it.'

'How deep is it?'

'Sorry?'

'I mean,' she said, her words coming out slower, 'is he lying in it regularly?'

'I think so,' replied Richard, surprised at Anne's sudden interest.

She looked at the ground, her eyes rounder and greyer, seeming to consider something. 'What does he say about it?'

'What do you mean?'

She paused. 'Why does he do it?'

'It's something his mum used to do. She had preoccupations with death and what it means for life.'

Anne rested her elbows on her knees and clasped her hands together. It was the most animated Richard had seen her in months.

'So now he does too?' she asked.

'He's trying to understand things.' Richard paused. 'I suppose he's trying to be closer to her. Grief can have many manifestations.'

Anne stared at him, giving a wry laugh.

'How does it feel? To be able to give vague philosophical answers to things that happen in real life? Tragic things?'

Richard wanted to comfort her, but he knew she'd keep pushing him away. He looked out of the window at the sky that was teeming with a flock of birds. Anne turned towards the perfect v-shaped formation too. They had the right idea, thought Richard.

'No-one has answers to things like this,' he said. 'We just make do with whatever we can to try and understand it.'

'Well, I don't. I don't understand it at all.' Her voice was suddenly sharp. 'It's like I'm waiting for some kind of miracle. Either for him to come back – as if the whole thing was an elaborate, horrifying joke – or to just move on from this feeling that nothing makes sense. Can your God give me that? Can he give me a miracle?'

Richard paused. He knew the answers he had weren't the ones she'd want to hear.

'Well?'

'The real miracle are those birds, flocking together; us sitting here, being able to speak to one another.' He looked outside the window again. 'This world. It's all a miracle, don't you think?'

She'd stopped listening. It was too much: birds flocking together – a miracle? What comfort is that to a mother of a dead child? Sometimes he wished he'd keep his thoughts to himself. He tried to change the subject, ask her questions, but he'd lost her. Much like he seemed to have lost the ability to inspire people to faith. He had to reconcile himself to the fact that we no longer lived in an age of wonderment.

Even his own wonderment might be suffering from a rapid decline.

chapter seven

'I AM GOING TO BUILD a mosque.'

Bilal swallowed hard as he looked at himself in the mirror. He breathed in, wondering when he'd produced a paunch for a stomach.

'Firm. Resolute,' he added to himself, approving of the charcoal grey suit he'd decided to wear. The tailoring of a man's suit said something about where he was in life.

He'd done the proper thing and had waited for his conviction to wane. Unfortunately, with each day his need to tell Babbel's End that he wanted to build a mosque had only expanded. Tonight this conviction was taking him to the council meeting. There was no accounting for feelings when they took a hold, except for the general rule that they strengthened in the face of opposition.

Bilal had expected a different reaction from Richard. A

part of him wanted his friend to tell him it was a brilliant idea, just what the village needed – a symbol of how far we'd come as a country.

'Where are my long johns?' asked Bilal, coming into the living room where Mariam was tapping away at her laptop as usual, and Khala Rukhsana was sitting on the sofa with her rosary beads. She'd been here a month now and had said nothing about being ready to go back, although he couldn't deny that there was something comforting about her presence. The same couldn't be said about the whistle around her neck, which she refused to take off in case she needed to whistle for help. Some fears you just couldn't rationalise.

'They're your long johns,' Mariam replied without looking up.

Bilal hadn't told Mariam what he was about to do. Her questions would make him tense and confuse him, but they'd force him towards rationality, which was usually a good thing.

Not today, though.

⁓

Bilal approached the village hall and got out of the car, his heart thudding. He reminded himself that he was wearing a suit and must act like it.

He walked into the hall with its high ceiling, chipped yellow paint and wooden floor. The back of the hall was empty, bar a small stage with equipment that had been covered in a white sheet. The windows were all open, letting in the fresh, late summer breeze as Harry and Bilal sat in the seats set out for the public. Shelley and Jenny – no sign of Copperthwaite, on account of a chest infection – also took theirs at the rectangular tables in front. Jenny looked around, smiling and chatting to people, while Shelley surveyed the audience she liked to keep captive.

'Bill.'

Bilal looked up to see his employee, Bruce, in his pale blue T-shirt, ill-fitted jeans and forgettable face.

'Thanks for staying late today to sort out those spreadsheets,' said Bilal.

'It's what you pay me for,' replied Bruce, taking his seat behind him.

Bilal looked at the agenda that was left on their seat. *Democratic time.* That was the time used to talk about issues from the previous meeting's agenda. His palms felt sweaty and he had an unexpected urge to go and get Mariam so she could be by his side. *A mosque.* It suddenly felt so absurd, sitting here with all his friends, in the hall where fetes and meetings took place. It just didn't *fit*. Bilal watched the room fill – more people than usual for some reason. Was his conviction purely circumstantial? Only forceful when standing in front of a mirror? Why hadn't he inherited his mum's talent for confrontation? Why was his body, now rigid in his seat, betraying signs of protest? Why hadn't he told his wife? And if it was the right thing to do, why was the whole thing giving him indigestion? Each white face suggested that his mum's legacy should simply be kept alive in his own, unimpressive memory.

'Hello.'

Richard came to sit next to Bilal.

'I'm going to do it,' blurted Bilal to him in whisper.

Richard held his gaze for a moment. Bilal would have to ignore the look of doubt. Ignoring uncomfortable things, after all, was the habit of his lifetime.

'I see,' replied Richard. 'Today?'

Bilal nodded.

'Do what?' asked Harry, who tended to spread his legs in direct proportion to how badly he wanted a question answered. He often looked in danger of doing the splits.

Bilal swallowed hard. 'You'll see.'

'Going to liven this party up?' said Harry, his bare knees now knocking against Bilal's trousers.

Richard gave what Bilal supposed was meant to be a supportive nod, but could as easily have been a twitch.

The room went silent as Shelley stood up, nodding to Richard. She scratched her skin, which looked red and blotchy in her V-necked chiffon dress.

'I know we're all busy, so your being here is a testament to your dedication to Babbel's End. We've lots to discuss, so let's get on.'

The main door swung open, hitting the wall so hard that the sound reverberated in the room. Everyone turned towards it. There, stood in his flat cap and boots caked with dry mud, was Tom. Shelley frowned.

'Good evening, ladies and gentlemen,' he exclaimed, bowing.

'Tom. We'd just begun.'

'Well, don't let me disturb the peace, please,' he said.

Tom walked in and took a seat at the front, looking around and smiling at everyone. Bilal saw him catch Richard's eye and wink. He picked up the paper on his chair.

'I see my bush is on the agenda,' he said.

'This'll be interesting,' muttered Harry.

Bilal wonderd if Tom's bush would eclipse the proposal of a mosque in Babbel's End. He suspected not. Bilal wiped his clammy hands and took long, deep breaths. He could see Shelley's mouth moving but couldn't hear her. Just then he saw a Pakistani woman in printed shalwar kameez, her dupatta over her head, standing behind Shelley, laughing at her. It was his mum. Bilal had to blink several times before Sakeena disappeared.

'Bill, are you all right?' whispered Richard.

'Hmm?'

Richard looked concerned.

'Yes, yes. Fine.' Bilal rubbed his chest.

'It's time,' said Richard.

For a moment, Bilal froze.

'No-one?' said Shelley, about to move on to the next item on the agenda.

Richard prodded Bilal's thigh, prompting him to jump up.

'Actually . . . ' Bilal cleared his throat, taking in the sea of familiar faces who were now looking at him expectantly. Except for Mr Pankhurst, who was nodding off in his chair. 'I have something.'

'Oh,' said Shelley.

Bilal looked again at Richard. He buoyed his courage and said: 'It's really about building new things.'

Bilal could feel the uneasy shuffle of bums on chairs.

'Well then,' said Shelley. 'You have your three minutes.'

Bilal cleared his throat. 'Right, yes, the thing is . . . ' He looked around the hall and laughed nervously. 'We . . . *it* is a cultural time.' What the hell did that even mean? 'And as you all know, I'm Muslim . . . '

Now he had everyone's attention.

The words sounded foreign coming out of his mouth – as if he was asserting an identity he hadn't quite recognised. Yet it didn't feel unnatural either.

'And, well . . . as such there are certain things Muslims need.'

What was he saying?

He detected the reserved alarm on everyone's face and knew he should sit down. Forget the entire thing. Change was meant for fascist states and oppressive governments, not serene, bobbing-along, minding-its-own-business Babbel's End.

'And so I propose – for the sake of . . . '

For the sake of who? His dead mother?

' . . . unity . . . ' Bilal glanced at Richard, who was looking at him intently.

Mrs Pankhurst nudged her husband, who awoke with a snort.

' . . . That, maybe, we should consider building . . . a mosque.'

Time stopped.

Twenty-eight meeting agendas halted and trembled in people's hands.

Harry closed his legs.

Richard folded his arms.

Mosque.

The word hissed in the village hall.

Bilal was sure he saw the first signs of beads of sweat on Jenny's forehead. Mr Pankhurst leaned forward, as if his hearing deceived him. Mrs Pankhurst's facial features seemed to have crumpled into each other. Bruce looked down at the ground. As for Shelley, the redness from her neckline had spread up to her face, her hands clasped together as if gripping the key to St Swithun's petty cash box.

Bilal attempted a smile, but his mouth was dry, his lips stuck to his teeth. 'I realise it's a bit out of the blue . . . '

The vocal tremors of mistrust were already beginning, echoing in the hall as well as in the spaces of Bilal's thumping heart.

Shelley gave a tight smile as the evening sun washed her face with its light. 'A mosque?' she asked.

Bilal could sit down and pretend it was a slip of the tongue, rather than a slip of the heart. He could tell them to forget what he said. He should ignore what his mum had asked of him. So why did he feel without choice?

Bilal's emotional tangle was interrupted by a loud laugh and clapping. There was Tom with his eyes closed in unmodulated mirth.

Shelley looked more than a little put out. 'Do you mean the type of mosque that has a minaret? With the call to prayer *five times* a day?' she added.

There was mumbling. Mr Pankhurst leaned back, whispering in his wife's ear. Harry slowly turned away from Bilal.

'Well, yes,' he replied.

Heat rose to Bilal's cheeks as he clenched his fists together, trying to feel resolute in a wavering room. Tom was now staring at him in wonder. Why couldn't he look away?

'I realise it's rather unorthodox . . . '

Someone scoffed.

'But, you see,' he added, hands shaking, 'I'm part of this community, aren't I?'

He looked around the room, which seemed to have become unsure of exactly what Bilal was. Did they think he was becoming one of those *extreme* Muslims? He had, after all, spent his whole life trying to be *un*-Muslim. The idea made him want to reach for a beer and a packet of pork scratchings. Though he was Muslim enough to hate the idea of pigs, at least.

'Of course you are,' said Richard.

Shelley gave another tight smile.

'So, I feel it would be good . . . *important* to have a mosque to show that.'

Mr Pankhurst scraped back his chair and stood up. 'Is this some sort of joke, Bill?'

Bilal's face flushed deeper at the indignity of having his mum's request reduced to a stunt.

'I'm quite serious,' he replied.

'Hear, hear!' exclaimed Tom.

The mumbling had turned into a commotion as Bilal felt the blood rush to his ears.

'Quiet. Quiet, please,' called out Shelley.

She straightened up as the voices died down.

'Well, Bill. We had no idea you felt so strongly about your faith. Not that you shouldn't, of course.'

He wanted to say *he didn't*. Until now his Muslim and Pakistani heritage had been purely anecdotal – good for an interesting story in the pub, or a quick laugh about how they'd eat tandoori chicken at Christmas while wearing Christmas cracker hats. But that image he'd had while lying in the grave, of being *in* the mosque, had imprinted itself in his mind. Plus, there were all kinds of inoffensive mosque initiatives throughout the country nowadays – chai-at-the-mosque, meet-a-Muslim – opening doors to open minds etcetera. Because it was largely agreed that open minds (and doors) were better than closed ones. Perhaps *he* could host one of those. It struck him so forcefully and gave him such a warm feeling he had to unbutton his suit jacket.

'Not just me, but Mariam too. And Haaris. Maybe more Muslims nearby?'

'More Muslims?' people muttered. 'What kind?'

He imagined Mariam reading their collective thoughts: were these *other Muslims* the tandoori-chicken-but-without-the-Christmas-hat-wearing sort, or another breed altogether? Did all Muslims eat tandoori chicken?

'Exactly how many? And how nearby?' spat Mr Pankhurst, his thick, grey moustache tremoring.

'Wouldn't it be a nice sign to the outside world, John?' Richard intervened, addressing Pankhurst. 'Considering the times we live in.'

'Yes,' replied Bilal, his confidence rising. 'That too.'

'Yes, well, of course,' said Shelley, looking around the hall, attempting to widen her smile. 'Thank you, Bilal. Let's move on, shall we?'

Was that it? Had they heard him? Bilal's heart felt wedged somewhere in his knees when someone spoke up.

'Where exactly would this mosque be?'

It was Guppy, looking at Bilal as if he'd just told him he'd stolen his golden retriever. Bilal had always had a soft spot for Guppy, who was often mistaken for a woman – one who'd *let herself go*, but a woman nonetheless – because of his long, lank hair, delicate features and broad hips.

'I've not really thought about that,' replied Bilal. 'I wanted to present it to the council before I take . . . practical steps.'

'*Practical* steps?'

'*He can't be serious!*'

Richard angled his head.

Bilal frowned. Why *shouldn't* he be serious?

'It's very good of you,' replied Shelley, her eyes boring into Bilal's.

'Excuse me, Bill,' said Mrs Pankhurst, 'but this really is . . . *out of the blue.*'

Murmurs of agreement pervaded the hall, but Bilal's resolution began to lift his heart from his knees, into his lower abdomen, at least.

'Racist!' Tom stood up, an ominous smile playing on his lips as Mrs Pankhurst flushed red.

'Well, wha . . . no, I . . . Tom Lark,' said Mrs Pankhurst, recovering, 'don't you go causing trouble.'

'Do sit down,' said Shelley, closing her eyes as if she were talking to a child.

'I'm sure you didn't mean it that way,' said Bilal to Mrs Pankhurst.

'*Of course* I didn't.'

'Bill, my boy, all she meant was that it's just not *English*,' added Tom. 'Isn't that right?'

No-one contradicted Tom. Not even Mrs Pankhurst. Bilal balked. What did everyone even mean by English? Bilal *was* English. Though he could concede that having a mosque in the middle of the village might not be. Surely you could be and want two different things at the same time? More than two things, even. He also enjoyed golf, for example.

'If I may?' Richard stood up, cutting a large and distinguished figure. He radiated calm and it served as a tranquiliser to Bilal's errant nerves. 'We know that St Paul's isn't exactly brimming with a full congregation. And as for St Swithun's . . . ' He looked around at the people who lowered their eyes, guilty of long-standing apathy. 'Anything that brings a little faith can only be a good thing, no?'

'With all due respect, Reverend, that's hardly the same thing,' replied Shelley.

'Isn't it?'

There was a pause as the two held each other's gaze.

'God's man!' exclaimed Tom.

Shelley let out a sigh.

'Smartest thing he's said in years.'

'Thanks, Tom,' replied Richard, sounding tired.

Tom surveyed the room, squinting at everyone.

'You look at these people, Bill,' said Tom. 'Take in each and every expression. They tell you truths you'll never learn from their mouths.'

Bilal couldn't help but look at the familiar faces that were now somehow foreign. He glanced at his hands; the cut of his suit couldn't hide the fact that he was brown, and never before had this distinguishing feature felt like such a hindrance. It didn't matter how much of his faith and culture he shed – quite happily – he could never shed the colour of his skin.

And why had he felt he had to?

'Tom . . . ' began Shelley.

Tom put up his hands. 'Say no more.'

And he swept out of the room, leaving nothing but a pervasive mistrust behind.

chapter eight

'A MOSQUE!'

Shelley's demeanour unravelled as soon as she stepped into her Volvo and drove off down Skiffle Road.

'*A mosque.*'

(If only she knew that Bilal had felt similar surprise when he first heard it from his mother's lips.)

She thought of when he moved here with his family and attended the first council meeting, back when Shelley was just a parish councillor – he had been rapt at her words. A quiet discomfort had lingered in her. She wasn't a racist – heavens! She had, after all, rather taken to Bilal's wife, despite her monochrome clothes. (That was until Shelley discovered that Mariam still referred to herself as 'Ms'. For Shelley this was dithering under the guise of feminism, and if there was one thing she couldn't abide, it was dithering.) No, it had nothing to do with the Hashams' skin colour. It was the unknown. Unknown people harboured unknown ideas. And ideas could be a dangerous thing.

She strode into the house and looked around for her intellectually vacant husband. Holly came barking at her feet as Shelley patted her head.

'A *mosque*, Holly.'

Arthur was sitting in the garden on his red and white striped deck chair, staring at the night sky.

'You'll never guess the *absolute treachery*.'

Shelley posed in the door frame, on the decking, expecting her husband to turn around. He didn't. His hearing was becoming increasingly selective. She wasn't sure whether it was age or stubbornness. Maybe they were the same thing.

'Well? Don't you want to hear what happened?'

Shelley walked over to Arthur and leaned over him. She realised she leaned over him a fair bit, so took a step back. She wouldn't have it said that she stifled him. Not when she felt stifled so much of the time.

'If you want to tell me, no point in objecting.'

Arthur had the knack of sounding cleverer than he was and the deceit of it irked Shelley, but she couldn't stop the words coming out of her mouth. As she related the events of the meeting, his expression began to change, until he looked at her full in the face and said: 'A mosque? In Babbel's End?'

Here was validation. Even her husband managed to emit emotion.

'You couldn't make it up, could you?'

'Bill?' he asked.

She nodded.

'I thought he was Sikh.'

Shelley exhaled.

'It's nonsense,' said Arthur. 'Wouldn't look right for one.'

A joy sprawled in Shelley's chest. The last time they had agreed on anything was probably when Arthur, for reasons now forgotten, thought they should spend the rest of their lives together.

'We can't let this happen,' said Shelley.

'You're going to stop him?'

'You said yourself it's nonsense.'

'Aye, but a man has to make his mark,' replied Arthur.

'You can make a mark without building a mosque.'

Arthur turned his head away and Shelley knew she'd lost him to the night sky. It didn't matter. She had been losing him every day for the past forty years.

Shelley went back inside and picked up the phone tree, which every household in the village had in case of an emergency. Below Shelley's name was Copperthwaite's.

'What?' he'd exclaimed, coughing, still in bed with his chest infection. 'A damned mosque?'

'Language, Copsy.'

She always could rely on his outrage. He'd been a part of this village his whole life – just as long as Shelley had. In fact, it was the only thing he had been a part of, on account of what had always been considered his *predilections*.

Copperthwaite had looked on the unfolding of gay

pride and celebrated 'coming out' with increasing disbelief; men and women affirming their sexuality on speakerphones and marches while he had barely affirmed his to himself. He'd failed to live by his own desires and, looking at these young (and old) people, had the impression that he must've failed others too. There wasn't even a lost love he could mourn and consider the question of 'what if' to fill his redundant days. There'd been one particular event, but it had meant more to Copperthwaite than the young man in question. A classic case of misdirection.

Back then, sitting in his home, Shelley had pressed his hand for a moment, carefully avoiding the full details of his upset. Her then strawberry-blonde hair fell over her shoulders rather charmingly, her face not yet lined with the vagaries of her own life. She'd just begun her teaching course and felt anchored enough to offer some anchoring to others, whatever their unfortunate circumstance.

'Goddamn country going to the dogs,' he added now.

Shelley listened patiently to his ensuing tirade, then told him she had a meeting to organise. The next call she made was to Mr Pankhurst.

'Shelley,' he said, as she heard Mrs Pankhurst talking in the background.

'You really must calm down . . . '

'I am *quite* speechless,' he added.

Shelley may very well have lost her husband, but there would be an ice show in hell before she lost her village.

That night Shelley tossed and turned. When she finally managed to sleep she dreamed of minarets and calls to prayers in Babbel's End, until her village had morphed into some Moroccan landscape. Shelley woke up in a cold sweat and resented the peace with which Arthur slept.

It didn't take long to rally the majority of people for an emergency meeting the following day at The Pig and the Ox. Shelley hesitated when calling Richard and was relieved when he didn't answer. At least she had done her duty as Christian and churchwarden by making the call. She got to Margaret's number. That woman had seen *too* much of the world, so Shelley – for the sake of keeping focused – skipped her name too.

'We're here to discuss the . . . the *outrageous* event at yesterday's parish council meeting,' said Shelley, calling the meeting to order.

'Yes, yes.'

'Quite.'

'*Outrageous.*'

The lights in the pub were always low, exactly how the villagers liked it. Mick came with everyone's drinks, wishing them luck, making extra space for them after he'd heard what the meeting was for.

Shelley took a sip of her sherry and looked around at the heaving crowd she'd managed to gather, the pine tables dotted in the middle of the room with their matching chairs, a cart wheel hanging against the burgundy wall, beside which was a wheelbarrow filled with logs, the fireplace next to it, which would be roaring come winter. People from neighbouring villages – Little Chebby and Swinknowle, Romsey and Baerney – had also come. Because what if Bill's idea caught on? What if *more* Muslims came out and decided they wanted to bring foreign ideas into their green spaces? There was a reason people chose to live in a quiet village. There was a certain way of doing things in these parts.

'I didn't know what to say when I heard,' exclaimed one voice.

'Oh, I said exactly what I felt,' came another. 'That Pa—'

'It is indeed a very trying time,' interjected Shelley quickly, unsure where that particular statement was going. 'But I don't think *any* of us have the intention of letting this abomination go ahead.'

'Absolutely not!'

'Hear, hear!'

Shelley's gaze rested on Anne. Why was she here and how had she even heard about the meeting? The people sitting around Anne shifted around her apologetically, still sorry for her loss, but sorrier for their inability to articulate their sympathy. It all rather detracted from the current problem. Aside from the discomfort of Anne's characteristic silence, the last thing Shelley needed was for Tom to come bounding in.

'Are we sure Bill's in his right mind?' asked Mrs Pankhurst, taking off her hot pink scarf. Never had Mrs Pankhurst's incessantly cold body temperature bothered

Shelley more. 'I've thought about it and his mother's death hit him rather hard, you know.'

She detected a few people nodding, as if this hadn't occurred to them; at least one looked pensive. Empathy, after all, wasn't always a given, but there was a time and a place for such a thing. This wasn't it.

'He's a good man,' added Mrs Pankhurst.

'No-one's denying that,' replied Shelley, annoyed. 'Even good people can have very bad ideas.'

'Exactly, Linda,' exclaimed Mr Pankhurst to his wife, who in turn gave him a stare hard enough for everyone to look away from the usually happily married couple.

A Mexican wave of nodding heads rippled through the gathering.

'I wouldn't have pegged Bill as a fanatic,' said another. 'But then he's Asian, so who can tell?'

'Stay in the sun long enough and you'll be brown-skinned too,' replied Mrs Pankhurst. 'Honestly, he wants to build a mosque, not a Jihadi centre.'

'I mean, it's not as if he's a refugee or something,' said another voice.

Shelley wasn't comfortable with the mumbles of agreement here. She had more than surface feelings for the refugee crisis. It never took too long after a news story for her to make a donation to a Christian Aid appeal. But if they spent all evening discussing the whys and whats, they'd never get anywhere.

'Listen to you people.'

Shelley looked at Copperthwaite, his finery distinguishing him in the crowd, the creases in his maroon Ascot tie as deep as the ones in his brow.

'He and his wife were fine enough when they came here, but see what's happening? Do you have any idea what this would mean?'

'Remember, this isn't *personal*,' said Shelley. 'It's about the bigger picture. It's about preserving our heritage.'

'Of course it's personal, Shell,' said Copperthwaite. 'When you start destroying things to *build* new ones. Where do you think this mosque will go, hmm?'

'I mean we're not going to get nasty,' replied Shelley.

This was her meeting and Copsy wasn't going to push her off her usual spot on the moral high ground.

'We're civil people and we'll take the civilised approach. We'll let the Hashams know, via petition, that we're against *anything* new that threatens to spoil our land.'

People banged their glasses on the table. 'Hear, hear!'

This must've been the moment Shelley's life had been leading up to – everyone watched her, in need of leadership. And she *would* lead. The ambassador of the village's conscience.

Mrs Pankhurst folded her arms, refusing to raise her wine glass with the rest of them. Mr Pankhurst seemed put out.

'It's not as if any of us have *problems* with Muslims,' said Shelley. 'But one should practise one's religion in one's own home.'

'Exactly.'

'Quite right.'

'Who will the mosque serve, anyway?' Shelley added, glad that everyone seemed to understand this was a rhetorical question. 'We must present a united front. Like the community that we are. Agreed?'

More voices of assent.

Had Shelley been less enthralled by her own speech-making, she would've noticed the two figures walking through the pub door.

She'd have seen them make their way towards the group and stand at the back of the crowd.

She would've observed Richard glance at Bilal, who for the first time was left, literally and metaphorically, out of the circle.

'Shelley,' Bilal said quietly. 'This *is* my community.'

Silence.

Everyone turned towards Bilal.

Shelley's cheeks flushed at the sight of Richard, whose eyebrows were creased enough for her to detect anger.

'Bill,' she replied, pulling herself together.

She gave him a small smile but his gaze rested on every face, as if to say, 'You too?' Copperthwaite was the only one who met his stare without wavering. Mr Pankhurst looked away, his lips clamped together. Jenny Ponsonby took a prolonged sip from her Pinot Grigio as her husband, James, looked into his pint glass. Harry was sitting with his arms folded, looking down solemnly, as if he didn't know how it had come to this. Then the blood rushed to Bilal's face when he saw Bruce.

'We weren't told about the meeting, Shelley,' said Richard.

Shelley maintained her smile. 'I tried calling you, Reverend.'

'I must've missed the message,' he replied.

Richard scanned the crowd, his sight resting on Anne. Shelley detected the sinking of his shoulders, the softening of his eyes.

'Let's get another table,' Richard said to Bilal.

But Bilal was still staring at the crowd, his mouth drooping at each familiar face.

'Bill?'

Bilal turned and followed his friend.

Shelley's heart hammered as hard as her thoughts. Feelings shot around her body, her arms tingled (they were apt to go to sleep). She swallowed hard. She had never felt more alive.

chapter nine

RICHARD CAME TO THE table with two beers, noticing Bilal's eyes darting towards the throng. What was Anne doing there? It was so unlike her to be in public, let alone such a meeting. Richard slammed the drinks in front of his friend, spilling some on the table.

'Sorry,' said Richard.

Bilal shook his head as Richard sat down, intentionally blocking the crowd from Bilal's view.

'Don't pay attention to that,' he said, reminding himself that this was about Bill, not Anne.

It wasn't up to him which meeting she should or shouldn't attend, no matter in how much poor taste he found it. Richard may have had doubts on the mosque matter, but it was his personal challenge to free himself of preconceived notions. Learning was a lifelong process, and he had taken it for granted.

He focused on his friend. 'Bill?'

'Shouldn't you be over there too?' asked Bilal.

'I'm right where I need to be.'

Bilal looked at him, holding on to his beer. 'Harry . . . and *Bruce*. Is that why he was even quieter at work today? Mrs Pankhurst sent us lamb chops the other week.'

Richard knew Mrs Pankhurst had a soft spot for the Hashams. When she lived in London her children had a Pakistani childminder who still sent the family Christmas cards – there was nothing like the yearly communication via festive cards, signed *with love*, to keep affection alive.

'Were they good?' asked Richard.

Bilal shrugged, angling to look over Richard's shoulder. 'Mariam made me give them to Sam's parents. She'll never go non-halal.'

Bilal was about to take a sip from his beer but paused, staring at the pint. 'I haven't had a drink since my mum died.'

Richard realised that he was bearing witness to a man in crisis.

'I even prayed once,' added Bilal. 'Maybe I'll do it again.'

'I've found that much of faith is practice.'

Richard couldn't help but think that the same went for kindness. And, often, hate.

'I know you think this is a bad idea, but I can't turn back now.'

Richard paused, unsure of what to say in lieu of lying. 'What has Mariam said?'

Bilal hesitated. 'I've not told her yet.'

'Oh. I see.'

'She's a little preoccupied, what with Khala here.'

'You'd better tell her soon – word doesn't stay quiet here for long.'

Bilal pushed his beer away and nodded.

'All the more for me,' said Richard, trying to sound upbeat.

The hurt lingered on Bilal's face as they watched people rise from their chairs, Shelley nodding at everyone, her face pinched. One by one they left the pub, avoiding Bilal's gaze, and Richard felt a sense of foreboding, which he instantly regretted as dramatic. Anne came into view as the crowds dispersed and she stopped in front of Richard, crossing her arms.

'Bye then,' she said.

'Bye,' he replied, resisting the urge to ask what she was doing there.

She looked at Bilal. 'How's Mariam?'

'Fine. Thanks.' He fidgeted with his beer mat. 'You . . . you were at the meeting from the beginning?'

Anne gave a small smile. 'Spying for the greater good.'

Richard admired her all the more for the way her humour managed to permeate her sadness just then. Bilal gave a relieved laugh.

'I know Mariam's been meaning to come and see you. But, well, you know . . . '

'Busy lives,' Anne added, turning to leave.

Before Richard could say to Bilal that it wasn't all bad, Mr Pankhurst had stomped over to him, his face red, his moustache trembling. Mrs Pankhurst turned around to see her husband pointing at Bilal with his thick finger, barely two inches from Bilal's face.

'Don't.' Jab.

'You.' Jab.

'*Dare.*' Jab.

Bilal had gone pale, his chest rising and falling as if he could barely breathe.

'John . . . ' began Richard, getting up.

But Mr Pankhurst gave Richard a withering look as he swept around, marching out of the pub, Mrs Pankhurst and her pursed lips in tow.

'Bill, are you all right?' asked Richard.

Bilal was staring at the door from which the Pankhursts had left.

'I hope you know – this *isn't* personal.' Shelley gripped her purse in one hand, a notepad in another.

She'd seen what had happened. The flush of her face gave her away.

'Shelley,' replied Richard, the sight of her notepad increasing his indignation. 'That was a *very* big meeting.'

'With all due respect, Reverend, it's a *very* big issue.'

Bilal cleared his throat, straightening his back as he looked at her. 'It is.'

'You understand?' she asked.

'Maybe. But even so, Mrs Hawking–' Bilal never referred

to Shelley as Mrs Hawking – 'We will not go gently into that good night,' he added.

Richard closed his eyes and took another sip of his beer.

'No,' replied Shelley, looking at both of them. 'We most certainly will not.'

❦

Bilal had to go home and lie in his grave.

Don't. You. Dare.

'Can't talk,' he said to Mariam, Haaris and Khala as he walked past.

He sensed their lingering gaze on him as he went into the garden, but he felt too harassed by the meeting, knocked sideways by Mr Pankhurst, and then too elated at his apt use of poetry with Shelley to have the ability to explain himself.

This isn't personal.

Mr Pankhurst's finger in Bilal's face felt *very* personal. Each averted gaze, each shake of the head was a denunciation; an *attack*. And it was all for Bilal. He settled into the grave, the earth smelling sweet as he looked up at the night sky. For a moment he thought he saw the shape of his mum's face in the stars, but checked himself for becoming sentimental. Action was alleviating his guilt, a feeling of concreteness came to him, sharpening the edges of what he always felt was a watery personality. He sat up, facing the wall of earth, and reached for his phone, checking for reception.

'Hello? I mean, salamalaikum?'

'*Walaikumasalam,*' came the voice on the other end of the line.

Bilal took a deep breath before introducing himself to the imam at what used to be his mum's local mosque in Birmingham.

'Sakeena's son?'

'Yes,' replied Bilal, shuffling on the uncomfortable ground.

'Sakeena Hasham?'

'Yes.'

'Oh haan. Your father left her, haina?'

Bilal had to take a deep breath – it was thirty-seven years ago. 'Yes.'

'Tst tst. Very strong woman, mashallah. And you sent us very generous donations when she passed away.'

'Well . . . '

'May Allah reward you. How can I help?'

Bilal explained his mum's dying wish and his newfound endeavour to fulfil it.

'Mashallah,' exclaimed the imam. 'This will be a *sadaqa jaariya* for your ammi – rewards in her afterlife for what she's left behind.'

'That's all very well, but I need money and I was wondering whether . . . ' He cleared his throat. 'Whether you might be able to help raise it. She was so dedicated to the mosque.'

There was a long pause. 'There is nothing better than building a house of worship. It is our duty as Muslims to help you. But . . . '

'But?'

'Who will be the imam?'

Bilal gulped. Of course! How could there be a mosque without an imam?

'I'd not thought that far ahead,' he replied.

'You must think of this. Where is your village?'

'West Plimpington.'

'West?'

'Plimpington,' replied Bilal.

'One minute.'

Bilal heard tapping as he waited.

'I see only one mosque in the county.' He paused. '*Bloat-isstone?*'

'Blotistone?' said Bilal. 'That's on the other side – hours away.'

'Yes, beta, it's far. What a name. Anyway, you will need to call them and ask for an imam.'

'Yes.'

'You can't have a mosque without a leader,' the imam added.

'No.'

'As for the money . . . well, people will have to know *why* they are giving it. Our own mosque is needing so much work, but we will help for sister Sakeena. Do you have plans?'

'Plans?'

'For funding?'

'That's why I called you.'

The imam laughed. 'We are only one mosque. How much can we raise for a place people haven't heard of?'

Bilal rested his elbow on his knee. 'Right.'

'You bring me a funding proposal and I'll put it to the board members.'

Bilal never thought he'd live to see the day there'd be board members at a mosque. 'Okay.'

The imam congratulated him again on doing God's work. Bilal muttered his thanks, not entirely sure whether he should tell the imam it was rather his mum's work he was doing.

chapter ten

RUKHSANA WAS ABLE TO walk a little more each week and thanked Allah for modern medicine with each step.

Being the type of woman who wasn't partial to a lot of movement, Rukhsana had never before thought about the freedom of it. Sakeena had been the curious one – discovering new shops, unearthing different restaurants, looking at the world map she'd tacked on the living room wall and talking about the countries they'd visit once she'd saved enough money. Rukhsana would've gladly trodden the path that Sakeena laid out, but now it was another unfulfilled future. Rukhsana knew her life was a series of promising failures and so she couldn't be blamed for the regular sighs she emitted. She knew Mariam – whose sighs seemed to remain on the inside – sometimes wondered about their origins.

Shagufta and Gulfashan called her regularly, asking whether Mariam was looking after her, eager for gossip. Mariam wasn't exactly warm, but every morning she'd come into the room and ask Rukhsana how she was feeling and what she'd like for breakfast. Rukhsana had never slept under a duvet or on pillows that moulded themselves to her body, and the white sheets and eggshell walls with their paintings of things she couldn't quite make out were all nice, but she was a woman who was consoled by familiarity. Even the beauty of the quiet country roads, the grey-stone churches with scattered honeysuckle, the sheep dotted around the green fields couldn't distract her from feeling that there was no sense of direction here.

She was saying her *Astaghfaars* – seeking freedom from hellfire – when there was a knock at her bedroom door.

'We thought we'd take you to the park, if you wanted?' said Bilal, coming inside. 'Get some fresh air.'

If you wanted? Did that mean they didn't want it? She had already lost her sister; she didn't want to lose her self-respect.

'I don't mind, beta.'

She *did* mind. She let out an imperceptible sigh when they heard a car park up at the side entrance of the house. Bilal walked up to the window by Rukhsana's bed and inspected outside.

'It's Saif, bringing Haaris back from Birmingham.' He was able to see them without being seen, if he leaned against the wall.

'Who can blame girls who don't want to marry men

from Pakistan?' Rukhsana said, knowing the story of how Saif had left Mariam.

Some people had no God-consciousness.

'Looks like he's put on weight,' said Bilal. 'And God, look at his beard.'

What a kind heart Bilal had, marrying a divorced woman with a child who he treated as his own. Rukhsana remembered when her husband died how no-one had wanted to marry her – apparently bad kismet was infectious and marriage was complicated enough. She'd had her dose of happiness one day and it had cracked, split and shattered the next. Imagine being born in this age where women weren't cast out for being divorced, merely judged.

'What are they talking about?' he mumbled.

'Hain?'

'Nothing,' he said, still looking out of the window.

'You're very good to Haaris,' she said.

'Am I?'

'Mariam has very good kismet,' replied Rukhsana. 'Mashallah,' she added. She didn't want to give anyone the evil eye, after all.

'I suppose he likes me a little more than he likes his stepmother. I spoke to him over the phone. He said he hadn't seen her properly.' Bilal shook his head. 'We can guess what that means.'

'Tst, tst. No-one can replace a real mother,' she offered.

'No,' said Bilal, softly. He stared at her for a moment. 'Come to the living room when you're ready. I have some news.'

As he left, Rukhsana wished Sakeena was there to tell Bilal that she wanted to stay in her room, think about her life and pray to Allah, not go to this park shark. She touched her gold necklace with *Allah* written on it. He, after all, was a constant; a person could lose everything, but He would still be there, a presence unseen but always felt.

Rukhsana had lived so long in Sakeena's shadow, she mistook herself for one. What she hadn't yet realised was that shadows were a reminder that we're still alive.

❦

'*What?*' Mariam asked, folding her trembling hands under her arms.

They'd sat at the table for their Thai green curry as Mariam had tried to keep her smile intact after her conversation with Saif. And then her husband declared that he'd announced to the village he wanted to build a mosque. Bilal gave a minute-by-minute account of what happened as he looked at her and Haaris with barely suppressed enthusiasm, before his gaze rested on Khala. 'I did it.'

'Why has it taken you *two* days to tell me?' Mariam demanded, almost knocking over her plate of food.

Bilal paused. 'You seemed preoccupied.'

Stay in the moment. Feel the sensation of the dry chicken struggling down your throat as you try to wash it down with cold water.

With Khala Rukhsana around all the time, Mariam had

been feeling on edge – of what, she didn't want to inspect – and unable to concentrate on her mindfulness videos. The result was increased irritability.

Khala looked between the two, as if trying to translate each word. Bilal repeated himself in Punjabi.

'Beta!' she exclaimed with excitement. 'You're fulfilling your ammi's wish.'

He smiled with satisfaction. Mariam tapped her fingers on the table, causing his smile to falter.

'Anne was there,' he said. 'She asked about you.'

Mariam took a long sip of water. 'How is she?'

'I told her you've been meaning to come and see her.'

For once Mariam had a reasonable distraction from the gnawing feeling of guilt, coupled with the self-knowledge of having failed as a friend.

'How will this even work?' she said, glancing at Haaris, who was looking intently at Bilal. 'Firstly, you'll have to prove there are enough Muslims around to actually need a mosque.'

'I know.'

'They're literally all in this room.'

She noticed him swallow hard.

'Then there's a question of *where*.'

'Of course,' he replied.

'Oh, beta, I'm so happy.' Khala Rukhsana beamed as she pulled out her rosary beads and began reciting *Allah hu Akbar*.

'Of course?' Mariam repeated, incredulous. 'So, where?'

She knew when Bilal didn't have an answer. Was love

simply knowing someone? Mariam shook the question from her mind – this wasn't the time for emotional analysis.

Bilal looked at Haaris. 'You think it's a good idea, don't you?'

Haaris shrugged. 'Will we pray in it?'

'Of course not,' said Mariam. 'It's never going to happen.'

'Why not?' said Bilal.

It was that bloody grave. It had made him emotional and he didn't understand how this would change things. Didn't they have enough change with Saif now back in Haaris's life?

'You know,' added Haaris, 'if the architecture reflected both British and Islamic identity, that'd be pretty cool.'

Khala Rukhsana leaned forward. 'Hain?'

'Yes,' Bilal said, considering this. 'You're a clever boy.'

'I've got chest hair now. I'm a man.'

'For God's sake,' interrupted Mariam.

How could Haaris know what this could mean for him? She looked at him – a combination of pride and uncertainty swelling inside her.

'They're all details to be worked out,' said Bilal. 'I know, I know,' he continued as soon as Mariam opened her mouth. 'But this is *right*. I *feel* it.'

'We have enough to worry about, you know.'

'Like what?' Bilal asked.

'Would Sam be able to come to the mosque?' asked Haaris.

Mariam raised her eyebrows, waiting for Bilal to answer.

'Why not?' said Bilal, unsure. 'Though strictly speaking, he's not Muslim . . . but that doesn't matter. Does it?' he asked, looking at Mariam's stony face.

Just then, and to Bilal's evident relief, the doorbell rang. Mariam went to open it and Margaret strode past her, into the kitchen.

'It's outrageous,' she exclaimed, putting her hands on her hips as she looked at everyone around the kitchen island. 'The whole village acting as if this is one imam short of a catastrophe.'

She shook Khala Rukhsana's hands vigorously and complimented her on her shalwar kameez. Mariam translated as Khala smiled uncertainly, probably because they were the same clothes she'd slept in.

'I'd love one of those. So elegant,' said Margaret.

Mariam paused as Margaret looked at her expectantly, waiting for her to translate.

'Khala, the *buddi* thinks your shalwar kameez is nice,' said Mariam.

'Tell her I'll sew her one,' replied Khala.

Mariam had to take a deep breath. 'Margaret,' she said, not without a little exasperation. 'She'll sew you one.'

'How heavenly.'

Margaret smiled so keenly her wrinkled jowls tightened momentarily. Mariam glanced at Bilal, feeling they were getting rather side-tracked.

'How can we help?' Mariam tried to add a smile to her question. She was keen on always trying, at least.

'That god-awful meeting last night was an abomination,' said Margaret. She looked at Haaris and nodded. 'Young man.'

'Thank you, Margaret—' started Bilal.

'We can understand people being wary,' interrupted Mariam.

'*Don't. You. Dare*,' said Bilal, jabbing his finger at Mariam, repeating Mr Pankhurst's outburst. 'That's more than wary.'

She couldn't lie: hearing Mr Pankhurst's reaction roused something in Mariam, which she promptly quashed in order to stay focused.

Margaret's nose twitched. 'I never took you for an apologist.'

'We're not apologising,' added Mariam. 'Just that we can see how they might be—'

'Racist!' exclaimed Margaret.

Haaris got up and put his plate in the sink. What was he thinking? Did he care? Was he going to prefer staying with Saif now that he was acting like an actual father?

'Is she angry about the mosque?' asked Khala.

'No. She's angry that other people are angry,' explained Mariam.

Khala nodded. 'White people don't like us, I think. But your ammi is your ammi.'

'Sorry for my incompetence, but who's Khala?' asked Margaret.

Mariam and Bilal both pointed to Khala Rukhsana. Margaret nodded.

'Mrs Pankhurst called me to say she was *not* pleased with the meeting,' she added.

A flicker of relief came over Bilal's face before it drooped, and that earnest look which he seemed to have acquired only after they got married took hold. 'You should've seen the way they looked at me. As if they didn't know me at all.'

'If Giles were alive, he'd be incandescent with rage,' said Margaret, folding her thin arms.

Bilal's smile faltered. They both knew that Margaret's late husband, Giles, was barely able to remember his name towards the end of his life, let alone form an opinion on the latest social backlash in Babbel's End.

Haaris rinsed his plate and put it in the dishwasher. 'That's a good word, Mrs Filibert.'

'Use it well, my dear,' she replied.

'Why don't you go and do your homework?' said Mariam to Haaris.

'Why?' he whined.

'Because I asked.'

'But I want to know what happens.'

Mariam raised her eyebrows as he exhaled loudly and left the room, her gaze following him, her nerves trembling.

'We won't take this lying down, Bill,' added Margaret. 'I've come to show my solidarity and whatever you need from me to help build this mosque. It'll be the village treasure, one day.'

'You know there aren't enough Muslims,' he replied.

Margaret scanned the room and seemed to understand

the problem. 'I'll sign up as one. I'll start a petition to convert people.'

Mariam massaged her brow, remembering that she still had an article to file about another latrine being abandoned in the lay-by. She sighed at the inconsequentiality of a forsaken latrine in the face of cultural upheaval. Or cultural evolution, depending on how you looked at it. 'I don't think that's the answer, Margaret.'

'This world,' said Margaret. 'Always quantity over quality.'

'Though we're very grateful,' added Bilal. 'What we need is land.'

'Hmmm,' responded Margaret. She glanced at Khala Rukhsana. 'I feel rather rude speaking in English when your aunt can't understand.'

She gave Khala an emphatic smile. Khala did the same, between her whispered *Allah hu Akbars*.

'Shelley Hawking won't get the better of us,' said Margaret. 'You mark my words.'

With that, Margaret gave everyone a nod and whisked herself out of their home.

'See what you've started?' said Mariam to Bilal.

'It is bad?' asked Khala.

Bilal looked uncertain. Even if the mosque had been his own idea, Mariam *couldn't* support it. She thought of Haaris in his school of a hundred and twenty pupils, one of whom was Korean and the other Irish, joining Haaris in the ranks of the exotic. Mariam felt perfectly comfortable with compromising principle for the sake of ease. She had experienced enough difficulties not to want to pass any on to her son.

'Yes, Khala,' Mariam replied. 'It's bad.'

'We can turn it into something good,' replied Bilal. 'There *must* be more Muslims nearby.' He paused. 'Mustn't there?'

Mariam considered the pigmentation of her skin. Muslims came in all shapes and colours but something beyond her power was dictating the turn their life was taking and this lack of control felt both absurd and – as with most absurd things – acutely true.

'Wasn't that part of the point when we moved?' said Mariam. 'That we'd be the only brown people in the village. No interfering aunties, judgemental uncles?'

She detected a faint blush rise in Bilal's cheeks.

'Of course not,' replied Bilal. 'I mean, yes, it had its advantages, but we're not self-hating Pakistanis, are we?'

Mariam didn't think it was as dense as self-hatred, more a sprinkling of distaste. Like catching a whiff of a rotten egg and wondering where it was coming from. Hard to detect, but far more apt to linger.

'What is "self-hating"?' asked Khala.

She'd almost forgotten Khala was still there. 'Don't worry.'

Bilal looked increasingly helpless. Mariam didn't enjoy it, but she had to strike before the metaphorical iron lost its ability to burn. She took out her phone and Googled 'land for sale in Babbel's End'. It was just as she'd thought. 'I didn't realise we had a spare eight-hundred-thousand odd pounds.'

She put the phone in Bilal's face as he looked at the only two listings on the page. One of the pieces of land lay adjacent to the ruined pre-Reformation chapel in the woods. Mariam and Bilal would take Haaris there when he was younger for their walks, letting him leave an offering of boiled sweets at Jesus's altar. The other was a field behind St Swithun's church.

Bilal clenched his jaw. 'I didn't say I had it all worked out.'

'You don't have *any* of it worked out. And you didn't even *think* to speak to me about it.'

Mariam wasn't sure if he was silent because he had no retort, or because he was brimming with too much emotion. She wished he'd just tell her what an unsupportive wife she was, so she could reply that she'd pay the price for the sake of her son. A prickling of guilt surfaced again as Mariam thought of Anne – she always did when worrying about Haaris.

Mariam recalled the look she'd see in Teddy's eyes when she used to ask him how he was. Sometimes she tried to detect anything similar in either Haaris's looks or behaviour – you had to learn from tragedy, after all. Khala's own eyes were on Mariam now. They so often were that Mariam ungenerously wondered again when Khala would be taking her gaze back to Birmingham.

She tried to level her voice, lowering it in case Haaris heard. 'And you know Saif just told me that this isn't enough for him.'

'What do you mean?'

'He says he wants Haaris to be more in touch with his culture.'

Bilal scoffed. 'He's an earnest dad now, is he? I suppose for him Birmingham is the hub of culture.'

Mariam paused. She'd said exactly the same thing to Saif, but her prejudice shouldn't affect Haaris's happiness. That was the general rule, surely.

'So? What'd he propose?' asked Bilal.

'He wants Haaris for the coming half-term.'

She left out the specifics of how he'd said it.

'You can give that to me, can't you, Mariam?' His voice lowered, and he leaned in closer, increasing the flow of blood to her heart. She'd noticed the change in him – the new beard, the tiredness in his eyes that sometimes looked like remorse – and she felt a rush of affection, for which she naturally hated herself. 'He said himself he'd like more time with me,' he'd added.

'When?' she'd asked.

Saif had paused. 'I've missed him, yaar. I've got so much making up to do. And he *should* know more about our faith and culture, no?' He'd paused with a knowing smile. 'Don't worry. I'll teach him all the classics too.'

Mariam wouldn't be taken in by it.

'What about just being a decent human being?' she'd replied, steadying herself. 'Like keeping promises?'

She couldn't help it. The sight of his beard, this growing religiosity, his sombre, thoughtful manner irked her.

He'd nodded and took a deep breath. 'I hope I'm

becoming a better person.' She'd clenched her fists in her folded arms. 'Right.'

Bile rose to her throat but she refused to ask herself why he'd almost touched her hand. She should be glad that Saif was becoming an active father. Instead Mariam felt something slipping away. What if half-terms turned into longer holidays? What if Haaris realised he preferred his father to his mother – and his stepmother became an increasing influence? She turned around, gathering all the plates and putting them in the sink.

'Are we going to the park?' asked Khala gently.

Bilal looked between the two women. 'Some fresh air would be good, I think.'

Fresh air felt frivolous when the kitchen cupboards needed organising. And then there was her exercise. The story she had to send Jenny. Shouldn't she instead look through old photos of Haaris when he was a baby and she was a single mother? And then learn to un-love the man who leaned in towards her only when he wanted to take her son further away? She took a deep breath and thought of Anne. *Be grateful that you still have a son.* It was a shame when guilt and gratitude had to go hand-in-hand.

'No,' said Mariam. 'We're not going to the park.'

❧

Rukhsana did the only thing she had the power to do in such situations: pray. She sat on a chair (due to her bad back and knees), listening to the cows outside, and said her afternoon prayer, followed by a long supplication. It included asking that Sakeena be resting in *jannat-al-Firdaus* (despite Sakeena's faults, Rukhsana believed her sister deserved the highest place in heaven), for money for the mosque, land, and more Muslims in Babbel's End. Even she felt the improbability of it, but she believed in God's miracles, and since He'd created the universe and mankind, He could surely send Bilal a bit of land.

'Khala,' came Haaris's voice as he appeared through the door, plate in hand. 'You like carrot cake? Icing's a bit sweet, but it's soooo good.'

He walked over and put the plate on her bedside table.

'You look after me, beta.'

He shrugged.

'Mum's angry,' he said.

Rukhsana shook her head. 'Sometimes people just need time to get used to an idea, na.'

Haaris perched on the edge of the bed. 'Do you think having a mosque will change things?'

'Hmmm?'

Haaris scrunched up his face and managed to string the sentence in Urdu – his dad had always preferred it to Punjabi.

'You will mind if things change?' asked Rukhsana.

'Like, yeah, and no.'

'Haaris,' called out Mariam. '*Homework!*'

He sighed as he got up, rolled his eyes at Rukhsana and left the room.

There'd been a lot of tension at lunchtime but Rukhsana was sure that this is what happened when people lost touch with God.

She thought about Margaret. Goray – white people – could be so kind. Of course they'd be angry about a mosque but see how she barged in and offered her support? Rukhsana's heart lifted and she got up to rummage through some of the material she'd brought with her, wondering which pieces she'd use to sew Margaret a shalwar kameez. She felt the full shame here of not knowing proper English. She'd never needed it in Birmingham but here she was losing things in translation. She could learn, but by the time she'd manage to speak fluently she'd probably be dead.

Her bedroom window overlooked the expanse of Margaret's green farm, where she noticed a woman's figure in the distance, accompanied by a dog. These goray loved their animals – almost more than they liked people – probably more than they liked Bilal.

'Holly!' she heard her shout, before the dog raced back and licked the woman's face.

'*Gandi*,' muttered Rukhsana, disgusted by all that dog's saliva on the woman's face.

Something about the scene, though, evoked a surprising impulse in Rukhsana to walk in the open air. Instead, she shuffled back to her bed, stretching out her plump legs. If only things didn't weigh her down, she'd walk around the green; if only she had more time, she'd learn to speak English. If only, if only, if only. No matter how she looked at it, she was all alone. It only confirmed what she knew about love: that it was both fleeting and timeless; that it could break and sustain you; that it could be limiting in its infiniteness. She ate the slice of carrot cake before looking in the bedside drawer for a pen and paper. Without much thought, her hand drifted from right to left, writing lines of poetry.

She looked at the sky getting overcast, a spatter of rain, and for a moment realised this English weather suited her soul. Rukhsana hadn't been back to Pakistan in thirty-seven years, but she remembered the smell of the soil after it had rained, Jahangir holding her hand, putting a shawl over her shoulders, and she wondered about the geography of love. Yes, she missed her country, re-imagining the steps she and Jahangir had taken, even though the English air settled something otherwise turbulent within her. If Pakistan was passion and love, then England was where its particles had scattered and settled, absorbed into its soil, becoming part of its earth. Her eyes filled with tears but she smiled at recognising and identifying a feeling. The last time she'd written anything was before Sakeena died. Why had she taken so long to pick up her pen?

She finished her sentence and shifted her weight off the bed again, feeling a twinge in her back. But she didn't sit back down. She hobbled towards the window – the clouds greyer, the rain coming down harder – and opened it. Rukhsana breathed in the air, holding on to her necklace. *Ya Allah*. It was nothing like Pakistan. And it was nothing like Birmingham. This smell was something new altogether.

⁓

Every restoration process had its boundaries. For Richard it was Tom.

He closed his umbrella – the weather preparing for autumn – and knocked on the door, ready with a priest-like smile.

'The good reverend,' said Tom.

Tom's eyes were red, his skin blotchy. Richard had expected Anne to answer and felt his smile falter.

'Anne,' Tom called out. 'It's the man of God. Doing his philanthropy.'

'Miserable weather,' said Richard, wiping his shoes at the door.

'That old bitch Shelley's got something new to worry about,' said Tom as Richard followed him into the living room.

Richard flinched. 'I wouldn't be so harsh.'

'Spare me the sermon. I don't need to add nausea to my list of ailments.'

If there was one common denominator in the tragedies of Tom's life, it was Shelley. Her presence during the time of Teddy's death reminded him that she should've done more when she was his headteacher. That she'd been the reason Isabelle had left him and Anne. If he'd thought deeply enough about this, he'd have recognised he was being unfair. But he always had been fond of apportioning blame – without excluding himself, of course. He was egalitarian like that.

'How's the gout?'

'Rotten,' Tom replied.

'And your heart?'

Tom raised his eyebrows. 'Amazing that Arthur didn't leave Shelley years ago. She couldn't be worth a damn in bed.'

'Yes, thanks, Dad.' Anne emerged from the kitchen.

Richard paused when he saw Gerald sitting at the dining table with a glass of juice in his hand.

'All right, old man?' Gerald said.

'Hello. This is a nice surprise.'

Gerald looked at his glass, a plate of half-eaten biscuits by his side.

'What can we do for you?' asked Anne.

'I was just checking in,' he said. He looked at Gerald's downcast face. 'Everything okay?'

There was a pause before Gerald held up a sweater to him. 'It was Teddy's.'

'I thought Gerald might like to keep it,' said Anne.

There was a long pause. After a while, Gerald said: 'Is it true? About that Bill guy wanting to build a mosque?'

'Yes,' replied Richard, sitting next to him, laying a hand on the crocheted table cloth. 'And it's Mr Hasham to you.'

Gerald exhaled and shook his head. 'Dan thinks it's typical, isn't it? That people fool you into thinking they're something they're not.'

Anne caught Richard's eye. Teddy, Gerald and Dan had bonded in high school when a Year Eight had tried to push Gerald and Teddy on their first day. Dan, always having been big for his age, had intervened, and quite literally packed a punch. It was an unlikely trio – the butch, the clown and the dreamer – but each personality type seemed to cancel out the excesses of the others: Teddy being a soothing voice for Dan, Gerald lending humour to teenage angst, Dan looming over anyone who threatened his friends. Despite that, Anne would happily put an arm around Gerald, but never quite managed more than a handshake with Dan.

'Well,' said Tom. 'We all know Dan's a thieving little shit. Don't know why you and Teddy gave him the time of day.'

'He's all right,' said Gerald.

'Bad influence all round,' said Tom.

Gerald shrugged. 'Teddy always liked talking sense into him. Dan's dad says Bill's—'

'Mr Hasham . . . ' interjected Richard.

'Mr Hasham's a nice bloke, but says if you've got money from working in this country then you should use it to help the English people who let you in, isn't it?'

'Dan's dad,' interrupted Tom, 'is a fucking imbecile.'

'Is that how you feel?' Richard asked Gerald.

He shrugged. 'Whatever. Don't know why they need a mosque. Not as if there's a god, anyway. Sorry, Rev.'

'No,' said Anne.

Anne's lack of belief made Richard impatient with

himself. Conjuring faith via prayer, after all, was a lengthy process.

'In all honesty, Bill's going to have problems with the funds and the space,' said Richard.

'You sound relieved,' said Anne, watching him closely.

'I thought you were a progressive,' added Tom.

'However things turn out, it's God's will.'

'Always so damn proper. Almost makes me like you,' said Tom. He stared at the tablecloth when he added: 'You wouldn't say that if you lost a son, though.'

Richard noticed Gerald wipe something off his face as Anne looked at the ground. Tom's expression changed to something bitter, then he said: 'You know, the only good thing about that damned Shelley is her dog. Cracking animal.'

His voice sounded thick so Richard decided not to call him up on the 'damned'. Even though Richard sometimes felt that everything *was* damned.

'Dad,' said Anne, seating herself next to Gerald. 'You know our guest hates that word.'

'It's your house, Anne. Your rules,' replied Richard.

'Don't you think we *are* all damned?' she asked.

Richard shook his head, despite himself. What was the point if he couldn't at least offer some hope? 'No.'

'What about my son? If he took his own life, isn't he damned?'

She crossed her arms and Gerald looked up at him, vulnerable, as if he'd been waiting for the answer to this question.

'Anne,' muttered Tom.

'We prefer to focus on salvation,' said Richard, softening his voice.

'He once laughed, saying he'd do it,' said Gerald, lowering his voice. 'Like it was only a joke. I pushed him and laughed too. Dan told him he was a being a dick. We didn't know he might actually . . . '

'We still don't know,' said Richard.

They all went silent as he watched Anne's chest rise and fall faster.

'No-one here cared,' said Tom. 'Living in their fairyland, thinking nothing's more important than a fete or a stolen ceramic pot; in the meantime, to hell with what anyone's going through.'

'A lot of people cared about Teddy,' said Richard.

'Where were they then?' said Tom. 'Oh, yes they came over with their watery sympathy and watery stews, but what about when he was actually alive?'

'Mariam was the only one who stopped to talk to him like a normal person,' said Anne, her voice low. 'Everyone else made him feel awkward, as if they couldn't wait to get away from him. Just because he was unwell.'

Tom looked at Gerald. 'I swear if you carry or take that filth again I'll be banging at your nan's door so fast you won't even see my fist coming for your face.'

'I wish you'd see that you aren't alone,' said Richard.

'Of course we're alone,' said Tom. 'And don't think, just because you have your god, that you aren't either.'

chapter eleven

*F*UCKING MUSLIMS, GO HOME.

      Bilal stared at the letters sprayed in red on his office door, heart pounding, face hot, feelings displaced.

As he'd walked down the hall, he'd noticed his secretary, Kelly, scrubbing furiously away. She'd looked up at him with a green scourer in hand and a wild panic in her eyes.

'I was trying to get rid of it before you got in.' She pushed herself up, the water from the scourer dripping. 'I'm so sorry.'

What disconcerted Bilal most was the tears that prickled his eyes.

'Don't look at it,' she said. 'I've made some fresh coffee.' She paused, biting her bottom lip. 'Maybe I shouldn't scrub it off? Oh, God, I should've called the police.'

'Oh, no. Let's not worry them about it,' mumbled Bilal, straightening his Hugo Boss tie, the only thing about him in that moment that felt dignified.

'Of course we have to worry them,' said Kelly, taking off her yellow rubber gloves. 'There was no sign of a break-in from the main door. I asked. No-one's sure how they got in.'

Kelly's words weren't quite penetrating Bilal's brain.

'Are you okay?' she asked.

Bilal tried to smile. 'Yes, it's fine. It's just . . . ' He looked at the door again. 'Someone was having a bad day, I suppose.'

Kelly paused again and lowered her voice: 'I think it's more than that.'

He looked at her earnest face, curly brown hair and the anxious look in her eyes. 'Has anyone else seen it?'

She nodded. 'I told them to carry on with work as normal.'

Bilal smiled and patted her on the arm. 'Thank you.'

As the boss of his own accountancy firm, it was the first time that Bilal had walked into the mid-sized office as if he was the new guy. Five cubicles sat parallel to one another, the fluorescent light giving everyone a ghost-like hue, the walls painted cream, apart from the one on the right, which Mariam insisted he painted red to bring a bit of character to the place. A large oil painting of an eighteenth-century English village landscape hung in the middle. Even now, years later, it looked out of place. Some things never would blend in.

The company was small – two senior accountants, one junior, a trainee and a secretary – but that was still four sets of eyes, excluding Kelly's, on him as he nodded in greeting. These eyes were attached to four heads, which were no doubt having their own thoughts on the matter of the unfortunate graffiti, which had appeared, presumably, on account of the unfortunate mosque.

'Morning, everyone' said Bilal, falsely bright, as he walked into his personal office, wishing that it wasn't made of glass.

His gaze rested on Bruce, Bilal's most senior accountant, who seemed to look determinedly at his screen. Since seeing him at the meeting in The Pig and the Ox, Bilal had been struggling with his sense of professionalism, power and intense self-pity. Conversations between them had become stilted, since Bilal wasn't sure if he wanted to admonish Bruce, or try to win him over. There was a time when he'd offer Bruce a lift to work but it would be declined, until Bilal had stopped asking. He had the feeling that Bruce didn't like his then-BMW pulling up next to his Nissan Micra. But perhaps it had been something *else* altogether.

Now Bilal's heart thumped so hard he had to take several deep breaths. He opened his drawer and took an Ativan before knocking back some Gaviscon, letting out a protracted burp. There was a knock on the door as John, who'd only joined the company a year ago but seemed to act as if he'd been there the longest, came in.

'Now, Bill. Don't worry about that stupid . . . *incident.*

There'll be CCTV cameras and I've already asked security to check the tapes.'

Bilal found himself rushing past John and out into the building's lift to the fifth floor. He knocked on security's door.

'Oh, yeah. You're the guy with the sign.'

The only sign Bilal felt he now had was 'Muslim' written on his forehead. The security guard sighed and shook his head.

'Graffiti,' Bilal corrected, albeit mumbling.

'Hooligans, mate.'

The guard was already forwarding the camera tape for their part of the building. Bilal watched, his nerves sprawling to the ends of his fingertips.

'So what? You really building a mosque?'

'Sorry?' asked Bilal.

'I asked your staff member who rang up to report it, "Who'd graffiti an accountant's door?" No offence,' he added to Bilal. 'And your colleague mentioned it.'

'And what did they say?'

The security guard's response was to exhale deeply. 'I mean, no need for graffiti, if you ask me.'

'Look, there,' said Bilal, pointing to the screen as a figure approached the office door.

'Typical. Covered his face, hasn't he?'

'Can't we check the other cameras? He can't have walked into the building like that.'

The security guard scratched the back of his head. 'Afraid that's broken. Meant to have got it fixed last week but the company sent a bloke who didn't know what he was doing . . . '

Bilal had stopped listening. He couldn't believe his eyes as he looked at the figure shake the can and spray the door as if performing a work of art.

'Sorry, mate. Bad luck,' said the guard.

'The graffiti or being a Muslim?' he mumbled.

'Both, I guess.'

Bilal took a deep breath. He supposed he couldn't be offended. Being one, after all, had led to the other. They made several attempts to catch the figure on the other cameras but he (or she, because Bilal wasn't gender-biased) had dodged them rather skilfully. Did they know the building? Of course. They *had* to know where Bilal worked so did this mean they knew where he and his family lived too? Were they dangerous? Suddenly, Mariam's reservations all made sense – what if someone decided to harm her? Or Haaris? A plethora of questions began to tumble around his aching head as he returned to the office.

'Well?' asked Kelly, wringing her hands.

All his employees had turned towards him.

'They were wearing a mask. None of the cameras caught anything,' he replied.

'We all think it's a bastard thing to have done,' said John.

'Oh, yes, awful,' another colleague added.

'No matter what,' said John.

'No matter about what?' asked Bilal.

'Well, you know . . . the circumstances,' replied John.

They all glanced at each other and Bilal wondered whether they were saying what they were thinking, or what they thought they should say to their boss. Bruce gave him a nod as he turned back to his spreadsheet on the computer.

'Are you *sure* you don't want to call the police?' asked Kelly.

'No,' Bilal replied. 'I don't want a fuss. Let's just get someone to paint over it.'

'You should report it, Bill,' said John. 'You don't want to take any chances.'

He gave him a knowing look but all Bilal could notice was Bruce, who had very little consolation to offer. Bilal had always trusted people and he'd rather not let one unfortunate incident mar a history of optimism. There were parts of his character that couldn't falter. Yet maybe he'd been holding on to facts about himself that turned out to be a fiction of his own making.

A memory seemed to pluck itself from his mind. A group of boys, jeering.

'*Go home, Paki.*'

His mum turning on them as if she were ready to take her shoe off and beat them. Then she had looked at Bilal – he'd been Haaris's age – and instead grabbed his hand and marched home, face screwed up in anger as she swore under her breath. *Kuthay de puttar. Zaleel maaray harami.* The whole thing had felt so unsavoury to Bilal he seemed to have deleted it from his memory bank. Until today.

Everyone left that evening, taking extra care to smile at

Bilal, say goodbye, and pat him on the back to alleviate any potential feelings of displacement. Bilal paced his office, hands in his trouser pockets, head lowered. The present insult was trying enough, but it was the past insult, which he'd all but forgotten, that was troubling him. This *going home* nonsense had to be nipped in the bud. When he first came to Babbel's End he was incessantly asked: 'What are your roots?' Bilal wasn't often annoyed but he had to admit he had to take a few deep breaths when asked that question the thirteenth time.

Roots.

He strode outside the office and looked at the smudged graffiti again, ensuring this time that he imprinted it into his memory. Then he went back inside, picked up his phone and called Vaseem Bhai.

'What's up, bro?' came the familiar voice. 'No, bruvs. *In* the van not on top of it, you *lallu*. Sorry, doing a delivery.'

'I need a favour, Vaseem.'

'Everything all right?'

'Yes, yes. Fine. You said the estate agent who sold your house was good, yes?'

'Yeah.'

'Well, can you ask him what kind of offer we could expect if we . . .'

This was impulsive. But to build a mosque he'd need money, and he had to start somewhere.

'If I sold Mum's house?'

Bilal leaned back in his chair, taking a deep breath, not

thinking about where Khala might live, the memories he would have to sell in order to buy new dreams. But everyone was *so* interested in this 'having roots' business. Bilal had no choice but to take the necessary steps in order to plant them.

When he got home that evening Mariam was preparing dinner, darting between the oven and steaming vegetables.

'Listen,' she said. 'I don't suppose you've asked how much longer Khala's staying?'

Bilal sighed, caught between agitation and the anxiety of having been impulsive. 'Why?'

'It's not easy with her in the house. I've got things to do and, you know, I *do* look after her.'

It occurred to Bilal that Mariam was a little selfish. But he buried his annoyance – because he could only grapple with one annoyance at a time. He cleared his throat, watching his wife as strands of hair fell over her face, her cheeks flushed. Soon he was sure it'd be in indignation.

'Mariam, I want to sell Mum's house.'

Mariam looked up, colander of broccoli in hand, her head almost popping out from her neck as she leaned forward. 'Sorry?'

'It's not enough to buy land, but it's a start.'

The steam from the broccoli rose and obscured her face. A protracted silence. 'You want to sell your mum's house?'

'Yes.'

'To buy land?'

'The field behind St Swithun's.'

'Oh, right, of course. Naturally there should be a mosque behind a church.'

'Mariam . . . '

If Bilal were honest, he thought the whole thing was quite poetic.

'This is getting out of hand,' she said, throwing the broccoli in a dish.

'Yes, it is,' he exclaimed, louder than he'd intended, making Mariam start.

He told her about what happened at the office. Mariam looked at him hard for at least thirty seconds, pressing her lips together as if she didn't trust what she might say.

'Right.' She grabbed the glasses and marched into the dining room. 'Bring the plates.'

He really wanted to lie in the grave.

'What did the police say?' she asked more gently, still clutching a glass in each hand.

He swallowed hard, placing the plates on the dining table as he told her he hadn't called them.

'*What?*'

Haaris came sauntering in and looked between Bilal and Mariam. 'Why's Mum about to break the glasses?'

They both paused.

'It's nothing,' said Bilal, attempting a smile.

Mariam put the glasses down as gently as the force of her emotions permitted and walked out of the room. Bilal went to follow when Haaris took one of the glasses and observed it.

'What's wrong?' he asked, distracted by Haaris's sullen face.

Haaris shrugged. 'Nothing.'

Bilal went to leave when Haaris said: 'Why a mosque?'

'Not you too.'

Haaris looked so innocent it hit Bilal, quite forcefully sometimes, how much he loved him.

'Why not a mosque?' replied Bilal.

Haaris continued staring at the glass. 'Hmm. You know I'm basically holding sand in my hands?'

'Yes,' replied Bilal, hearing the clanging of dishes from the kitchen. 'How'd you know that?'

Haaris put the glass down. 'Education.'

Bilal smiled, despite himself.

Haaris slipped his small hands into the pockets of his jeans, looking at the floor. He was petite for his age, lithe like an elf as he stood there. Bilal stepped closer and found himself putting his arm around him.

'All okay at school?'

Bilal swallowed hard, peering down at his stepson's face with his perfectly straight nose and thick lashes. Were things changing for Haaris too? Would he find out what had happened at the office? Worse still, what if someone told *him* to go home? And would all this push him closer to his dad?

'Well?' said Bilal.

'Yeah,' replied Haaris, unconvincingly, eyes still lowered, putting his arm around Bilal too.

'Are you sure?'

'Don't be like Mum.'

Bilal squeezed Haaris's arm and told himself that trials and tribulations were all character-building stuff. Of course, there was a fine line between character-building and character-breaking, but Haaris had Mariam's genes. He brought Haaris into a rare hug – rarer still was Haaris hugging him back. Mariam walked in and Bilal was sure he felt a pause in her step when she saw them. Her eyes darted around the room, her hands fidgeting over the dining table.

'Excuse me,' she said and left the room.

This time he followed her into the passage.

'Who *are* you?' said Mariam, turning around, whispering loud enough for her not to have bothered. 'Suddenly a mosque is important?'

'I don't understand why you're so against it. You actually pray – more than I ever have, at least.'

Mariam paused, biting the skin on the inside of her mouth.

'All I care about is Haaris fitting in.'

Bilal nodded. 'And what about him standing out?'

Mariam flashed him a look. 'Says the man who's made an art of trying to blend in.'

Bilal looked at her, the hurt visible on his face.

'Listen, forget all that,' said Mariam. 'I just . . . I don't . . .'

'What?'

'I don't want him to end up like Teddy.'

'What?' He scratched the back of his head. He didn't want to sound insensitive but what did Teddy have to do with it?

'You don't understand what I saw,' she said, barely audible. The anger had drained from Mariam's face. 'It's like someone just scooped out Anne's soul.'

His wife wasn't prone to hyperbole, so naturally the statement disturbed him.

'It's an awful thing to have happened, but she's getting better, isn't she?' said Bilal. 'She'll never get over it, I know. But still.'

Mariam looked worried, staring at the ground. He hadn't seen her this agitated before and went to hold her. She looked up at him.

'I don't know what to say to her any more. My friend of eight years, who's the only one I laughed with in this place. And all that she'd been through with her mum . . . and then this.'

Bilal rubbed her arm, telling her that she had time to make up for it. Nothing was too late.

'Isn't it?' Mariam said. 'I'm *embarrassed*, Bilal. Not only of that, but . . . '

'What?'

'That I'm grateful it wasn't Haaris.'

'But that's just human. Teddy was always troubled. Haaris sprints around, giving us random facts and trying to beat us at Scrabble. You're being hard on yourself.'

She pulled away. 'Not hard enough.'

He sighed. His wife had always been complicated.

'Oh, hey,' said Mariam as Bilal turned around to see Haaris looking at them. 'We'll be through in a minute.'

'You know a cold dinner is depressing,' said Haaris.

'Bring in the rest from the kitchen, we're coming,' said Mariam.

They both stood there, quiet for a while, before Bilal said: 'You know, you didn't ask me how I felt.'

'About Teddy?'

He shook his head. 'When I saw the graffiti.'

Mariam paused. 'No, I didn't. Sorry.'

'It's okay.'

'Well? How did it feel?'

He stared at her, barely believing the day he'd had. 'Well. Shit, quite frankly,' he replied.

'Hello! Guys, where's Khala?' said Haaris, coming back out of the kitchen with the bowl of salad.

'I'll get her,' said Mariam, giving Bilal a sorry smile and turning away.

Five minutes later they hadn't come in so Bilal looked in Khala's bedroom. There he saw Mariam, folded into Khala's arms, neither of them looking as if they were going anywhere.

❧

Shelley hadn't been able to sleep properly – yet again – and Arthur's body clock still woke him up at four-thirty in the morning. He was listening to the dawn shipping forecast as she tapped away at her PC keyboard.

She was not the type of woman to forget about one problem just because another, bigger one had reared its unseemly head. She had done her neighbourly duty, given due warning – multiple times – but if Tom was not going to trim his bush then she had no option but to lodge an official complaint to the council.

'Anyone would think I enjoyed this,' she muttered, squinting at the screen.

Arthur increased the radio's volume. Shelley read the letter to herself, half-hoping her husband would ask what she was doing. She glanced over at him, sitting on the sofa, his head back and eyes closed. How easy it was for his main concern to be the weather around the isles.

'Well, that's done,' she said, louder than usual. 'I didn't want to, but no-one can say I've been unreasonable.' Arthur didn't move. 'This isn't coming out of the blue,' she added.

'Were you going to make tea?' he asked.

Oh, yes, of course. He spoke to her when he wanted tea or had lost his slippers.

'Yes. I suppose you want some.'

'Is there toast?'

What did he think? That the bread magically toasted itself?

'Just butter?' she asked.

He nodded. Shelley walked into the kitchen, wondering what it would take for Arthur to ever just . . . *get up*. She looked outside the kitchen window. A few stars still flickered in the emerging morning sky, the warmth of summer now over. Mrs Pankhurst's curtains were still closed and would be for another two hours, at least. Shelley had tried to speak to her a few times since the pub meeting but she was always rushing off somewhere. Some people just didn't *care* about preservation, or the natural order of things. They lived in an age of flippancy. No-one sought longevity, or got attached to things because they didn't last the way they used to. Shelley and Arthur had had their stove for twenty-one years but the moment she had to get a new one she knew she'd be counting down the days to its demise. Shelley buttered her husband's toast as she thought of profound matters of conservation and the gravity of loss in the face of all this newness.

'Islam and mosques are hardly new,' Mrs Pankhurst had said at the pub meeting, just after Bilal and Richard had walked in.

Shelley dipped the knife into the butter again (Arthur was the slathering type).

'They're new to Babbel's End,' Copperthwaite had replied with feeling.

Shelley wielded the butter knife absentmindedly, uneasy that she might be seen as a woman who lived in a bubble. She might not be well travelled but anyone who'd been married to her husband would acknowledge that she knew the tumults of living.

'Why shouldn't we have something new?' Mrs Pankhurst had said.

Everyone looked at her, a wave of loud grumbling.

'But-but-but,' Mr Pankhurst stuttered, shocked at the

notion of *anything* new. More so that his wife should suggest it. 'It would change the whole *look*! It's unthinkable.'

'This is *England*,' another had replied.

'Isn't Bilal English?' Mrs Pankhurst had leaned forward, a challenging glint in her eye.

They had all looked at each other. Even Shelley didn't have an answer to this one.

'He's Pakistani, isn't he?'

'He was born here though, eh?'

'It's all about *links*, isn't it? You send me to any country to live and I tell you, England will always be in my blood,' said Copperthwaite.

'But your children would no longer be English,' replied Mrs Pankhurst as the crowd's eyes narrowed. Copperthwaite's frown contracted because he had no children, and the sadness of it never quite left him.

'Well, if I had, they damn well would be. They'd be white.'

Why had this conversation turned into a debate about identity? She had no time for that kind of pseudo-intellectualism. People started greying the edges of things that were quite clearly black and white.

'Listen,' replied Mr Pankhurst, while his wife glared at him. 'I've no problem with Bill but by God—'

'Don't you?' said Mrs Pankhurst pointedly to her husband.

He looked equally defiant 'A *mosque*, Linda? You *must* be joking.'

Mr Pankhurst's face had gone red, his eyes as narrow

as everyone else's, his fist in a ball. Everyone's head turned from one Pankhurst to the other.

'I most certainly am not,' she replied.

'*Linda*,' he'd exclaimed, banging his fist on the table.

Silence.

'We'll talk about this when we get home,' she said, furiously crossing her arms, eyebrows raised in defiance.

Shelley was undeterred. In numbers there was power. A few dissenters were nothing in the grand scheme of things – and even Mr Pankhurst was siding with Shelley. She didn't enjoy the idea of married couples arguing but she did feel more beneficent towards Mrs Pankhurst for at least the next half hour.

She walked back into the living room as Arthur looked at the plate she handed him.

'I wanted two slices.'

For a moment Shelley considered taking the toast, putting it in her mouth and eating the whole thing while Arthur stared on. But her body – or mind – wasn't designed to make movements so contrary to its usual practice. So, instead, she walked back into the kitchen and buttered his second slice, while she watched for the first ray of sunrise.

chapter twelve

MARIAM WOULD NOT TAKE it lying down. If Bilal didn't want the drama of calling the police, she'd have to take matters into her own hands. (Which was more than she could do about Bilal wanting to sell his mum's house. What would happen to Khala? What other impulse was going to take him? Was he even the man she'd married?) When he'd gone to sleep she took her laptop into her study and typed out:

We Will Not Go Home. We Are Already Home.

'*You* can go to *hell*,' she mumbled as she banged at her laptop's keys.

She didn't write that into this particular article because that might've been unprofessional. The whole incident had been offensive to Mariam on several counts, not least the graffitist's unimaginative words. This was followed, in a close second, by her exasperation at Bilal, who thought a hate crime could be ignored. She sat back and folded her arms. No – in fact, her exasperation came a close third. Second was that these unimaginative words had rendered her speechless. This sweeping, general statement, personalised for her and her family, for her eleven-year-old precocious son, had momentarily stifled her voice. And all the while Saif was already on her case about faith and culture and things like belonging (and didn't she want him to say that she still belonged to him?). Then there was Khala, who'd hugged her. Just like that, without explanation or reason. And Mariam had sunk into her comforting arms with no thoughts of feeling suffocated. She wouldn't be silenced a moment longer and banged out each word to the beat of her thumping heart.

Words have power. They're absorbed into a person's mind and can shift the sands of perspective. But so does action. As for the question of going home – the writing might be on the office door, and spray paint may leave its mark, but it can't crack the foundations upon which a home is built.

Mariam looked at the screen and read the words several times. She took a long, deep breath as she typed in Jenny's email address and pressed the send button.

'That will show them,' she said.

Whoever *they* were.

❧

Bilal and Haaris had already left for work and school when Mariam woke up the following morning. She checked her

email on her phone, but it was still early. There was something about the stream of words she'd poured out the
night before that gave Mariam a hankering for more words.
Ones that didn't have to do with broken church bells and
village fetes. She sat at the kitchen table and, without even
making coffee, began to write. What she was writing she
had no idea, but sometimes words formed the ideas rather
than the other way around.

'Salamalaikum, beta,' said Khala, ambling into the
kitchen.

Mariam jumped. 'I'll make breakfast,' she said, embarrassed in the cold light of day by what had happened the
night before. What must Khala have thought? When
Mariam broke away from her she had simply said: 'Shall
we have dinner?' As if crying into someone's arms was
normal.

'No, beta,' replied Khala now. 'I'll make breakfast. This
much I know about the kitchen, na?'

Mariam flitted between carrying on with the free flow
of sentences and wanting to maintain order in her kitchen.
You must learn to let go. This, she realised, could be applied
to Tupperware as well as ex-husbands. So she smiled,
ignoring the clanging of cutlery. A plate of fruit, all cut
up, was put in front of her, along with a mug of green
tea, then Khala left the kitchen without saying another
word. Mariam managed to shout out a thank you as she
ate a forkful of blueberries.

Two hours later she emerged from her writing stupor
– something creative about a woman who'd lost her

memory and couldn't find her way out of a forest. She felt a sense of vigour, which she usually only experienced when exercising her body or exorcising her mind. She checked her email again but still nothing. Jenny usually responded promptly. Of course, that was pre-mosque days. There was no impartiality in this place. But she waited. She listened to another Adalrik clip – this time on purging the past – exercised for an hour, had lunch with Khala, and then did some more writing. As three o'clock approached, she went to collect Haaris, who walked towards the car, shoulder slouched under the beating rain.

'Hi, baby,' she said as he got into the passenger seat.

Haaris looked out of the car window, the windscreen wipers furiously sashaying side-to-side.

'How was school?'

'Fine,' he replied.

She looked at him, waiting for more. Haaris was usually as monosyllabic as Bilal was pessimistic.

'What'd you get up to?' she asked.

'Usual.'

She paused at the front gate and noticed Sam's dad, Harry, pull up by her side. She tried to smile through the rain, but he stared resolutely ahead. Haaris and Sam did the same.

'How's Sam?' she asked, feeling anxious.

'God, Mum, what's with the million questions?'

Before she could reply there was a knock on her window.

'Hell-o,' sang Terri, Haaris's form teacher, waving at Mariam from under her umbrella in her jumper and flip-flops.

'This weather! Gosh, you're looking well. Sorry, it's just a quick word about the bake sale next month for the church bell – almost there with the money! We wondered if you'd like to make something *traditional*?'

'Sorry?'

Terri glanced at Haaris, who looked down at his lap.

'Something . . . Hang on, let me check because I don't want to offend anyone.' She laughed. 'You are Pakistani, aren't you? I mean *your parents* are from there. I understand that's a very important distinction.'

Mariam felt her nostrils flare. 'Quite.'

'Well, if you could make something *Pakistani*, that'd be wonderful.'

'Right,' said Mariam. 'Like what?'

Terri bent lower, clasping her hands between her knees. 'We were hoping you'd help with that.' She laughed again.

Try to see the best in people. Dig deep. Deeper than your husband's grave.

'Okay,' she finally replied, even though she'd never made a Pakistani dessert in her life. 'Why not?'

'Oh, I'm so glad,' said Terri, clapping her hands, despite still holding on to an umbrella. 'We want to be *inclusive*. It's so nice to experience other cultures, isn't it? No matter what's happening.'

Mariam gripped the steering wheel. 'Of course.'

Terri stepped back and waved so hard Mariam thought her hand might fall off.

'So now I have to learn to make ladoos?' Mariam joked to Haaris. 'The height of cultural experience.'

He didn't reply. By the time they got home the rain had subsided, the skies cleared with a rainbow arching over the green fields. Haaris went to go straight to his room but then paused at the stairs and looked back. 'Am I going to Dad's this half-term?'

Mariam hung the car keys on the key rack. 'Did you want to?'

He shrugged. 'Be good. Different.'

Different? Why did he suddenly want something different? 'Okay.'

Khala Rukhsana called out to Haaris, who brushed past Mariam and went into her room, closing the door behind him. She looked at her phone for an email but there was still nothing. Whatever had happened between Haaris and Sam, she knew it was something to do with the mosque. In a bout of impatience, she called Jenny.

'Hi. Mariam. I was just about to take the dog for a walk—'

'Did you get my article?'

'I did.'

'And?'

Jenny paused. 'I'm not sure it's quite right for the paper.'

Mariam gripped the top of the kitchen chair. 'Oh?'

'It's quite hard-hitting. You're a good writer, but—'

'You don't want to address racism?'

'Oh, God, no, it doesn't all boil down to that,' said Jenny. Jenny who was obviously on Shelley's side. 'What happened is *appalling*. Even Shelley thinks so. But do we need more provocation in an already provocative situation?'

Mariam had to level her breathing. 'I see.'

'It's September so too early to write about the Nativity. Your write-up about the harvest festival was *great*, by the way.' Jenny paused. 'Why not write something about the broadband?'

'Excuse me?'

'I know everyone's complaining about the new telephone poles, but I *do* wish people moved with the times.'

Mariam's heart beat faster as she looked around the living room for a sign, *any* sign, of her Muslim-ness. She strode out of the room, looking in the passage, the kitchen, searching the house for anything that might tell a stranger who the Hashams were. It turned out that the most visible sign of their being Muslim had been on Bilal's office door.

'The connection is dire for people working from home and raising a family,' carried on Jenny. 'It's not easy being a woman, is it?'

Then Mariam heard Haaris and Khala's faint voices, a hodgepodge of English and Punjabi.

'Jenny,' said Mariam. 'An article about my husband's office being graffitied with: *Fucking Muslims, Go Home* isn't important, but substandard Wi-Fi connectivity is?'

There was a long pause.

'Hello?' said Mariam.

'I'm sorry. There's just no need for foul language.'

'No, we don't like it much ourselves,' replied Mariam. Her shoulders stiffened. An attack on her family dismissed in favour of broadband! It was absurd. Absurd, how perfectly unsurprising it was. 'I'm sorry, but I don't think this will work.' Mariam swallowed hard. 'I'm resigning.'

'Mariam,' said Jenny. 'That's quite dramatic.'

Dramatic! Mariam paused. 'Oh no, Jenny. You've not even begun to see dramatic.'

She put the phone down, her hands shaking and mind reeling. Mariam paced the living room. Had she really quit her job? What choice did she have? She tried to rein in her panic – she still had other freelancing jobs. Except for some reason it all felt vacuous. They were jobs of no importance and it made her feel like a woman of little importance. What if Mariam finally had nothing – other than Haaris – to show for her life? She'd spent so many years apathetic about her career – why? She wiped her sweaty palms on her jeans and took deep breaths. *One, two, three, four.* It was times like this she wanted to pick up the phone and call Anne. It was just the kind of thing that would've started as a rant and ended up in laughter. Before Teddy. Mariam played with her phone, thinking of Haaris. And then she dialled Anne's number.

'Hello,' said Mariam. 'It's me.'

'Oh. Hi.'

'How are you?'

'I'm okay. Fine.' There was a pause. 'You?'

'Fine,' replied Mariam. 'Listen, I—'

'I heard about the graffiti.'

'Oh, yes, that.'

'That was pretty nasty,' said Anne.

'I know. Thanks.' Mariam sat on the sofa, staring at the

TV screen on their wall. 'I'm sorry I haven't been round for so long.'

There was a long pause. 'Yeah, well . . . '

'I just . . . '

But there was nothing Mariam could say that could begin to explain it. She remembered that day with clarity. Mariam had witnessed a woman losing her mind and it had terrified her. Not just because she wasn't sure whether Anne would ever come back from it, but because she'd glimpsed herself in Anne: the wild, unfiltered breaking of a heart and life. Mariam had spent every night in the house with her for a week, refusing to leave her side, and all she'd been thinking was: what if that had been Haaris? When she returned home, she would hold on to him whenever he said goodbye. Grab his face to kiss his cheek, even though he'd exclaim, 'Mum! Get off!' Every morning when he left the house she agonised: will he come back to me?

'It's not like I've been in the mood to see people,' said Anne. 'Though you never were people.'

Mariam's guilt swelled, her heart cracked a little. 'People are hard work.'

'Aren't they?' replied Anne.

Mariam missed her friend. She was mortified at how little she could do to help her. Mortified at how little she had tried.

'It's just, if it was me—' began Mariam.

'I know.'

They were both quiet for a few moments before Anne said: 'How's Bilal taking the whole thing?'

'How do you think?' said Mariam.

'Pretending it didn't happen?'

Mariam let out a small laugh.

'Richard mentioned . . . he said something about a grave.'

'Oh. Right. Yes,' said Mariam, feeling a flush of embarrassment, but the least she could do was explain the backstory.

'Does it help him?' asked Anne.

'I'm not sure. But it hasn't done us any favours,' said Mariam.

Silence.

'How's your dad?'

'Fine. I keep telling him to stop getting so angry about things, his heart's rickety enough. Although I should thank Bill.'

'Why?'

'Mariam, even in Dad's wildest dreams he'd never have come up with a plan as antagonising as building a mosque in Babbel's End.'

There was a pause before they both burst into laughter.

'Well,' said Mariam, 'I'm glad the token brown people have come in handy.'

'After this, there'll be nothing token about you.'

Mariam laughed again. How could she help Anne with her sorrow, so that their lives might tally with each other's again? But Anne's type of grief couldn't be watered down to something as mild as Mariam's discontent. It was a force too strong and isolated; it could make room for nothing and no-one.

'Anyway, I just wanted to say hello. It'd be nice to see you soon.'

Another pause.

'Maybe,' said Anne.

'Give me a call when you're free.'

Anne said she would as she put the phone down, while Mariam knew full well she wouldn't. How could they bridge the gap of the random injustice of one of them having a son, and the other losing one?

❧

After their conversation, Bilal was the first to put the phone down on his impulsive wife. Yet he *was* annoyed with Jenny. Mariam had written something important – and since she'd written it he knew it would be more than just good . . .

'Sorry,' said Bruce, coming into his office. 'Is Mrs Neil's cat's wicker basket tax-deductible?'

'No. I'm afraid you'll have to give her the bad news.'

Bilal had seen Bruce parked in the car that morning with his son, Dan, clearly in the throes of an argument. Would he and Haaris ever argue like that? Bilal felt an unexpected pang of pity for his employee, trying to forget he was at that meeting, and forced a smile.

Bruce went to leave as Bilal asked: 'How are things?'

'Fine.' Pause. 'Thanks.'

'And Dan?'

'Still not quite himself. After Teddy.'

'Hmmm,' replied Bilal as sympathetically as he could for a person who knew that Dan would be Dan, with or without Teddy. 'They were close.'

'He's just distant, you know,' replied Bruce, before his face reddened, as if he'd said too much. 'Anyway,' he added. 'Lots to do.'

Bruce left and sat back at his desk. If he could just have said *something* about the graffiti to Bilal, Bilal might *try* and understand why he had been at that meeting. Instead Bilal went back to staring at the page with the land listing. Vaseem had called to let him know that his mum's place had been valued and was worth less than a quarter of the money Bilal needed to actually buy and build on the thirty acres behind St Swithun's. Perhaps he could buy a small section of the plot? So Bilal had given Vaseem the go ahead. With or without Mariam's consent, a plan for Khala, or an idea about where the rest of the money might come from. Then he looked at the proposal he'd written to send to the imam in Birmingham, which was more of a one-page document begging them to help him in the name of *spreading peace*. Bilal shifted uncomfortably at the idea, since it was rather spreading discord. He picked up the phone and took a deep breath before dialling a number.

'Hello, I'm enquiring about the land for sale – between Babbel's End and Little Chebby? I wanted to speak to the owner about applying to the council for planning permission.'

Apparently he didn't need to own the land to get permission, provided the owner was in agreement. The agent told him that Mrs Gardiner, who now lived in Scotland, was visiting her son in Australia and wouldn't be back for a few months. He'd drop her an email.

'What's the planning permission for?' asked the agent, after taking Bilal's email address.

Bilal cleared his throat. 'A mosque,' he mumbled.

'Sorry?'

'A *mosque*.'

'A what?'

Bilal sighed. 'You know the place of worship? For Muslims?'

'Oh. All right. Fine. I'll, er, I'll let her know.' The agent paused. 'Though I should probably warn you – Mrs Gardiner's agnostic.'

Bilal put the phone down. 'I'm not asking her to convert,' he added when there was no-one on the other end to hear him.

He grabbed his jacket and keys and drove towards Babbel's End, parking up in the lay-by next to a fence that stopped the gathered cows from escaping. He stepped out into the cloudy day, the chill of autumn already in the air, and made his way towards the land behind St Swithun's church. There was a steep, hilly road and when you got to the top, beyond the low stone wall, you could see miles of rolling hills and the sea. Sheep were bleating on the patch on his left, a row of pine trees lining the road as Bilal reached the top, panting. The vast expanse of the country was spread before him, hills of green and yellow with the sea just about visible. Slivers of white light lined

the grey clouds, the sun pushing through, casting the fields
in shadows and illuminated light. Bilal's heart swelled with
pride. He imagined the mosque behind St Swithun's and
a warmth filled up within him. He always assumed that
you created yourself in whatever shape you wanted, but
it turned out that people didn't trust the art of shape-
shifting. He looked up at the sky. *Go home*, indeed.

He'd show them who was home.

chapter thirteen

BILAL PARKED UP OUTSIDE his house. When he got to the doorstep he noticed the red tin box on the welcome mat. He looked around – perhaps someone had left it there by accident? But there was no-one in sight. He put the box under his arm and opened the front door.

'Mariam!' he called out. 'Anyone ring the doorbell?'

He walked into the kitchen to see Khala peering into Mariam's laptop screen. Mariam came in a few seconds later in her gym gear and Bilal appreciated what good shape his wife was in. This was immediately followed by regret that lately, she didn't seem to want to share it with him.

'You're home early,' she said, frowning.

She was twitchy, her eyes searching for something to do.

'Been a bit of a day, hasn't it?' he said, trying to be as still as possible, to counter Mariam's constant movements.

'That Jenny,' began Mariam. 'So now I don't have a job—'

'Well, you have other freelancing and you didn't *have* to quit,' he said.

She stared at him. 'Didn't I?'

Haaris then walked in, addressing Khala directly. 'Do. You. Seeee?' He then turned to Mariam. 'Khala said she'd help make zarda for the bakesale.'

'Are you happy with that? Or do you just want cupcakes? Like everyone else?' asked Mariam.

Haaris shrugged. 'Whatever.'

'What?' said Bilal.

Mariam explained. 'We are literally giving them bite-size culture.'

He had visions of bright yellow rice with almonds and raisins in the midst of all the cupcakes.

'Right,' he said, looking at Khala. 'What's she doing?'

'English,' explained Haaris.

'She asked whether Mum spoke English,' added Mariam. 'What with her being a housewife. And I said, yes, of course. But it's not a matter of course, is it?'

Khala looked back at them. 'I seeeee.'

'Anyway, Haaris told her it's never too late. *Onnay kya see na?*' Mariam continued in Punjabi, mentioning to Bilal that Khala said she felt too old to learn new things. 'So, we're going to get her a phone, download an app and she can learn. It was Haaris's idea.'

Khala beamed at Haaris.

'Oh. Okay. Great idea,' Bilal replied.

His mum had told Khala a hundred times to learn English. What had changed, he wondered.

'What's that?' asked Mariam, seeing the box in Bilal's hands.

'Thought you might know? It was on our doorstep.'

'No note?' asked Mariam.

Bilal shook his head as she snatched the box, put it on the table and pulled Haaris back.

'What?' asked Bilal.

'You decide to build a mosque, your office gets graffitied, and now we're left a mysterious box?'

Even Khala dragged her chair back as everyone stared at the potentially offensive item.

'Do you think . . . *really*?' said Bilal.

He wanted to tell Mariam that she was being ridiculous, except perhaps she wasn't. She hardly ever was.

'Maybe it's a dead rat?' suggested Haaris. 'Anthrax?'

'What's in it?' asked Khala.

'How do you say Anthrax in Punjabi?' asked Haaris.

'Khala,' said Bilal, looking warily at the box. 'Can't you . . . I don't know, pray *Ayatul Kursi* and blow over it or something?'

His mum used to say that prayer over him whenever he left the house and since no physical harm had ever befallen him, he imagined there might be a possibility that it worked.

Khala nodded, muttering the prayer before she took a deep breath and blew over the box. Then she blew over

Bilal, Mariam and Haaris, he supposed for good measure.

'This time I'm calling the police.' Mariam got her phone out.

'Police?' said Khala, clearly shocked. She understood words that suggested danger.

'What will you say? That someone's dropped off a box?' asked Bilal.

'*Yes!*' Mariam had the phone to her ear as Bilal watched her, incapable of overpowering his wife's paranoia.

'You should've done this in the first place. Hello? Oh, hi, Olly? I'm glad it's someone we know. It's Mariam.'

Was it the same person who'd graffitied his door? Or someone new? Bilal lost count of how many people were angry with him, and it was distinctly depressing.

Mariam explained to Olly about the box on the doorstep and the reasons behind her suspicion. 'He's on his way,' she said, putting the phone down.

Bilal opened the door, a chilly breeze wafting in as the sun began to set, tinging the sky with a pink and orange hue. Ten tense minutes later and there was Olly with his round face and rosy cheeks, looking like an overgrown baby. His police tractor was parked up behind him as Bilal checked for the twitching of curtains.

'Bill,' said Olly, without the usual smile or offering of an apple (he always carried a bag).

Bilal waited. 'Well,' he said, finally. 'Through here.'

They entered the living room and Olly got his notepad out.

'Hello,' said Khala.

Olly gave her the smallest of smiles. 'This is it then?'

'We didn't want to open it, just in case,' said Mariam.

'Hmm.' Olly shook the box. 'Not heavy.' He scratched his smooth face and put the tin back on the table. 'You think this is hate mail?' Olly said, almost as if the very idea was a joke.

'Well . . . it *could* be. Considering,' replied Bilal.

Olly sighed.

'I guess I'll have to take this down to get it inspected at the station.'

'Yes,' said Mariam. 'I guess that would be part of your job.'

Bilal cleared his throat. Olly gave Mariam a look. He picked up the box and turned around as it slipped from his hand and landed with a crash on the kitchen tiles.

'Oh,' exclaimed Mariam, looking at the cracked tile and then noticing that the box had opened.

Olly tried to pick it up but Haaris had already grabbed the brown envelope that had fallen out.

'Don't!' said Mariam.

But it was too late – he'd already opened it and for the first time in a while Haaris managed to show a strong reaction.

'Oh. My. God.'

He looked up at Mariam and Bilal as Bilal took the envelope from him.

'Oh my God,' repeated Bilal.

There, in the envelope, was a wad of fifty-pound notes. Bilal looked up at Mariam as he took the wad out.

'What the . . . ?' Mariam stared at the cash.

'Hang on,' said Haaris. 'There's a note.'

'Who sent that?' said Khala Rukhsana, staring at the money.

Mariam read the note aloud: 'Bill – I trust you'll put this to good use. Yours, A Supporter.'

Olly cleared his throat, looking annoyed. 'Well. Not everyone's out to get you.'

'But this is . . . '

'Incredible,' said Bilal.

'Mad,' added Mariam.

'Could it be Richard?' Bilal asked Mariam.

'Richard wouldn't be secretive – and he doesn't have this kind of money,' said Mariam. 'Could be a hoax.'

Olly cleared his throat again. 'You're going to have to declare it. Tax man will want his bit.'

'Of course,' said Bilal. What did Olly take him for?

'Won't you have to do a write-up of this?' suggested Mariam after Olly made no sign to leave.

'Hmm? Yes, well . . . ' Olly stared at the envelope still in Mariam's hand.

She handed it to Bilal and led Olly to the door.

'Did you see how he spoke to us?' she said when she returned.

Unfortunately, Bilal couldn't argue with her. But he was thinking: was this a divine sign?

'He seemed annoyed,' said Khala Rukhsana. 'Should we make him zarda too?'

'This is almost ten thousand pounds,' said Mariam.

'Whoa,' exclaimed Haaris.

'*Das hazaar* pounds,' Mariam repeated for Khala.

'*Hai Allah*,' she replied.

'I can't . . . '

'I know.'

'Who would . . . ?'

'I don't know.'

'Do you think . . . ' Bilal glanced at Khala Rukhsana and switched to his broken Punjabi. 'God heard me?'

'What? God dropped off the money?' said Haaris.

Bilal smiled at his stepson's logic, yet perhaps a larger force was at play.

'Baby,' Mariam said to Haaris. 'Don't be so literal. It's what gives Muslims a bad name. Anyway, it's not nearly enough to buy a piece of land.'

'But that's not the point, is it? This money, Mum's . . . ' Bilal stopped short. When would he tell Khala about her sister's home?

'What?' Haaris asked.

'Nothing,' replied Bilal.

Khala looked at Haaris and said: 'Beta, when you ask Allah for something he makes *sabbab*.'

'What?' asked Haaris.

'A conduit,' Mariam explained.

'Allah knows best,' said Khala, looking up at the ceiling.

Bilal and Mariam also looked up at it. Their respective reverie was interrupted by Haaris.

'Guess we should find out who the conduit is then?'

chapter fourteen

'Yes, yes, I understand,' said Richard into the phone to Mr Pankhurst. He was sitting in the church office, his head in his hands for the second time that afternoon.

Bilal had just called and told him about a mysterious donation. It was so very *odd*. Richard wondered if someone might be setting his friend up and then shook the notion from his mind. So much doubt was bad for both soul and society. Outside the church window the leaves were beginning to flicker with oranges and red, which would soon be ablaze, much like Mr Pankurst's temper on the other end of the phone.

'*Do you?*' exclaimed Mr Pankhurst. 'Planning permission! Heard it from my nephew's friend's own cousin.

How could they do this? We voted for Mariam and Bilal's turnip at last year's fair.'

Richard sighed with exasperation. 'Well, John, what can I say? Sometimes voting for someone's turnip isn't quite enough.'

Silence.

'Hmph. I suppose we all know how you feel about the whole thing then,' snapped Mr Pankhurst and put the phone down.

Richard rubbed his eyes, wishing he'd exercised more restraint. He would have to apologise. Christmas was still three months away and he was already nervous about the Nativity. Every year, a friend lent his barn for a Christmas party. The place would glimmer with fairy lights and crackle with a logfire. The whole community would sing Christmas carols, drink sherry and mulled wine, perform the Nativity and his heart would feel at ease: celebrating the Lord and the love He wanted us to spread. How would the party fare this year? Richard prayed that news of the money would stay quiet. That they could at least get through the next few months without any more discord.

❧

Of course he hadn't banked on Olly telling his wife. Their daughter, who also went to Haaris's school, overheard. She told Sam, who naturally told his parents, until the Pandora's box of Chinese whispers had overspilled. The irony that Bilal should have got ten thousand pounds – exactly the amount of money they had needed at the beginning for St Swithun's bell – was lost on no-one. It was a mockery, though no-one was sure of what.

Mariam had left Khala alone that morning and went to see Margaret to find out if she had been their mysterious benefactor. She was sure Margaret would love the very idea: a story to tell her grandkids about how she helped build that mosque in the middle of their village.

'No, dear, I'm afraid not. Got to keep this farm running, see? Setting up the children with their own homes has quite depleted my funds, even with the subsidies.' She shook her head. 'Upkeep's a bore.'

Mariam looked around the black and white chequered tiles, the sweeping staircase with a gargoyle next to it.

'Quite the exciting mystery, though, isn't it?' said Margaret, resting both hands on her hips. 'You'll get that mosque. Mark my words.'

Mariam had given her a weak smile and gone back home to start Googling 'how to trace money'. She'd gone through the vast websites of serial numbers and databases and security cameras but it was all rather nebulous. This place wasn't that big – surely it should be simpler than this?

But she had to put that to one side to finish a freelance article about library cuts for an online magazine.

'What the hell am I doing here?' she asked herself.

After sending the article she sat on the chair, staring at the laptop.

'I am from Liverpool,' came Khala's strong Pakistaniaccented voice. 'Oh, Mariam, I thought you were out.' She took her earphones out, the phone in a bumbag tied around Khala's waist, whistle dangling around her neck. Khala was, after all, a creature of habit and apparently the whistle, like her necklace, gave her comfort. She looked set for an expedition. 'Where is Liverpool?'

It was incredible – a lifetime in the country and Khala still had no sense of Britain's geography.

'Just a few hours north of Birmingham.'

'I am from Birmingham,' said Khala, her eyes animated, a smile on her lips. 'Haina?'

'That's right,' replied Mariam.

She went to make tea when Khala said, 'No, beta. You work. If Sakeena showed me one thing, a woman must always work.'

Khala ambled towards the hot water dispenser, getting two mugs out while emitting a grunt here and there. Her recovery was slow, but apparent.

'Don't you ever regret, you know . . . not working?' said Mariam.

Khala's dupatta slipped off her head, ruching around her neck. She pulled it back up. 'Beta, I regret many things.'

She said it with a smile but an immense sadness came over Mariam for Khala.

You can only regret the things you could've changed.

'I am from Rawalpindi,' said Khala as she made the tea.

Mariam wondered why her own mum had never had the same soft voice. Khala gave her the tea, patted Mariam's head and ambled out of the kitchen, placing her earphones back in. 'I am from Babbel's End.'

⌒

When Bilal came home that evening Mariam was boiling the rice, her back to him, as she said: 'Not one person said hello at school drop-off today.'

Bilal sighed. 'Right. How's Haaris?'

'I don't know because he won't speak to me.' She turned around, biting the inside of her cheeks. 'I think you should hand the money in to the police.'

He looked at her, his brow creased in childish despair.

'I don't think Sam and him are speaking,' she added. 'Adults aren't the only ones with issues.'

Mariam was unable to look at Bilal as she took up her phone. She'd download a podcast on guilt and what to do with it.

Bilal sat down and lowered his head in thought. 'Someone's made an offer on the house,' he said.

She paused.

'And I'm going to accept,' he added.

'I see. And where's Khala going to live?'

He cleared his throat. 'We'll sort something, but for now, can't she just stay here?'

Mariam had a strange twinge of conflict: the principle of being asked to continue to look after Khala, and the growing sensation of comfort in her presence.

'Doesn't look like there's much choice.'

Mariam turned around and stabbed at the dinner.

'Where is Haaris?' asked Bilal.

'Said he wasn't feeling well. He's gone to bed.'

They ate dinner in silence. Khala Rukhsana sat with headphones in her ears.

'*Hau-are-youh!*'

She looked at Mariam and Bilal, but not as if she actually saw them.

'*I-am-fine.*'

Mariam tried to smile.

To relinquish control is to liberate yourself.

Her liberation, however, was beginning to feel too much like resignation.

❧

There had been a lot of *shoon shaan* about the mystery money this past month. Or, like Mariam had said: hoo-ha. Rukhsana recognised the similarities of language here and it rather excited her. She'd looked on as the case of the mysterious money had unravelled, catching snippets of English, but realised that it took too much concentration, so instead focused on reading emotions: the furrowing of a brow, a small sigh. She feared the way Mariam looked at Bilal and the way he didn't seem to see it. The policeman didn't have a friendly tone. She made a note to put extra almonds and raisins in his zarda. If Rukhsana had believed in spirits, she'd think that her sister was sweeping around this village, sprinkling seeds of disquiet.

Rukhsana laid the material for Margaret's shalwar kameez on the bed. She'd decided the dusky pink chiffon with pale gold embroidery would suit the *buddi*. She needed her measurements but was too embarrassed to ask, and anyway, she wanted to see the surprise on Margaret's face when she handed it to her, so she guessed. Rukhsana looked outside her bedroom window at the leaves on the trees that were orange and red, and she smiled at the beauty God bestowed on white people's land. She never got to see much beauty in Birmingham and as for Pakistan . . . her life had been as geographically static there as it had been here.

Lately, an idea that had been lurking in her mind was becoming an unexpected yet overwhelming urge. She crept down the passage, even though no-one was home. There was always a spare set of keys hanging by the door. The clouds were overcast and it was spitting, but Rukhsana eyed Mariam's wellies in the shoe stand. They wore the same size. All she wanted was to walk in that green and open field. Rukhsana put on the anorak, which belonged to Bilal, so didn't zip up. She tucked her necklace and whistle into the folds of her scarf and grabbed the bannister, easing herself on to the step at the bottom of the stairs to put the wellies on. By the time she had finished she'd broken into a sweat, her legs in greater pain than usual and her back hurting. Plus, her calves weren't slender like Mariam's so the wellies ruched, cutting into her flesh. Her urge wasn't in line with her physical abilities and the fact of her age swept over her like a Bollywood drama.

She had spent her youth in mourning and now her youth was another thing she mourned.

Nevertheless she gathered herself.

'*Bismillah*,' she uttered, pulling herself up.

She walked over to the door, opened it for the first time, and stepped out into the great outdoors.

❧

At first, Shelley wasn't sure what she was seeing. A bulging figure ambled towards her, head bent low, attire flapping in the wind. She couldn't help but walk towards it, to take a peek at who it might be. Then the clothes came into clearer view. The loose trousers – which is the only thing she could call them even though they weren't exactly trousers – were tucked into wellingtons, billowing like Aladdin pants. The top looked far too thin for this chilly weather. It came down to the woman's knees – a sharp purple colour against the black of her unzipped anorak and Hunters. The woman looked up, as if to see where she was going, and Shelley realised: of course, it was Bilal's aunt. The vision of this foreign figure only added insult to the injury of finding out about Bilal seeking planning permission. She'd heard about the aunt, but to Shelley she'd become something of a mad-woman-in-the-attic figure – locked up in a room, never seen to leave the house. Shelley was about to turn around when Holly bounded towards the aunt, who backed away, flapping her arms and shooing Holly.

'Honestly,' sighed Shelley. 'Holly! Here, girl. Back. Back.'

The aunt yelped every time Holly barked.

'You have to stop that or she'll think you're playing,' shouted Shelley, picking up her pace towards them. 'Holly! Down!'

'Hai Allah, daffa dur!'

Holly had leapt up at the aunt, who would've fallen flat on her bum had Shelley not got there in time to save her.

'You have to stop waving at her,' she exclaimed. Shelley grabbed a stick and threw it as far as she could, which Holly dutifully ran after.

'Kya?'

'What?'

'Kutay ne saaray kapre pleet kerdite.'

'Sorry?'

'Gandi.'

'Gandhi?'

What did Gandhi have to do with anything?

'Haan, *gandi*.' The aunt looked like she'd eaten a rotten egg as she tried to wipe her top.

'Right, well. I suppose you're all right.'

The aunt looked at Shelley closely, as if observing every wrinkle on her face. Honestly, didn't these people know not to stare?

'I'll take that as a yes,' added Shelley, ready to walk away.

'Isslow,' said the woman.

'Sorry?'

Bilal's aunt put her hands out. 'Ispeak isslow.'

Ah, here was the rub. Of all things! To be told to speak slow in her own language.

'She. Thought. You. Were. *Playing*.' Shelley's voice rose a few decibels.

'Hau-are-youh?'

Shelley felt her brows contract.

'Hau. Are. Youh?'

Shelly cleared her throat. 'Fine. Thank you.'

The aunt smiled. 'I also fine. Thanking you.'

They both stared at each other before the aunt put her hand out and said: 'Me, Rukhsana.'

Shelley extended her hand. She wouldn't have foreign people thinking the English were rude, after all.

'Shelley.'

Rukhsana squinted into the distance, her face scrunched up in concentration. 'Pleasing . . . to meet you.'

Shelley looked at her, from wellies to anorak. What an ensemble. The aunt smiled. Shelley cleared her throat. The aunt still smiled.

'Well . . . ' said Shelley.

Smile.

After a minute of this, Shelley decided to say goodbye.

'Goodbye,' the aunt replied, taking Shelley by the arms and pulling her into an unprecedented hug.

Shelley was so taken aback that she didn't have a chance to reach out her hand instead. It felt like a long time until Bilal's aunt released her and Shelley realised that she'd forgotten her name. Something with a K?

'Come, Holly,' Shelley called out as she made her way towards her car.

As she walked away she glanced back. The aunt was still there, waving and smiling. Shelley honestly didn't know what to make of it.

chapter fifteen

MARIAM ARRIVED HOME AFTER a yoga class to feelings of agitation and saw her wellingtons, muddied and collapsed on the floor.

'Khala, I'm home,' she called out, noticing Bilal's wet anorak. 'Khala?'

She knocked on Khala's door and opened it to see papers scattered on the bed with writing in Urdu. She wished she'd paid attention when her mum tried to teach her to read and write in it. Except what could've been more mortifying than identifying with your heritage when growing up? And what could be more karmic than regretting it later in life?

Mariam found Khala in the living room, lying comatose on the sofa, headphones in her ears.

'How much are the tamatars?'

'Salamalaikum, Khala,' Mariam said, raising her voice.

'Oh, beta. I didn't hear you.'

'Did you go out today?'

Khala broke into a smile and nodded. Mariam hadn't ever noticed what lovely teeth Khala had, and how beautiful her smile was.

'I saw the cows. And a woman.'

'What woman?'

'Oh, beta – I can't remember. English names confuse me. She had a big *kutha*.'

'Everyone has a dog around here, Khala.'

Khala began to describe her: average height, short, curly hair, sharp nose, medium build. Black, brown and white dog.

'Shelley?' said Mariam.

'Haan! Shelley.'

Mariam sat down. 'That's the woman who's after Bilal.'

'Hain? She was very nice to me.'

'Well . . . what did she say?'

'I don't know.'

'Then how do you know she was nice?'

'Beta, she tried to understand me.'

Mariam sat back.

'How much are the tamatars?' said Khala, who'd already put her headphones back in.

'Tomatoes, Khala.'

'Hmm?'

'Tomatoes.'

'That's what I said. Tamatar.'

An image came to Mariam: Khala, in her shalwar kameez, wellies and anorak, walking towards Shelley, and she felt a flush of embarrassment. She'd speak to Bilal about going shopping to get Khala some country clothes, so at least she could fit in. Until she left – whenever that might be, wherever she might have to go.

Mariam sighed. Saif would be collecting Haaris for half-term tomorrow.

She went to her room with her laptop and opened up YouTube.

There is nothing to fear, but fear itself. You are sufficient. To live without hope is to not live at all.

Mariam got irritated and paused the video. She'd heard it all before, so why had nothing changed? She wondered why she still felt her life to be too small, as if she was running out of oxygen? The only time she'd felt alive – in months, maybe years – was when she'd written that article for Jenny, and look how that turned out.

She decided to write more of whatever story she was telling. Could it be a book? Whatever it was at least it was giving her *some* sense of achievement. She didn't even feel the need to dust behind the shelves. Then Khala's voice called out to her.

'Let's make the zarda, beta.'

Mariam started, shutting down her laptop before going to the top of the stairs.

'For the sale bake tomorrow,' added Khala, looking almost energetic.

'Bake sale,' corrected Mariam.

And so they began the process of making the sweet, fragrant, yellow rice, to give everyone in Babbel's End a taste of what was to come.

〜

Of course, even Mariam couldn't force zarda down someone's throat.

'Maybe people don't like almonds? Or the raisins?' said Khala as she, Haaris and Mariam walked past the table with their rice in a dish, untouched.

'Or us,' replied Mariam.

Regardless, Mariam walked through the bustling school hall, with its white, blue and red bunting strung across the walls, people chattering around stalls packed with cakes and flapjacks, brownies and cookies. Mariam was resolute, buying a cupcake here, getting Khala a mud cake there, spending a pound every time she noticed Haaris's shoulders droop, reminding her of Bilal. Sam's mum saw Mariam and turned her back; Brenda, with whom Mariam had organised the summer fair two years ago, whispered something into Sam's mum's ear. Leanne walked past without so much as a hello. Mariam should've felt angry at Bilal – this was all his doing, after all – but instead she made a mental note to ask how things were in the office.

If Teddy were alive, Anne would be here today too, to do her bit.

Then she saw Jenny.

'Oh, God,' she mumbled as their eyes met.

There was nothing for it but to walk up to her and pretend she didn't want to shove Jenny's face into the dish of zarda.

'Hello,' said Mariam, painfully aware of Khala by her side, who was looking from one face to the other.

'Mariam,' said Jenny, flicking a lick of hair from her forehead, glancing at Khala. She buttoned the collar of her blue and brown chequered dress.

'Hau are you?' Khala put her hand out.

Jenny shook it, her mouth clamped together. Then she leaned in and raised her voice. 'And how do you like Babbel's End? Rather perfect the way it is, yes?'

Mariam had never partaken in physical fights, despite having lived in the scrappy side of Birmingham, but rugby tackling Jenny on to the school hall lino wasn't improbable. She caught sight of Haaris, hands in his pockets, kicking at the floor, soon to be collected by his dad.

Just then a lady in a grey polo neck, pearls and bumbag around her waist came up to them, a plate of zarda in her hand. 'Dear, you *must* try this.'

Jenny introduced the zarda-eating lady as her mother, visiting from Winchester.

'Mariam used to work for the paper, Mum. Until recently.'

'Oh, really? And did you make this?'

'My aunt did.'

Khala Rukhsana shook Jenny's mum's hand, smiling emphatically. 'Pleasing to meet you.'

'It's heavenly,' said Jenny's mum, taking a spoonful. 'So, what are you doing now?'

Mariam hesitated, feeling Jenny's eyes on her, expectantly.

'I'm writing a book,' said Mariam.

She noticed Jenny's shoulders stiffen. Ha! Take that, holier-than-thou, Shelley's lapdog, Jenny.

'Oh, how lovely,' said Jenny's mum. 'I do admire you creative types. You must tell me when it's published. I'll have my book group read it,' she said, looking at her daughter.

'Well,' said Mariam, waving her hand, a mild panic at raising expectations. 'It's early days.'

Mariam's mild panic came across as modesty, which was probably even more annoying to Jenny.

'I'm sure it'll be wonderful. Now,' added Jenny's mum. 'Will it be in English?'

She watched Mariam, awaiting a response, only Mariam didn't know *how* to respond.

The pause grew into a protracted silence.

Khala's gaze shifted from one face to the next.

'Of course it'll be in English, Mum,' said Jenny eventually, trying to smile, before steering her mum away.

By this point Khala had wandered off towards the zarda table with Haaris, and Mariam saw, with more than a pinch of alarm, her trying to give zarda out to people, while speaking to them in Punjabi, Haaris translating. Then he whispered something in Khala's ear. She cleared her throat as people ambled past and she pushed plates of zarda towards them. 'For the church bell.'

'Oh, we're certainly going to that pub quiz now,' Mariam told Bilal.

Who'd have thought that a bake sale could ignite such passion in his wife? Or maybe it was that ex-husband of hers who'd picked Haaris up afterwards that had unnerved her again.

'"Will it be in English?"' she repeated. 'What else? Mandarin?'

'It's funny, if you think about it,' Bilal said, smiling.

Mariam gave him a look and he promptly fixed his face.

She took a deep breath. 'Just because something *might* be funny doesn't make it right. Treating us like we're . . . we're . . . *fundos*.'

'That's a bit extreme,' said Bilal. 'Pun intended.'

Bilal caught the flicker of a smile from his wife. It all boiled down to everyone ignoring the zarda. More importantly, though, why hadn't Mariam told *him* she was writing a book? Mariam had been in a bad mood for a while – several years, maybe – but this zarda business, along with Haaris leaving with his dad, seemed to have tipped her snappiness over the edge. And Mariam wasn't the type to snap and have sex, so there was still that problem.

'Maybe we should ask Khala?' said Mariam later as they got ready for it.

'What's she going to do in a pub?'

'It'd be rude not to,' said Mariam. 'It's not as if she'll come. And you know you're going to have to tell her about selling her home before one of the aunts do.'

'*Mum's* home. And I've told Vaseem Bhai to make sure they keep quiet until we have a plan.'

Mariam raised her eyebrows. Bilal sighed and went into Khala's room. She was on the sewing machine, having borrowed it from Mariam, stitching together two pieces of material. A sense of guilt came over him – he should have at least spoken to her about selling her sister's house.

'Khala,' he said, attempting a warm smile. 'We're going out. For a quiz. Do you want to come?'

She looked up from the machine, contemplating his question. He'd expected her to say: 'what will I do there, beta? You young people enjoy'. Instead she pushed herself off the stool, holding on to her hip, and said: 'I will get my coat.'

Bilal watched in semi-horror as Khala put on her clunky, black sandals, revealing her white socks.

'Do you want to borrow a pair of Mariam's shoes?' he asked.

Khala said something about her big toenail and was already making her way out of the room.

'Oh, Khala,' said Mariam. 'You're coming?'

'I can practise my English,' she replied, going into the kitchen, as Bilal and Mariam watched her in wonder.

She emerged again, this time with a plastic bag full of containers.

'Zarda. For your friends. There's so much leftover, na? Wasting food is a very big sin.'

Bilal had never seen his khala move with such speed nor heard so much about zarda in his life. Nothing could be done. So the three of them got into Bilal's Lexus and drove towards The Pig and the Ox.

Bilal steadied himself in the pub car park, only to catch sight of Khala's shoe and socks combo again, which did nothing for his anxiety. He felt the weight of her, leaning on him, Mariam on his other side, carrying the plastic bag.

'I wish she'd put on some other shoes,' she whispered.

He took a deep breath and opened the door. It slammed against the wall and everyone turned towards the trio; an unfortunate time for a gust of wind to sweep the room, filling it with what felt like winter's first chill. A hush fell across the room. Bilal nodded vaguely to everyone.

'Smug,' he thought he heard someone say, and it melted any steeliness Bilal managed to conjure.

'Bill!'

Richard's hand was in the air, beckoning him. The murmurings got louder as they made their way towards Richard, past the log fire that had now been lit. Khala walked past everyone, smiling and nodding, people pretending they hadn't seen her. Mariam walked behind her, head held high – the shape of her square, erect shoulders prompting Bilal to stand taller.

There was Mr Pankhurst, sitting with Copperthwaite, Jenny and Shelley, surrounded by her slew of supporters. Tom was sitting at the bar nursing a glass, which he raised to Bilal. On another table was Bruce with his wife, who gave Bilal what could've been a smile, but it wasn't a certainty.

Bilal turned around to see Khala waving at someone. His eyes travelled and rested on Shelley with some confusion. At first, Shelley didn't seem to know what to do. Now everyone was staring at her as well – their eyes darting between the two women. Her face was unmoved as she nodded towards Khala.

'Hau-are-you?'

'Fine. Thank you.'

Another low murmur spread as people exchanged looks, peering at Khala's clothing. Bilal had never wanted to bury his head in his grave faster. They joined Richard, Margaret and Mrs Pankhurst, who was dutifully ignoring her husband.

'Good to see you again,' said Richard.

Khala paused. 'Yes,' she finally responded.

It came out as more of a question than an answer.

'Excellent!' exclaimed Margaret. 'Your English is coming along wonderfully. Though, honestly, if I were you I wouldn't bother with it – I'd rather you teach us your language, Khala.'

Margaret winked at a bemused-looking Khala.

'It's Rukhsana,' corrected Bilal.

'What did I say?'

'Her name's Rukhsana. Khala means aunt.'

'Splendid,' said Margaret, looking Khala up and down. 'I shall say it all the time, even when you're not around.'

'Mariam. Glad you made it too,' said Richard. 'I heard the bake sale was a bit, let's say, trying.'

'Well . . .' said Mariam. 'Is this all of us?'

Mrs Pankhurst paused. 'A few people moved.'

Bilal felt a rush of gratitude towards Mrs Pankhurst and Margaret. He concentrated on the act of taking off his coat, each movement concealing the anxiety in his stomach, his chest.

'They're all buggers,' said Margaret, loud enough for people to turn their heads.

Richard cleared his throat.

'Should we ask Tom to join our team?' said Bilal.

Mariam told Khala that he was the one who'd lost his grandchild, whose daughter had been her friend.

Khala put her hand to her necklace. 'Allah give them patience. Why haven't I met your friend?'

'Leave the old codger alone,' replied Margaret, whose face flushed.

'Quite. And your aunt's a welcome addition,' said Mrs Pankhurst, nodding curtly as if that was the end of the matter.

Khala Rukhsana leaned in at the mention of 'aunt'. She and Mrs Pankhurst looked at each other, unable to speak anything other than the language of uncertain smiles.

Mariam had brought them three Cokes as Mrs Pankhurst sipped her red wine. 'You people must have exceptionally clean livers.'

Bilal felt that now would've been a good time to have something a bit stronger, but there was Mariam and now Khala to think of. He sighed inwardly, taking a sip of the watered-down Coke.

'I didn't know this was a *sharaab-khaana*,' said Khala Rukhsana, eyes widening at realising she was in a pub. She shifted on her wooden chair.

It wasn't the done thing for good Muslims. Bilal knew she was thinking this was just another link to their religion broken. The very thing that Sakeena had complained about when he'd decided to move.

'Right, teams. We ready?' called out Mick, standing stout and proud. 'You've all put in your five-pound participants' fee?'

Everyone assented.

'Let's make our target to get that bell fixed then!'

Cheers came from around the pub as they began.

'Who said: "One small step for man, one giant leap for mankind"?'

'Neil Armstrong.'

'Hitler.'

Jenny and Guppy called out at the same time.

Laughter erupted as people said: 'Good, old Guppy.'

The next hour saw the escalation of spirits and de-escalation of mosque-centric angst as they came closer to the end.

'Which two body parts continue to grow in a person's lifetime?'

There was a pause.

'Nose and ears,' whispered Bilal to the table. 'Trust me. Haaris is always coming at me with odd facts.'

Khala Rukhsana nodded in a way that suggested she understood.

'Surely not,' said Mrs Pankhurst.

Richard put his hands in the air and Mariam folded her arms.

'Nose and ears,' called out Bilal.

'And that is . . . *correct*! Which earns The Babbling Brooks a whopping seventy-eight points, putting them in a two-point lead ahead of The Quail Eggs . . . ' The implications of this seemed to dawn on Mick as his voice slowed down. 'Which means . . . *they* are the winners tonight.'

Everyone turned to their table as Margaret raised her skinny arms and clapped. A scattering of applause came from various corners of the pub, but none outlasted Margaret's, who only stopped at Richard's request.

'We've done a count and we're still £703 short,' said Mick.

Disappointed groans permeated the room.

'Hang on, hang on . . . ' he continued. 'Our very own Shelley came up to me earlier and said she'd make up the difference needed with a *personal donation*.'

Everyone looked at Shelley, who smiled with the self-satisfaction of a woman who tried to hide it.

The room erupted in cheers as they raised their glass to her.

'Good on you, Shell.'

'What a woman.'

'Unlike some others . . . '

There was a knowing pause in the room. Should Bilal have offered part of his mysterious donation? What was the etiquette of social warfare?

'So . . . we've met our target. Great team effort everyone.'

Margaret looked a little put out by Shelley's kindness. Not all acts of kindness were equal, after all.

'*Hum jeetgaye*?' asked Khala Rukhsana.

'Yes, Khala,' replied Mariam. 'We won.'

Khala got the plastic bag, taking out three containers and handing them to Richard, Margaret and Mrs Pankhurst.

'*Mubarak*,' said Khala.

'Gosh, where?' said Margaret, looking around the pub.

'No,' said Mariam. She sometimes wondered whether Margaret was really of this world. 'Not Hosni Mubarak,' Mariam added, looking as agitated as Bilal felt. '*Mubarak* means congratulations. It's the sweet rice, leftover from the bake sale.'

Khala then, unaware of people's stares, and much to Bilal's consternation, went over to the bar and gave a box to Tom. She didn't notice Tom's look of surprise as he nodded at her, then asked Mick for a spoon. She couldn't *not* give him some, not when he'd lost a grandchild, and all she hoped was that it was the box with the most almonds in it. But the real surprise came when Khala made her way to Shelley, two more boxes in hand. Shelley looked like she might want to hide under the table.

'Share?' said Khala, handing her the containers. 'Sorry.'

Everyone looked uncertainly at one another. Shelley gave her a tight smile, thanked her and took the boxes. As Khala ambled back to the table, smiling widely, everyone stared at the woman who looked as if she'd given them their just desserts.

How all white people enjoy their life, thought Rukhsana. This was the type of thing her friends in Birmingham would never do. Old women looked after their grandchildren, cooked and cleaned; they didn't sit and relax in the evenings, or go out walking, like that Shelley with her dog. And this Mrs Punkhurst: she was such a large woman but she didn't move, as if her whole body was in pain.

Every time Rukhsana had tried to catch Shelley's eye she looked the other way. What did it matter if she was against building the mosque? It was her country after all.

If Rukhsana's husband could see her, what would he have thought? All this alcohol . . . *astaghfirullah*. It was *haram*. Maybe that's why Sakeena always said: 'gora place, gora ways.'

After she had given out the zarda, Bilal said it was time to leave.

'Stay, Khala,' said Margaret, pressing her hand on Rukhsana's arm with such force she sat back down.

'Rukhsana,' Bilal said to Margaret, perhaps for the third time.

'O-ho,' said Rukhsana. 'Let her call me khala, even though she looks like she could be my khala.'

The *budda* – Tom? A nice, simple name – sitting on the stool, was looking at Margaret, his brows furrowed, cheeks red. He had finished his zarda, which pleased Khala. But why did everyone look so serious when the game was won and money for the bell raised?

All the chatter and the clinking of glasses filled Rukhsana with energy. She'd go for another walk tomorrow. Maybe she'd get closer to the cows.

Someone then came up to Richard (how strange that a man of God was in a place like this), who paused at the question he was asked, and then said Mariam and Bilal's names.

Everyone stopped.

Rukhsana wished she'd picked up more English but peered into everyone's faces, reading their expressions. The man (though he looked like a woman) talking to Richard didn't look pleased, but Richard patted him on the shoulder, smiling. She caught words like 'Christmas'.

'What's happening?' she asked Mariam.

But Mariam was distracted and said something to the man. Guppy?

'Mariam,' said Bilal, as if warning her.

Then Margaret shook her finger at Guppy, who glared at Mariam and Bilal. Richard put his hand up to her before Guppy stomped back to Shelley's table. Mariam and Bilal both started speaking very fast to Richard – serious and frustrated – and even he couldn't seem to keep up.

Margaret looked pleased, but Mrs Punkhurst was thinking hard. Richard tried to calm things; the vein in his neck was getting bigger. Tom was looking at everyone, laughing.

Then Shelley's table got up.

They all walked out of the pub, not one person looking their way.

After a few more minutes of confusion, and feeling disconnected, Rukhsana left the pub following a visibly flustered Mariam and Bilal. She looked up at the full moon, the shape of the trees against the misty sky, the dimly lit street lamps, tinging everything with an orange hue, and she felt that this place could be as haunting as it was beautiful.

Then: 'What the—' came Bilal's voice, grabbing a piece of paper from the windshield.

'What?' asked Mariam.

For a moment, Rukhsana was so pleased she'd understood their English she didn't see their faces fall. Mariam folded the paper and put it in her pocket.

'What is it?' asked Rukhsana. 'What's happening?'

'Someone wrote a note,' replied Bilal.

Mariam had already opened the door for Rukhsana.

'What did it say?' asked Rukhsana.

Bilal's shoulders drooped, his eyes sad. Had his hairline receded more since she'd got here? That look would have had Sakeena march around the house, shouting that Mariam just *didn't* look after him; that Bilal had inherited none of his mother's *or* father's genes – he was *too* kind.

'*You're not welcome here,*' he replied.

Rukhsana glanced at Mariam, whose eyes were glassy with either tears or fury.

'Hain?' said Rukhsana. 'What do you mean?'

'They don't want us here, Khala,' replied Mariam, her voice cold.

'But . . . this is your home.' She looked between Bilal and Mariam. 'Maybe you will have to re-think your ammi's request, beta. Maybe these people aren't ready. Everything has its time.'

The break in Bilal's heart was apparent on his face.

'Absolutely not,' replied Mariam.

Bilal looked at her.

'Who are they to say we're not welcome?' she added.

They held each other's gaze. If only Sakeena could have seen the strength Mariam seemed to give Bilal.

'You've got the piece of paper?' asked Bilal.

Mariam gave a small laugh that didn't come from a place of happiness. 'Oh, *yes*.'

They all got in the car and Rukhsana noticed Bilal put his hand on Mariam's leg and squeeze it. She covered his hand with hers and that's how they drove back, all the way home.

chapter sixteen

Dear Reverend,

You must understand why we categorically object to assigning the roles of Mary and Joseph to Mariam and Bilal. In the past three months the Hashams – who you full well know we had respected as a part of our community – have become intent on destroying everything Babbel's End stands for.

This petition, with names attached, should show how strongly we all feel. Surely it is your duty to consider the feelings of the masses rather than succumb to the pressure of a minority.

Respectfully yours,
Shelley Hawking

Richard knew cages would be rattled. It was inevitable when people lived in such small ones. A month had passed and winter's chill was settling into the village as well as people's hearts. Despite several conversations with Shelley, she had finally delivered her petition. Richard had spent much time considering the feelings of everyone in the village, but then the graffiti had happened, and the bake sale had been unfortunate, so that moment in the pub when Guppy asked him about the Nativity and Richard had looked at Bill's withdrawn face, the decision was obvious.

But, of course, with conviction would come conflict.

'Oh, don't be such a dry old stick, Guppy,' Margaret had said, watching his sweaty face turn red. 'Mariam means Mary in Arabic.'

'So?'

She rolled her eyes. 'They were *all* brown.'

'Who?'

'Jesus's lot, of course.'

Guppy's eyebrows had collapsed from their disbelieving heights. He, along with most, believed history and holiness to have always been white.

After the Hashams had left, Tom had come and sat at Richard's table.

'For a man of God you have a wicked sense of humour.'

'Tom, go and sit at the bar where you belong,' said Margaret.

'This isn't for entertainment, Tom,' said Richard.

Tom scoffed and shook his head. 'Those two could head the next ten village spring cleans and they still won't be a part of this place. Not if Bill actually succeeds. And you know what? I hope he bloody does.'

'Why?' asked Richard.

'Teach these people a thing or two.'

'And what do you think they'll learn?'

Tom stared at Richard, holding his gaze. 'That the fucking earth isn't theirs.'

~

Shelley's hands shook as she read Richard's letter.

Dear Shelley,

Thank you for your letter, which I've admittedly received with regret. You seem to think that the pain of many is greater than the pain of a few. It's disappointing that a family that has done so much for the community these past years can have that respect and love taken away so easily.

I sympathise with your position, but I cannot, in good conscience, take away what has already been offered to Bilal and Mariam. They are delighted to undertake their roles and I believe it will show everyone that it is better for us to live in respect and harmony than to begin to sow seeds of doubt – an evil that only grows unless it's countered with neighbourly love and, of course, faith.

Yours truly,
Richard

Here was pure evidence: the all-embracing reverend was every bit as heretical as some people suggested. A clichéd product of the times – too scared to hold on to what was dear for fear of offending, happy to forsake his own roots so that others could plant theirs.

'Arthur!' she shouted, banging the kitchen door.

She almost knocked over the framed embroidery on the wall as she walked in to find him in his usual place. She shoved the letter in his face.

'Another letter?' he asked, without reading it.

She saved him the trouble, looking at him expectantly when she'd finished.

'New age hippie,' he said.

Her face flushed with relief. 'Exactly.'

'I told you: a man of God who's that good-looking can't be trusted,' Arthur mumbled.

What did Richard's looks have to do with anything?

'Pfft, Margaret,' he added, shaking his head. 'Anyone who tells you that Mary and Joseph were brown are plain brainwashing you.'

Shelley paused at the gap in her husband's knowledge. Of course they'd been brown, but she wished Arthur could stick to the point. Shelley needed to think. She grabbed her coat and summoned Holly, and they made their way towards the usual path through the fields, wishing she'd also brought her gloves. The inconvenience of this, however, was nothing compared to seeing Bilal's aunt. At least this time she was in *normal* attire – trousers, a red jumper, an anorak that zipped up. Before Shelley could turn the other way, Bilal's aunt was already waving to her.

'God help me,' exclaimed Shelley under her breath.

⌇

Richard pounded the treadmill and pushed himself on the leg press, before pulling at the wide-grip lat until he'd run out of breath, feeling mildly nauseous. His letter was perhaps too candid, but if one sought truth, then surely they must be truthful. The village had a right to feel wary about the mosque, but Bilal had a right to have one in the place he called home. Somehow two rights were making a wrong.

But if the village saw Bilal and Mariam play Mary and Joseph, they might realise that together they were in fact creating a new history.

At the bench press, Richard clenched his jaw, grunting at the extra five kilos he'd added to today's workout, wondering what Jesus would've done.

'All right, old man?'

It was Gerald, looking even skinnier than usual, a dimness to his sunken eyes. Next to him was Dan, with his solid form and overly groomed eyebrows.

'You up for a bit of competition?' said Dan, already lying on the neighbouring bench press, pushing weights before Richard could say yes.

Eventually, Richard had to stop, perturbed by Dan's strength and composure as he benched 120 kilos.

Dan finally stopped. He wiped the sweat off his face and gripped Richard's hand, looking smug, pressing it tighter than necessary.

Richard held on to it, meeting force with polite force.

'Let go of him, man,' exclaimed Gerald.

'What?' said Dan. 'Rev's all right, isn't he?'

'Don't mind Dan. He's just a knob.'

It was as Dan got his rucksack to take out a bottle of water that Richard noticed the spray can. He wasn't a suspicious man, but he was a man of instinct.

'Do you always carry spray paint?' he asked, folding his arms, which he knew were the right shape of threatening.

Without hesitation Dan took the can out. 'I like the colour red.'

'People will start making assumptions,' said Richard.

'And . . . ?' Dan held Richard's gaze.

Gerald stared at the ground. 'Rev's not got time for your bollocks.' He looked at Richard, stuffing his hands in his pockets. 'Say hi to Mrs Lark, yeah?'

Dan's face seemed to flicker with something like emotion.

Yes, to counter people's burgeoning hate, Richard had to show more than just dutiful love. Except as he watched Dan walk away with Gerald, he knew it was easier said than done.

❧

It took Rukhsana longer to walk in these new clothes – everything felt so *tight*. The rolls of her flesh felt exposed, as if her body was on display. She didn't know how goray wore them. Maybe that is why they also sometimes seemed so uptight. Still, she couldn't ignore Shelley once she had seen her, even though she might laugh at her for dressing like someone she's not.

'Hellaw,' she called out.

Shelley didn't look happy, but then she had such a face and you shouldn't question what Allah has given someone.

'How are you?' Rukhsana asked.

She could now say this fluently, as if she'd said it her whole life, and it made her excessively proud.

'We walk?' she added.

Shelley paused. 'Oh, *fine*.'

Rukhsana decided that there must be something, other than Allah's wisdom, that made Shelley's lips so thin.

'Game. Was . . . fun, haina?' Rukhsana offered, keen to comment on the positives.

Plus, the quiz *had* been fun, despite what came afterwards. But Shelley whipped her head around, eyes narrowed. That dog started barking so Rukhsana had to keep muttering prayers under her breath. Then Shelley's words came out in waves, Rukhsana barely catching two of them together before Shelley took a breath to continue. She caught things like 'Christmas' and 'husband' and 'home'. *Hai hai.* Why wasn't there someone to translate? Shelley went on like this until she stopped abruptly.

'I'm sorry.'

That, Rukhsana understood, even though Shelley didn't sound sorry.

'It's just how it is,' Shelley added.

'Hmm?' asked Rukhsana.

Shelley shook her head, her eyes rolling around as if she were considering the future. Or maybe the past? 'Oh! Life!'

Rukhsana nodded. '*Zindagi*,' she said.

'Sorry?'

'*Zindagi* mean life,' Rukhsana explained.

'Right.'

'You have husband?' she asked.

'Well, yes . . . I just said . . . Oh, doesn't matter. Yes. I have.'

Rukhsana smiled. '*Twaadi kismet changi hai.*'

'I don't understand.'

Rukhsana tried to think of the translation. 'You.'

'Yes?'

'Are . . . '

'Go on.'

Rukhsana concentrated. The word was on the tip of her tongue. Then it came to her.

'Lucky.'

For a moment Shelley seemed surprised, and then had a look – something like pride, but also regret. Rukhsana would think of that look for a long time.

chapter seventeen

BILAL WALKED THROUGH THE narrow hall of his mum's home in Birmingham – there to finalise the sale and organise storage until he knew what he'd do with everything. He should've told Khala by now, brought her with him, but he wanted to wait until they had a nice retirement community to show her. Selling the house was a *good thing*.

She would understand.

Ultimately.

Taking out his phone he chased the Titchester agent about the owner of the land, but no news there. He swallowed hard, remembering his mum's words: *look after your khala*.

And now, since this whole Mary and Joseph drama, there was a new feeling. Whereas Mariam's cynicism usually evoked feelings of endearment in him, they were recently evoking exasperation. Her cynicism seemed to be ageing disagreeably and he was beginning to see just how difficult his wife found it to let go of things.

He peered into his old bedroom and remembered something. Walking to his wardrobe he battled through to the back where the boardgames were kept. There it was: his backgammon set. After paying the garden a visit, where the grave was now unkempt, he went to leave and paused at the door. He took in the house one last time and finally walked out, backgammon set nestled under his arm and a gnawing sense of guilt in his chest.

⁓

It was, quite frankly, patronising. Of course, Bilal didn't see it that way. In the stark light of the Nativity, Mariam wasn't sure why his incessant optimism had once appealed to her. On top of which, she'd gone into every stationery shop in town with the red tin box, to see if she could find out where it'd been bought, but had found nothing.

Bilal had returned from Birmingham, so she should've been kinder, but he *still* hadn't told Khala and this cowardice didn't induce affection.

'I've nothing against Richard, but the way he just assumed we'd jump at the chance at being Mary and Joseph . . . ' Mariam had said.

She unfolded the letter on the table for the tenth time.

'Are you *sure* you don't recognise the writing?' she asked. 'It's not similar to the graffiti?'

Bilal didn't even pretend to look this time. 'I don't go around inspecting people's handwriting.'

Mariam paused. Such snark wasn't Bilal's habit. That was her domain.

'And I don't think Richard's gesture was patronising,' added Bilal, looking her in the eye.

'Of course you don't.'

'He's trying to bring us back into the fold,' Bilal explained.

'Really successfully,' said Mariam, flattening the hate mail on the table with her hand.

Bilal snatched the piece of paper from the table and tore it into pieces.

'What are you doing?' exclaimed Mariam.

He threw the pieces in the bin, Mariam looking at him in dismay.

'That was evidence,' she said, rushing to the bin.

'There's no point dwelling on it.'

Mariam took a deep breath. 'Why do we even want to be in this fold?'

Why was she so intent on Haaris fitting in? Maybe Bilal was right, maybe Haaris should learn to stand out. It was happening anyway, whether they liked it or not.

Accept the things you cannot control because you will never be able to control how someone sees you.

It had been true of Saif, and now it was true of Babbel's End.

Bilal looked too deflated, too soon. He sat in his chair, rubbing his forehead. 'It's our home.'

Mariam could almost feel Bilal's mum's *I told you so*. God, that woman was clever, even beyond her grave. But Mariam had wanted to live here too, partly to prove Sakeena wrong, but mostly to get away from the place that reminded her so much of her past life. She wished Bilal would sit more erect so she could soften towards him. Doleful eyes just made her irritable.

'Isn't it?' he asked.

Bringing the kitchen chair around, she sat opposite him. Mariam hadn't bargained for his doubt on the matter, but she wondered: did you build a mosque in a place that *felt* like home? Or to *make* it feel like home?

'You see the best in people,' she said. 'Between us, it's probably a good thing. Because when this is over you'll at least be able to look them in the eye and not want to . . . I don't know . . . pummel them.'

'Pummel?' Bilal looked amused.

'Or something less violent.'

He got up and kissed her on her head.

'Where are you going?' she asked as he grabbed his gardening coat and scarf.

'Outside.'

She watched from the window as, despite the cold and damp of the November day, her husband lay down in his makeshift grave, a place he seemed to find more respite from the world than with her.

⟨⁓⟩

Bilal picked up the earth next to him in his gloved hand and played with it absentmindedly.

'I thought this mosque would make things clearer,' Bilal mumbled at the sky.

His mother appeared, wearing a white shalwar kameez with a bright red dupatta and matching red Nike trainers. *His* trainers. She'd refused to let him throw them out when he'd grown out of them. With two pairs of insoles, she'd said, they were practically made for her. He'd insisted they didn't go with her clothes – she only ever wore shalwar kameez. But she wouldn't be deterred. Now, not even in his imagination.

Just then he felt his phone vibrate in his pocket.

'Hello. It's Richard. Are you busy?'

'Oh, just pondering life.'

'Decent pastime.' Richard paused. 'How's work? No more graffiti? Notes?'

'No. But there's always tomorrow,' said Bilal.

Richard paused again. 'Listen, I wanted to ask about Bruce . . . Does he talk about Dan?'

'Not much,' replied Bilal. 'He's a quiet man, but I mean, it's Dan . . . '

'Hmmm. I've never felt that he's the best influence on Gerald and . . . '

'And?' said Bilal, finding himself sitting up. 'Hello?'

'Hi. Sorry. It's nothing. You know kids. He had a spray can—'

'What?' Bilal swallowed hard. 'You think the graffiti was him?'

He waited for Richard's reponse.

'No,' he replied, finally. 'No . . . I'm just worried about Gerald. Anyway,' added Richard, 'you and Mariam still set to be beacons of the Nativity?'

Bilal gave a barely audible 'yes'. His friend's generosity only heightened his wife-weary state. Richard said bye to Bilal, who closed his eyes again, the image of his mother etched into his retinas. Why was the process of building this mosque beginning to show the cracks in the foundation of their marriage?

༄

Rukhsana returned from another walk with Shelley, who had actually laughed once in their conversation.

'*Tusi aithay masjid kiun nahin chaanday?*' Rukhsana had asked.

She wanted to understand why everyone was so against the mosque, but, of course, Shelley didn't understand the question. A small crease appeared on Shelley's brow as she spoke (if only Rukhsana had learnt English sooner, she'd have understood the origins of that crease). Rukhsana caught the words *English, Punjabi* and something like *melloddius*. She'd have to ask Haaris what it meant.

By the end her heart would be lighter and even Shelley's

lips wouldn't be so pursed. Rukhsana had shared things she'd never voiced to her friends, because if Shelley couldn't understand then she couldn't judge. Sometimes, though, Shelley would give her a look so sympathetic that perhaps pain transcended language.

Rukhsana's life now brimmed with a routine of walks, words and prayers. She'd spend a little time every day sewing Margaret's outfit, which was coming along nicely. At least a quarter of her notebook was full of poetry. She wished she could share her words about the pot-holed streets in Rawalpindi and the rolling hills of Babbel's End, the mountains of Sawaat she'd never seen and the pebbled beaches she didn't want to visit – the endless sea being something that frightened her. She wanted to unravel the mysteries of these two lands, but she'd seen too little of either. Her life had been small but her feelings vast, perhaps as vast as the world she never explored. But these were the matters of her heart, and they weren't easy to explain.

What would Shagufta and Gulfashan make of her wellies, and what do they call this coat? *Boar Boar*?

For the first time Rukhsana felt the urge to speak to her friends – she actually had stories to share. She picked up the phone and called Gulfashan.

chapter eighteen

FEELINGS WERE A COMPLICATED matter. Bilal had tossed and turned all night and every time he woke up he'd stare at Mariam's sleeping face, wanting to stroke her hair and shake her at the same time.

He got up early and went downstairs to make coffee when he saw the light on in Khala's room, door ajar, a muffling of voices.

'And then Henry the Eighth . . . ' Haaris gestured, slitting his throat, speaking in his English-accented Urdu. 'To *that* wife too.'

'*Hai Allah*, so many wives,' said Khala.

'Test!' Haaris knelt on the edge of Khala's bed in his Spiderman pyjamas, hair flopping over his face. 'What is *marwaana* in English?'

Bilal let out a small laugh. It took a while before Khala replied: 'Ummm, *kill*?'

Haaris high-fived Khala.

'You know, I wish I was a king,' continued Haaris in English. 'I mean, I'd put a stop to wars and stuff, *and* I'd make sure everyone could afford video games. But, like, if people wanted to build mosques or churches or synagogues or whatever, I'd let them.'

Bilal wanted to go in and kiss Haaris on the head.

'Speak slow,' laughed Khala.

'Or do I want to be a superhero?'

'What?' asked Khala.

He flexed his arm muscles and in Urdu managed to say: 'Make Sam disappear.'

Khala paused, just the ruching of the blanket over her legs visible to Bilal.

'Beta, what is the use making people disappear when it's how they think that is the problem?'

'Weird,' said Haaris, looking sombre. 'That's what my dad says.'

His bloody dad, the shadow of a past, lurking in their present.

Bilal showered and crept out of the house, vapour emanating from his mouth, the morning sky still in the process of waking up as he made his way to work early. *Haaris is not happy and it is my fault*. He walked into the office and switched on the lights. As he passed Bruce's desk he stopped. A Post-it was on his computer.

Without thinking, Bilal took it and looked at the handwriting.

Get Kat M&S shoes she wanted
~~*Ask Bill for afternoon off for Dan's dr appointment*~~
~~*Thu 2pm*~~
~~*Send off T's docs to archives.*~~

Bilal's heartbeat quickened. He knew this handwriting, didn't he? The neatness of each letter and word, the forward slant, the orderliness of it. He held the paper, staring at it in disbelief.

'Bill?'

Bilal turned to see Bruce.

'Is this yours?' asked Bilal.

'Yes,' said Bruce, looking confused and, Bilal noticed, rather tired. 'I've come in early to—'

'This is *your* handwriting?'

It began to make sense. Bruce had never actually *liked* Bilal. Mariam was right. Bilal *was* too optimistic. Bruce's quiet manner was actually curtness. His indifference about the graffiti, his presence at the anti-mosque meeting . . . Didn't Richard say he'd seen Dan with a spray can? The apple, after all, fell close to the tree. Bilal's simmering doubt boiled over into conviction; he only wished he hadn't torn up that note. Why hadn't he listened to Mariam?

'Bruce, did you write this?' said Bilal.

'Well, yes,' Bruce said, taking the Post-it. 'You said it was fine to have Thursday off.'

'I . . . Why were you at Shelley's meeting? Against the mosque?'

Bruce clenched his jaw. 'We all have the right to an opinion.'

'You've certainly made yours very clear.'

Bruce looked unmoved. Oh yes, now he could see where Dan got it from. Bilal was absolutely *certain* that it was the same handwriting.

'Did you . . . I can't believe I'm asking this . . . Did you leave that note on my car windscreen?'

'Wha . . . ? *What's* given you that idea?' asked Bruce, his face going red.

He tried to read Bruce's expression, but it looked so confused it made Bilal doubt his own conviction.

'And the graffiti?' asked Bilal, noticing a nick in Bruce's chin from where he must've shaved.

'Graffiti?' said Bruce, his look wavering.

'Yes,' said Bilal. 'Was that . . . Dan?'

Bruce paused, stony-faced as he looked at his desk.

'No, it wasn't.'

'Bruce, I'm sorry, but I find that hard to believe with everything he . . . well, you know . . . gets up to.'

Bruce stared at Bilal. 'It wasn't him.'

'Richard himself told me he caught him with a spray can.'

'It was *me*.'

Bilal's heart sank. They'd never been friends outside the office, but they'd always been civil. Before the mosque debacle, every now and then, they'd even shared a joke about tax deductibles. Bilal had given Bruce a job. But in all that time he'd never actually *accepted* Bilal.

'It was *you*?' said Bilal.

'Will you press charges?' said Bruce, his voice low.

Bilal couldn't believe it. Bruce was covering for Dan – of course he was – but it didn't matter. He'd written that note; his son had graffitied his office door. They were both the same.

'I'll pay for the damages,' said Bruce with such a severe expression Bilal's anger turned into something solid. There wouldn't be enough Gaviscon in Babbel's End to alleviate his heartburn.

'You realise this is gross misconduct? That you're fired?' said Bilal.

Bruce paused, as if steadying himself. 'I understand.'

He began to gather his things: a few photos of his wife and family, but not much else.

Without another word, Bruce gave Bilal a nod and made his way out of the office.

'And yes,' said Bilal, the anger bursting in his chest, 'I *will* be pressing charges.'

❧

'Oh, beta, I've done something terrible,' said Khala as Bilal emerged in the living room, his tie loosened and hair windswept. Khala held her rosary beads, other hand clutched to her necklace, looking as if she was about to cry.

'Sshh, Khala,' said Mariam, relating to Bilal that

Rukhsana had inadvertently invited Auntie Gulfashan and Auntie Shagufta to stay with them over Christmas.

'What?'

'I tried to tell them,' Khala exclaimed. 'I said you are busy, it's cold here, but Gul just said instead of being cold in Birmingham they'd be cold in Babbel's End.'

Mariam's life had become a series of taking deep breaths. She tried to sound sympathetic but Bilal *had* to tell Khala it wasn't going to work. He *had* to tell Khala he'd sold her sister's house.

'I'm sorry I acted as if it was my home,' said Khala, wiping her tears.

He handed her a tissue and for a moment Mariam thought he looked like he might cry too.

'Of course it's your home,' said Bilal. 'We'll make space.'

'You don't mind?' said Khala.

He paused, his mouth twitching, unable to commit to a full smile. 'No, of course we don't.' He turned to Mariam. 'Do we?'

What could she say? *Recognise the negative parts of who you are and try to ask: why am I feeling this way?*

'No,' replied Mariam. 'It's fine.'

Rukhsana put her hand on Bilal's face and kissed him on the cheek. 'Your ammi would be so proud.'

Mariam supposed her dead mum's pride didn't matter, and was then annoyed at her own ungraciousness. Khala managed to get up, telling them she had to go and pray.

'Thanks for the support,' said Mariam.

'Keep your voice down.'

'It's not as if she can actually understand.' Mariam was being mean. 'It's just . . .'

I feel tired. And alone. And I don't know if I ever loved you because I'm still in love with the man who broke my heart.

She'd known this for longer than she cared to admit, but something about her life's recent events had made the truth of it come to the surface. What chronic emotional issue did you have to dislodge in order to love the right person? It felt like such a waste. She felt a wave of sympathy for Bilal, for what he deserved and what he'd ended up getting.

'Not now,' he interrupted, sitting on the sofa and putting his head in his hands.

'What happened?'

When he told her about Bruce, she couldn't believe it – he'd always seemed so harmless. Distant but harmless. Then she took Bilal's hand, pressing into it, holding on tight – he probably thought it was out of affection. But it was just another way of telling him how sorry she was.

❧

Shelley saw Richard drive out of Tom's garage. It was this kind of thing that piqued her. What made Tom more in need of spiritual support than her?

'Hush, Holly,' she said as the dog's barking interrupted her thoughts.

She swerved around that stupid bush, recounting all the things she had to do: thank Jenny for the carrot cake even though it was dry; chase the district council for an update on the planning permission; gather *more* signatures against Bilal and Mariam being in the Nativity. How many numbers did it take to be *heard?* She'd parked up in the lay-by by the field when her mobile rang.

'Hello?' she snapped.

'Guppy here.'

She sighed as he launched into the details of his day until she sighed again, this time loud enough for him to get to the point.

'Well, now, I don't mean to disturb you but you ought ter know there were some very suited and booted men at St Swithun's today.'

'What?'

She saw Khala in the distance.

'I was checking on the new bell – it's looking grand as anything – and strimmin' the grass and I said, "Excuse me, sirs, but you'll have to go while I finish up."'

'*Holly, be quiet.* What's that?'

'Suited folk. Never listen. They said that *I* could come back later. I told 'em: "I always do my strimming on a Wednesday, eleven o'clock. Never missed a week". One of them – black fellow, nice enough – said sorry, and then another had the cheek to offer me a fifty-pound note to leave.'

Shelley held the car door open, intrigued. 'Did you ask who they were?'

'Said they were looking at the area. "For what?" I wanted to ask 'em, but the black fellow apologised and the lot of 'em left.'

This was very odd. Although they were probably from some kind of film production company.

'Honestly. We're always good for a scene, aren't we?' said Shelley, shaking her head at the world and its preoccupations as she put the phone down.

As if real life wasn't dramatic enough.

Shelley walked through the damp field, with her wide-brimmed hat, quilted jacket, scarf and dark sunglasses, looking – to her mind – inconspicuous. It's not that she had anything to hide, conversing with Khala, but still . . . There was something cathartic about revealing her innermost soul to a woman who didn't understand her. Shelley didn't believe in this therapy nonsense – paying a *stranger* to listen. But here was a mutual exchange of stories and feelings. And there was something melodious about Khala's voice, and even, dare Shelley say it, the language? Listening to the dip and rise of Khala's intonation she knew, whatever life story she was telling, it was a sad one. It made sense to discover that Khala wrote poetry; it was only a shame Shelley would never be able to read it – she fancied herself quite cultured when it came to matters of the arts. Shelley walked up the frosty mound with Holly and saw Khala approaching, her strides more confident, her smile assured. She almost looked like she belonged in the countryside. Khala waved and Shelley felt the hint of her own smile emerging. She had a niggling anxiety that someone might recognise her.

But on these walks, she barely recognised herself.

chapter nineteen

RICHARD LOOKED UP AT St Swithun's bell tower where the restored bell, which weighed a modest 650 pounds, was now tolling through the village. He wondered who exactly it tolled for. Going into the empty church, he sat on the front pew and looked up at Christ on the cross, feeling the coldness of the unused altar. He considered Bilal firing Bruce. They both knew Bruce was covering for Dan's graffiti, but the note on the windscreen was inexcusable. If, of course, it had been him. Richard felt unsure – it just wasn't like Bruce.

Bilal insisted he was going to press charges. 'I don't want Haaris growing up thinking that there aren't consequences to actions,' he'd said.

But Richard had asked him to reconsider. Was it right for Bruce to be charged with a crime he didn't commit?

And hasty retribution for another crime he claimed he didn't commit would be bad for Bruce and, indeed, Bilal.

'It was *his* handwriting,' he'd insisted.

Still, Bilal listened to his friend and agreed that he wouldn't do anything for now.

Richard heard the creak of the wooden door and turned around.

'I came to check on the bell and saw your car parked,' said Shelley.

He noticed the envelope she held. Before she could push the new petition into his hand, Richard said: 'I was planning to come and see you today.'

'Oh?' Shelley's eyes narrowed in suspicion. 'What was the occasion?'

'I wondered if you'd like to play the angel Gabriel in the Nativity?'

He kept his tone light. Shelley wasn't to be fooled by earnestness.

'No-one else has taken you up on the offer?' she asked, taking a seat next to him on the pew.

Richard held back his sigh. 'I've not asked anyone else.'

Shelley's shoulders visibly relaxed. 'Well . . . I see. What about the wise men? Copperthwaite's hip's playing up. He could do with a distraction.'

Richard tried his best at a neutral face. If ever there was a person to take the magic out of a moment, it was Copperthwaite.

'And Mr Pankhurst could be the other,' added Shelley.

He saw where this was going. 'Good idea. How about Margaret as the third wise man?'

'She's a woman.'

'And Gabriel was an angel,' Richard responded with a smile.

Shelley sniffed. 'Fine.'

'So . . . you'll be an angel?'

Shelley nodded curtly. 'But it won't stop me from giving you this.'

She handed him the envelope he'd hoped she'd put back in her handbag.

'I see. Even after what happened at Bill's office?' asked Richard.

Shelley crossed her ankles. 'I don't make any excuses for vandalism or threatening letters, but the principle still stands, Reverend.'

He held the envelope, not wishing to see who else had now signed. Instead, he looked again at the figure of Christ. The sun pushed through the grey clouds for a few moments, shining through the stained windows and casting a light on the chancel.

'Won't you even look at how many more names there are on the petition?' she said.

'I understand people are upset but—'

'What'll be next? Maybe a Muslim-only school?' Shelley's now high-pitched voice reverberated in the church. 'And pardon me for saying, but at least Mariam doesn't wear one of those scarves. Can the same be said for the type of people who'll want to visit?'

'You object to them?'

'Well, no, it's a free country, but you understand that kind of thing can make a person feel *uncomfortable*.'

'Does her aunt?' Richard asked.

Shelley paused, as if recalibrating her thoughts. 'I'm sure we all seem very closed-minded, but in this day and age it takes some bravery to say exactly what's on one's mind.'

'Yes. It does.' Richard observed the colour rise in Shelley's cheeks. 'Would you like to have a cup of tea?' he asked, already getting up and leading Shelley through the ambulatory into the vestry.

She hesitated. 'I didn't realise we kept a stock of tea here.'

'I try to come here once a week, just so I know the church is in use.'

Shelley entered the small office space and looked at the wooden table, where there were papers and a few old books. 'You're reading C.S. Lewis's reflection on Psalms.'

'Yes, it's always interesting to me,' said Richard, as he handed the tea to Shelley before taking a seat. 'Don't you think that sometimes dislike can taint your vision as much as love?'

Shelley rested her tea cup on her saucer. 'It was clever of you to stay away from the word *hate*, but not clever enough. How many times do I have to say that this *isn't* personal?'

Richard leaned forward. 'Of *course* it is. Especially when you're forming petitions to stop Bill and Mariam from being in the Nativity. When they're being left threatening notes and their property is getting vandalised. You've stirred something in people, Shelley.'

Shelley stared at him, and for a moment Richard thought he'd pierced through this barrier of preservation. He tried to keep his irritation in check. She straightened up in the chair as it creaked. Richard noticed the swelling in her ankles and felt sorry for the inevitability of old age. Sorry that it could surpass wisdom.

'I've lived in this village my entire life,' said Shelley. 'As did my parents. As did theirs. Do Bill's opinions about what happens here matter more than mine?' She put her unfinished tea on the floor. 'I think it's time for me to go.'

'It'd be a shame to start measuring whose opinions are more important.'

'Except when it suits you, of course.'

'Especially when it *doesn't* suit me. How else are we to learn?'

Shelley took her purse and stood up. Richard had no option but to follow her out to the nave.

'If you insist on Mariam and Bilal playing Mary and Joseph then I'll have to insist on separate rehearsals—'

'Shelley . . .'

'I won't be dissuaded,' she said. 'And as someone who's *meant* to be impartial and think of everyone's wishes, I expect you to respect that.'

On Richard's way home the pale sheet of darkness began to thicken as dusk set in. Mitch had already strung up fairy lights outside The Pig and the Ox, as he did every year, six weeks before Christmas. A dispirited Richard found himself driving towards Anne's.

He knocked on the door several times, about to turn away, when Tom walked through the gate.

'Hello,' said Richard. 'I thought Anne might be in.'

'Hmph.' Tom walked past him, scowling as he opened the door and switched on the dim passage lights. 'Anne! The reverend's here, doing his charity.'

Richard sighed inwardly. 'How are you?'

'Just been to my grandson's grave, so cracking.'

Richard didn't respond.

'*Anne!* Where is she?'

They walked into the living room. The coffee table in the middle was bare, a tall floor lamp lit in the corner, the curtains drawn. The quiet of the house was disquieting. Tom peeked through the curtains.

'What the hell . . .?'

Tom, with a newfound energy, marched into the garden. Richard followed, only to find Anne sitting on the edge of what appeared to be a hole in the ground, a shovel abandoned next to her.

'What are you doing? Why aren't you wearing a coat?' demanded Tom. 'You'll catch your death.'

She looked up as if barely registering him. The dark was settling in around them, a few stars making an appearance.

'What is that hole?' said Tom.

She looked into it – it was barely big enough to fit a dog, but Richard understood. He bent down and wrapped his scarf around her cold, bare neck.

'Let's go inside.'

'Well? What's going on?' Tom's face was scrunched up in confusion. 'Don't go worrying my already addled brain.'

She glanced at Richard, squatting next to her, and he wasn't sure whether it was with contempt or for help.

'Anne,' said Tom, his voice softening. He looked increasingly worried as he went to sit next to her, grunting at the effort it took him. 'You can tell your old man anything, can't you?'

'It's just . . . ' She looked over at Richard again, her teeth beginning to chatter as he took off his coat and wrapped that around her too. 'You're the one who put the idea in my head.' She looked so distressed it was all Richard could do to stop himself from wrapping his arms around her too. The entire thing was getting out of hand; no Nativity rehearsals and now Anne digging herself a grave. *Jesus*.

'I'm sorry,' he said.

'What the hell have you done now?' exclaimed Tom to Richard.

Anne looked at her dad, her gaze troubled as she told him about Bilal digging his own grave and lying in it, because his mum used to.

'What?' Tom looked at Richard. 'What in your god's name is all this?'

He took the shovel and threw it across the hole. 'Everyone's lost their fucking mind.' Then he paused, looking at his daughter again. 'Why were *you* doing it?'

She looked at her hands, resting on her legs. 'I don't know. To feel something. Even if it was just fear.'

'Of what?' asked Richard, gripping his arms, pretending the cold hadn't penetrated his skin.

'Death.'

'Christ almighty,' exhaled Tom, watching his daughter as if he was experiencing a physical pain.

'It's okay, Dad. I'm fine.'

'And do you?' asked Richard. 'Feel fear?'

A sad smile played on Anne's lips as she shook her head. 'No.'

'What do you feel?' asked Richard.

She looked at him beneath the large yellow moon, tears surfacing, looking sorrier than she ever had done. 'Nothing,' she said. 'I feel nothing.'

❧

'. . . *Ar-Rahman. Allamal Qur'an. Khalaqal insaan. Allamahul bayaan.*'

Bilal had never imagined he'd hear it again, and there it was – a surah from the Qur'an. In Babbel's End. He'd just started the fire in the living room, trying to bring warmth in the midst of December's cold, amongst other things, and went to get Khala. He stopped in his tracks. Her door was ajar, the words floating into the passage, a stillness taking hold. His mum would recite this surah aloud once a week. A memory ploughed itself into his mind.

'Denying the truth of God,' she'd said, trying to explain its essence, 'is like denying the truth of the beauty of the world.'

She'd taken his face in her hand, smiling, and then raised an eyebrow, as if to challenge him.

He peeked in to see Khala sitting by the window, looking out of it, some papers and a pen in hand. A few minutes in and he could hear carol singers, singing 'Silent Night' outside Margaret's house. Only three weeks to go until Christmas, and the aunts and the Nativity still to get through. The voices were distant, a harmonious background to the surah filling their home. Every week his mum would sit on their green and brown velvet sofa, rocking back and forth while reading, as if swaying to a tune, before she'd wipe her eyes, muttering, 'The greatness of the world.'

She never expanded on that, and now that the world was feeling small to him, he wished he'd asked her about its greatness.

The surah had finished and it took a few moments for Khala to gather her papers and lay them on the bed.

'Sorry,' said Bilal, setting foot into the room. 'The door was open.'

'Come in, beta. I was looking at the stars.'

'Oh. Yes.' He looked up at the star-studded sky.

The carol singers had quietened; he waited for them to

sing outside their home, but the night was indeed silent for the Hashams. He shouldn't have been surprised that they passed them by, but it still pinched. Mariam enjoyed carol singers. With quiet regret, Bilal left his khala and went back into the living room to find Mariam on the sewing machine.

'You heard that then?' she said accusingly.

'Yes.'

'Mob mentality.' Mariam shook her head as the sewing machine whirred and she pressed her foot on the peddle.

Bilal picked up a few small logs from the basket and added them to the fire, poking them with the tongs. 'They're hardly a mob.'

Mariam whipped the brown, linen cloak from the machine and pressed it against Bilal.

'Put it on.'

Bilal sighed, inwardly. He pulled the cloak over his shirt and chinos and looked down, outstretching his arms, the sleeves flapping around.

'How do you feel?' she asked, standing back to inspect her handiwork.

'Nothing like Joseph.'

She had insisted on making the costumes for the Nativity. If they were going to be the centre of attention, without a chance to rehearse as one cast, then she'd make sure they both shone.

'It's short,' said Mariam. 'Give it back.'

She began unstitching the bottom of the hem. 'To just pass our house like that . . . Not that I'm surprised. You know someone said to Haaris that his stepdad was a bastard for firing Dan's dad?'

At that point Haaris came and placed a small box under the Christmas tree.

'Who's that for?' Mariam asked, faking a smile.

'Khala,' he said, and walked back out.

Last year he'd run into this room as if scoring a goal when putting his present for Bilal under the tree. Mariam's brows were etched in concern as she watched Haaris leave. Was it all worth it?

'Any more ideas about who gave us that money?' said Bilal.

'No. There's no way to trace it and . . . oh, I don't even know why it matters any more.'

Bilal's stomach churned at this change in tune – he was losing his constitution as well as his wife. She'd stopped telling him to forget this mosque business since they'd been left that note, so he should've been grateful, and yet something jarred. Mariam slid the cloak into the machine again.

'You're not mad about this any more, are you?' he asked.

'Bilal.' Mariam paused and looked up. 'I don't know what I am.'

chapter twenty

To the Hashams,

The mini-van in your drive has extended into the road, causing cars to swerve. It's also been noted that the van's bumper is broken. Should it fall off in the middle of the road, it could cause considerable harm.

We'd appreciate the van being moved so as to not impede oncoming cars, and that the bumper is checked so that it goes back with the van, as soon as possible as intended.

Best,
Jenny and James Ponsonby.

'All right, bro? Got ourselves into a bit of a mess, innit.'

Vaseem's arm dangled out of the van window, e-cigarette in hand, as he revved the engine again in an attempt to hurtle *Vaseem's Removals* van out of the ditch. The vehicle stuck in the middle of the quiet village's Rayner's Lane was already giving Bilal heartburn. Auntie Shagufta – hair immaculately set with light brown highlights – and Auntie Gulfashan – grey bun hidden beneath her Russian hat – peered out of the van windows. The curtains in the Ponsonbys' yellow house twitched.

After his failed attempt, Vaseem Bhai came bounding up to Bilal, gripping him into a bear hug.

'Look at you,' he said, his e-cigarette prodding Bilal as he grabbed his friend's face with both hands. 'Told Khala R yet about the house?'

'No, and please don't say anything.'

'Buyers are getting itchy, you know. My boys are gonna have to remove all that stuff soon,' said Vaseem.

'I know, I know.'

Bilal was delaying the inevitable – but he couldn't have Khala's things removed without her knowing.

Vaseem Bhai pulled Bilal's head forward, inspecting his head. 'Losing your hair, bro. I got stuff for that. Buy two and I'll give you the third free. Special family discount.'

Vaseem Bhai laughed his belly laugh, ruffling Bilal's head without thinking of Bilal's feathers. He glanced over his shoulder to check if Jenny and James were still watching. A few months ago they'd have been out here offering their AA insurance and a cup of tea. Bilal wished that his guests could have arrived at a less curtain-twitching time. It just so happened that fate had conspired to heighten everyone's twitchiness when he heard the chugging of a car and saw, from afar, Copperthwaite approach in his unmistakable 1920s red Willys-Overland Whippet. A smaller car might've been able to pass through, but there was no way that Whippet was going anywhere.

'Oh, God,' muttered Bilal.

'Look at that car,' said Vaseem.

Auntie Gulfashan started knocking at the window. 'Will we be stuck here all day?' came her muffled voice.

Copperthwaite, in his grey trilby, slowed down before his car came to a stop. He peered over the steering wheel, looking straight at Bilal. Bilal walked over to him, gesturing for him to roll down his window.

'Bit of a disaster,' he said.

Copperthwaites' furrowed his brows. 'Hmph.'

Vaseem Bhai was already walking around Copperthwaite's car, rubbing his cold hands together, surveying it. 'What model is this?' He poked his head into Copperthwaite's window. 'All right, mate?'

Copperthwaite looked at Vaseem's outstretched hand before reluctantly taking it.

'Pleased to meet you,' Vaseem added.

For a moment Bilal's heart swelled with affection for his childhood friend – protector from bullies, attacker of his head of hair – for his sheer attempt at politeness. Vaseem, for the sake of propriety, relinquished his 'innits' and 'bros', even though he couldn't relinquish his brummie accent.

'Trouble?' Copperthwaite barked, frowning at the van.

It was this moment that Auntie Gulfashan had stopped waiting for the men to answer and bundled out of the van, gripping her walking stick, almost slipping in the mud. Copperthwaite's frown deepened.

'*Ki syaapa pegya?*' she exclaimed.

Bilal felt his face go red. 'She's just wondering what the calamity is,' he explained to Copperthwaite.

Copperthwaite looked at the Pakistani woman in her Russian hat, multi-coloured shalwar kameez peeking from beneath her long winter coat, her eyes buzzing about the place and resting on Copperthwaite.

'Shagufta! Careful,' exclaimed Gulfashan.

Auntie Shagufta's dupatta – a paisley printed chiffon scarf – that was wrapped around her neck, over her brown fur coat, caught in the door as she too attempted to come out.

'O-ho!' Shagufta exclaimed as she heard it rip.

'It might be best if you turned around,' Bilal said to Copperthwaite.

But Copperthwaite was too busy aunt-gazing.

'Why didn't you bring your car, instead of this van?' Bilal muttered to Vaseem.

'Got it cheap, innit? Sold the car, got the van to drive around with me bits.'

Copperthwaite shot Vaseem a look. 'Bits? What bits?'

'I'm a salesman, sir. Get you a good deal on anything you need.'

Just then, Jenny and James's door opened, both of them coming out in their wellies and jumpers.

'A bit of a problem here, Copperthwaite?' called out Jenny.

'Shall we call someone?' asked James.

'Jenny,' Bilal nodded.

She pretended she hadn't seen.

The cold-shoulder hadn't eluded Vaseem Bhai. 'Don't need nobody. Got me muscles. And me bro' here. But if you . . . what's your name, bro?'

'James.'

'Jaam-es! Just kidding.'

Oh, God.

'If you jump in the car and start the engine, we'll push the van.' Vaseem thumped Bilal on the arm. 'Come on, then.'

Before James could do as instructed, a noise, familiar to Bilal, but rather foreign to his neighbours, broke out in the middle of the country lane.

Allah hu Akbar. Allah hu Akbar. Allah hu Akbar. Allah hu Akbar. Ashahadu an la illa ha illa la. Ashadu an illa ha illa la.

Everyone paused. A look of sheer bemusement came over Copperthwaite, Jenny and James. They looked at each other, around them, to the heavens above, wondering where this – little did they know it, Godly – commotion was coming from.

Vaseem got his phone out of his back pocket. 'Sorry about that,' he said to the befuddled trio as he switched the *azaan* off. 'Time to pray. Mind like a sieve, me. Downloaded it on my phone so it reminds me.'

He put his phone back into his pocket as Bilal watched his village neighbours exchange sideward glances.

'The call to prayer, that is,' added Bilal. 'Not his mind.'

Vaseem looked at him and laughed. 'Wish I could download me brain. Mind if I pray then?'

This couldn't be happening.

'O-ho, Vassu. You're travelling,' said Auntie Gulfashan. 'You can pray when we get to Bilal's home.'

Vaseem raised his eyebrows at his mum. 'Say your prayers, before your prayers are said for you.'

Vaseem's allusion to potential funeral prayers was best left unexplained, Bilal felt. Just when Bilal thought the unfortunate interval was over, Vaseem went into the van, came back out with a bin bag and placed it on the ground, before placing a prayer mat on top of it, presumably to keep it from getting muddied.

'Vassu, it's so cold, *paagal*,' said Auntie Gulfashan.

'Nothing like praying in God's fresh air,' he exclaimed, smiling.

Vaseem did a three-hundred-and-sixty turn to take in this air as he said: '*Subhanallah*,' before he raised his hands in prayer and was lost to God.

'*Chalo*, I will read too then,' said Auntie Gulfashan, climbing back into the van for the sake of privacy. There was nothing to do but wait until they had finished.

Finally, Vaseem put his hands up in prayer, mumbling something in Arabic and then in English: 'And give these good people in Babbel's End health, wealth and happiness.'

Copperthwaite's brows furrowed so deep they'd merged into one entity.

'What?' he barked.

'Health, wealth and happiness,' repeated Bilal.

'Ready, bro?' Vaseem said to James, who looked towards Jenny for approval.

The aunts stood to the side to save their shalwar kameezes from getting splashed by all this English mud. James revved the engine and Bilal, Jenny and Vaseem managed, after multiple tries, to push the van out of the ditch. Bilal looked up to see Jenny give Copperthwaite a meaningful look. Yes, perhaps the aunts should have considered their colours-of-the-rainbow attire, perhaps Vaseem shouldn't have prostrated to God in the middle of the English countryside, but didn't they think about how *rude* they were being? Couldn't they have gone home and gossiped behind closed doors like respectable English people?

'Come on then,' said Vaseem, getting into the van. 'Let's go finally see my bro's house.'

Bilal dutifully got into his own car, letting Copperthwaite drive past first. Their eyes met as their paths crossed and it was with considerable fortitude that Bilal refused to cower under Copperthwaite's scowl.

He had been putting if off for a while, though he didn't know why. The Christmas lights were up in town, festive displays up in Babbel's Bric-a-Brac and James's bookshop.

The towering tree in The Pig and the Ox, with its yellow fairy lights and red and golden baubles. But why was his family always on the receiving end of looks and accusations when they hadn't harmed anyone?

Bruce had.

And so had his son.

It hardly seemed fair, and maybe Mariam was right: maybe it was time for Bilal to be more assertive in life.

He arrived home and walked out into the garden. As he looked over his makeshift grave, he took out his phone and finally called the police.

Vaseem had dropped the aunts off and returned home to his family the same day. He was so charmed by Babbel's End though, so taken at the idea of a Christmas party in a barn that – much to Bilal's dismay – he decided he'd bring his wife and three children to the village over the Christmas holidays.

The village's feelings, however, weren't mutual. It wasn't long before news of the mass influx to Babbel's End spread. By the time Shelley found out, Vaseem's five-minute prayer had turned into a half hour devotional act with the call to prayer's apocalyptic undertones startling everyone in the village. And when Bilal's cousin wasn't praying, he was a swindler, selling things in the back of his van. To add to all this, not only had Bilal fired Bruce – although he'd been quite deserving of it, given the circumstances

– but he'd actually called the police and now Bruce would have to pay a fine as well as face unemployment during Christmas and beyond. Poor Bruce, who no-one had ever thought of before, was now at the forefront of their pity.

Was this the Muslim spirit? Whatever happened to things like forgiveness and mercy?

chapter twenty-one

TWO WEEKS BEFORE CHRISTMAS and the day of the
party arrived (along with Vaseem, his wife and
gaggle of children). The place felt more like a
Lahori bazaar during Eid than Christmas in a quiet
village. Mariam was in the laundry room, wrapping the
presents, and Bilal was bringing in the third load of
laundry when he paused outside, hearing her voice
within.

'No, Saif, we'd agreed that he'd spend Christmas and
New Year here.'

Bilal leaned closer to the door.

'It's not *celebrating*, it's just a tree and a party. Yes, and
lunch. So what? You loved it when we . . . when you first
moved here.'

She paused.

'You keep mentioning you've changed but generally it's nice when it's for the better.'

Bilal smiled at Mariam's refusal to put up with anyone's nonsense, though rather wished she'd make an exception for him. The following silence lasted so long Bilal wondered whether he should go in. God, Saif was insufferable. This was exactly the reason he'd wanted to move away from Birmingham – everything was subjected to so much scrutiny. For eight years he'd lived peacefully in Babbel's End, until now, when his life choices were being questioned again. He was beginning to see there was no escape from it.

'I see.' Mariam's voice had softened, quickening the beats of Bilal's heart. 'When? I didn't even . . . You hadn't mentioned anything. Nor did Haaris.'

Bilal gripped the laundry basket tighter.

'Right, well, I appreciate that. He's at that age. Shall I speak to him?'

Speak about what? Another long pause.

'Saif . . . now's not the time.'

Bilal couldn't listen any longer. He opened the door with his free hand, plastering on a smile as Mariam looked up with worried eyes, which did nothing for his worried mind.

'Let's speak about this later, Saif, I have to go. No, I get that, but Bilal and I were in the middle of – yes. Fine. Bye.'

'What'd he want?'

'Haaris, over the Christmas holidays.'

'He had him during half-term.'

'Yes, I know.'

Mariam sat down on the floor amongst the ribbons and wrapping paper. 'What was Vaseem Bhai's youngest one's name again?' Her hair was slicked back in a ponytail, her eyes flickering around the scattered objects – two teddy bears, a stationary set, Lego set, three scarves (for the head), another scarf (for the neck), a photo-frame (with a picture in it) and a set of earrings (pierced).

Bilal placed the laundry basket on the washing machine.

'Saima?'

'I thought it was Sammia?'

'Or Samina,' he replied.

'*For Sam*,' she said, writing the name on a card, which she sellotaped to the Rudolph-themed paper. 'Shit!' she exclaimed. 'The chops.'

She ran out of the laundry room as Bilal watched her go, then closed the door after her. He'd emptied the load into the machine before switching the light off, placing the basket upside down on the floor and perching on it. Saima, Samina or Sammia was crying. Haaris was locked in his room as the aunts were in the throes of deciding what to wear for the party that evening. Bilal put his head in his hands. He'd have slipped into his grave only it was too conspicuous at this time. The presence of so many family members only pronouncing the lack of his mother's.

What had Saif said to Mariam that caused her to soften her voice? It was, after all, a rarity.

'All right, bro?' A flood of light came through the door

as Vaseem Bhai's figure loomed in the doorway. 'Got some Pepto-Bismol?'

Bilal had to squint. 'Will Gaviscon do?'

'It's for the wife. You know what it's like.'

Bilal nodded. Vaseem closed the door behind him and looked around before clearing the Christmas paraphernalia and sitting on the floor.

'You look a bit stressed,' said Vaseem.

'I . . . No, I'm fine.'

'Sitting in a laundry room in the dark?' Vaseem looked around the small space. 'The wife's going on about having one of these now. Says if she has to iron my shirts, least I could do is give her a room to do it in.'

'She irons your shirts?'

'She's a good one, you know.'

'Because she irons?'

Vaseem gave a small laugh. 'Because she looks after me. And I look after her, innit. Works both ways. But someone's got to put the other first,' he said, rolling his eyes to the ceiling.

Bilal knew Mariam would have something to say about . . . what did she call it? Co-dependency. He remembered how she'd spent weeks reading up on attachment theory as he waited patiently for its conclusion. When had Mariam ever put him first? Then he wondered when he'd ever put her first. In the race of life, they always seemed to be neck-and-neck. But her mind was like shifting sand and he never knew which way it would go.

'That's why your mum always looked at you so proudly, innit. Taking in a divorced woman with a child.'

'She wouldn't be so proud of me now – failing to get this mosque built,' said Bilal.

Vaseem began puffing on his e-cigarette. Quitting cigarettes was another thing he was doing for his wife.

'Got to admit,' mused Vaseem, 'never thought you'd even try.'

'No. Nor did I.'

'It's mad. Selling your mum's place to raise the money too. Brave, but mad.'

Of all the adjectives there might be to describe Bilal, 'brave' wasn't one that sprung to mind, although he didn't mind the attribution.

'They really hate me now.'

'What did you expect?' laughed Vaseem. He opened up his arms and put on a posh accent. 'Yes, come along – build a mosque on our green land. We invaded and ruled your country for hundreds of years, so it's the least we could do.' He shook his head.

'Well, they never did *me* any personal harm,' replied Bilal. He wasn't fond of this historical blame ideology. 'You can't move forward if you hang on to the past,' he added.

Vaseem thought about it. 'No, bro. But you can't move forward without thinking about what went wrong in the past either.'

Bilal's thoughts kept coming back to Mariam. Had he ignored her past for too long? Did it stop him from understanding her? What made him think that just because he loved her, he had a right to be loved back in the same way? He let the question he'd kept from asking himself surface in his mind, sitting there in the laundry room with Vaseem Bhai.

Did his wife actually love him?

Bilal was lost in this reverie when his phone beeped. It was an email from the agent for the land. *Please, God, let this be the hope that I need.* Bilal clicked on the email, hands trembling.

From: Adam, James
To: Hasham, Bilal
Subject: Land

Dear Mr Hasham,

Mrs Gardiner has come back to me about your query. I'm afraid she's already in the middle of talking to two parties interested in the land and doesn't wish to complicate matters.

Sorry not to have been able to help.

Best wishes,
James Adam

Bilal re-read the email, heart sinking.

'What's wrong, bro?' asked Vaseem.

Then he scrolled down and realised James Adam had pressed 'forward' instead of 'reply'.

From: Gardiner, Agatha
To: Adam, James
Subject: Land

James, are you mad? Grant someone permission to build a mosque?? On my land! You've quite rattled me while I wait to catch sight of some whales (the season's almost over). You can tell him I'd sell my soul before selling him my land.

Now, I've misplaced my binoculars. Honestly! Mosque!

'Right,' said Vaseem. 'Let's get that Gaviscon.'

Never had Rukhsana's wardrobe evoked such conflict. She looked longingly at her shalwar kameez. It was a gora occasion and so she should wear her new gora clothes. But then there were her friends. She noticed how Shagufta looked at her up and down. Sakeena never got those looks when she wore gora clothes. Why were some people's characters bound by certain expectations more than others?

'Do you have any . . . *news*?' asked Gulfashan when she and Shagufta went to see her room.

Rukhsana paused, confused. How could she express how much news she had! Bilal's mosque, the mystery donation, the Nativity, her new friend, Shelley, who everyone called Bilal's enemy. (It wasn't as clear-cut as that.)

'Why are you friends with *her*?' Shagufta laughed.

'Oh, Rukhsana. You are still the same!' added Gulfashan. 'Even still wearing that whistle around your neck.'

Rukhsana wondered why she'd brought her friends and their opinions into her village life.

'She is not a bad person,' replied Rukhsana. 'These are nice people.'

'Are they nice, or do you just not understand them?'

Rukhsana knew she'd always been measured against the quickness of Sakeena, but she hadn't realised that her friends thought she was actually stupid.

Gulfashan paused. 'So, you are happy here?'

Shagufta adjusted the lace of her shalwar kameez as she continued to take in the clean, vanilla-scented room.

'Yes,' replied Rukhsana.

'Bilal hasn't said anything about . . . you coming back?' asked Shagufta.

'No.'

She must not be such a hindrance, and it pleased her more than she'd realised. It was a great consolation in the face of knowing that she would be seeing Shelley with the whole village present. Was she to say hello, or were they to ignore each other? Their companionship seemed to only exist in the context of their walks – outside that

Rukhsana wasn't sure what the etiquette was. So much etiquette! A new anxiety to go with each new rule. There were people in the world who managed whole companies and she could barely manage her feelings.

The Christmas tree hadn't helped. Sakeena used to put a small plastic one up every year because it was a reason to use tinsel. It wasn't anything like the towering tree that Bilal and Mariam had – the gold and silver ornaments that were taken out of the storage box and placed on the tree with care, next to the fireplace that now roared every evening. Sakeena's tree was a novelty; this was a celebration. Jesus had his place in Islam – a very important one! Wasn't that enough? Rukhsana took out her trousers and a sequinned jumper, hesitated for a moment, but knew it was the only thing that would do for the occasion.

❧

Mariam hated that the idea of fitting in played on her mind. She saw the way the aunts looked at the Christmas tree and Khala's attire, her life reduced to tinsel and clothing. She began to see it the way they must. It was all a façade. A beautifully packaged gift with nothing inside. The simplicity of the realisation diffused her sense of self, as if she wasn't an individual at all – just another person who'd lived a life of self-deceit.

Now, Saif's wife was leaving him. His declaration on the phone earlier had slipped into her ear like a wisp of smoke, morphing into a two-tonne weight that crushed her chest as she wrapped another present in Rudolph-themed paper.

'I made a mistake,' he'd said.

Mariam would have smothered his words if she had had a moment to reflect, breathe and *let go*. But letting go can't have witnesses. Reasoning with oneself can't have interruptions, and the onslaught of activity was at an all-time high. After she checked on the chops, she went into her study, locking the door behind her as she leaned against the wall. What did he mean that he'd *made a mistake*? Was the mistake his increasing self-reflection, which bored his current wife into an exodus?

Or was it leaving Mariam?

Her heart pounded.

She put one hand over her mouth, grabbing the bin with the other, thinking she might be sick.

'Mum!' came Haaris's voice as he rattled the door handle. 'You in there? It's locked.'

'Coming,' she called out, taking deep breaths, closing her eyes and doing what Khala did whenever she seemed overwhelmed. '*Allah hu Akbar*,' Mariam whispered. '*Allah hu Akbar, Allah hu Akbar, Allah hu Akbar.*'

'Do I *have* to go with you?'

Mariam took another deep breath, steadied herself and opened the door. 'Yes, you do.'

'But why?' he whined, looking so desperate she almost gave in to him.

'You loved it last year.'

'That was last year.'

She pulled Haaris into a hug, kissing his head as many times as she could before he pulled away from her.

'*Mum*, my hair.'

She grabbed his face, willing herself not to cry. 'I made that hair.'

'Actually,' he said, 'according to Khala, God made the hair, so . . .'

She turned him around because her tears *would* surface, and pushed him towards the staircase, steeling herself as they entered the living room.

'I think we're all ready,' she said to the aunts as Vaseem walked in with a concerned-looking Bilal. She got the bag with their costumes. 'Haaris, grab the stick.'

'But I don't want to see anyone, Mum,' he murmured. '*Please*.'

She swallowed hard, her heart cracking as she pressed his head to her chest. 'I'm sorry, baby,' she whispered. 'Sometimes we just have to face up to things.'

❧

'*Hai hai*,' exclaimed Gulfashan from the back of the van.

'So cold.'

'So foggy.'

'How can you see?'

'Careful of the bush just there,' said Bilal, pointing to Tom's hedge.

'Slow down.'

Mariam leaned into Haaris and whispered, 'Quite loud, aren't they?'

He managed to give her a knowing look – her son, the only unique thing in this world; an anchor to her otherwise frenzied feelings; the one distinction in the blur of her life. Mariam put her arm around him, savouring the solidity of his form as he took out his Nintendo Switch. But he simply held on to it and stared out of the window. Bilal turned around and looked at them. They drove through the village green, strewn with lights – James had put up a reindeer in a sleigh and Santa Claus outside his bookshop – past The Pig and the Ox, and arrived at the barn, which sat across from a row of houses. Behind the barn the field stretched out, obscured by the fog, but from where they could hear a cow or two. The thatched roof and two bushes that stood either side of the entrance had been decorated with fairy lights that twinkled through the mist; a wreath of frosted acorns and mistletoe hung outside the door. A line of bright white bulbs hung from the barn's gable, attached to two poles on the other side of the road. They all teetered out of the van, the aunts complaining about the uneven ground, the slippery mud, the cold that seeped into their bones. Where were the street lamps? Thank God they didn't live in a village.

Then they saw the spectacle before them and let out an appreciative breath.

A hum of chatter came from within, people walking in, greeted by Richard in jeans and a Christmas jumper – this year it was one of Rudolph with stars sprinkled around him – Richard's collar intact underneath. Mariam took a deep breath, pressing her gloved hands together.

'You're here,' exclaimed Richard, rubbing his arms and looking at the line of brown people, the bulbs' warm light shining on their awed faces.

Bilal introduced him to everyone as Vaseem clasped Richard's hand in his.

'Merry Christmas, Reverend.'

'And to you. Come in, come in. Can't have anyone catching a cold before the Nativity. Plenty to eat and drink.'

The aunts meandered cautiously into the unknown territory, a wave of warmth enveloping them, the smell of mulled wine and the heat of the crackling fire thawing their cold hands and suspicious hearts. Candles were dotted around, fairy lights looped around the wooden beams on high ceilings. Mince pies and Christmas puddings, gingerbread men, pigs in a blanket and roasted chestnuts were laid out on tables, glasses and wine some feet away, ice buckets in the corner.

The room paused. It was always going to.

The diamantes on the aunts' golden and purple shalwar kameezes, the bronze thread-work on their scarves felt like an assertion here.

What did Mariam's black trousers and white angora jumper say about her?

Focus less on the material and more on the heart of life's matter.

Candle flames still flickered, the fire still roared, but the people were still.

'Marvellous!'

Margaret came up to them in her green sequinned jumper and gillet, shaking hands with each aunt so vigorously, taking in their demeanour with such pleasure that Mariam made a note to bake Margaret something nice for New Year's. Khala then handed a bag to Margaret.

'Christmas present,' she said.

'What? For me?' Margaret peered into the bag, taking out material of some sort. She held up a pale gold and dusky pink kameez as people glanced her way. 'Oh, gosh. It's *heavenly*.'

She hugged Khala, who looked so pleased Mariam wondered why her own mum had never done that for people? Why hadn't she hugged them so readily, offering to sew things and make zarda?

'You like?' asked Khala.

'Like? I *adore*. Shall I wear it now?'

'Please, no,' said Mariam, trying to smile. 'I don't think a wise man would turn up wearing shalwar kameez.'

'Such a boring lot, weren't they?'

Mariam scanned the room: there was Copperthwaite, today in a red and green Ascot, coupled with deriding gaze; the Pankhursts, standing uncomfortably apart; Jenny and James, the interchangeable couple; Sam and his parents. No Bruce. Mariam noticed Haaris turn his back, pretending to observe the concrete floor. People from Little Chebby, Long Chebby, Swinknowle and other neighbouring villages were also present. And there was Shelley, staring at Khala and Margaret.

'Are you ready?' Richard asked, leaning into Mariam.

'Oh. Yes,' Mariam replied, lifting up the bag with hers and Bilal's costumes. 'Can't wait.'

'I'm really glad you didn't back out,' said Richard.

Bilal was engaged in conversation with Margaret – largely as a translator – even though the aunts, apart from Khala, spoke fluent English.

'Why would I?'

'A lot's happened,' he said, looking over Mariam's shoulder towards the door. 'But then, all the more reason to stand one's ground.'

'I thought we were just doing the Nativity.'

Richard smiled at her. 'Politics and religion . . . '

Mariam returned the smile.

Be receptive to kindness. Offer it yourself so that it comes your way. You receive from the universe what you give to it. Give love.

My ex-husband is going to be single.

'Why don't you both go and start getting ready?' said Richard. 'I'll tell the wise men *et al* to do the same.'

Mariam nodded as she and Bilal walked towards the back of the barn, where there was a screen and a door to a toilet. Behind the screen were a couple of blocks making a stage and set for the Nativity. Bilal and Mariam were momentarily taken aback.

'Richard really does go all-out, doesn't he?' said Bilal.

Wooden beams framed the stage that glittered with lights and homemade ornaments, which Richard had inherited from his predecessors. There was a manger,

and a makeshift donkey, which was slightly disconcerting.

Bilal was staring at Mariam as she was handing him his
costume.

'Are you happy?' he asked.

'What?'

'Happy?'

*Happiness is transient and is dependent not on what you
have in life, but how you perceive it.*

'What do you mean?' she said, more curtly than
intended.

His face seemed to deflate.

'That face doesn't make me happy,' Mariam said. It was
meant to come out light and frothy, but instead came out
like shards of glass.

'Right,' said Bilal.

'You honestly ask the oddest of questions at the oddest
of times.'

'Mariam . . .'

She pushed the robes into his hands but couldn't quite
meet his gaze. He could've warned her before asking such
a direct question.

'You're not, are you?' he asked.

Persistence! It made her so uncomfortable.

'I mean, what's happiness anyway?' replied Mariam.

'Mariam . . . ?'

'I have to think about it.'

'You either are or you aren't. If someone falls over they
don't have to think about if they're hurt.'

'If they've fallen over then of course they're hurt.'

Was it the the flames of the candles that played a trick on her, or were Bilal's eyes watering?

'Don't do that,' he whispered. 'I have a right to know, don't I?'

'Says who?'

'The man who's tried to make you happy.'

Life was a constant flux of honesty versus not hurting feelings – even one's own. You could do plenty of damage to yourself, simply by recognising the worst parts of who you are.

'It's my own job to make me happy,' she replied.

And she believed it. Why should anyone else bear the burden? And it was a burden – the constant need to be *happy*. As if sadness was like a cancer that should be fought at every stage. What if the real fight was accepting the sadness?

Gratitude.

List three things for which you are grateful.

1. *Haaris.*

2. *Health.*

3. *A home.*

What was home, anyway? Her first had been with her parents, and that was a non-starter. Her second with Saif had been the light at the end of the depths of anxiety – only it had been extinguished as quickly as it had burned. And then there'd been her home with Bilal. The light here flickered, but had never before felt in danger of going out.

'Look at that donkey.'

Mariam looked over her shoulder to see Shelley, Copperthwaite, Mr Pankhurst and Margaret approach.

'Excellent!' exclaimed Margaret. 'Not ready yet? Don't worry, there's plenty of time – not as if we need a dress-rehearsal or anything,' she added, nudging Copperthwaite in the side. 'Excellent family you have, Bill. Pakistanis do have beauty on their side – it's the colouring.'

Margaret looked at her companions.

Silence.

Copperthwaite cleared his phlegmy throat.

'I'm not dallying around here. Give me that,' he said, taking his costume from Shelley and barging past Bilal and Mariam into the toilet cubicle.

Mr Pankhurst remained stony-faced, refusing to look at either of them. Mariam stood closer to Bilal.

'Well, isn't this the Christmas spirit?' said Margaret.

One by one everyone went in and changed into their costumes, coming out in biblical attire, if not manner.

'Look at us,' said Margaret, beaming.

Bilal was draped in his beige cloak next to Mr Pankhurst and Copperthwaite, who'd donned a rather elaborate outfit for a wise man. Shelley adjusted her unwieldy wings.

'Is Anne coming?' said Mariam, peeking through the curtains.

She'd bought and wrapped a present, hoping today would give her a chance to hand it to her. It would be her first Christmas without Teddy and if Mariam was going to atone for her shortcomings as a friend, now would be the time to begin.

'If her bugger of a father comes, I'll throw Jesus's crib at him,' said Copperthwaite, inspecting the jewels on his fingers.

'You'll give yourself a hernia,' said Shelley.

'I'd pay good money to see you bowled over by a hernia at Tom's feet, Copsy,' replied Margaret. 'Say Jeeeees-us.' Her flash caught the actors off guard. 'Shelley, perhaps smile a little more – you're an angel, not a fascist.'

Margaret winked at Mariam.

'It's my flock,' said Richard, entering the performance arena. 'That crown suits you, Margaret.'

Mariam thought he looked as proud as if the birth of Jesus was his idea. She hated her cynical observations sometimes. *See the best in people. How else will they see the best in you?*

'Ready to act, as you please,' Mariam responded.

She sounded too chirpy. Bilal looked at her. Richard smiled. If he detected her disingenuousness, he didn't show it. He was a better person than she. Most people were.

'Now, I know you've not had a chance to rehearse together but we know the story well enough, yes?' said Richard.

There was a reluctant murmuring of assent.

'Right. In your positions then, please.' Richard moved the screen to reveal the seated audience. 'A round of applause for our thespians.'

There was a scattering of claps. Mariam wondered if Saif were here what he'd make of it. *Why do you try so hard to fit in? These people don't even want you here.*

What did it matter? Why were her thoughts constantly filtered by what he might think? Thoughts of him gave him relevance – and he had never felt more so than now.

She should've put her foot down and said no to being in the Nativity. How long were you meant to stand in front of a crowd that tried to bowl you over with their looks? The energy it took to not be moved was diminishing. She saw Haaris, sitting between Khala and Vaseem Bhai, looking down at his lap, and Mariam had a sudden urge to go and slap Sam for being so fickle.

'Two thousand years ago,' began Richard's narration, 'in the town of Nazareth, lived a young woman named Mary. An angel came and told Mary: "Do not be afraid, you have found favour with God."'

The aunts' faces in the crowd contracted, eyes narrowed, throats cleared. Mrs Pankhurst sat with her arms folded, staring at her husband on stage. From the corner of her eye Mariam could see Copperthwaite twitching behind the curtain, Shelley's wing poking above his head, Margaret with her crown and phone.

What had she learnt? That things splintered.

Remember to breathe. Stay in the moment. Feel the ground beneath your feet.

Mariam looked into the crowd and saw Sam filming the play, then her eyes rested on Haaris again. He'd grown so much in this past year and soon he'd leave her in order to live a life that was fully his own, stories that wouldn't include her, and worse still – he'd face the challenges of daily living, the world falling away from him, or closing in on him. Then she felt a nudge. It was Bilal. She glanced around the stage at Jenny, the innkeeper, who was looking at her expectantly.

'Is . . . ' Mariam had to clear her throat. 'Is there any room at the inn?'

No! There isn't any room. And if you thought there ever had been it was an illusion.

James, whose jeans were peeking out from under his robe, led them towards the stable, where Mariam was about to give birth to Jesus. The curtain closed before the indelicacies of labour had to be shown.

'You stepped on my robe,' came one voice.

'Gosh, accident. Sorry,' said another as Bilal, Mariam and James went behind the screen to give way to the shepherds.

'I am here with good news for you, which will bring joy to all nations,' came Richard's voice as they imagined the shepherds' scene taking place.

'Good job, you two,' said Margaret. 'No time to stop, the shepherds are in Bethlehem.'

Mariam and Bilal shuffled back on stage.

'We have been following a star for months,' enunciated Margaret. 'And we knew that it was a sign that the king of the world was to be born.'

Margaret picked up the plastic baby and Mariam saw Shelley's brow twitch – the white doll had been painted brown.

'Jesus would bring the light of love into the world – it

would remind us for all eternity of God's love for us.'

Richard paused and looked around the room, pointedly. He waited. Then he waited a few more moments before he said: 'The end.'

The room gave a generous applause, moved by the scene, or perhaps Richard's stern eye. Haaris clapped too. The aunts and Vaseem Bhai were varying shades of pleased and Richard turned around to give the actors a broad smile.

Mariam grabbed Bilal's hand on the way off the stage and she felt him squeeze it.

'That was excellent. *Excellent*,' said Margaret.

'I need to speak with Richard,' said Bilal as the audience broke out into chatter and he let go of Mariam's hand.

❧

The moment she held his hand Bilal had decided: it was better to abandon ideas of the mosque than to abandon his family. Saif's shadow was beginning to eclipse Bilal's marriage. Looking out at everyone, watching them all on stage, the gathered community had lifted his heart as much as Mrs Gardiner's email, with her transatlantic tension, had quashed it. He ignored the prodding thoughts of succumbing to peer pressure, giving in as if he wasn't allowed to be more than just Bill, the brown guy in Babbel's End, because wasn't it easier if he just were? Instead of the man who pressed charges against the employee he fired? He smothered feelings of doubt and his mum's voice that reverberated in his head. Anything this difficult must mean it's just not meant to be. Hadn't his mum always quoted that saying by the prophet (Muhammed, he was sure, but there were others and he really couldn't keep up): *What has reached you was never meant to miss you, and what has missed you was never meant to reach you.*

This, he had to concede, was kismet. He'd fill in the grave when he got home; no more of that nonsense either. He took the cloth off his head and lifted his robe, realising the absurdity of what he'd been attempting. Something would have to be done about that mystery donation, and the selling of his mum's house, but he'd have to worry about that later.

It's a wonder Mariam was still with him. That Haaris still spoke to him – just look at him sitting alone while Sam joked around with their friends. Trying to plant roots really could cut you off.

'I find mulching at this time of year excellent for suppressing weeds,' said Richard to Mrs Newbury.

'Richard, we need to speak,' Bilal interrupted. 'Mrs Newbury.'

Richard paused long enough for Mrs Newbury to acknowledge Bilal, but she pretended he wasn't there. Bilal didn't care about that any more. He had to tell Richard before he changed his mind. Before he forgot the way Mariam had gripped his hand. He led Richard to a quieter spot in the room, noticing his aunts huddled in a corner where Margaret and Mrs Pankhurst had joined them. How grateful he felt to them for making his family feel welcome.

'What's wrong?' Richard asked.

Bilal hesitated.

'I've changed my mind.'

His friend's eyes bore into his. 'About?'

'The mosque. I'm going to forget it.'

Richard crossed his arms.

'I know you're relieved really,' continued Bilal. 'And that's okay. I understand. It's not worth it in the end, I don't think.'

He waited for Richard to speak. It was taking a while and he wasn't sure what to make of his friend's stare.

'You don't think?' repeated Richard. 'Or you know?'

'Does it matter either way?'

'It does.'

Bilal saw the village thespians still in their stage attire: Shelley in her wings, Margaret with her crown. Sometimes he wished that Richard would just say, 'yes' or 'no', call the spade a spade. The devil really was in the detail.

'The land I wanted to buy . . . well, she won't sell it to me. She knew it was for the mosque and she refused. This whole thing's just caused too much trouble.'

'I see.' Richard paused. 'But you always knew that it would.'

Except Bilal had underestimated his constitution for conflict. And back then he hadn't realised that his marriage needed saving as much as his mother's memory.

'Look at Bruce. It brought out the worst in him and see what happened? And aside from that . . . things are tricky at home.'

'Right.'

'It's all taken a bit of a toll.'

Silence.

'Well, say something,' said Bilal.

Richard rubbed the back of his neck. 'Do you think it's just the mosque that's done that?'

'I don't know,' exclaimed Bilal, turning a few heads.

He had too many thoughts and that was nothing compared to his cocktail of emotions. Even Gaviscon couldn't help. He took a deep breath, waiting for Richard to speak. Again.

'Well?' Bilal asked.

'You know what's best for you.'

'It's all too much,' said Bilal. 'The planning permission, the money, the looks we all get. No-one invites us over any more, no quick coffees, no chat about the weather – nothing. It's like we're invisible. And Haaris – his friends have all deserted him . . . '

Richard's expression looked pained.

'Listen, it's not your fault,' added Bilal. 'I'm just giving you the facts.'

Bilal could almost see the flurry of thoughts occupying Richard.

'What?' asked Bilal.

'It's not right,' said Richard, scratching at Rudolph's nose. 'A mosque's just another building.'

'Yes.'

'Just another house of God,' added Richard.

This was getting rather tedious. Bilal wanted to go and tell Mariam what he'd done. 'And?'

'What's the use of a church bell if no-one actually uses the church?'

'What?'

'Just empty,' said Richard, almost to himself.

'Yes, it's all quite sad,' replied Bilal, unsure of Richard's point. The place was getting hotter, people close by.

'Bill . . . ' said Richard, now tugging at a thread on Rudolph's nose. 'What if we converted St Swithun's into a mosque?'

Bilal leaned forward. 'Excuse me?'

'We'd have to get it deconsecrated,' said Richard quietly, deep in thought. 'And there are channels I'd have to go through, but . . . ' He looked at Bilal, as if this was his battle as well as Bilal's. 'It's the answer.'

Bilal stared at his friend. 'Convert St Swithun's? Into a mosque?'

Richard nodded.

'But . . . it's a *church*,' said Bilal.

'A holy space.'

'For Christians.'

'Right now it's just for decorative purposes.'

Bilal loved the small, stone building, surrounded by grass and flowers, with the characteristic wooden door that had to be pulled with some force in order to get in, the rows of carved pews, the two memorial columns erected in memory of Henry and Elizabeth Elliot, who'd lost their baby in 1702 and had donated money to the church. All those names on the plaques – the stories behind each life transcended the years and were kept alive in that space. The village had a fundraiser when the church's roof needed fixing, and they made target, just like they had for the bell – so intent were they on patching up and preserving old things.

'But what about everything it means?' said Bilal.

Richard folded his arms again, looking at the ground in thought. 'Yes. Yes, I know what you mean, but looking too much into the past can stop you from considering the future.'

'What's brought this on?' asked Bilal, recognising something troubled in his friend.

Richard paused. 'We have to push past ignorance, Bill. Even if we don't like doing it.'

Before Bilal could reply, there came a very loud voice amongst the chattering din.

'*Over my dead body.*'

The room went quiet.

There stood Shelley, face red, wings shaking.

'Now, Shelley—'

'Absolutely *not*,' she interrupted. 'Convert the *church* into a *mosque*?'

Murmurs vibrated.

'This is *too* much,' she exclaimed.

'What's going on?' asked someone.

'Our reverend and his friend here are plotting to convert St Swithun's into a mosque.'

The room erupted in expressions of collective shock. Shelley's fists were clenched, the vein in her forehead protruding.

'Don't worry, Shelley, I wasn—'

'I am very sorry, Bill – *Bilal* – but I *will* worry.'

'This is alarming,' said Jenny, stepping forward.

'Please, everyone,' said Richard. 'Let's carry on with the party. Shelley, let's talk about this later.'

'I'm tired of being ignored—'

'Ha! Couldn't if we tried,' exclaimed Margaret, nestled between Bilal's aunts.

'I'm sorry, Reverend, but is it true?'

Silence descended, all eyes on Richard. Bilal saw Mariam's confused face. What was happening?

'Well?' said Copperthwaite. 'Speak up. Is it?'

'This isn't the time,' replied Richard.

'It is!' someone exclaimed.

'Well, now, let's stay calm,' said Mrs Pankhurst.

'Being calm has brought us nowhere,' replied Shelley.

Mariam had weaved her way through the crowd and was already by Bilal's side.

'I don't wish to be dramatic,' Shelley added, looking around the fairy-lit room, the faces flushed with indignation. 'But it's time to pick a side.'

The crowds gathered closer to Shelley, dispersing from Bilal and everyone related to him.

'Shelley . . .' came Richard's slow, pronounced warning.

'Let her say it, Reverend,' shouted Margaret, putting an arm around Khala.

Shelley paused, looking at Khala, almost as if she were re-considering things. But with what seemed like some effort, Shelley looked away and added: 'If you are for this mosque that now threatens to destroy our much-loved church, then it follows that you mustn't care very much about the place in which you live.'

'Oh, come now, Shelley.'

Shelley closed her eyes upon hearing the voice. Bilal looked around and saw Tom standing with Anne.

'Sorry we're late to the party,' he added, stepping closer to the crowd. 'We know there's no-one in the world who cares about this place as much as you, Shelley.' He paused. 'Except for me, obviously. Why'd you think I gave Bill that money?'

It was the confession that broke Shelley's composure. She strode up to Tom, glaring at his self-satisfied face as if she might push him into the ice bucket. Instead, without another word, she marched out of the barn. She sped all the way home. She didn't even say hello to Arthur, didn't care he was sitting in the exact position she had left him in. She stalked through the house, into the garden shed and got out her electric hedge-cutter.

'Where in the hell are you going with that? And why are you wearing wings?' he shouted as she slammed the door behind her.

Shelley's car screeched to a halt. She got out her torch and banged it on to the car's bonnet. The buzz of the hedge-cutter trilled through the quiet country air, the fluorescent glare of the torch shining a light on her winged figure.

'That man!' she exclaimed as she hacked off a towering chunk of Tom's overgrown Red Robin bush.

How dare he? She hadn't thought to pick up her gloves and her hands were as icy as her resolve. It wasn't even as if he *cared* what happened here. He just went around making life difficult for everyone. Shelley had had enough. After a few very satisfying minutes a set of headlights flashed at her. She turned to see an oncoming van. It halted and out stepped Bilal and Haaris, with phone in hand, by his side.

'Shelley.'

'That man has no regard,' she shouted over the noise of the cutter, going at the bush again, bits of red and green leaves flying in the air like confetti.

Another car pulled up behind the van, lights flashing on Shelley's face.

'What's going on?' called out Richard as he approached Bilal. Seeing Shelley with the hedge-cutter answered his question. But before he could intervene another car had pulled up and out came a voice.

'What the hell's going on?'

Tom's figure emerged, bathed in the glow of headlights as he looked on at his neighbour and fallen bush.

'This is private property' he shouted, marching towards her.

'And this is public land,' Shelley retorted.

Before long a line of several cars were backed up, people rolling out of their vehicles to watch the spectacle, inky figures against the dark night and times.

'You can't leave things be, can you?' said Tom, red-faced.

'Dad, calm down,' came Anne's voice. 'Shelley, stop that now.'

'Not when people like your father don't care a jot about others,' Shelley replied.

'You all seeing this?' Tom said, turning to look at the gathering, which looked on in disbelief. 'Stop that right now!' he shouted as Shelley continued to hack at the bush.

But short of rugby-tackling Shelley, there was no stopping her. It wasn't long before the bush had been cut and slashed, opening up Coowood Lane, making room for two-way traffic. Shelley switched off the cutter and threw it in the boot as a scattering of applause came from the shadows.

'*This* is who you want in charge of things?' exclaimed Tom. 'Sticking her nose in, ripping things to pieces?'

Quiet.

'Ugh, you people,' he said. 'Well! You heard her before,' Tom continued. '*Pick a side.* And by God, let it be the right one.'

chapter twenty-two

SHELLEY SLAMMED THE PHONE down. It was the fourth media call she'd received in forty-eight hours.

'Take the phone off the hook,' Arthur called out, eyes glued to the television.

'It might be important.'

She received a grunt in response. Her neighbours were also calling – updating her on news of which she was already aware. Shelley *had* lost her mind. It *wasn't* the right way to have done it. The hedge-cutter *had* been a bit much. But despite all that, there wasn't much doubt about the fact that in the eyes of Babbel's End, Shelley was a hero. Her lapse in judgement meant Coowood Lane was no longer a hazard. Even the Hashams couldn't deny that. And, after all, the provocation was at its peak. St Swithun's a mosque!

Unfortunately, in all the commotion in the barn, no-one

had noticed Sam recording the entire scene on his phone. Then, later, between flashing lights and hedge-cutters, no-one paid attention to Haaris, catching Shelley's meltdown on his own phone, (which rather trumped the barn in terms of visuals). Honestly! Children nowadays! A little bother at school and all this competition. Then Sam and Haaris forged a team – called a truce! – put the clips together and uploaded it on YouTube.

Now Babbel's End was *teeming* with outsiders. Reporters fizzed around the village green, pouring out of The Pig and the Ox, scattering around people's *houses*, for God's sake. They were everywhere: wrapped in their coats and scarves, putting their smartphones in the air to find reception – the indignity of it all. Jenny had been interviewed by at least two reporters and Mr Pankhurst – who refused to speak to anyone – had to put his hand up to three others. The quiet Christmas spirit had been punctured by interfering busybodies.

Were Bilal and Mariam getting similar calls from so-called journalists? What if their version of events cast Shelley as the wicked witch of Babbel's End? She could see it now: the minority couple being publicly shamed for simply wanting a place of worship in their village, their home; the unreasonable white bullies, driving hedge-cutters at any supporter. The fire in Shelley's belly inflamed her cheeks. People wouldn't see or hear about how Bilal was met with open arms in his wishes to be part of the parish council before he got too busy and had to leave. Of course not! No-one cared about kindnesses of the past when there seemed to be so-called hatred in the present, though no-one ever forgot past hatred, even in present kindnesses. Shelley clicked again on that pesky site, YouTube. She typed in *Nativity, Muslim mosque,* and there it was: the familiar still frame of the barn.

She clicked play and this time noticed new things: the Jones's odd looks, not quite giving away who they were in agreement with. Bilal's aunts came in and out of view; Rukhsana, her face caught between pain and panic. There was no use dwelling on that though. Then the camera was on Shelley. When people looked at her, is that what they saw? The sag of the jowls, a frame that looked larger on video than it did to her in the mirror, a patchy red face borne of fury, which didn't paint her features in the most favourable light. Thankfully Shelley was good at correcting frivolous thoughts like vanity. There was Mariam, striding over to Bilal's side. Shelley had to pause the video as Arthur's cough turned into a hacking one, bad enough that she should offer to get him water, but he had legs after all. She played the video again. Copperthwaite was there behind her, his narrowed eyes speaking his support.

'But it's time to pick a side,' came YouTube Shelley's voice.

Did she really say that?

Bilal's face was flushed almost a deeper shade of red than hers and for a moment she felt a twinge of guilt. She remembered the time he came and helped her put up the fence in her garden because Arthur was unwilling.

'So what?' reasoned Shelley.

How powerful words could be. You could sentence someone to a feeling by using the right ones. Shelley was overwhelmed by her own sense of authority; the way her speech could cause ripples in the minds of those around her. Then came Tom's voice, changing the whole dynamic, usurping her freedom of speech by insisting upon his own. She fast-forwarded to the scene with her and the hedge-cutter. Why hadn't she taken her wings off? Shelley shook her head. It was one thing to be indifferent, but to actively help by giving money to buy land . . . *Unforgivable*. Tom's words beat down on her: '*Pick a side. And by God, let it be the right one.*' The video ended and she looked at the number of people who had watched it growing by the minute. Over 132,000 *hits* – that's what they called it – in forty-eight hours. Shelley scrolled down the 'comments' section:

Yeah, watch what would've happened if a Muslim went mental with a hedge-cutter. Now tell me England ain't racist.

Shelley felt her heart beat faster. Of course she wasn't racist! Why did people misconstrue opinion for racism?

Fuckin muzlims. Go bk to Saudi where you belong!!

This particular comment had over 4,500 'likes'. Shelley didn't approve of the language or sentiment. The idea didn't even make sense! Bilal and Mariam were originally from Pakistan. Shelley, troubled by the comment, phoned Copperthwaite.

'Ha!' he exclaimed. 'And they call village people backwards. I bet you two-to-one that half of these ingrates live in council housing and the other half are bankers. Put your husband on the phone. He'll take the bet.'

'Isn't it horrific?' she said. 'I mean, what's out there?'

'It's a jungle, that's what it is.'

Shelley put the phone down and got out her glasses to scroll through the rest of the comments. The really disconcerting ones were those that called for the mass murder of Muslims. It made her so uncomfortable she decided to make herself some camomile tea. She'd have to respond to some of these remarks, because invoking violence would be a terrible outcome. Leaving an anonymous comment was all rather complicated but she went through the necessary steps because let it not be said that she wasn't a woman of principle. She pressed on the reply button to the swearer:

You should mind your language and geography. The people in question are originally from Pakistan.

There. Her duty was done. Except within minutes she received a reply:

Fuck you, you raghead loving bitch.

Shelley's heart thudded as she quickly clicked the cross button on the window. What was a raghead? Her hand shook as she sipped her tea. She knew that the world wasn't always a civilised place, but such barbarity! There was little point in visiting this scene on YouTube over and over. It had taken place and there was nothing to be done about that now.

Shelley just really wished it hadn't gone viral.

⚬⚯⚬

The front door slammed shut as Auntie Shagufta stormed back into the living room with rollers in her hair, her face ghostly without her usual layers of make-up.

'When will these *chavval* journalists leave us alone? Who is your MP here? Let me write to them.'

She'd only stepped out to check if she'd dropped her lipstick in Vaseem's van.

Mariam turned the television's volume up as the news-caster's face filled the screen. Shagufta came and squeezed herself between Auntie Gulfashan and Bilal, Haaris perched on the arm of the sofa, Khala Rukhsana in her sofa chair, rosary beads in hand, Vaseem and family on the floor.

'*A recording of a Nativity play has gone viral, but Muslims, rather than Jesus, were at the centre of it . . .*'

Mariam looked at Haaris, whose head was bowed.

'I honestly don't know *what* you were thinking.'

'I told you,' he said. 'Sam was all in my face, showing off his new iPhone. Then Mrs Hawking, you know, went mental, and you can't let opportunities like that pass, can you? Do you think I should go into film?'

Mariam shook her head. 'I think you should be sorry for what you've done.'

'I didn't mean to!' exclaimed Haaris. 'And Sam started it.'

'Yes, and then you both put your heads together and did *that*,' she said, pointing to the television.

'The unfolding events have opened up a great debate around the nation: What exactly does it mean to be English? Here's a clip of the video that was uploaded on to YouTube . . .'

'Just look at the venom the woman is spewing,' said Mariam, observing YouTube Shelley.

'Ki?' asked Khala.

Mariam repeated herself in Punjabi. Khala looked like she was about to respond but Auntie Gulfashan spoke.

'See how calm Bilal looks. Well done, beta.'

'As if that'll matter. Though your propensity to go silent in the face of argument worked in our favour,' added Mariam, looking at Bilal and unable to resist a small smile. 'At least you're not brandishing a hedge-cutter.'

'Reporting from Babbel's End is Henry Miller. Henry, tell us, what has been the local reaction?'

'Well, Harriet, you saw from the video how many people are worried about what converting a church to a mosque would do to the village's cultural heritage . . .'

'But not everyone is against it, are they? One member had actually donated a significant sum of money . . . ?'

Mariam had tried to give the money back. Tom had swept out of the barn and she had rushed out after him.

'We can't take it,' she'd called out.

'Why the hell not?'

Anne had come out too and Mariam told her to make her dad see sense. It was too much. They couldn't possibly afford it – though she kept this thought to herself.

Then Anne took Mariam's cold hands into hers. 'It's yours.'

'But I don't—'

Anne lowered her voice. 'Let him do this. *Please.*'

God, she missed her friend. Before Mariam could say anything else Anne had taken Tom's arm, sat him in the car and driven off into the dark, foggy night. Then, of course, the hedge incident happened. Mariam and Bilal's conversation about happiness had to be put on hold, floating around their heads like bits of tissue in water as they darted between the insanity of what transpired in the barn, why Tom would do such a thing and how they could accept it. Then news of the YouTube clip erupted.

Mariam took out her mobile and looked at her Twitter account:

@TiradeTyrant
WTF 'types of people'?? Well done @C8News on spewing racist shit #Babbelsend #Teamhasham #Buildthemosque

@SaimaShaaaargh
A mosque in a village! Yes! We are here to stay #Babbelsend #ProudBritishMuslim

@AbbeyFielding
Jus another exanple of Muslims takin over n white libtards cozying up to em #Babbelsend #EnglandFirst #withusoragainstus

@John_Adams
Why can't they do a vote? This is a democracy. If the village doesn't want a mosque, shouldn't their opinion matter? #Babbelsend

@Em_Hurst
@John_Adams Yeah, John. Three Muslims Vs entire white village. Real fair democracy #Babbelsend #Givemeabreak

Em and John went on in this vein for a while. Never had Mariam felt so exhausted at people's capacity to argue. She wasn't going to take to Twitter like some social media warrior when the physical battleground had been laid out. Plus, she had to cook dinner. She just wanted to know what people were saying. Though keeping abreast of hate was a rather arduous thing.

'Joining us today is renowned anthropologist Fabiola Tocci. Fabiola, can you tell us a little about your thoughts on what's transpired in this remote village in England?'

'Certainly, Harriet. As we know, from time immemorial, civilisations have been encroached upon—'

Mariam's mobile rang.

It was Saif.

'*How representative do you think Babbel's End is of the rest of the UK's attitude to Muslims?*'

'Hello?'

'Mariam,' he said.

She steeled herself. Every conversation with him was a lesson in steeling herself.

'What am I seeing on the news? When did Bilal become a *mawlvi*? A mosque? In your village. *Paagal hogaye ho?*'

'No-one's gone mad,' replied Mariam.

She was surprised that Haaris hadn't mentioned it to his dad sooner.

'This isn't good for Haaris.'

Mariam crept up the stairs and closed the bedroom door. 'You said yourself he needed more culture. Well, here it is. And don't worry, I know what's good for Haaris.'

'I wondered why he's been so quiet and now I know. Yaar, these goray don't want religion shoved in their face.'

'What is it you want? Culture or not? Make up your mind.'

He paused. 'Listen, that place gives me the creeps, but I want him to be safe and happy.'

'This is none of your business,' said Mariam.

'I'm his *baba*. Of course it's my business.'

'Were you his *baba* when you decided to leave us?'

She had spent years pushing down the bile of that accusation. The legitimacy of it was somehow dampened when said out loud. It almost sounded petty. But things were different now. Never had Mariam needed answers more.

'Mariam . . . '

'Well?'

Pause.

'I shouldn't have left you.'

The pace of Mariam's heart quickened.

'I always knew it, Mariam. You and Haaris were the best thing that happened to me and God is punishing me now with this regret I have living inside me . . . Mariam?'

'Yes.'

'You heard me?'

'I heard you.'

She thought of Bilal sitting downstairs, making tea for everyone to distract himself from watching that YouTube clip for the hundredth time.

'You remember the letters we used to write? I still have yours.'

This can't be happening.

'I have to go, Saif.'

'Is Austen still the master of irony?' he asked, a smile in his voice.

'Stop.'

'You won't tell me what I want to hear?'

'No.'

The answer came so fast it surprised Mariam.

'It's okay, Mariam. You've always needed time to think about things. I'll give you however long you need.'

And instead of saying that she didn't need time, that she certainly didn't need him, she found herself saying: 'Okay.'

'No, I understand that,' said Richard into the phone as he rubbed his forehead.

It wasn't quite the Christmas Eve he'd imagined.

The archdeacon had been on the phone now for ten minutes. 'Had you asked me privately, I'd have granted the request.'

Richard had the urge to smash the phone over someone's head. Unfortunately, this wouldn't be very Christian.

'But you can understand the problems it's causing. Ah, John's here with the custard creams. Just put them down there, thank you. As I was saying, it'd be different if the purpose of the deconsecration was not widely known but . . . '

'Yes,' said Richard. He took a deep breath. 'But still—'

The archdeacon interrupted with a sigh that was as long as it was deep. 'You're a good and thoughtful man, Richard, but I can't grant this favour.'

'Can't you—'

'At a time when the church is weak we can't be seen to give way to *the other*.'

'But—'

'We must look strong.'

'Isn't there strength in granting neighbours a holy sanctuary?'

The archdeacon paused. 'It's a noble thought, Richard.

But strength is also in perception. And the whole country is watching us.'

Everything, it seemed, was perception.

'Merry Christmas,' added the archdeacon as Richard put the phone down, his heart heavier than his head. He picked up the *Daily Reporter* again. Merry Christmas, indeed. He'd never buy such trash but someone had left it at the gym. On the front page was the headline: *Babbel's END . . . of the English countryside and everything we know.* Under it was a picture of a quaint village church being overshadowed by a mosque. Of *all* the stupid things. He flung the paper across the church office, nearly toppling the Christmas tree. What would he tell Bilal? How could he go back on the hope that he had given? And why was there no longer nuance in an argument? Why did it have to be as simple as Christian vs Muslim; preservation vs change; old vs new? Wasn't there a happy medium in which something fresh could be created? Richard realised he'd become too comfortable with his life. If he were honest, Anne almost digging a grave had affected him more than he thought possible. There was no miraculous outcome, but at least she was *trying* to feel something, and as long as she kept trying he knew there was hope.

He picked up his Bible and opened it at random. Deuteronomy 21:22 – To not let a man who's been sentenced to death stay hanging on a tree: 'You shall not defile your land that the Lord your God is giving you for an inheritance.'

To some that last line might suggest that it was Bilal

who was defiling the land with his mosque, but not for Richard. He nodded in understanding.

This is God's land. Don't hold on to things that have no life.

Richard closed the Bible and opened it at random again: Jeremiah 1:5 – 'Before I formed you in the womb I knew you, and before you were born I consecrated you; I appointed you a prophet to the nations.'

Everything that happens is inevitable.

He did this several times and it didn't matter which verse he opened, it seemed to tell Richard that he must maintain his ground. It wasn't because he was superstitious. He believed that religious texts didn't just reveal things *to* you, but *about* you. What you made of them was who you were and Richard would *not* be a person who balked at the idea of a church becoming a mosque.

He looked out at the darkening sky and noticed a figure approach. Another journalist. The congregation would be arriving for children's mass at six o'clock. St Paul's would be brimming with people wrapped in furs and woolly hats, bathed in the warm hues of twinkling lights, framed by mistletoe and holly.

He grabbed his coat and scarf and made his way out of the church.

'Excuse me, Reverend Rich—'

'It's Christmas Eve. Go home to your family,' said Richard, striding past and getting into his car.

Five minutes later he was knocking on Anne's door. She looked surprised but Richard strode in without ceremony.

'It's all nonsense,' he exclaimed.

'Do you want to sit down?'

There was no Christmas tree. The BBC news was on in the background: '*Will it be the last Christmas for St Swithun's in Babbel's End?*'

Anne got the remote and switched it off.

'St Swithun's doesn't even hold mass at Christmas,' said Richard, whipping his scarf off, throwing it on the back of the dining chair.

'On the plus side,' said Anne, 'Babbel's Life Art gallery has probably never had so much business.'

He stared at her in her woollen grey jumper, jeans and red socks, and he felt a sense of regret: that he wasn't at liberty to hold and kiss her when he wanted. What was this? Richard knew he suffered from saviour complex. That's what his feelings must amount to. And of course there was the human flaw of desire; the carnal appetite to which he refused to be a slave.

'What *was* Tom thinking?' He waited for her to answer. Nothing.

'You won't be surprised to hear that the archdeacon won't allow the damn deconsecration,' he added.

Anne raised her eyebrows.

'You know what I mean,' replied Richard.

'Right.'

He glanced towards the garden window. 'Have you done anything with that . . . hole outside?'

Silence.

'No,' she replied.

He breathed a sigh of relief. Though he didn't know why. It wasn't her sadness. He'd seen the kindness and spirit in her before she lost Teddy. He loved the fact that she'd get more icing on her clothes than on the cakes when there'd be a bake sale; that she'd be able to quieten Shelley with a friendly retort that doubled as a rebuke. This felt like a bad state of affairs. But Richard was no stranger to self-denial for the greater good.

'How's Tom?' asked Richard.

'Furious, of course.'

'He did a lot of damage,' replied Richard.

'I know,' replied Anne. 'Dad's destructive tendencies are just that bit greater around Christmas.'

Anne turned around and stared at the fire. Richard had read many articles on ownership disguised as love – and though he felt sure he had no desire to control anyone, he couldn't help but feel protective towards Anne. He'd have to give the matter some thought.

'I do want them to get that mosque of theirs,' she added.

'Me too,' he said, trying to level his voice.

'Do you?' she asked, turning around.

He clenched his jaw. 'Yes. I do.'

Richard stepped towards her then took a deep breath, praying to God that he might collect himself. It had just been a bad day and he needed to untangle these emotions. Richard paused and looked around the room. It was better than staring at Anne.

'Do you want to sit down?'

Richard hesitated. 'I have to get back for first mass.'

'Are the family coming over tonight?'

'They'll be here in time for midnight.'

'Just like every year,' said Anne.

'Hmmm.'

'Hope you manage to hide how frazzled you are. I can't imagine it'd be very uplifting otherwise.'

Anne saw everything. He must conceal his emotions better.

'I wish people could realise that sometimes what looks like a problem is just another facet of life to be reconciled with,' he said.

'People don't want to be reconciled. We're pretty selfish as a race . . . You wanting me is selfish,' she added.

Richard felt his face flush. 'Excuse me?'

'I said: you visiting me is selfish. It is, in the end, isn't it?'

Richard was hearing things. His mind was clearly beginning to fail. He was at a loss about what to do. So, he prayed. In his head, of course.

'Yes. I suppose you're right.'

Anne looked mildly surprised. 'I thought we'd argue about that for a while before you said you had to go in case you lost your temper.'

'You know I never lose my temper with you.'

Richard held her gaze for a fraction longer than was appropriate.

He was going too far. What right did he have to burden her with his feelings? On top of all the emotions she was already wrangling with. Anne was right. Humans *were* selfish, but he'd fight against it.

'I'd better leave,' he said.

Anne paused before walking him out. 'It's not easy, trying to manage everyone's emotions. I don't envy your job. Showing sympathy to everyone, though you know which way your heart goes.'

'And always falling short, don't forget,' Richard replied.

Anne nodded. 'Yes. Always falling short.'

She turned the doorknob and Richard made it out into the foggy night air. He'd be able to see things more clearly when he got to church.

'Hello?'

'*Assalam-o-alaikum,* Bilal, beta. It's the imam, Sheikh Mirza. From Birmingham.'

'Oh. Salamalaikum.'

'I've seen it all, beta.'

Bilal had come to the office for respite, knowing it'd be empty on Christmas Eve. His plan had clearly failed.

'I see.'

'May Allah reward you.'

Bilal held back his sigh. 'Yes.'

'No-one will give you that church and so we are raising money here for the land. Everyone knows Babbel's End now it's in the national news. You, beta, are giving every Muslim in this country hope.'

Bilal gulped. Actually, his Facebook was a virtual heap of hate and hope, death threats, calls to bomb their home, other unsavoury things. Amongst which were messages of support from non-Muslims, but what affected him were the ones from Muslims, hailing Bilal as some kind of saviour, rejuvenating faith within communities across Britain. *Gosh*. This was not what he'd anticipated.

'Right. But no-one's going to sell us the land.'

'Have faith in Allah. But listen to me. Carefully, yes?'

Bilal held the receiver closer to his ear.

'No violence.'

'Violence?'

'Keep calm.'

'Of course.'

'Our Islam teaches us peace. Not this nonsense we see on the news.'

'Well, quite.'

'Ah . . . one minute.'

Bilal heard shuffling on the other end of the line.

'Salam, brother Bilal.'

'Hello?'

'My name's Taufiq. I'm one of the new imams at the mosque.' He sounded very young.

'I see.'

'I know Uncle's spoken to you about making sure everything's done with *adab*. You know, etiquette,' added Taufiq. 'You're now an example of what a Muslim should be, mashallah. Allah has granted you this position. Use it wisely.'

Surely Allah had the wrong chap. How could Bilal in any way be an exemplary Muslim?

'Yes, Taufiq, that's very well, but . . . how old are you exactly?'

'Brother,' replied Taufiq, a smile in his voice, 'old enough to know that, unfortunately, people can be impulsive.'

'Yes,' Bilal replied, who had some experience with impulse.

'There'll be the racists coming out of the woodwork, others justifying their Islamophobia by saying we're *taking over*.'

Oh dear.

'But our people might do stupid things too. Ones without the capacity to reflect,' he added with enough scorn for Bilal to recognise. 'You must lead by example.'

'Right.'

'We'll do all we can for you here, brother.' Taufiq paused again. 'Our prayers are with you.'

chapter twenty-three

W E'RE OFF TO SEE *the wizard, the wonderful Wizard of Oz.*

'Ugh, this is *boring.*'

'It's a classic, you little brats.'

'Mariam! How do you put this oven on?'

'Put on Zee TV, they're showing a Christmas special.'

Rukhsana had been driven to anxiety by all this *shoon shaan*. The frosty stillness outside her window was the only thing that calmed her.

It had got too cold for her daily walks, but after the barn party she'd still attempted a few in the vain hope that she might run into Shelley and try – in her broken English – to make her see Bilal's point of view. Just like she'd tried to make Bilal and Mariam see Shelley's. But they'd turned on the television and there was everyone's

face on the news in the clip they'd shown from that
YouTube. Rukhsana clicked on the counter that Haaris
had got her for Christmas (a much more modern way of
praying, he said), and tried to reason that she mustn't
despair, that things were beyond her control, and yet she
had this urge to fix things. If Sakeena were here she'd
know what to do. Better yet, she'd do it herself.

'Haaaaaris!'

Mariam was probably calling him to lay the table. The
others were in the kitchen preparing Christmas Day lunch.
Mariam and Bilal had taken ownership of the turkey but
Shagufta and Gulfashan had decided to make complemen-
tary dishes: biryani, koftay, dahi pakoriyan with homemade tamarind chutney, kebabs and garlic naan. The smell
of fried onions, chicken tikkas sizzling and pilau wafted
through the house. Rukhsana decided she'd better join
them before everyone thought she'd fallen into a depression.

As she opened the kitchen door she heard the sound
of old Bollywood songs playing.

'O-ho, what are you doing to the rice, Shagufta?'
exclaimed Gulfashan, shoving her out of the way.

Mariam had her back to Khala as Bilal made the stuffing.

'There are too many people here, Rukhsana,' shouted
Gulfashan, who hardly looked at her.

Mariam turned around and raised her eyebrows. So,
Rukhsana went to the living room, where Vaseem, his wife,
children and Haaris were playing a board game, the television muted in the background. The fairy lights around

the tree were lit, the presents had all been opened, Rukhsana's favourite old Bollywood singer sang in the background. She wondered if Shelley had family members around her? She wished she could invite her over so she could smell the turkey and the spices, and hear Rafi sing in his harmonious tones.

Then the phone rang.

No-one paid attention. She'd never have dreamed of it before, but her English was getting better and so, in a bout of confidence, Rukhsana picked it up.

'Hellaw?'

'Do you have something to do with this?' came a voice. Khala recognised it, but before she could say anything the voice continued. 'I want to know why on God's green earth – and on *Christmas Day* of all days – Babbel's End is swarmi . . . *packed*, with Muslims.'

'Shelley?'

'Khala?' Shelley snapped.

'What is wrong?'

'Bill, Khala. I need to speak with Bill. *Now.*'

❧

Bilal felt that his personal acquaintance with the idiom 'spiralling out of control,' had become rather intimate.

'Cold out, innit?' said Vaseem as he drove past Tom's house, the hedge now neatened and in keeping with the rest of the village order. It was too cold for the aunts to walk and Bilal had tried to keep them back, but it was no good. Most surprising was Khala, who wouldn't be deterred.

'I did not like the look of that woman when I met her,' said Gulfashan, referring to Shelley. '*Sarree*.'

Bilal rubbed his temple. 'Turn right at the village notice-board.'

He was just about to give further directions but he didn't have to. The lane leading up to St Swithun's was lined with cars, people getting out in their hijabs and jubbas. Vaseem parked the van and Bilal jumped out and strode towards the church before he stopped in his tracks.

'What the . . . ?' He stared up at St Swithun's bell tower, only there was no bell.

The crowds parted as he entered the churchyard and there he saw Shelley, her palms up, saying things he couldn't hear amongst the din. She locked eyes with Bilal and shouldered her way past all the Muslims. He'd have thought he was in Birmingham if it weren't for the stone church set against the rolling hills.

'Will you take responsibility for this?' she exclaimed, mist emanating from her mouth.

'I don't know what *this* is,' he replied.

'For God's sake, someone *stole* the bell. On Christmas Day.'

'Where's Richard?'

'Inside, trying to get to the bottom of it,' she said.

'Why are all these people here?' said Bilal. 'I don't understand.'

From the corner of his eye he saw a reporter taking

notes furiously. If Bilal pinched himself, would he wake up?

'Young man,' came a voice as a man came towards him.

His long, grey-speckled beard gave the impression of Gandalf in the shire. If it weren't for the skull cap and jubba he was wearing.

'You are Bilal?' the stranger asked. 'Bilal Hasham?'

There was nothing to do but admit it. The man broke into a smile and pulled Bilal into a hug. He then grabbed him by the shoulders, surveying him.

'May Allah give you *jaza* for what you are doing.'

He recognised *jaza*. If Bilal recalled correctly it meant reward. All these old words were coming back to him, anchoring themselves into his present.

'I'm not doing anything.'

Bilal's eyes flickered around – there must be forty people here. He searched for Mariam, but couldn't see her. The man slapped him so hard on the back Bilal almost choked.

'Humble as well. Allah bless the woman who gave birth to you.'

There was a girl, she looked Somalian, no more than sixteen, in hijab, skinny jeans and a duffle coat speaking to the reporter.

'Do you feel your religious needs aren't being met in this county?' asked the reporter.

'Well, no. Not really,' she said. 'There aren't any mosques around here. But we just got on with it because . . . well . . . ' She gestured around her. 'Anyway, my parents always told us not to make a fuss of things, so . . . whatever. Right? But then *he* came along.'

The girl smiled brightly, pointing to Bilal.

'What exactly happened, Shelley?' said Bilal, turning to her.

'We'd just got home after the reverend's morning service in St Paul's, and I was in the kitchen when Copperthwaite – you know he never goes to church – called to say he'd noticed lots of cars driving past. Then Jenny called to say there were people gathering around St Swithun's. And, well, I abandoned my cooking and came down, only to find the bell had gone missing and all your *people* here.'

Bilal ran his hand through his hair. 'Okay, I think we need to stay calm.'

'Mr Hasham,' called out the reporter, coming towards him.

Bilal felt the distinct need to run away, but his eyes searched for Mariam again and this time he saw her. She was on the phone, the look on her face a mixture of tension and surrender.

Lead by example.

'What do you make of all this?' The reporter cast his arms around the church.

'I've certainly never seen this many Muslims in Babbel's End before,' said Bilal with a wavering smile.

'Who do you think stole the bell?'

Bilal hadn't realised that the bearded uncle was still there until he intervened. 'When I saw this man on television I praised Allah . . . '

Bilal wanted to sit down, right there, on the frosty grass.

'I'm the imam for a small mosque in Blotistone. Unfortunately,' he cleared his throat, 'not all Muslims agree that a church is a place for a mosque.'

Shelley scoffed.

'I wanted to come and see it myself but my plans, as you can see, weren't kept secret for long. My wife told her sister what I was doing, who then told her uncle, who told his cousin's niece and . . . ' They looked around them. 'And then *this* happened. Plus, you know, no traffic on Christmas.'

'You're telling me that you being here and the bell going missing is just a coincidence?' said Shelley.

'Nothing God does is by coincidence,' he replied.

Shelley was caught off guard by this spiritual logic.

'So,' said the journalist, 'you think this is a faith-driven crime?'

'Who do you report for?' snapped Shelley. 'Are you here to just stir trouble?'

The journalist carried on as if Shelley hadn't spoken. 'I have all I need here. And you are Mr . . . ?' he asked the imam.

'Hannachi.'

'Can I add that the deconsecration and conversion probably won't—'

But before Bilal could finish his sentence the shriek of a whistle filled the air. He looked around to see where it was coming from. It went on and on until the crowd was forced into silence.

Bilal watched in amazement as Khala Rukhsana waddled past and began telling people off in Punjabi.

'*Taanu sharam nai aandi?* Christmas *de din angraizan nu khapana?*'

Some faces stared blankly but others understood. Someone whispered to the Algerian imam, who passed it on to his neighbour, who repeated the translation to the Somali girl's mum: *Aren't you ashamed, disturbing English people on Christmas Day?* Everyone looked at one another sheepishly as their eyes fell on Shelley.

'Sorry, ma'am, very sorry.'

Shelley looked bemused.

'*Hun saaray apne kaar chalo. Assi vi* Christmas *manaani hai*,' added Khala.

Bilal couldn't believe his eyes or ears. Khala, in a crowd, ordering people to go back home so they could celebrate Christmas.

'*Baji*,' said one man, walking up to Khala. 'You know celebrating Christmas is *haram*.'

Khala looked like she might blow her whistle in his face. 'You spoiling this day for everyone is *haram*.'

The aunts looked at one another, clearly wondering what had possessed their friend. The crowds began to disperse, looking back at the church. Shelley scrutinised every gaze, each one seeming to agitate a separate nerve. Richard came out of the church with Olly in his PCSO uniform, looking more than a little harassed.

'Well?' said Bilal to Richard.

'It must've happened in the middle of the night.' Richard rubbed his forehead. 'I imagine they'd have needed several people to carry the ladder and to bring the bell down the tower, but the new bell's not as heavy as the old one and you see the tower's not very high, so . . . '

'And?' said Shelley.

'Well . . . ' Richard sighed. 'There's no clue as to who might've done it.'

Without evidence pointing to any one party, both sides were free to uninhibitedly blame the other. It didn't matter that no-one currently standing under the tower had taken the bell themselves – logic mattered very little in times of vast emotions.

'And I ask that no-one jump to any conclusions,' added Richard, his tone stern.

But minds that weren't anchored to reason would jump.

Shelley nodded to everyone, her eyes settling on Khala. She pointedly looked away and made to leave.

Khala stepped into her path. Was she going to blow the whistle in Shelley's face too?

Then they witnessed the most extraordinary thing: Khala opened her arms, wrapped them around Shelley and pulled her into a hug. Even more disconcertingly, Shelley, after an initial reluctance, wrapped her arms around Khala too.

Everyone stared.

What was going on? Should Bilal break this whole thing up?

They remained in that embrace as Khala said something in her ear. Shelley seemed disturbed. Then they let go and

Shelley walked, as if trying to keep her balance, towards her car, and drove off without looking back.

❧

Muslims gathered in droves in what looked like a pilgrimage to St Swithun's on Christmas Day, only to discover that the church bell had been stolen. The culprit is unknown, but this hasn't stopped anyone from making plans.

'We'll have to get rid of the stained-glass windows,' said one gentleman by the name of Abdullah Green, a convert to Islam. 'And, of course, the crucifixion of Christ. I suppose we won't have to worry about the bell now.'

There were many languages being spoken, few of which seem to be the mother tongue of Mr Green's country of birth, and it makes one wonder – how will this affect a village that's so quintessentially English?

❧

Bilal threw his phone on the bed in frustration and switched on the radio.

' . . . as a Muslim, I've got to tell you, *I* don't support this mosque. I mean, you're taking a perfectly nice village and—'

'Ugh,' mumbled Bilal, switching the radio off.

He sat on his bed, staring at the fluffy carpet. Had he

been blind? He had spent the majority of his life believing that people were generally good sorts. That this racism thing people complained about was a figment of their own cynicism. *Victim mentality*. It was people never taking responsibility, blaming bad luck on phantom prejudices. It was only now that he began to wonder whether they might have had a point. He had to distinguish between the ones who liked to complain and the ones who actually had something to complain about.

'Do you think it was one of our lot that stole the bell?' asked Mariam, watching him from the doorway of their bedroom.

Bilal sighed. 'I hope not, but who knows?'

He picked up his phone again.

'Have you read the comments section?' she asked.

'No sense in that.'

'Think we're past the realm of sense, aren't we?'

'You know . . . '

Did he want to say what was on his mind? Was that particular can of worms worth opening right now?

'What?' asked Mariam.

'If you'd been a bit more supportive in the beginning . . . '

That was all he had. There were all sorts of ways that sentence could go.

'Then what?' Mariam snapped.

'*This* might not have happened.'

It wasn't a very imaginative end to the sentence, but it wasn't any less true for that.

'Someone wouldn't have stolen the church bell and a bunch of Muslims wouldn't have turned up outside it on Christmas Day?'

He sighed. Mariam always threw logic at his feelings.

'Even if they did,' he replied, 'even if it had all happened exactly the way it has, I could've done with knowing you're on my side.'

'Whose else's side would I be on?' she asked, folding her arms.

'I don't know.' He shook his head. 'You've always been a law unto yourself.'

He noticed her breathing get deeper. Were her fingers gripping her arms tighter? Bilal looked away and turned his phone over in his hands, just to distract himself from Mariam's gaze. It was that gaze that had him hooked the first time they met. He was pretty sure it could weave the same magic now that it had then.

'I'm sorry,' she said.

She came and sat next to him, arms still folded.

'You are?' he asked.

Mariam nodded.

'I'm sorry too,' Bilal replied.

Then she was shaking her head. 'No.'

'What?'

Tears had surfaced in her eyes. 'I'm sorry because I lied to you.'

He gripped his phone.

'What did Saif want when he called?' asked Bilal, quietly.

'How do you know it was him?'

Something had been set in motion and Bilal knew he shouldn't answer the question, but he had to face the inevitable. Hadn't he learnt that there was no grave-pit deep enough in which to bury himself?

'Because you have the same look whenever you speak to him.'

She lowered her gaze and he noticed her wipe away a tear. 'I'm so sorry.'

Bilal felt his own eyes fill with tears. He was free-falling into that grave-pit and he wasn't sure if he'd ever get to the bottom.

Arthur's grunting tipped Shelley's irritation into an altogether new emotion. The church bell had gone. *Stolen!* The audacity. After all that work fundraising. Donating from her own pocket! Worse still was that she just *knew* it was someone from Bilal's side. He might not know who, he might have nothing to do with them, but that wasn't the point. And then when she returned from the Christmas Day debacle, Arthur and his brother were sitting on the couch, in front of the television! Shelley's sister and her family were about to arrive and the kitchen was askew with dishes, cake batter in bowls, vegetable peelings, and smoke billowing out of the oven.

'Arthur!' Shelley exclaimed as she entered the kitchen.

He must've heard a unique urgency in her tone, because he managed to get off the sofa and look through the kitchen door. Shelley flung open the oven door to take out the burned turkey, slamming it on the kitchen counter.

'I asked you to check on it in twenty minutes if I hadn't got back,' she added, her voice shaking, tears prickling her eyes.

'Hmm. TV was on too loud. I forgot.'

She shook her head at his nonsensical excuse. 'Now what?' she said, giving him a full view of the remains of Christmas Day lunch.

Arthur looked at her blankly.

'Well?' she said.

Shelley realised, in that moment, that Arthur had never provided a solution to anything. He only created problems. The main one being that he had to be a consideration in all the decisions she made, without sharing any of the burden. The smell of burned turkey and doubt filled her senses. It was Khala's fault. Khala with her warm arms and words that had no place being spoken at all.

I. Hope. You. Are. Happy.

What a thing to say! Whoever had the right to hope on another's behalf, as if their life was to be pitied?

'Maybe it looks worse than it tastes.' Arthur picked up a knife and stabbed through the burned meat. 'There,' he added. 'It's all right on the inside. We'll just slice the burned bits off.'

It was too late. Khala had ignited the question of happiness and it inflamed Shelley. She watched Arthur as he sliced off bits of burned turkey and threw them in the sink. Didn't he know there was a bin for food waste? It struck Shelley with the clarity of the church bell tolling.

She *wasn't* happy.

'Stop it, Arthur,' she mumbled as he carried on ruining the turkey further. 'I said stop it!' she shouted.

He froze.

She grabbed the knife from him.

Arthur retreated, but just as he was about to walk out, Shelley said: 'And if you could lay the table.'

She felt him pause.

'I'm watchin—'

'If you're eating then you're helping.'

She waited for a response.

'Where are the plates?'

'If you don't know by now, I suggest you find them.'

With a final grunt Arthur left the kitchen. Shelley knew that he'd not do it properly. Eventually he'd expect her to take over from his own ineptness. And she would. Just as she always had done. So, Shelley buttered the parsnips, knowing she could not, would not, forgive Khala's words.

chapter twenty-four

27 December

Dear Reverend,

I pray this finds you in good health.

I am writing to you from the Christians for Muslims Alliance, an organisation of individuals who started this charity after the increased Islamophobic attacks since 9/11 and 7/7. We have watched, with regret, the events unfolding in your village. As devout Christians we believe in loving one another, living under the umbrella of one human race. We must help our Muslim brothers and sisters feel a part of the community, and so urge you and the bishop to reconsider the deconsecration of the church.

Of course, the ultimate decider is the good Lord Himself, but we must do what we can and this is why we plan to come down from London to Babbel's End to peacefully protest against the protesting of the mosque.

We have contacted some news outlets for the purpose of bringing the nation together, reminding us all to love thy neighbour.

Please let us know if there are any protocols you wish us to follow. We do not want to offend anyone, merely show the Muslims in the area, and in Britain, that they have friends.

Warm regards,
Timothy Popper

Richard sighed. He should be grateful for the Timothy Poppers of the world but even so . . . Babbel's End was not a hub of multi-culture. Popper had clearly been in London too long to see that there was a world outside it.

༄

Notice to all residents of Babbel's End

Dear residents,

Please be advised that there will be a peaceful protest outside St Swithun's on 29th December at 2.30 p.m. The Christians for Muslims Alliance are making their

way from London to show their support for the mosque.
Also be advised that news outlets will be present.

Yours, as ever,
Reverend Richard

This had to be some kind of elaborate joke.

'I just saw it with my own eyes,' exclaimed Copperthwaite down the phone to Shelley.

'Christians for Muslims?'

Copperthwaite scoffed.

'Only in London,' added Shelley.

'Who are they to come down here and tell us what to do? How to live? As if I've not had enough of that,' he mumbled.

'Yes. Quite. But calm down or you'll aggravate your hernia.'

Copperthwaite was right, of course. Shelley wasn't trying to change other people's lives, or stick her nose into their affairs, she was merely thinking of the piece of life and land that concerned *her* community. If only this ridiculous Christians for Muslims Alliance could do the same.

'If they want to protest then we can do the same,' said Copperthwaite.

'Of course. But I really need to know who took our bell.'

'Do you think it was one of us?'

Shelley paused. 'I hope not.'

'That Tom. I saw him walking the dogs while I was

reading the noticeboard. Self-satisfied bastard. "Be joining the protest, will you, Cops? See you there," he said. I knew I should've left more than just a note on Bill's windshield.'

Shelley had been about to say something but paused. 'Copsy . . . '

'And I wish you'd cut off more than Tom's bush.'

'What did you say about the note?'

There was a long pause. 'Well, it didn't do any harm, did it?'

'*Copsy*,' Shelley said, her voice low, disbelieving.

'Don't you go getting holier than thou, Shells. You know damn well he deserved it. I've not been in this village my whole life to have it turned upside down.'

Shelley, for perhaps the second time in her well-intentioned life, was lost for words.

'I've put up with a lot, Shells, goddamned nearly lost my life to fit in, and to think some entitled . . . *foreigner* . . . could come in and want to change things.' He scoffed. 'No chance.'

'But that was . . . it was . . . '

'What? You know you're glad *someone* did it. I've known you too long to believe your mock outrage.'

'I–wha–you . . . '

'Hmph.'

Silence.

Shelley was relieved when Copsy abruptly hung up. It took a few moments before she was able to put the receiver down. Her long-term friend, confidant – however grumpy he was, there'd been no other in her life – had written that horrid note to Bilal. What's more is he was *right*. She *had* felt a sense of satisfaction that Bilal had received it. That someone – *Copsy* – had taken matters into his own hands.

She took a deep breath. There were things to do. Focus had been her life's work and it couldn't fail her now. She got the phone tree out to rally the troops. Then she drove into town, because you needed things for a protest.

The roads were still quiet as Shelley parked up and made her way to the shops with her list. She noticed the few people in town stare at her. Shelley wasn't prone to exaggeration – the looks couldn't be a figment of her imagination. Then one person actually smiled. It should've lifted her spirits but it only dampened them.

Holier than thou.

As she walked over the small bridge she saw a tall hooded figure in the distance. He was facing the Waitrose wall, a can in his hand. He began to spray it all over the brickwork, not noticing Shelley or that she had got out her phone to call the police.

What was the world coming to?

The sirens didn't deter the boy. As the police got out of the car he didn't even try to run away, merely leaned against the wall before being handcuffed and shoved in the back of the car. And that's when she saw.

It was Dan.

Her heart beat faster.

Poor Bruce. What was most odd was that her sympathy

also extended to Dan. The intimidating nuisance Dan, who'd lost his friend.

Should she have seen who it was before calling the police? She could've tried to talk to him first, at least? It was too late now though. Some things were just always too late.

As Shelley walked into Waitrose and took out her list, she reminded herself that she had done what was her duty by law. Except she wasn't sure any longer whether duty was quite as black and white as she had always thought.

❧

'That old windbag's at it again,' said Margaret as Mariam opened her front door.

She hoped her mascara hadn't smudged from having just cried in the toilet. It was the only place she had enough privacy.

'Sorry?'

'Shelley! Mrs Pankhurst called to tell me that Jenny had called Mr Pankhurst to tell him about this protest.'

'What protest?'

'My God. You've not heard? Christians for Muslims.'

'Sorry?' said Mariam.

'Are you okay, dear?'

Perhaps it was because Mariam missed the mother she never had, or that she now had to choose between her ex-husband and current one, or that Margaret's face was so kind, but she couldn't help but burst into tears.

'Heavens,' said Margaret.

Mariam stepped out into the grey, icy cold in case anyone heard.

'What *is* the matter?' asked Margaret. 'You know – we won't let prejudice win.'

Mariam shook her head, teeth chattering, unable to stop the tears from flowing as Margaret pulled her into a hug. She took off her woollen polka dot scarf and wrapped it around Mariam.

'Now, that's exactly what it is, no matter what anyone says. Why . . . any counter protest should be seen as a hate crime.'

Mariam sniffed, smelling a mixture of farm and Poison on Margaret. She shook her head again. 'It's not that.'

'Then what? Hmm?'

'It's *me*,' said Mariam, a new barrage of tears taking over. 'I'm all wrong.'

'Are you? You seem perfectly fine to me. Aside from the crying, of course.'

Why was Margaret so *nice*? Showering Mariam with a kindness that she didn't deserve.

'I can't control anything,' Mariam said, catching her breath.

'Whoever can?' replied Margaret.

'But feelings,' cried Mariam, looking up at Margaret's lovely, wrinkled face. 'If they belong to me then why can't I control them?'

Margaret smiled. 'My dear, that's like saying we can control our thoughts. The day we manage that is the day we master our feelings. What's wrong with your thoughts anyway?'

'I told Bilal that I don't love him.'

Margaret paused. 'Don't you?'

'How am I meant to know?'

'Hmm,' replied Margaret.

'It's just that I . . . '

'Go on . . . '

'He knows.'

'What?'

'He knows that I . . . '

'Yes?'

'That I still love my ex-husband. And now his wife's left him and he says he wants me and Haaris back.'

A fresh wave of tears took over and the cold, just like Saif, got under Mariam's skin.

'Come on,' said Margaret, leading Mariam by the hand down the road, through the grand black gate and along the gravelled path into her home.

'Now you sit here while I make you some tea.'

Mariam looked around the scruffy, open-plan kitchen: cookbooks stacked haphazardly on wonky shelves, dishes in the sink, whitewashed wooden counters and exposed brick walls, from before they were trendy.

Margaret went about the kitchen, talking to herself as she put the kettle on: 'Teabag in the mug, milk from the fridge for me . . . Ah, what biscuits do I have . . . ?'

'I'm sorry,' said Mariam.

Watching Margaret like this, widowed and living

alone, Mariam was ashamed that she didn't visit her more often. How did Margaret manage to stay so incessantly *bright*?

'What for?' Margaret smiled as she handed Mariam a peppermint tea. 'Now tell me. Properly.'

Mariam looked into her steaming hot mug, ignoring the watermarks on it, the flecks of dirt, which she subtly wiped off. And so she told Margaret everything. The first marriage, the betrayal, the comfort of Bilal, his love for Haaris and her, the way the reality of her life and heart didn't align. And now the choice she had to make.

'Yes.' Margaret nodded. 'That is a tricky one.'

'It *is*,' said Mariam. 'I couldn't lie to him any more.'

'Does he know that your horrid – sorry – ex is now single again?'

Mariam shook her head. 'I already feel awful enough.'

'Hmm. Yes. Bilal's a good man.'

Thanks, Margaret. It would be so much easier if he weren't.

'So, what is it you *want*?' asked Margaret.

Mariam gripped her mug. 'I don't know.' She paused. 'To feel like I'm living the life I *chose*, not a life that just . . . happened.'

'Ah. Control.'

Mariam nodded.

'I read a lot of psychology books. The best thing to do with something like that is to just, you know, let it go.'

Mariam smiled at the simplicity of it. She'd tried. Then she thought that maybe – during a run, drinking tea, or writing a passage of what she dared to hope could one day be a book – things would let go of her.

'Except now I have a choice to make and Haaris to think of.'

Margaret considered this as she peeled a banana and ate it, both ladies sitting in silence for a while.

'Liberate yourself, dear. Read the signs. What's the point in being Muslim and having faith if you can't relinquish control to the God you believe in, see the path he's showing you, et cetera?'

'Signs? Sounds a bit mystical. I'm obviously not a very good Muslim.'

'Appalling, if you ask me,' replied Margaret.

Mariam laughed.

'Not mystical at all. People show themselves to be who they are and you just have to make sure your . . . *love*, or whatever you want to call it, doesn't hamper your view of things.' Margaret laid the banana peel on the table. 'You know my Giles had been ill for six years before he passed away into the next realm.'

'I liked him a lot.'

Margaret raised her eyebrows. 'You don't have to lie. He'd always been a difficult bugger – it's my weakness, I'm afraid – but there was more to him.'

'Like?' asked Mariam.

'He was *interested*. He cared about the details of everything I did – the attention he paid to the most trivial matters, simply because they were my matters. It was quite the killing combination.'

Margaret looked at a photo of her and Giles on the sideboard. 'You can only embrace the lows, along with the highs, but let me tell you one thing for sure.' She leaned forward and gave Mariam a look she recognised as quintessential grit. 'You only have yourself. All that is inside you, all that you have lived through is your own. It can't be redistributed, only untangled.'

Mariam felt her eyes fill with tears again, but this time it was thinking about her parents and how miserable her dad had been when her mum had died. How he'd shut himself off from the world, including Mariam. She thought he'd change, but he soon began searching for the arms of a new woman to comfort him, just like he had when her mum was still alive.

'Is that what brings happiness?' asked Mariam, wryly.

'Ha, the pursuit of happiness is the single most ridiculous lie we've been fed. All flapping about for the next best thing to numb the searing pain of loneliness.'

Mariam paused and smiled. 'Say it how it is, Margaret.'

'No point in hiding the fact that we all feel it; the loneliness. That's also part of the problem. And now you young ones have this social media nonsense to contend with too. The real pursuit is of understanding. And not just ourselves. See?'

Perhaps Mariam had focused so much on her own version of events, she hadn't really considered anyone else's.

'Anyway,' continued Margaret, observing Mariam more keenly than she liked. 'You'll have to put all of that on hold.'

'Why?'

'The protest, dear.' She beamed. 'You have to focus on the protest.'

chapter twenty-five

RUKHSANA SAW SHELLEY FROM her window. Never
had she changed into her wellingtons and shalwar
kameez so quickly. She pulled on the knitted hat
that Mariam had got her for Christmas and called out to
her.

Shelley turned around, not returning Rukhsana's wave.

'How are you?' asked Rukhsana as she approached her.

'Fine,' said Shelley.

Rukhsana felt her own smile falter. English people were
just like this weather sometimes – one minute sunny, one
minute grey.

Shelley paused. 'You?'

'Fine,' replied Rukhsana.

Another pause. 'I'm sorry, Khala, but I have to go.'

Rukhsana had found that reading people's body

language, along with their words, made the task of understanding simpler.

'Why?'

Shelley showed the hint of a smile. 'Your English is quite good now, no?'

'Better than your Punjabi, haina?' replied Rukhsana.

It was a relief to see Shelley laugh. Even if it was like a rock hitting the ground.

'Arthur needs you?' asked Rukhsana.

Shelley's brow twitched. 'No. Not quite.'

'We walk?'

Shelley put on her black leather gloves. 'No, really—'

But before Shelley could finish, Rukhsana had walked ahead of her. The grass was dewy, the clouds grey; this damp weather did nothing for Rukhsana's bones, but she still regarded her wellies as a pair of rubber miracles. She'd abandoned the uncomfortable sweater and trousers and picked up her warmest shalwar kameez, put a cardigan over it, before pulling on her raincoat. Breathing in the cold, fresh air, she enjoyed the low mist, able to see the hills beyond the clearing. Rukhsana had spent the majority of her life accepting the rightness of Sakeena's decisions. Until now. How could her sister not understand why her son was drawn to this place?

'You not talk?'

Shelley stopped.

'I just have to say, Khala, that you shouldn't say *you hope someone is happy*.' The colour in Shelley's cheeks rose, her voice clipped as she rubbed her gloved fingers in agitation.

'Hain?'

'On Christmas Day. You said, "I hope you are happy."'

Khala nodded, waiting for Shelley's point.

'It's not the done thing.'

'Hain? What is "done thing"?'

'Something that isn't proper, Khala,' replied Shelley.

'Hmm?'

'Like this protest. It's not right.'

Why did Rukhsana never say the right thing? Why did she never understand the rules? And whose rules were they, anyway? Holly ran around both of them, panting and stopping by Rukhsana, who still balked and twitched around dogs.

'I know he's your nephew, but I can't change my stance on the matter.'

'Stance?' asked Khala, getting increasingly bewildered. And what did Bilal have to do with her wishing Shelley happiness?

'You know. Position. About the mosque.'

Hai hai, the mosque. Had Sakeena any idea what she would be doing to her son's life? People die and then leave you with the guilt of carrying on their wishes. This did not feel very Islamic.

'Of course you'll be on Bilal's side, it's only fair, but I hope—'

'Why you don't want it?' interrupted Rukhsana.

'Would you want a church in your home in Pakistan?' asked Shelley.

'Where is home?' replied Rukhsana.

Could a place she hadn't been back to for decades really be called home? Even Birmingham had felt like a kind of limbo.

'Where you were born, of course,' replied Shelley.

Rukhsana wanted to say that home must be where you feel most alive, but she wasn't sure how to construct that sentence. Never had she wanted Shelley to understand the expression on her face, the thoughts she couldn't articulate, more.

'It's not personal,' said Shelley.

Rukhsana stopped and Shelley had to turn around. *Personal.* She'd heard Mariam and Bilal say this. It sounded like *person.*

'We all are persons,' she replied.

'Yes. I suppose so.'

A sense of pride swelled in Rukhsana that she had understood something. The wind whistled in Rukhsana's ears as the sun cleared through the clouds.

'But,' continued Shelley. 'You have to put your point across . . . ' Shelley observed Rukhsana's confused look. '*Fight* for what you believe in.' She raised her fist to demonstrate her point.

'Fight no good.'

Shelley sighed. 'Khala, you ignore too much.'

Rukhsana looked at Shelley. It was as if for the first time someone had actually understood her. She nodded.

'Anyway,' said Shelley. 'I must go.'

It occurred to Rukhsana that Shelley was always the one to end their meetings.

'Tomorrow walk?' asked Rukhsana.

Shelley paused. 'No. Not tomorrow.'

'Then?'

Shelley put the lead around Holly's neck as she said: 'I don't know. Maybe no more walking.'

'Why?' asked Rukhsana, her heart in her throat.

'Because all things must end eventually,' replied Shelley, pursing her lips.

Without another word, a wave or a hug, Shelley left. Rukhsana had been sentimental. Just because she and Shelley shared what was in their heart, they didn't understand each other – they'd merely scraped the surface. Perhaps Shagufta and Gulfashan were right. Maybe that's why Sakeena – who basked in variety – didn't like it here. There were some divides you could not cross, that just made you feel *bad* about yourself. A heaviness took over Rukhsana as she opened the front door and walked into the noisy din of the household. Maybe it was time to go back to the familiarity of her sister's home, sitting next to the grave that Sakeena had dug. At least there she didn't make mistakes. At least there she was in no-one's way. She'd speak to Bilal. Tell him it was time to leave, omitting the details of why – how she had said too much to Shelley and lost another thing in her life.

❧

Bilal and Harris had made up the placards. Focus, after all, was the key. Vaseem Bhai had collected thirty wooden sticks from a man who knew a man in Titchester. The aunts were making snacks. Heaven forbid there should be an occasion without samosas. They'd moved the sofas out of the way and spread everything out in the living room. Bilal knelt over one of the signs: *Faith and Peace for One and All.* He hoped that no-one thought he'd come up with it. It was difficult to dissuade Vaseem Bhai though, who fancied himself to be quite poetic.

Bilal looked up and saw Mariam, standing with a mug of tea in her hand.

'It might be okay if you helped, Mum,' said Haaris.

'I'm already occupied,' she replied, lifting her mug.

Haaris rolled his eyes. 'Control your woman,' he said to Bilal.

She's not my woman. She's not anyone's woman. Bilal looked down at his placard again. These past few days he had tried to conjure anger. Though he wasn't a man prone to excessive feeling, he thought that his wife practically admitting that she was in love with her ex-husband might drive him to it. Instead a strange numbness had prevailed. One which helped him apply his attention to things like clearing out the attic, taking the rubbish to the dump, calling around and asking who'd support the Christians for Muslims Alliance. He'd fixed the drain in the second toilet, and set up a Twitter account to keep abreast of national opinion – especially after the latest story in Newcastle about some bacon being thrown at a mosque (awful waste of food), after which someone retaliated by throwing a brick through a UKIP member's house with a verse from the Qur'an (waste of a brick). Passions had been ignited without much creative outlet it seemed. So, Bilal oiled the hinges on all the doors, and took a copious amount of Gaviscon, and an Ativan or three.

Mariam settled next to him. He could smell her lemon and tea-tree oil shampoo. Her knee just about touching his thigh.

'What do you want me to do?' she asked.

Her eyes were on him. What did this mean? Why did she look at him if she no longer loved him and why couldn't he be angry with her? Anger could lead to hate and then he could get somewhere. Haaris handed her a black felt-tip and told her to go over the writing in pencil. Mariam went to work quietly and Bilal wondered: was her ex-husband still in love with her too?

～

Richard's family had just left, so he'd been changing the bed sheets, loading the dishwasher and clearing up the remnants of the festivities when the doorbell rang.

'Hello,' said Anne, nuzzling her face in her scarf because of the wind.

He had made a conscious effort to avoid her. Their last meeting had muddled up the straight paths of his intentions and he needed some time to properly draw them up again.

'Is everything all right?' he asked.

'Not quite,' she said.

That's when he noticed she wasn't alone.

'Gerald?'

He walked in behind Anne, giving Richard an unsure smile.

'Well, come in. Don't mind the smell. I burned my toast,' said Richard, as they walked into his living room.

'Gerald has something to tell you,' said Anne.

Gerald stood in his puffa coat, jamming his cold, red hands in his pockets as he avoided Richard's gaze.

'What's going on?' Richard asked, trying to ignore the fact that Anne looked flushed and it heightened the brightness of her eyes.

'Well,' said Anne to Gerald. 'Tell him, or I will.'

Gerald slumped into Richard's chair and looked up at him. 'I'm sorry, yeah? Like really, *really* sorry.'

'For what?'

'Ugh,' exhaled Gerald. 'I did it, all right?'

'Did what?' said Richard.

'I stole the bell.'

Richard stared at Gerald for a few moments before he turned to Anne. 'Is this true?'

'You're hearing it from the horse's mouth,' she replied.

'What?' Richard sat down in front of Gerald, clasping his hands together. '*Why?*'

Gerald shrugged. 'It was stupid. Da . . . '

'What?'

'Nothing,' he replied.

'You didn't do this alone, so you'd better tell me,' said Richard.

So, Gerald revealed all. According to him, he'd gone to see Dan, who was now in custody until his hearing because of breaking the terms of his recent parole. He thought that stealing the bell was a matter of principle. Richard glanced at Anne, who looked equally dumbfounded by the logic.

'It's 'cos Bill fired his dad and his dad didn't even do nothing,' said Gerald, his flushed face matching the hue of his pimples. 'He said taking the bell would serve him right 'cos obviously everyone would blame him. So, me and some mates . . . we called a person.'

'Are you . . . is this . . . ' Richard looked at Anne before facing Gerald again. 'Have you *absolutely* lost your mind?' exclaimed Richard.

Gerald stared at the ground.

'Well?' demanded Richard.

Gerald unzipped his coat and took it off. 'Also . . . ' he mumbled.

'*What?*'

Gerald looked at Richard. 'Dan didn't do the graffiti.'

Richard had to take a deep breath as he clenched his jaw. 'Listen, I know he's your friend, but—'

'It was me.'

Gerald looked at the ground again.

'What?'

'It wasn't my fault,' he cried. 'I dunno. My nan was doing my head in and my mum was just as bad and I thought . . . '

'*What?*' snapped Richard.

Gerald shrugged. 'I was *bored* and then I was at Dan's one Friday and his dad's office keys were there and I just . . . you know. I returned them the next day. No-one even noticed they'd gone.'

Gerald looked up, his face sorrier than ever. 'I guess I thought Dan would think it was funny.'

Richard had to take a few moments to absorb this. 'Right.'

'He properly laughed his face off—'

'That's enough, Gerald.'

'And it was weird—'

'*I said that's enough.*'

Anne started at Richard's raised voice. He had to grip both hands together in case they did something he'd regret.

'That is the *stupidest* thing I've ever heard,' he said.

'Richard . . . '

'*What on earth were you thinking?*'

'Richard, your voice—'

He stood up, towering over Gerald. 'This is what happens when you don't *think*.' He turned to Anne. 'Has everyone lost the capacity to use the brain God's given them?'

'I—'

'You'll put this right, Gerald,' said Richard, cutting him off.

Gerald nodded.

'We're going over to Bill's now so you can tell him and his whole family what you did. You're lucky I'm not making a call straight to the police.' Richard pointed at Gerald, barely able to stop his hand from shaking. 'And after that you're telling me where that bell is and we're going to get it back.'

Richard grabbed his coat and car keys, slamming the car door in Gerald's face as Anne got in next to him.

'I think you should calm down,' she whispered.

'Like hell I will.'

∼

Of all the unfathomable, ill-thought-out, ridiculous things. Young people just had *too* much time on their hands. *No responsibility*. Richard had called Shelley to let her know what had happened, and she set out for Bilal and Mariam's immediately. As she stepped through their front door she glanced into the room filled with placards and God knows what else, the aunts and cousin with his family, a hubbub of noise, a baby crying, all of them speaking over one another. No Khala.

Mariam hurriedly shut the door, leading Shelley into the second living room.

'The thing is, we sold the bell to this guy,' said Gerald, looking at the faces that still glared at him, after his confession about the graffiti and profuse apology.

Bilal rubbed the bridge of his nose.

'Which guy?' said Mariam, voice terse.

'Gavin. Lives past Titchester – you know? Peatsland. Melts metal and stuff for scrap.'

Shelley let out a groan. Voices came from the other living room but where was Khala's?

'What if . . . ' Bilal began. 'What if Bruce *didn't* write the note?'

Richard seemed to breathe a sigh of relief.

Shelley's nerves fluttered.

'It's worth considering,' said Richard.

'He *did* look confused when I confronted him and I . . . oh, I'm doubting everything now.'

This wasn't the moment for Shelley to out her friend and yet something *had* to be done about poor Bruce. Oh, there was so much to think about!

'Give me this Gavin's number,' said Shelley. 'I'll go and see him this instant.'

As if on cue, Khala walked in and looked at everyone, her eyes settling on Shelley. She spoke to Mariam in Punjabi, who must've explained what was happening.

'Dunno, Mrs Hawking. He's kinda dodgy, if you know what I mean.'

'Gerald Smith, if you'd been as committed to your lessons as you were to stealing this bell, I dare say you'd have made a success of your GCSEs.'

'Do you have *any* idea how hard we all worked to raise the money to get that bell fixed?' said Mariam. 'I learned to make zarda.'

'What's *zaadaa*?' he said.

'You want zarda?' Khala asked him in English. 'I bring some.'

With which she left the room.

'So, what do you propose we do?' said Shelley, looking at Richard.

'Excuse me,' said Bilal. 'Richard, can I have a word?'

The two men left the room, Shelley reeling at the idea that her church bell should be used for *scrap*. Khala came in with a tray of zarda as Shelley's eyes locked with hers.

'No time for that,' she said. 'Come on you.' She grabbed Gerald by the arm. 'You're taking me to see Gavin.'

'Shelley,' said Anne, her voice cold. 'I don't think that's a good idea.'

'It certainly *is*.'

'Well, you can't go alone,' replied Anne.

Shelley was already marching down the passage, Gerald in tow.

'Shouldn't we tell . . . Right, no,' said Mariam as Shelley left the house, bundling Gerald into her car. A few moments later, out came Anne and Mariam, waving a set of keys, Khala waddling out behind them.

'We're taking the van,' Mariam called out.

Shelley hesitated. In the end, she decided that this was a far more sensible plan.

Peatland was a thirty-minute drive away, which was an awfully long time to spend in an enclosed space with people who didn't really speak to one another.

'So, is that *zaadaa* thing sweet?' Gerald asked Khala.

Khala looked at Shelley, who was sitting in the back with them, Mariam driving and Anne in the passenger seat next to her.

'Her English is a little poor,' Shelley explained.

'Oh. Bit hard, innit?'

'As is yours, it seems,' added Shelley.

Mariam put the address in the SatNav.

Silence.

She turned to smile at Anne. 'How was Chri—' Mariam stopped herself. What a stupid question to ask. 'How are you?'

'Fine,' replied Anne. 'You know . . . '

There was a pause.

'You?' Anne asked.

Mariam gave a short laugh. Anne looked in front of her.

They drove on, Mariam rummaging in her head for other banal things to say. It was enough for her to lose her own self-respect.

'So, like, you don't want the mosque?' Gerald asked Shelley.

'Acute observation,' she replied.

'Still snarky then, Mrs H?'

She gave him a withering look.

'Sorry. Anne's well up for it,' Gerald added. 'The mosque, that is.'

Mariam glanced at Anne.

'Everyone's entitled to their opinion,' said Shelley. 'It's when people start donating money that it becomes a problem.'

'You know, Shelley,' replied Anne, 'it's not much different to raising money to fix a bell.'

'*Hardly*,' said Shelley, bristling. 'Your dad doesn't care

what happens here. I don't know why he stayed after your m—'

Anne whipped her head around. There was a palpable silence.

'Well,' Shelley added. 'It just never made sense.'

'Maybe he does care about the place, just not its people.'

Shelley looked exasperated. 'That's nonsense. A place *is* its people.'

'Only the ones that suit you,' replied Anne.

'*Excuse* me?'

Anne paused. A few moments passed before she said: 'You *knew* Teddy had a drug problem. You *knew* he had trouble, but not once, not *one* time did you or anyone think to help him. To even ask if there was anything you could do. You ask people about their turnips and topiary, or whatever, you *still* gossip about the woman who abandoned me – you really hated her, didn't you? I don't even blame you, because so do I. But didn't you *think*? Didn't it occur to you that it might be a kindness to ask me, Dad, *anyone* about your ex-student's drug addiction?'

'*Of course* I worried. Your dad had no time for me. Never has. And Anne, dear . . . ' Shelley's voice softened. 'Some things are beyond our control, no matter how hard we try.'

Mariam gripped the steering wheel, realising that she'd just agreed with Shelley about something.

'But what did you *do*? You're so good at rallying people, but what about when a life actually depended on it?'

Shelley had nothing to say. Anne turned back around.

Khala clutched that necklace of hers. The van went silent.

'If you ask me, it's not like the best idea,' said Gerald, clearing something that seemed to be stuck in his throat. 'Mosque would look a bit weird, innit? Can't you just pray at home or something?' he added to Mariam.

'You would think,' she replied.

'Never mind your opinion,' said Shelley, visibly shaken by Anne's words. 'What were *you* thinking, stealing the bell?'

Gerald shrugged. 'Dunno. You know how sometimes you think things and don't even know *why*? Teddy was always saying people don't think enough. He was the one who used to say: "Why you saying that, Ger? Where'd you even get that from?"' He paused, looking at Mariam. 'I'm well sorry about that graffiti.'

Mariam drove over a pothole, everyone holding on to their seat.

'Well, at least we know how you feel now,' replied Mariam eventually, her voice cold.

'*No*, I don't. Honest. I just didn't think. It was just for a laugh. I'll do anything to make it up to you, yeah? I'll clean your garden for a year. Just don't tell me nan, please.'

Mariam sighed.

'I should've asked myself what Teddy would've done,' added Gerald.

'Not stolen a bell, I'm sure,' said Shelley.

'Or he might've,' said Anne, staring out of the window. 'He wasn't an angel. Who knows who he'd be if he were still here.'

They all went quiet for a few moments.

'I remember when Haaris was learning how to ride his bike,' said Mariam. 'He'd gone off ahead, leaving Bilal behind, lost his balance and would've hit his head if Teddy hadn't been there.'

Anne stared at her. 'Your silence was the worst,' she said, voice low.

Mariam swallowed hard.

'Of all the people, I never thought you'd back away,' Anne added.

They'd come off the A-road and were following a narrow, winding road. She wanted to stop right there and ask for her friend's forgiveness. All she could do was whisper: 'I'm sorry.'

Anne stared ahead.

'I don't even have an excuse. Just, you know, regret.'

'Don't we all,' said Anne.

Silence.

'I mean,' began Shelley, as if she'd heard nothing spoken between Anne and Mariam, 'it has to be said that Teddy was always very polite.'

'Yeah,' said Gerald. 'Like, *really* polite. I mean, he'd give money to homeless people in town and stuff, wave to kids, pretend he was an aeroplane and all kinds of shit. Sorry. Then he'd get this look, yeah, this faraway look and said it hurt to be in the world sometimes.'

Anne looked away, tried to wipe her eyes but couldn't help the sob from breaking through.

'Sorry, Miss L,' said Gerald.

She shook her head, unable to speak. Mariam pulled

over, ignoring the car behind that beeped at her, and drew Anne into a hug, the gearstick digging into her thigh.

'Please, don't,' said Anne.

'Oh, dear,' said Shelley, shuffling forward and patting Anne's shoulder. 'There, there now. It's a horrid thing, I know. Horrid.'

Anne's sobs got louder. 'I don't know what to do,' she said. 'I just don't know what to do with any of it.'

'Of course you don't,' said Shelley. 'Look at us. None of us know what to do with anything and you . . . well. Let's just say you're a very brave woman.'

Anne caught her breath, breaking away from Mariam.

'I should've told you that sooner,' said Shelley, sitting back again and looking at Khala, whose eyes flickered between everyone.

'God, I'm sorry,' said Anne, wiping her tears.

Mariam took Anne's hand and squeezed it. She'd never let this happen again. Wasn't life about breaking through the barrier of discomfort, trying to get to the other side? Isn't that what you *had* to do to keep any relationship worth having?

'Since we're apologising, yeah,' said Gerald, turning to Shelley, 'I'm *well* sorry to you too, Mrs H.'

'You certainly *should* be,' said Shelley.

Which made Anne laugh. Then Mariam laughed.

'It's not at all funny,' said Shelley.

This just made the two of them laugh even more as they carried on towards Gavin's house.

chapter twenty-six

MARIAM DROVE THROUGH PEATLAND'S centre, unable to see much in the dense, freezing fog. The streetlamps were too dim to make much difference. Everyone peered out of the van's windows.

'SatNav's not gonna be much use now,' said Gerald. 'Just follow this road to the top, yeah? And then make a right down the lane.'

When Mariam got to the turning she insisted it wasn't a lane.

'Trust me,' replied Gerald.

She dutifully turned right, only without the streetlamps she couldn't see much, so slowed down to Khala's pace, who was, incidentally, muttering prayers under her breath.

'Gerald, where on earth is this place?' said Shelley.

'There aren't any houses,' she added, squinting outside the window.

'Middle of nowhere, innit?' replied Gerald.

Just then Mariam's phone rang. She picked up to Bilal on the other end of the line.

'Wh-ell-ou.'

'What?'

''ere-ai's-an?'

'I can't hear you,' she said. 'Hello? Bilal?'

She looked at her phone. No reception. Shelley, Anne and Gerald also looked at their phones. *No Service.*

'*Kithay agaye?*' came Khala's worried voice. She was staring out of the window.

'I have no idea where we are, Khala,' mumbled Mariam.

Gerald continued to lead them towards the house, Mariam continuing to trust him.

'I can't see,' he said, pushing himself forward, hands either side of Anne and Mariam's headrests.

Mariam turned her full beams on, the misty outline of a house no more than six feet away.

'Yes,' said Gerald, pumping his fist. 'Got you here, didn't I?'

'Quite a feat,' said Shelley.

Gerald paused. 'I guess I'd better get him.'

He didn't move.

'Go on then,' said Shelley.

He swallowed hard before he opened the van door and jumped on to the frosty ground. They heard a dog barking.

Mariam edged the car forward, watching Gerald walk up to the house.

It was a few minutes before Gavin came out in jeans and a black vest showing his hulking arms, a silver chain glinting around his neck. He pulled at the Rottweiler, who looked quite frantic and ready to jump on Gerald.

'Isn't he cold?' said Anne.

Gavin's gaze rested on the women in the van.

'Do you think Gerald's okay?' said Mariam.

'*Hai hai*, what a disgusting dog,' said Khala. 'Why won't he stop barking?'

The blue house paint was chipped, the picket fence broken and Mariam could just about see an old shed behind the property. After a few minutes the situation looked heated, so Mariam got out of the van, followed by Anne. There were the faraway cries of some sort of bird, the cold causing both Anne and Mariam to shiver, the stillness of the place feeling like a threat.

'I paid you for it so we're square, all right? You ladies can sit right back in your van.'

'Listen,' said Anne. 'We'll return your money. The bell's very important.'

Mariam was looking at Anne so didn't notice Gavin frowning at her.

'You the family that's going on about turning that church into a mosque?'

For the first time, Mariam thought she might actually

become a victim of racist violence. It was more troubling than she'd imagined.

'Yes,' she replied, straightening her back.

He stared at her. Even Gerald looked nervous. Another bird screeched from somewhere in the distance; the Rottweiler foamed at the mouth.

'My girlfriend's Buddhist,' said Gavin. 'She could do with a centre around here. But you don't get those in these parts, do you?'

Mariam cleared her throat, hopeful, if somewhat confused. 'No.'

'Anyway,' Gavin added. 'It's too late, so you'd best get out of here, before I set my dog on you.'

Maybe not so hopeful.

'You mean the bell's gone?' asked Anne.

He eyed her up and down.

'Gav—'

'And you'd better leg it too,' interrupted Gavin, jabbing his finger at Gerald. 'Before I show you what happens to people who disturb my Christmas break.'

'Now, listen here,' said Shelley, who had also got out of the van. 'What will you gain by keeping this bell? Let's be civilised.'

'This your nan?' said Gavin to Gerald.

'I most certainly am not.'

Gavin stepped forward, loosening his Rottweiller's leash as Gerald took a step back. 'Get out of here, Ger. I'm giving you thirty seconds, all right?'

Gerald glanced at the three of them, Mariam increasingly

aware that her husband had no idea where she was. Shelley looked like she wanted to give Gavin a good talking to. Just then Khala, wrapped in a big black and white tassled shawl, bundled out of the van.

'Khala, we're leaving,' said Mariam.

Khala paused, flinching at the barking dog, but seemed to steel herself as she walked up to Gavin, took his hand and placed something in it. He gave her a dubious look before he opened up his palm. They all saw the glint of gold as he brought it up to his face. He turned on his phone's torch and inspected it.

'This real?' he asked Khala.

'Real,' she confirmed.

'What are you doing?' said Mariam.

'Sshh,' replied Khala. 'Tell him give the bell.'

'But your husband gave you that,' said Mariam. 'It has Allah's name on it.'

'Allah is everywhere,' said Khala, tears surfacing. 'Not just around my neck.'

'Khala . . . ' said Shelley.

She didn't need to know Punjabi to understand what was happening.

'Well?' said Mariam to Gavin. 'You can keep that if you give the bell back.'

'If this is fake, I know where you live, Ger.'

Gerald shook his head.

'All right,' said Gavin. 'This way.'

Giving that necklace had felt like Rukhsana's parting present, and though happiness wasn't quite what she felt, it was the sense of having done the *right* thing. And the latter could often lead to the former.

Her husband would've agreed.

They'd come home to Bilal striding out of the door, speaking to Mariam quickly, while Gulfashan and Shagufta attacked Rukhsana with too many questions. She entered the house to see another face in the room – the old man from the pub. Tom started talking loudly at Anne and Gerald, shaking his fist, and then Shelley looked so uncomfortable Rukhsana wanted to tell her to stay for chai. But she left, without anyone stopping her. Not to have someone stop you from leaving the warmth of a full house was a sad thing. And then everyone cheered for Rukhsana and the old man hugged her and she found the feeling.

Happiness.

It was late at night when she heard Bilal's footsteps and called out to him in a low voice, her heart in her throat.

'Beta, in the new year, it will be time for me to go back to Birmingham.'

Rukhsana felt a pull at her heart just at the mention of it. Bilal stared at her.

'You've looked after me enough. I've enjoyed my time, but you are all busy and . . . I should leave.'

She wasn't quite sure why he looked so still, or why he paused for so long.

'Khala, I . . . '

'Oh, don't worry about your khala. I overstayed my welcome already, na?'

'No, Khala, it's not that, it's . . . '

'What, beta?'

'Well, there is no house to go back to,' he said.

'*Kya?*' she asked.

What did he mean? Bilal came and perched on the side of her bed, looking at her blue veins snaking around her ankles.

'I sold the house. For money for the land.'

Rukhsana rested her hand where her necklace used to be, on account of being used to Allah being there. What did he mean he sold the house? But that's where she lived.

'I'm sorry, I should've told you, but there was never the right time and . . . we didn't want to worry you.'

'Beta,' she whispered, feeling overwhelmed and her eyes stinging with tears. 'That was my sister's home.'

Bilal looked down. 'I know. It wasn't easy. But I don't want you to think you have nowhere to go. You have us and we'll . . . we'll think of something for you. A nice communal place to live.'

They wouldn't even keep her with them. She'd be taken to some nursing home. No-one would visit. She'd die without any family or friends around her. *Ya Allah you are all knowing.* And He was the only one who knew Rukhsana's pain in that moment. The breaking of a heart for lack of a place to call home.

❧

'If we're doing this protest then you're going to have to get out of your grave,' said Mariam.

Bilal opened his eyes. There she was in her brown Barbour coat, hair falling over her face, looking down at him. The cold seeped through his layers of clothing and into his veins, the earth frosty and hard as he shifted his body weight here and there. It had begun to drizzle, the icy droplets falling on his face. Bilal was still agitated about Mariam going off with Khala to retrieve the bell. (What if something had happened to her? What would happen to Haaris? Would he go to live with his biological dad? Why did Saif seem to have everything that mattered to Bilal?) And then, of course, there was the selling of the house without telling Khala . . . Such thoughtless cowardice.

He might stay in his grave.

'Look, I said I'm sorry about last night but all was okay in the end and, you know, we got what we went for,' she said, crouching.

They had all returned the evening before to find a furious Tom in the living room.

'What's she doing here?' Tom had demanded, looking at Shelley.

Shelley seemed to swallow as she paused. 'Well, I'll be on my way.'

Before anyone could say much, Shelley gave Khala one last look, nodded, and left. It was only then that they cheered for Khala for having saved the day. Gavin would be returning the bell to St Swithun's in his lorry, for an extra charge, of course, paid by Shelley. Even Tom, who didn't care two bits about it, thought Khala had shown good form. She looked rather alarmed when he put his arm around her.

'We'd better go,' Anne had said.

'See you all at the protest tomorrow,' replied Tom.

'Oh no you won't,' she'd said. 'The doctor's said you need to rest. You've been too excitable lately.'

'What the hell does she know?'

'Maybe Anne's right,' Richard had added.

'I'd show you how fit I am right now if you weren't wearing that damn collar. And I'm not missing out on showing up that old bag.'

'She's all right, you know,' said Gerald. 'For an old bag, I mean.'

'Bell's rung out your brain, boy. Anyway, Bill's given me this placard,' said Tom, picking it up.

Babbel's End we just ask that you let us have our mosque.

'I said he should change it to: *Babbel's End can just fuck off, we'll make this church a fucking mosque.*'

'Not quite what we're going for,' said Bilal.

'Least you could do since I donated that money, but I guess it's that Muslim blood of yours. Makes you proper.' He paused. 'When we get that church deconsecrated you're going to use that for the conversion, all right?'

Bilal wanted to argue but was fearful of the brimming of his own emotions. He didn't think Tom would appreciate them.

Now, Bilal had been taking a moment in the grave to think about Bruce – had Bilal's passions manipulated his memory? Had it *definitely* been Bruce's writing? And about Khala, and possibly losing Mariam and Haaris.

'We're not pressing charges against Gerald, then?' he asked.

Mariam considered it for a moment and shook her head. 'No. Stupid boy. But we'll think of something for him to do to try and make up for it.'

Bilal closed his eyes. 'Yes. I suppose so.' Gerald had to be forgiven, even though it felt rather unjust. Bilal was only surprised that Mariam didn't hand him over to the police immediately. He took a deep breath, as if that would help how depressed he felt at the state of life's affairs. 'You should've seen Khala when I told her about the house.'

'She's not come out of her room,' replied Mariam. 'Haaris sat in there for a while.'

Life was all about rights, wasn't it? The rights we have over others, and the ones they have over us.

'What do you want to do, Mariam?' he said, sitting up.

'About?'

'You know. About us.'

She plucked the withered blades of grass, her hands red from the cold, unable to look him in the eye. 'I don't know.'

He pushed himself out of the grave, brushing down his trousers.

'I suppose one protest at a time,' he mumbled, about

to walk back into the house. Then he paused and looked at Mariam.

She was biting the inside of her cheek.

Bilal took another deep breath. 'We need to talk about Khala.'

chapter twenty-seven

'Y OU ARE GOING TOO?' asked Rukhsana as her friends scurried in and out of the kitchen, gathering the snacks they'd made for the people *on the right side.*

'*Le,*' exclaimed Shagufta. 'Of course we are going.'

There was a mosque at stake and suddenly the aunts were acting as if this was their village. The whole country was acting as if it was their village. Yes, Rukhsana could understand why Shelley was angry.

'Why are you staying home?' asked Gulfashan, wrapping foil over the tray of samosas.

Rukhsana wanted to tell her it was because she saw little reason in things now, but felt this might be rather too self-pitying.

'You can wear your goray clothes,' added Gulfashan.

'I'm not feeling well,' replied Rukhsana.

'O-ho,' whispered Gulfashan. 'How long did you think Bilal would keep the house for you? It was expensive. He was always going to think of his own pocket.'

Rukhsana didn't feel this assessment was fair, but didn't contradict it.

'Will you be okay?' asked Bilal, looking, for the first time in a long time, like a man in command of both his feelings and situation. Aside from the residue of guilt he clearly felt.

She gave him a wavering smile.

He'd been wrong not to tell Rukhsana before now, but then Gulfashan was right. It was never her home to keep. She couldn't blame him for having priorities. She even wished that Sakeena could see him now, taking charge of the village and his life. He lurched forward because Shagufta had bumped into him while trying to save the tray of samosas from flying on to the floor.

'No time to stand around, Bilal, beta,' exclaimed Shagufta. 'The samosas will get cold.'

Before Rukhsana could say any more, everyone bundled into their coats, hats, scarves and gloves. Vaseem picked his daughter up by her coat and carried her out. His wife refused to be left behind this time, so toddled out with their other two children.

'We'll try not to be too long,' said Mariam.

Haaris hovered at the door. 'Why don't you come, Khala?'

She smiled at him, putting her hand on his head. 'You come back and we have another English lesson.'

'Yeah,' he exclaimed. 'And now you're going to live with us we can learn Chinese next.'

Rukhsana looked up at Bilal and Mariam, who also caught her eye.

'Let's talk about it when we get back,' said Bilal.

'No, tell her *now*,' said Haaris.

Bilal and Mariam exchanged looks before Bilal said: 'Khala, we feel . . . '

Haaris cleared his throat.

'Sorry, *Haaris* feels that the house wouldn't be the same without you. He wants you to stay with us.'

She looked at the three faces, Haaris barely suppressing a smile.

'And you?' she asked, looking at her nephew and his wife.

Mariam put her arm around Haaris, smiling – but it wasn't her usual forced smile, though it looked a little sad. 'We feel exactly the same.'

'We do,' added Bilal. 'I'm sorry for selling Ammi's house. But you have a home. With us.'

Rukhsana felt her eyes fill with tears. Joy sprawled in her chest. And the bitter sadness of life seemed to dissolve in that moment. She pulled Haaris in to give him a kiss – since her words were lodged in her throat – which he accepted without fuss.

'Okay?' asked Bilal, putting his arm around her.

She nodded, replying in English: 'Okay.'

'Let's do this then,' he added, as Mariam pushed Haaris out of the door.

Rukhsana closed her eyes and took a deep breath. She should've gone with them. She had the mind to now. It didn't matter. *She was wanted.* When they returned she'd feed them zarda and hear all about it.

It was cloudy outside, the drizzle hadn't stopped since morning, but Rukhsana, in a burst of energy, put on her wellies, raincoat, scarf and gloves and went for a walk. The low clouds covered the hills and she had to squint to protect her eyes from the spitting rain. Out here she felt alive, and she would be able to feel this way every day from now on. She breathed in the cold, fresh air before deciding to return home. Rukhsana had just taken off her wellies when the doorbell rang.

'Shelley,' she said, opening the door.

Shelley's glasses had steamed up, her raincoat splattered with the misty rain.

'The van's gone. Saw you walking into the house.'

'Come,' said Rukhsana, opening the door for her.

'I don't want to be far behind them. I just . . . '

Rukhsana looked at this odd Shelley, with her pinched features and words. Yet Rukhsana tried not to think of that because she knew there was a sadness in her, even if she'd been short with her during their walk, and hadn't said a word to her when they were in the van, or when she had left. Rukhsana wished happiness for her – the kind that Rukhsana now felt.

'I wanted to give you this.' Shelley extended her hand, in which she was holding a gift bag.

'For me?' Rukhsana asked.

'Yes,' Shelley replied, nodding.

Rukhsana stared at the floral printed bag until Shelley shook it a little, forcing Rukhsana to take it.

'What it is?' asked Rukhsana.

'*What is it*,' Shelley corrected.

Rukhsana peeked into the bag.

'A small gift,' Shelley said. 'Present?'

'It is cold. Come in.'

Shelley hesitated, then stepped into the warmth.

'Because,' continued Shelley. 'Well, I know I can be taciturn. So . . . '

Did she say tax return? Sakeena would mention this a lot and it always put her in a bad mood – maybe that was the reason for Shelley looking so sour. Rukhsana took out a rectangular-shaped object that had been wrapped in red tissue paper and a gold ribbon. How nicely these goray presented things. She undid the ribbon and peeled the sellotape, without ripping the tissue paper.

It was a notebook.

A bronze hard cover, with leaves imprinted on all four corners.

'For your poems,' said Shelley.

She took the notebook from Rukhsana and opened the first page to show her.

'It's a note. From me.'

'What it says?' asked Rukhsana, embarrassed all over again at her lack of education.

'"So you can write the words that have sometimes failed us both",' said Shelley. '"Love, your friend."'

Rukhsana felt tears come to her eyes again. She wasn't sure what the message meant but she knew what *your friend* meant.

'I'm sorry, I not buy you present.'

Shelley laughed, staring at Rukhsana in mild surprise. 'You did quite enough yesterday. And, well . . . ' Shelley took Rukhsana's hand, gripping it before pulling her into a hug.

'You . . .' started Shelley.

But she didn't finish her sentence, only pulled Rukhsana in tighter before letting her go.

'Anyway, I must be off.'

'It must be like this?' asked Rukhsana.

'What?'

'You not join Bilal?'

Shelley straightened up. 'It's out of the question,' she said. 'I thought you understood.'

Rukhsana nodded. How was she to explain to Shelley that just because she understood didn't mean she didn't hope.

'We'll walk. In the new year,' said Shelley.

Rukhsana held her notebook to her chest, feeling the lightness of still having her friend. And now also a home.

'Yes.'

Shelley left and Rukhsana went into the living room, sitting by the fire that would probably die now Bilal wasn't there to keep it going, her notebook and pen in hand. Rukhsana hadn't given much thought to New Year in the past. She and Sakeena would sit and watch the fireworks on television, but this time something new flickered inside her. She thanked Allah as she flipped over a fresh new page and began to write.

~

Shelley got into the car, feeling satisfied. She had done something for another person, not out of duty, but because she was thankful to them and it made her feel rather . . . *light*. This was not in keeping with the task that lay ahead of her – she knew she should be feeling disgruntled but it occurred to her that being angry consumed an awful lot of energy, and wasn't this feeling of lightness preferable? These thoughts swiftly disintegrated when she turned the corner and St Swithun's came into view.

A barrage of people in raincoats held banners and plac-ards. Men and women in jeans and jubbas, hats and hijabs, people with cameras and video-cameras, taking pictures with their phones. The crowd's hubbub spoiling the peaceful look of the church that stood, unassuming, under the winter sky. The drizzling, freezing rain had deterred no-one, the people making a splash of colour against the grey day. Shelley's body convulsed, as if the grass being trampled on was her own skin and the church that was at stake, her own flesh. She slammed the car door and marched towards the crowd, spotting Mr Pankhurst, Copperthwaite, Guppy, Jenny and James with a large group of other villagers.

'There you are,' said Jenny, seeing Shelley approach. 'We were waiting for you.'

Sometimes Shelley wondered whether the village might fall apart without someone to give directives. She was as exasperated as a person who felt the satisfaction of still being needed could be.

'Christians for Muslims,' grunted Copperthwaite, shaking his head, glaring at the band of merry Christians (and non-Christians). 'Bloody Londoners.'

Shelley saw Bruce, looking as if he were burdened with the weight of the world. She still hadn't spoken to Copperthwaite since his confession about the note and it was something she'd have to tick off her list sooner rather than later. There was Bilal and his family, handing out food to the visitors. It wasn't long before Bilal's cousin, that great big man, was walking towards them with a tray.

'Honour thy neighbours,' he said, smiling.

His familiarity was almost as offensive as the food he was offering underneath his stripy umbrella. James looked like he was about to reach out when Shelley said: 'No. Thank you. We're quite okay.'

'You sure?' he asked. 'Freshly fried samosas don't get much better than this,' he added, waving the tray under Copperthwaite's nose.

Honestly. For all of Copperthwaite's complaining, there was nothing like food to make him waver. His eyes shifted to Shelley.

'He doesn't do well with spices,' she interjected.

Bilal's cousin took a bow as he walked backwards. Such smugness! Look at them! Then she caught Mariam's eye.

Well, she had been useful yesterday, hadn't she? Shelley couldn't help but nod a hello.

'As if they own the place,' said Jenny.

James cleared his throat. 'Well, we like democracy – isn't this it?'

Jenny shot him a look.

'I see your wife's adamant,' said Shelley to Mr Pankhurst, looking over at Linda Pankhurst, who stood near Bilal in her multi-layered outfit and hot pink woollen hat – the bobble bouncing around.

'We've had some heated discussions in our life together but nothing quite like this,' said Mr Pankhurst. 'But . . . ' It seemed to cost Mr Pankhurst to continue. 'There comes a point when you just have to agree to disagree.'

'I see.'

Shelley wondered how two people with such opposing views could live under the same roof – worse still, have such opposing views and *remain* under that same roof. A sense of grave injustice swept over Shelley. What twist of fate meant that Mrs Pankhurst was rewarded with such a husband and she with Arthur? For a moment Shelley felt as if she were looking at herself from the outside, and a cacophony of infinite possibilities that never transpired cascaded before her. In another reality Mr Pankhurst could've been her husband. Or even Copperthwaite, despite his *predilections* – they might've got married and lived a comfortable life of friendship. Marriages were were based on worse things. What if Babbel's End hadn't been her home? If it was someone else standing here, trying to save St Swithun's, and she was watching it all on television. It struck Shelley that the smallest of incidents could change the trajectory of our lives. Or not change it. What if Bilal, Mariam and Haaris had never moved to the village and because of that she had never met Khala? It wasn't like Shelley to be sentimental. Indeed, that's not what she was being, because Khala was no *great* friend of hers. Yet their walks had given her comfort, a safe space – free from the eyes and ears of others' judgement – which had awakened something in her.

'Shelley?'

'Hmm?'

'Shall we move closer. For effect?' asked Jenny.

Bilal had caught Shelley's eye and for a moment neither of them looked away.

'Let's do it,' said Copperthwaite, who was already leading the way with his placard in hand: *Home is where the church is.*

The sign had seemed like a good idea at the time to Shelley – it was true, after all – but in the cold light of protest it felt rather too hostile.

'We're here because we believe in a united Britain. One where people of all faiths, or none, whatever culture, can co-exist, learn from one another,' one man said into a reporter's camera.

'Listen, I never had a problem with Bill or his family,' came Copperthwaite's voice, now speaking to another reporter. 'But this is a church, dammit,' he continued.

'Some might say it's not your cross to bear,' replied the reporter.

Copperthwaite's eyebrows collapsed into each other. 'Are you being clever?' He leaned into the reporter. 'It's a jolly fine day when a man's told that his home, where he's spent a lifetime, isn't his cross to bear . . .'

'Shelley . . .'

Shelley turned around to see Richard holding his umbrella over her, even though she'd put up the hood of her raincoat. Before he could say any more, coming up behind him was Tom with his walking stick, dogs and Gerald. And Anne. She gave Shelley a small smile, and Shelley felt she had no choice but to return it.

'That Copsy going off again?' said Tom. He gave a smug smile as he took in the scene before him.

'Let's all be civil,' said Richard.

'Civil?' exclaimed Tom. 'To that old goat?'

Upon hearing Tom's voice, Copperthwaite turned around, his placard slipping in his hand a few inches. Shelley noticed his nostrils flare. Tom leaned forward, squinting.

'*Home is where the church is,* eh?' Tom laughed, pointing his stick at Copperthwaite's placard. 'Who came up with that genius line?'

He had spoken loud enough for the leader of the Christians for Muslims Alliance to turn around.

'Don't remember you putting on your Sunday best for church too often, Cops.'

Copperthwaite stuck out his neck, scrunching up his

face. 'Not like you gave a damn about anything but your-self. Your bush nearly killed my dog.'

'Calm down, Copsy,' said Shelley, glancing at Bruce, who'd edged forward.

'He's well within his right,' said Jenny.

'You're keen on *his* rights,' said Mariam, holding Haaris's hand, who looked at Sam standing with his father, Harry. The boys were back to planning new pranks to play at the next village fair.

'But forget other people's right to voice *their* concerns,' Mariam added.

'It just wasn't *West Plimpington Gazette* material, Mariam. You're writing a book now, anyway. Worked out for you, didn't it?'

'Oh, excellent,' exclaimed Margaret. 'What's it about?'

'You'd do well to take some things seriously, Margaret,' came Mr Pankhurst's voice.

'I take your overgrown moustache very seriously,' she replied. 'I find it terribly offensive.'

'This isn't helpful, Margaret, please,' said Richard.

'Listen, I think we should all take a moment,' Bilal added.

All eyes settled on him as everyone paused (bar several outsiders, who were recording the scene and taking pictures).

'*You*,' exclaimed Mr Pankhurst. 'Why couldn't you leave things *be*?'

'No need to point at my bro like that, yeah?' said Vaseem.

'We don't care for what outsiders think,' said Copperthwaite. *'You're not welcome here.'*

Bilal paused, taken aback. Shelley pursed her lips and put her hand on his arm.

'I'll explain to you later,' she said, glancing at Bruce.

'Oh, I'm too old to care,' said Copperthwaite. 'I wrote the note at the pub quiz.'

Bruce's face went red as Bilal met his gaze.

Everyone started talking over one another.

Tom pointed his stick at Copperthwaite, Mariam argued with Jenny, James looked from side-to-side, Haaris and Sam now stood together, widening their unimpressed eyes at the grown-ups, Richard was trying to keep Margaret away from Mr Pankhurst, while Mrs Pankhurst was telling a journalist off for recording the whole scene.

Shelley felt a nudge. *'What?'*

She looked around to see Guppy. 'There's one of them men.'

'What men?

'The ones who disturbed my strimming at the church.'

Guppy pointed to someone in his mid-thirties in thick-rimmed glasses, wearing a long navy coat and tapered trousers. He couldn't be with the alliance, not if Guppy had recognised him, nor did he look like a reporter with his hands jammed in his coat pockets. No, this man did not belong here.

'I knew Bruce didn't write that note,' someone said.

'Bill, it was a rotten thing you did to Bruce.'

Margaret volubly retorted with: 'Oh yes, let's put this on Bill when Copsy's the one to blame.'

'*Precisely*,' said Mariam.

'We're getting a bit off track here,' came Richard's voice.

Shelley walked towards the stranger, stopping next to him as she asked: 'Excuse me, who are you?'

He turned away from the unfolding drama. 'Sorry?'

'What are you doing here?' she said, narrowing her eyes as everyone talked over one another.

He paused. Then he took out a wallet from his inside pocket and handed her a card.

'Just look at you all,' exclaimed Tom. 'Shuffling around, dying over that old stone building because of some pie-in-the-sky-god but not giving a shit about actual people.'

Shelley read the card: *Turnpike Constructions*. She looked at him, confused.

'We heard about the protest and I was asked to monitor the situation.'

'What do you want?' she demanded.

He cleared his throat. 'You'll all be informed in due course.'

'Listen,' someone exclaimed. 'I don't even believe in God but this church should be used for whoever needs it.'

'*Traitor*,' came another voice.

'You will inform me *now*,' said Shelley.

'Who is he then?' Guppy had sidled up next to Shelley, who handed him the card. '*Construction*? What are you constructing?'

'Like I said to your neighbour: you'll be informed in due course.'

'Of course I don't want to destroy things,' exclaimed Bilal. 'Why can't we have a church *and* a mosque?'

There was a roar of mock laughter.

'Living with the fairies.'

'Turned this village into a hell-hole!'

'Get your camera out of my face.'

'WHO KNOWS THIS MAN?' Guppy's voice resounded.

Silence.

Everyone turned to Guppy, who pointed to the man in question. The man shuffled on his feet, attempting a weak smile under everyone's stare.

'You know him?' said Guppy, looking at Timothy Popper, the alliance leader.

Timothy shook his head.

'Any of you lot?' added Guppy, eyeing the reporters, who gave non-committal shrugs. They hardly even recognised each other such was their geographic diversity.

'Who cares?' someone exclaimed.

'Turnpike Constructions he says he's from,' Guppy called out.

Turnpike buttoned up his coat, looking everyone square in the face. Mrs Pankhurst and Jenny narrowed their eyes at him.

'A construction company?' Bilal had now pushed through everyone, Haaris by his side, to stand beside Shelley. 'What are you doing here?'

Turnpike cleared his throat and repeated: 'You'll be informed in due course.'

'I think we'd quite like to know now,' said Richard, with a smile that didn't altogether reach his eyes.

'Someone from a construction company has no business at a protest,' added Mariam.

Copperthwaite and Anne had joined them too, the rest of the village closing in on Turnpike – protestors, supporters, counter-protestors – all pushed to the back.

'Now, if you could give me some room,' Turnpike began.

'Let's not crowd our visitor,' said Richard. Everyone seemed to take heed of this as Richard added to Turnpike: 'Well?'

'You'll all be informed in due course.'

'Is the man a robot?' said Mr Pankhurst.

'Yes,' added Mrs Pankhurst. 'Be *transparent*.'

'You heard the lady,' said Harry, resting his hands on Sam's shoulders.

'I'm here to help,' said Turnpike.

'Help *who* exactly?'

'Got the face of a man who'd only like to help himself,' said Copperthwaite.

There was a murmur of assent.

'Perhaps it would be good to set up a formal meeting,' said Turnpike. 'I'll speak to the managers. Now, if you'll excuse me . . .'

But no-one moved.

'Now seems as good a time as any,' replied Richard.

Turnpike swallowed hard. 'Very well.' He straightened his back. 'Modernisation and innovation has long been a stance of Turnpike Constructions.' He paused, his nose red from the cold as he cleared his throat, facing narrowing eyes and stiffening bodies at the word *modernisation*. 'Never have there been more people travelling between towns and cities, contributing to our growing economy—'

'Spare us the company line and get to the point,' interrupted Mariam.

'You should underst—'

'You heard her,' interjected Shelley.

'We're straight-talkers here,' added Margaret. 'What do you want with our mosque?'

'Church,' corrected Shelley.

'Our *building*,' added Bilal.

'The reason . . . we see . . . its situation is that . . . '

'Spit it out, man.'

'The thing is, we need to tear it down.'

Silence.

'Excuse me?' said Shelley, stepping forward and leaning in close to the harbinger of the future.

'For the new road. All for your benefit. By 2035 we estimate that there'll be twenty thou—'

'Are you mad?' someone exclaimed.

At once, everyone's voices merged, pointing at Turnpike, telling him to get off their land, that he'd tear this church/mosque/building down over their dead bodies. Then Tom stalked up to him, pointing his finger into Turnpike's now sweaty face.

'Don't you *even* think about it.'

2035? Who knew what changes would metastasise tomorrow, let alone by 2035?

Tom's face flushed red as Turnpike laughed uncomfortably. 'Well, sir, it's already thought about.'

'You take your grubby, city-dwelling hands and get out of here.'

'Dad,' said Anne, holding on to Tom's arm. 'It's okay.'

'Like hell it is,' exclaimed Tom.

Shelley was taken aback by the force of Tom's words. His hand was mid-air in righteous indignation, everyone waiting for him to continue.

'Dad?'

But Tom didn't respond. He clutched his chest as his walking stick fell to the ground.

Richard strode forward and grabbed him before he fell.

'Call an ambulance,' exclaimed Richard.

'Where's my phone?'

'It's here.'

Suddenly everyone had their phones stretched out in front of them.

'I've got it,' exclaimed Mariam, dialling 999.

The crowds heaved forward as Richard eased Tom to the floor, his head on Anne's lap, and bent over him, loosening Tom's coat and scarf. Shelley pushed the crowd back, demanding they give Richard space, instructing them to remove any cars that might block the ambulance's way.

Everyone complied. Even the videographers put their cameras down.

'Is there anything I can do?' asked Turnpike.

Shelley stared at him hard. 'You've done enough.'

Then she looked at Anne, her face ashen.

Don't you go dying, Tom Lark. I'll deal with you a hundred times but don't you go dying on that daughter of yours.

At Evergreen Hospital, Shelley sat in the waiting room, along with Bilal and Mariam (he'd told Vaseem to take the family home), Margaret, the Pankhursts and Copperthwaite. Richard sat next to Anne, glancing at her every so often as she stared at the posters on the wall.

Margaret tapped her fingers impatiently. 'How long will it be, for God's sake?'

'Calm down,' grumbled Copperthwaite.

It was a surprise to everyone, except Shelley, when he'd decided to come too. The others hadn't considered the importance of consistency for Copperthwaite. He had never liked Tom, but he was *used* to him, and familiarity could breed even the most reluctant of positive emotions.

Margaret looked like she was about to say something but held her tongue. It wasn't long before a doctor walked in and everyone stood up.

'Who's Mr Lark's relative?'

'I'm his daughter.' Anne stood up.

The doctor smiled. 'He's out of danger. You can relax.'

She breathed a sigh of relief as she grabbed Richard's hand.

The doctor explained that he'd had a heart attack, but it had been a mild one, even though at Tom's age he was lucky it wasn't more severe.

Shelley cleared her throat. 'We should leave you to it,' she said, patting Anne on the arm, unsure whether to hug her or not.

Shelley shook her head as Bilal's phone rang. He spoke into it, his voice getting louder. Common courtesy seemed to have gone out of the window.

'What do you mean?' he said. 'What? We're still at the hospital.' Bilal sat back on his chair, putting his head in his hands. 'I don't . . . What do you mean?'

Shelley's heart began to beat faster.

He put the phone down.

'What is it?' said Mariam.

'It was Vaseem,' replied Bilal. 'He says . . . '

He looked confused, uncertain, as if he wasn't sure what he was saying, or who he was saying it to.

'He says Khala's died.'

chapter twenty-eight

**Protest for Mosque Threatens Life of
Babbel's End Resident**

The ongoing dispute over whether to convert a long-standing church in Babbel's End to a mosque took an unexpected twist when it was declared that it may have to be knocked down for an A-road. In the midst of the commotion that erupted, one of the residents suffered a heart attack. Tom Lark, who is in critical care, was one of the protestors, when the previously undisclosed plan was revealed, causing further waves of discontent in this already fractured community.

KHALA HAD BEEN FOUND on the sofa, as if asleep, in front of the dying fire. It was Shagufta who'd walked in on her, excitedly telling her to wake up and hear about these, quite frankly, uncivilised villagers. But Khala didn't wake up. Shagufta shook her friend as Gulfashan, Vaseem and his family walked in.

'*Ya Allah*,' exclaimed Shagufta, before muttering the first *kalima* prayer – which was always a good thing to remember as a Muslim in the face of death, if your emotional capacities allowed it. Rukhsana would've been very grateful for Shagufta, had she been able to hear her.

'*Inna lilla hai wa inna ilayhi raji'un*,' added Gulfashaan, once she had got over the shock of seeing her friend lying lifeless.

We belong to God and to God we shall return.

Vaseem called Bilal and he, Mariam and Haaris were back at the house within twenty minutes to find the ambulance's blue lights flashing outside the place Khala had, that very day, called home.

'Haaris, please go to your room,' said Mariam, her hands shaking, but her voice unwavering.

'*No*, I want to see Khala.'

Haaris hadn't had the experience of learning to control his voice the way his mum had.

'Baby.' She bent down and brought him into a hug, kissing his head. 'I promise I'll come and explain, okay? But you don't want to see her like this.'

'I don't get it,' said Haaris, his voice finally breaking. 'We were going to learn to speak Chinese.'

But it was too late. The paramedics were bringing Khala out on a gurney and Bilal couldn't help but remember it was how he'd seen her when he'd gone to collect her from Birmingham five months ago.

'Khala,' called Haaris, rushing to her side. 'Khala, wake up.'

This time it was Bilal that pulled Haaris back because Mariam's fist was pressed against her mouth, her body swaying as if she might lose her balance. She didn't. But it took something in her not to.

'I'm going with her to the hospital,' said Bilal to Mariam, handing Haaris over, who was now sobbing in his arms.

'Okay,' she was barely able to say.

Then she reached up and hugged Bilal tight enough for him to know that she'd be there when he got back.

❧

Bilal waited for the doctor to confirm what they already knew. Richard sat next to him on one side, Anne on the other, the three of them adrift in the reverie of loss. Few words were exchanged, just the solace of shared experience. He decided to go alone and sit with Khala's body before they took her to the morgue. Bilal wondered why he didn't feel anything. A numbness spread to the tips of his fingers and toes, suggesting that after a lifetime of knowing Khala, perhaps he had felt very little for her. But he remembered her face and his guilt when he told her he'd sold his mum's house – and it hadn't been guilt (he was so accustomed to the feeling, any new emotion just felt like an extension of it). It had been affection. Such a strong one that he had told Mariam he wanted Khala to live with them.

'Funny you say that,' she'd replied. 'Haaris said the same thing to me.'

Haaris had insisted that they tell Khala it was his idea, because he'd been feeling that for ages and why should adults get all the credit? Mariam had given a sad smile.

She hadn't argued, and he knew that was half the battle. Though perhaps that was because she knew she'd no longer be living in the house with him. A sob escaped Bilal. His chest appeared to concave as he pressed his head to his hands.

Khala's had been a life less lived and now their lives were lesser without her.

⁓

Haaris had fallen asleep in Mariam's arms. She pulled his Spiderman blanket over him, switched off the Iron Man lamp and kissed him on the forehead. Auntie Shagufta and Gulfashan were in the living room, mourning their friend, and also the realisation that one day, maybe their bodies would be discovered in the same way. All alone. Mariam found herself walking into Khala's room, sitting on her bed, in the dark.

When Bilal had asked that Khala live with them, Mariam was relieved. Relieved that she'd not have to argue with him, because no, she *didn't* mind. The entire thing surprised her. And then she had wondered, what if she

left Bilal? Packed her suitcase, took Haaris and went back
to Saif? She'd be leaving Khala behind as well, and why
was it in life that you could never gain a thing without
losing another?

But now there was no gain. Only loss. She wiped the
tears that fell, even though she hadn't emitted a sob. She
rummaged in the drawers for some tissue, but instead
found a bunch of loose papers. Switching on the bedside
lamp she looked at what seemed like hundreds of pages
of writing in Urdu. Saif had encouraged her to read Urdu
poetry, and though it took her a while and sometimes she
couldn't make out a word, she found herself able to read
Khala's words.

'Hey.'

She started and looked up through the tears still stream-
ing down her face to see Bilal standing in the doorway.

He came towards her as Mariam picked up the papers
and showed them to him. 'It's Khala.'

He took a crumpled piece and stared at it. 'Can you
read it?'

She nodded, wiping her tears with the back of her hand.
'Just about. They're poems. That she's written.'

'She wrote poetry?'

Mariam nodded again. 'And, oh, Bilal,' she said, trying
to hold back her tears again. 'I didn't know . . . I couldn't
tell. She was so *sad*.'

'What does it say?'

Bilal sat on the edge of the bed, looking from the papers
to Mariam as she skimmed through them.

'It takes me a while to understand,' she said. 'But look, this one: *Manzir-eh-kashti* . . . '

'Erm . . . destination of a ship?' said Bilal.

The English translation somehow didn't do the poem's title justice. Some things would always be lost in translation.

'She writes how the *kashti* – ship – never docks, only goes round in circles with her as a passenger with a view of nothing but the never-ending sea.' Mariam sniffed. 'Why didn't we see how sad she was?'

The light from the lamp highlighted Bilal's dark circles and sad eyes. He shook his head.

'Is she really gone?' she asked.

He was barely able to hold back his own tears. 'Yes,' he managed to reply. 'She's gone.'

chapter twenty-nine

'. . . WAVES OF DISCONTENT in this already fractured community.'
Shelley finished reading the article – a version of which had been printed in every major national paper – but there was not one mention of Khala. She reasoned that Khala hadn't been at the protest, why would she be mentioned? Yet it felt like an unbearable omission. She sat at her computer, staring out of the window for a minute. The stillness between Christmas and New Year was usually a specific kind. But this one had the particular shadow of loss.

To Whom It May Concern,

We, the undersigned, hereby demonstrate our condem-
nation of the demolition of our church building to make

way for the expansion of the A-road. As residents of the
village this will not only be the cause of severe disruption
to our daily lives, but also affect the nature reserves that
are a marked attraction of our wonderful county.

Please be advised that we will not let this matter
rest, nor will we be ignored by officials who deemed
it appropriate to begin such plans with complete disre-
gard for the community's thoughts and feelings.

I hereby petition for a public inquiry to be made.

Chairwoman of Babbel's End council,
Shelley Hawking

Each one of the 1,232 inhabitants in Babbel's End and its
environs – who were not away on holiday – had signed
their name. All names sitting side-by-side for the first time
in a while. Shelley had managed to garner 962 signatures
against the mosque, but somehow that no longer felt satisfying.

What came over Shelley in the next few days was a kind
of fever, which only people who had suffered from love
or loss could understand. Her hands trembled as she
knocked from door-to-door, village-to-village, with petition
in hand. She wrote with fervour and spoke with the air
of someone who looked ready to lose her life before she
lost her conviction. The numbers grew and grew and she
supposed the people of neighbouring villages had rather
more to lose from a new A-road than they ever did from
a mosque.

Upon hearing the news of Khala's passing, Shelley felt that she had some right to rush back home with Mariam and Bilal, but she was unable to articulate it to them, for obvious reasons. She had asked Richard to relay any news, and it had swiftly come back with the confirmation that Khala was 'no more of this world'. For all of Shelley's Christianity, it struck her as an odd sentence. Of which world was Khala a part? And whatever world she belonged to now, Shelley wondered whether she'd ever really belonged to this one. Did Shelley even belong to this world? Since we all eventually die, she supposed no-one did. We were all merely passing by.

Shelley was no stranger to death, having lost both parents, but she was surprised at how absurd it seemed to her in that moment. Just a few days ago, she and Khala were standing in Bilal's house, and she was unwrapping Shelley's present. The day before that they'd been speeding in the 'Vaseem's Removals' van to save the church bell. Khala had exchanged something she held dear for something that Shelley held dear and now the person behind the action was gone.

Shelley's phone rang.

'It's Richard.'

'Hello.'

'Just to let you know, Khala's body's been taken to Birmingham, where she'll have a proper Islamic burial.'

'Ah.' Shelley lost all the energy that she seemed to have had in the past few days. She closed her eyes and realised that she would never again go on a walk with her friend.

A lump formed in her throat, but she barely recognised what it indicated until a tear managed to push to the surface of her eye.

'That makes sense,' she added, wiping the stray tear.

'It would've been her wish.'

'Perhaps she'd have liked to be laid to rest here,' Shelley replied.

'I don't see why,' said Richard. 'It wasn't her home.'

The idea of home suddenly seemed so arbitrary to Shelley. 'She was happy here.'

'I wasn't aware you knew each other,' said Richard.

Shelley paused. 'Sometimes we'd walk together.'

Her voice sounded strained but it was beyond her control, as so much of life was.

'What happened on these walks?'

Shelley wasn't sure how to articulate it. What *did* happen? She unburdened her life to a person who hardly understood her.

'It's over with now,' she replied. Shelley opened the kitchen door to see Arthur still on the sofa. 'Did you know she wrote poetry?'

'Did she? In Urdu?' asked Richard.

'Well, obviously in Urdu.'

'No, of course. Excuse me.'

What a silly thing to ask, but she supposed the reverend was human too.

'Would you like to go to the funeral?' he asked.

The thought had passed some part of her consciousness, but with such speed that she hadn't dwelled on it.

'I'm sure Bilal and Mariam would be fine with it. And apparently Islamic funerals are open to whoever wants to attend,' added Richard.

Shelley imagined sitting in a mosque with strangers. What were the rituals? What would they think of her? Would she have to pray with them? She wouldn't even know what to wear.

'I wouldn't want to interfere,' came Shelley's reply.

'I don't think they'd see it like that,' replied Richard. 'They're very ope—'

'No, really, Reverend. I don't think it's appropriate.'

That ended that conversation as Shelley told the reverend that she'd wait to email the district council and their local MP with the petition until the first week of January. She'd be able to gather more signatures from neighbouring villages by then.

After all of that arguing about whether the church would be a mosque, wouldn't it be something to lose the place altogether? Shelley looked out of her window again into the night sky, the fog as dense as ever. She wondered if there'd be any fireworks tonight.

'I suppose I'll see you next year then, Reverend.'

He asked what she'd be doing that evening.

'Just a quiet one,' said Shelley. 'I'll pay a visit to Tom. Though God knows why I bother.'

Richard paused. 'Because we try,' he said, a heaviness in his voice.

'Yes,' replied Shelley, still looking out into the night sky. 'We try.'

chapter thirty

Take hold of the feelings you have and imagine a jar.

Now put each feeling into that jar.

Are you done?

No?

Take a few more minutes.

Pick up that jar and take a look inside. What are the emotions you see and recognise?

Mariam squinted at the empty space in her hand. The jar she imagined was murky – as were its contents.

'Ugh,' she exclaimed as she closed her laptop and chucked the fictitious jar through the room's window.

Perhaps it was being back here in Birmingham that skewed her feelings. Or maybe her feelings were skewed because of the gathering of people downstairs, praying for Khala, Haaris sitting there too, with her ex-husband, while her current husband made the arrangements for the funeral. They had to stay at Auntie Shagufta's across the road from her mother in-law's house because it now belonged to someone else. Here the walls were painted white, the light lino covered in rugs dotted around the house. But that earthy smell mixed with fried oil and vanilla was still Sakeena's. There was a knock on the door.

'Hi.'

'Oh, hi.' Mariam closed her laptop.

Saif came into the room and she wasn't sure how she felt about him closing the door behind him.

'How are you?'

'Fine,' she said.

'Poor Auntie Rukhsana.'

She considered him, the love of her life, in his plain white shalwar kameez, kempt beard and look of regret.

'Yes.'

'Haaris will miss her,' he added. 'I'm worried about him.'

'They'd got close.' Mariam managed a smile. 'But I'm

glad that he got to spend time with her – she was like the *naani* he never had.'

Saif folded his arms and looked at Mariam so intently it unsettled her, the fluttering in her stomach bordering on nausea.

'We shouldn't speak ill of the dead,' he said, softly, kindly. But it didn't matter.

It annoyed Mariam.

'Well, we can't lie about them either. And Khala acted more like a mother to me than my own ever did.'

'Maybe,' he conceded. 'But still.'

There was a knock on the door as it opened, pushing Saif forward.

'Oh, sorry.'

It was Bilal.

He looked between Mariam and Saif, and seemed to hesitate before committing himself to the room. Saif, however – despite the indignity of almost falling flat on his face – carried on staring at Mariam.

'I'll wait for you.' Saif paused longer than necessary, before adding: 'Downstairs.'

Mariam felt her face flush as he left the room.

'What was he . . . ' Bilal paused. 'Why are you sitting on the bed with your laptop?'

'Oh, nothing,' she replied.

But the lies felt too exhausting. She owed her husband some more truths and having lost the energy to play hide and seek with her emotions (there was such a thing as hiding too well), she shifted a little, inviting Bilal to sit next to her. Opening up the laptop, she replayed the YouTube video.

Now, take each feeling out of the jar and place it in front of you, asking where it came from . . .

'What jar?' He looked around the room.

'It's imaginary.'

'Oh,' he replied.

Mariam glanced at Bilal. He thought she was mad. It was etched in his furrowed brows.

She paused the video and turned to him. 'They're . . . you know. Self-help videos.'

This only fortified the crease in his brow.

'Self-help?' he repeated.

Mariam nodded. 'It helps me manage things.'

'What things?'

She took a deep breath. He was a man who, after all, sought clarity in everything – who couldn't understand unless the details had been explained precisely.

'You know what self-help videos are,' she said.

He looked at the screen again. 'Well, yes. But I've never "got" them. What's this jar business?'

'Forget about that, it . . . '

What was the use? A person either understood a thing, or they didn't. You couldn't teach it, not in any real way. Even if the audience was a willing one.

'Doesn't matter,' she added.

'But it does matter,' Bilal replied, looking at her. 'Is this what you've been doing every time I've come home unexpectedly, and you've looked flustered?'

'Have I?' she asked.

'Yes.'

'I thought I was always quite composed.'

'Which is why when you're flustered, it shows.'

'Oh.' Mariam paused to consider how much Bilal saw. Bilal looked at the screen, scrolling down other YouTube clips. 'Who is Starr Applebaum?'

'Oh no, she's awful.'

'Ever think I might've been more use than these videos? I mean, I don't have a jar . . .'

Mariam smiled and they sat in silence for a few minutes.

'Saif's probably waiting for you,' Bilal said.

After all, love was just a tug of war between remembering and forgetting. Mariam wasn't sure whether her dissatisfaction with her life – her feelings – arose because she thought too highly of herself, or not highly enough. She didn't need a jar, she needed an aeroplane-sized vessel to fit all of her feelings.

Saif was hovering by the front door, looking for his other shoe in the sea of ones scattered against the wall. She noticed it and was going to pick it up for him, but thought better of it. Instead, she came down the last step and kicked it towards him. He gave a small smile.

'Is that how you hand things to Bilal now?' he asked, putting the shoes on.

'I'd like to say she puts them on my feet before I leave the house, but that wouldn't be true.'

Mariam looked back to see Bilal standing behind her, his hands in his pockets. Saif also looked up.

'Mariam would beat a person with their shoe before doing that,' replied Saif.

There was something so self-satisfied in his look, so predictable in what he said, that it hit Mariam in a rather forceful way. It occurred to her that her silent dignity in the past several years had had no outlet. She'd relied on the power of logic and self-help videos to unknot her feelings, and, quite frankly, both had failed. What made her think that silently failing emotionally was somehow better than vocally trying to succeed? It struck her that going back to Saif wouldn't just be abandoning some kind of principle, it would tell her – and Haaris might also come to learn it – that this was the measure of her own self-worth. That she deserved to be a consolation prize. It wasn't so much that she found clarity in that moment, but that she was seen with clarity by the man she'd been married to for the past ten years. And she realised that she loved him for it. Once the barrier of her love – or illness, as she was beginning to see it – for Saif had been removed, she might realise the many other ways she loved Bilal.

'I think you should stop pretending that you know me,' replied Mariam, ignoring the two aunties who'd just come out of the living room, making their way into the kitchen.

Saif was visibly moved, but he recovered soon enough. 'Maybe I should. Maybe you're not who you used to be.'

It was always this kind of innocuous, passive aggressive comment that fortified Mariam. 'I hope not.'

'Mariam . . . ' Saif looked at Bilal, clearly annoyed that

he couldn't be alone with her, say all the things he wanted. 'I'll keep Haaris here for the weekend if you want.'

'I think he's okay with us,' said Bilal.

In that moment, it seemed a miraculous stroke of luck that Bilal was still by her side. She wondered if he would *stay* by her side – if their life hadn't collapsed within the boundaries of her silence.

'Okay. Well, we'll talk later?' said Saif.

'I'll be busy,' she replied.

He hesitated.

'Bye, Saif,' she said.

There was nothing for it. He had to turn around, walk out and close the door behind him.

'I don't think Khala ever really liked him,' she said, turning to Bilal.

'No. Why would she? She liked you though,' Bilal said.

'I'm not entirely sure why.'

'Maybe she thought you were kindred spirits,' he replied.

He looked at her as if he understood everything – more than he ever showed, anyway. He seemed new to her in that moment, even though he was familiar. Yes, she'd need the familiarity to anchor her and the newness to shift her perspective. How much of who you were could depend on another? So much interdependency mortified Mariam, but it was clear she'd have to rethink things.

'She came into her own in Babbel's End, didn't she?' said Mariam.

Bilal nodded. 'Mum had been . . . '

'A good soul,' added Mariam.

He nodded again. 'But even they have their flaws.'

'How do you feel about flaws?' she asked.

'Mine, yours, or generally?'

'You think I have flaws?' she replied, raising her eyebrows.

He laughed for a second but then thought better of it. 'Let's compare.' He brought out his hand and she took it in hers. 'Perhaps a list? You write yours and I'll write mine?'

Mariam had a fleeting thought about her imaginary jar, and how she'd put this feeling of contentment tinged with fear in it. She wished Khala were there to see her and Bilal holding hands, not out of solidarity or duty, but hope. For all of Khala's forlorn words and looks, she could recognise hope when she saw it.

~

'I just wanted to come and wish you a Happy New Year.'

Richard stood at the foot of Tom's hospital bed, Anne by her dad's side, reading the paper. Margaret was also sitting there, telling Tom she was keeping his garden in order, fluffing his pillows for him.

'No fireworks here,' replied Tom.

Anne was shaking her head. 'I never thought I'd see the day when a mosque would get upstaged by an A-road.'

Richard smiled. Was he imagining it or was there something of the old Anne back?

'Don't get me started,' said Tom, his face going red.

Richard took a seat. 'It's good to know you care, Tom.'

'Of course I bloody care. Serves those self-satisfied bastards right, though. Worrying about a damned mosque when we have bigger problems. They need to get their priorities straight. I still say build the mosque. Long as there's none of that call to prayer racket.'

'I like those a great deal,' said Margaret. 'It's very beautiful, you know.'

She then proceeded to imitate the call to prayer, though it sounded more like the soundtrack of a bad Hollywood film about Native Americans. Richard cleared his throat.

'Why, in Morocco,' she added, 'I used to enjoy it at least five times a day.'

'Oh, it's dreadful, Mags,' replied Tom. 'But then something's got to give.'

Anne held on to Tom's arm, the trace of a smile on her face. Richard remembered how she'd gripped his hand when they were here in the hospital, and then how she'd let it go as if it never happened. A chasm of isolation seemed to open up in front of Richard; hope on one side and him on the other. The idea was so startling it was almost as if he'd fallen *into* the chasm. Here was blasphemy! To be without hope when he had God. But Richard was suffering what could only be described as a terrible bout of yearning. Somewhere between his treadmill, Christmas turkey and protest for the mosque, Richard's affections – which he generally managed to rein in quite successfully – had turned into a new beast altogether. The shaky ground of reasoning was giving way to a sinkhole of what he could only describe as forlorn love. Being unaccustomed to such ardent feelings, Richard stood up.

'You all right?' asked Tom.

'Hmm? Yes. Quite. I just realised the time. I've a meeting.'

He dared not look at Anne.

'He'll be back,' she said to her dad. 'Our reverend is never too far away from bestowing sympathy.'

A few months ago Richard would have taken the comment in the spirit that it was intended: to test his patience, but today was a different day and he felt like a different man.

'Only where I feel it's of some use,' he said. 'Clearly, it's not here.'

Anne met his gaze.

'I hope you're better soon, Tom.'

Tom furrowed his brows, either in anger or confusion. Margaret cleared her throat, looking at him as if he ought to remember he was a man of the cloth.

'Reverend,' said Tom.

Richard nodded goodbye to Margaret, gave Anne one last look before he walked away. As he turned the corner of the ward he heard Tom.

'That man loves you, Anne, and you're a damned fool if you think otherwise.'

But the fury of desolate love drove Richard's steps still faster away from Anne, until he was in his car, foot on the accelerator, speeding all the way to Pineneedle Prison.

Brought face-to-face with Dan Barnes, Richard had hoped that he'd feel sympathy, but he couldn't quite muster it.

'How are you?' Richard asked.

Dan sat up and nodded. 'Fine.'

Richard sighed. 'I'll just cut to the chase here. Gerald told me about the graffiti and stealing the bell.'

Dan shook his head. 'He can never keep things to himself.'

'No,' said Richard.

They both sat and looked at each other – Dan in his grey sweatshirt and bottoms, Richard in his collar.

'Listen,' said Dan. 'If you think I'm going to tell the police about Gerald and that graffiti, I'm not. Dad's already taken the blame for it and I'm no grass.'

'Well, that's good of you. I think Gerald just needs a chance and with his previous conviction that could . . . '

'Put him here, with me? Don't worry, Rev. I've got selling drugs, buying drugs, oh, and that actual bodily harm thing to my name. Gerald's all right with his one conviction of possession of pot.' Dan gave a derisive laugh.

Richard felt inordinately angry and had to press his hands to his legs. 'How's your dad?'

Dan made no move to answer. 'Are we done here?'

'I suppose so. If you want.'

Dan was about to stand up when Richard added: 'Wouldn't Teddy have talked you out of stealing that bell?'

A flicker of sadness crossed Dan's face as he looked at Richard.

He shrugged. 'Probably.'

He went to walk out of the room but paused at the door. Without turning around he added: 'Tell Ger . . . '

'What?' asked Richard.

'Tell him to be more like Teddy.'

❧

When Bilal returned home after New Year with Mariam and Haaris, the first thing he saw was Khala's waterproof anorak. It jolted into him the memory of her passive face, her body wrapped in a white shroud, before being taken to be buried. The sentimental notion that the sisters were now together occurred to Bilal, and he didn't dislike it.

'What happens to her things?' asked Haaris.

'We'll sort through them,' replied Mariam, pulling him into a hug. 'Though she didn't have much.'

'Is it because she was alone?' he asked.

'She wasn't alone,' replied Bilal.

But even as he said it, he knew it was a lie. Mariam had asked Haaris if he had wanted to see Khala's face before they buried her and he had said yes. She had hoped that his curiosity for life wouldn't match his curiosity for death. He'd looked at Khala, her face a pale yellow, lips darkened, for a full three minutes before turning to Mariam and whispering: 'It's not her, Mum, is it? It's just a body.'

Now, they watched Haaris trudge up the stairs and Bilal

felt that the road of parenthood was to become rockier. Inside the quiet house, he felt a strange sort of nervousness with Mariam – as if the spaces, now no longer filled with muttering aunties, separated them.

'Are you hungry? I'll make some sandwiches,' said Mariam, going into the kitchen.

She was here, yes, but why? He recalled the scene on the stairs, but perhaps he was imbuing it with too much of his own hope. Bilal followed her.

'Are you here because you want to be or because there's no other choice?' he asked.

The funeral had many effects on him, the most prominent of which was to be bold enough to ask questions, even if he'd rather not know the answer. Mariam turned around from grating the cheese, observing him – was she calculating a diplomatic way to respond to this?

'Because if you want Saif then I don't think we can carry on like this.'

If he hadn't grabbed on to the chair in front of him, Bilal's legs may have given way.

'I need you to give me time,' she replied.

There it was: the bubbling of rage – that she should get to decide the terms, that her feelings took precedence over his, and all the time he let her. It was his own doing. No, he didn't want to lose her, but he couldn't abide being a second choice. He had seen too much death in the past year to not want to live.

'For what?' he asked.

She folded her arms. 'I can stand here and tell you that

I've realised this is exactly where I want to be, but somehow I don't think you'd believe me. Even if I did have a choice.'

'Do you? Have a choice?'

She paused. 'It's hard to tell sometimes.'

Bilal too folded his arms. He needed more warmth from her to counter his reticence, but he knew that was impossible – he couldn't expect her to be a different woman to the one he had married. It struck him then that a partnership in a relationship never was equal. One would require more patience and understanding than the other, and in that moment he had to decide if he was okay to carry on being that one. It felt rather too much like martyrdom.

'So?' he said.

'Let time tell,' she said. 'But right now, given the choice, I promise – there's no place I'd rather be than here.'

He watched her eyebrows contract a little, and her eyes, that were usually distant, seemed fully present.

'Okay,' he said.

He unfolded his arms and went to leave.

'Where are you going?' she asked, gesturing to the unmade sandwiches.

'Outside.'

Bilal grabbed his coat and gloves, a big towel, some bin liners and made his way into the garden.

chapter thirty-one

BILAL LAY IN HIS grave watching the dark sky, breathing in the foggy smell after too many fireworks, contemplating the absence of the two women in his life who'd brought him up. Khala had been the balm to his mum's fiery words and looks. His mum had brought bravery to Khala's indecisiveness – together he realised that they'd imbued him with rather more measure than should be allowed. He had seen two extremes and chosen moderation. Yet he didn't seem to love his wife in moderation. He teetered somewhere between awe and adoration, pride and a crippling kind of dependency. Nothing imbalanced him more than the idea that she might walk away with Haaris in tow. But he wouldn't hold on to her, not if she didn't want it. There were a thousand little intricacies that made every human being so different that it was a wonder to Bilal that anyone ever got along at all, let alone got married.

His mobile rang and he fumbled around before taking off his glove and answering it.

'Richard. Hello,' said Bilal.

'Hi.' Richard was panting.

'Where are you?'

'Gym. You?'

'Grave.'

'Ah.' Richard's breathing came down heavily on the phone.

'How's Tom?'

'Fine. He'll be fighting fit again sooner than we expect.'

A long pause ensued and Bilal rather wanted to go back to his thoughts when Richard said: 'How are things with Mariam?'

Sigh. 'Uncertain.'

'Right.'

'Well—'

'I . . . ' interrupted Richard.

'Yes?' asked Bilal.

'This is tricky for me,' said Richard.

Bilal felt distracted by the thudding of Richard's footsteps. 'Could you stop running for a minute?'

Bilal heard a beep, Richard's breathing slowing down.

'Well, go on,' said Bilal.

'It's always easier to listen than talk.'

'Give it a go.'

'You and Mariam are quite different, aren't you?'

'That's safe to say.'

'What is it that made you sure? That it would work,' asked Richard.

It was an odd question to come from his friend, yet he felt the pressure of giving him an answer that would in some way do justice to the eight years Richard had spent listening to Bilal.

'I don't think there was a *moment*,' began Bilal. 'Being young helps. There's more feeling than thinking, isn't there?'

'Thank God for age,' replied Richard. 'If with it comes wisdom.'

'Hmm.' Bilal paused. 'I think it was partly that she was the only woman I'd met who didn't suffocate me with her affection. Perhaps there was something about the way she gave her attention to Haaris, too. Not the over-zealous single mother. You know the type – the one who'd end up being emotionally dependent on her only child.'

Bilal wondered if he'd had siblings whether he'd have felt the guilt in the way he did. Would they have joked about *old mother Sakeena, at it again* – or shared the latest story of their mum's bizarre behaviour? Bilal shifted on his bin liner, looking at the fog emanating from his mouth. His mum had tried not to show it, but he'd felt the expectation in the tone of her voice, saw it in the way her life was just her and Khala. Bilal wondered whether it wasn't too dissimilar to the way in which he felt dependent on Mariam.

'Right. Yes,' said Richard.

'What's going on?'

Richard cleared his throat. Another beep, Richard's footsteps quickening again. 'I was curious. And I thought I might make sense of something in my life if I heard about yours.'

'You're being cryptic,' said Bilal.

'Sorry.'

'You're a man of God. People of God get all the answers.'

'Do we?'

'Of course. You're meant to be, you know . . . certain about things.'

'Death, I'm afraid, is the only certainty,' replied Richard. Bilal nodded in his grave. 'And taxes.'

There was a pause. 'And love,' mumbled Richard.

'Sorry?'

'Nothing. Don't mind me.'

'Richard . . .'

'Thanks for the talk, Bill. As for the mosque business, I promise it's not over.'

Bilal sat up in the grave. *Love*. He'd rather not talk about it if he could help it – it was such a sentimental subject, made more uncomfortable by virtue of the fact that he suffered from it. But friends had a duty to one another.

'Yes, but Richard . . . is it Anne?'

Of course. Bilal had been so wrapped up in his own crumbling marriage, he hadn't seen the potential of something blossoming elsewhere.

A long pause ensued.

'Yes or no will do,' added Bilal.

There was another beep as Richard's footsteps quietened. 'Yes.'

'I see.'

Another long pause. Bilal shifted in his grave again. 'And how does . . . how does she . . . you know . . . *feel?*' he muttered.

'Like a woman who's lost her son,' replied Richard.

Bilal thought of Haaris stomping up the stairs and a well of anxiety opened up, quite equal to the depth of the grave he was in. Life suddenly felt so precarious that he felt the earth might collapse in on itself, smothering him in his makeshift death-hole. He stood up.

'You're a good man,' said Bilal as he started to throw the towels and bin liners over the edge.

'I'm consummately flawed.'

Bilal laughed as he climbed out of the grave. 'Well then there's no hope for the rest of us.'

'I'm *angry*, Bill.'

The force of Richard's words made Bilal stop.

'There's a spark of rage in me that I feel . . . Never mind.'

'No. Go on.'

Spark of rage. Yes, he knew that feeling, having become newly acquainted with it.

'I have great faith in God. I do. Sometimes I flatter myself that I believe in humanity, too. But every now and again something in me makes me want to—'

'Do or say something terrible.'

Richard sighed. 'Yes.'

'Something out of character.'

'Or it's entirely in character and I've just been lying to myself – not to mention others – all these years. So you see, Bill, I'm not so good, after all.'

Bilal paused and thought about it. 'Perhaps Anne would like you all the more for it.'

'A fraudulent vicar? I give the impression of wisdom and knowledge and patience and all those virtues we're supposed to admire, but when I'm at the gym, on the treadmill, like now, all I imagine is running away from the tedious questions people have. And the people who *aren't tedious*? You can't save them. Even Gerald. I went to see Dan . . .'

'Did you? And?' Bilal's heart beat faster.

'There's something so cold about him.'

'What did he say?'

'Nothing. But I couldn't find it in myself to push past my own prejudices and help him.'

'You can't save everyone.'

'It's my job to try.' He paused. 'And then he surprised me.'

'How?'

'By showing that he has the ability to care.'

Bilal sighed. 'Right. You know, you should've just become an accountant.' But really, he was thinking about Bruce again.

Richard laughed and paused for a while. 'I was unforgivably rude to Anne.'

'Were you? Just say sorry. You're no prophet, Rich. No-one expects perfection,' replied Bilal.

'What do they expect?'

All these questions were uncharacteristic coming from Richard. He was always so ready with answers.

'There's something to be said about telling the truth about how a person feels. I . . . let's just say Mariam has told me a few things I'd rather not have discovered, but now, well . . . No use tiptoeing around a marriage. Or any relationship.'

'Hmmm. Silence can be its own tragedy,' replied Richard. 'Thanks, Bill. Sorry . . . '

'It's nothing. Don't mention it.'

Bilal put the phone down and felt a sense of calm. It wasn't the perverse gratification – which no-one admits to – that one gets when they learn that someone might be suffering a fraction more than them in life, but the realisation that everyone *does* suffer. That suffering can be shared, if not solved.

Bilal walked into the house a few minutes later. Mariam was staring into the fireplace, and as he went to sit next to her he felt something poke his leg. He reached into the sofa to find a bronze notebook that looked quite new.

'This yours?' he asked.

Before Mariam could answer, the doorbell rang.

'Hello.' It was Shelley, a woollen scarf over her head. 'I hope I'm not interrupting.'

It was more of a statement than a question. Her lips were pursed and her nostrils flared. Bilal couldn't understand what he might've done this time to make her angry. Perhaps it was just ongoing discontent. He heard a car approaching rather speedily. It zoomed past as he realised it was Richard. Shelley was surely about to say something about its speed, but her eyes were resting on the notebook.

'You've found it then?' she asked. 'The notebook. Notebooks, I'm sure. May I?' Shelley asked.

Bilal opened the door for her as she stepped into the house.

'You'll see there's an inscription,' she said.

Bilal flipped to the first page.

'That's from me,' she added.

'Oh.'

Shelley folded her hands in front of her. 'Yes, that's right.' She paused. 'Khala and I were friends. Good friends, I think.'

Richard knew that if he didn't go to see Anne now, he would lose his nerve. He stood at her door and hesitated. What would he say? He'd have to make do with the words that came to him. He was an articulate person, after all, and the worst thing he could do was think it through too thoroughly. He knocked on the door.

'Hello,' he said.

'Hi.'

They stood like this for a few moments, Richard's mind quite blank.

'Come in,' said Anne.

'May I?'

'Yes, Richard. You may.'

In the living room the fire had just been kindled, so he went and moved a few of the smaller logs, strengthening the flames.

'Sorry,' he said when he realised Anne was watching him.

'What can I do for you?'

'I owe you an apology.'

He waited for a response. None came.

'I shouldn't have spoken like that at the hospital.'

'Don't worry.'

Richard had to suppress his agitation at her apathy. Anger was an emotion to be mastered.

'Look, Anne, I know you must be angry, but you know—'

'Honestly. It's forgotten about,' she replied. 'You're free to go.'

It would've wounded him less if her face wasn't so impassive. She *would* be cold towards him – that might never change – but this just made Richard more resolute.

'I see how it has to be,' he said, suddenly feeling a solidity in both emotion and action. 'I came here to apologise, Anne, and to tell you that your father's right. I *do* love you and you *would* be a fool if you didn't see it.'

Richard noticed the colour rise to her cheeks.

'Perhaps I've known it for a while but have refused to believe it because . . . you're you and I'm me. I know how much this collar appalls you and if I had a choice in the matter I'd rid myself of these . . . ' Richard paused. *'Feelings*. I'm sorry to say it, but you know I'm not sentimental, and you'd respect me less – if you have any for me in the first place – if I pretended these things didn't matter, because they do. And, as it happens, so do you. A great deal. I did a poor job of managing my emotions in the hospital and took it out on the person who's put them in – let me tell you, because I'm not ashamed to say it – a bit of a tumble.'

'Tumble?'

'You don't have a right to know all this,' he continued, 'just as I probably have no right to tell you . . . ' Richard tried to read Anne's face – was she angry? Annoyed? Indifferent?

'So why did you come here?' she asked, her tone as steady as her gaze.

'Purely selfish reasons,' he said.

'Which are?'

'To see if you would – *could* – ever feel the same.'

'Do you have expectations of me?' she asked.

It was such an odd question. But then she was odd. If Richard was distressed at the idea of things never being the same between the two of them again, he didn't show it. He would meet her steadiness with steadiness.

'Just as much as you're willing to give.'

Anne gave a wry laugh as she looked away. 'No-one gives anything of themselves willingly. Unless they're very optimistic.'

Any other day he would've laughed and agreed, but he stopped himself.

'No,' he said. 'But I'm not sure what we gain by too much reluctance either.'

He stepped towards her so that they were just an arm's length away from one another. It was enough, he supposed.

'The problem is, Reverend—'

'Would you please just call me Richard.'

'Is that you'd spend your whole time trying to get back the Anne-before-Teddy-died, and she's gone,' she said, her voice cracking. 'Everything's gone. It'd be a bad deal for both of us. But especially for you.'

'That's not for you to decide.'

'The last thing I need is the burden of making sure you're okay, when I'm content in my own misery.'

'You won't have to worry about me. I'm quite self-sufficient.'

'So, what's the purpose then?' she asked. 'For someone who's meant to be wise, don't you see the flaws in your plan?'

'I don't have a plan,' he replied. 'Some things aren't as complicated as you think they are.'

'Sometimes they're more so.'

Richard paused. He wished he didn't see the reason in Anne's rationale, but it was impossible not to. To continue right now would be to press upon her the very feelings that she didn't want to be in charge of.

'I understand,' he said.

She looked at him, a slight crease appearing in her brow.

'And don't go playing the martyr, waiting for me to suddenly change my mind,' she said.

'If I did, you'd be the last person I'd tell.'

'Don't manipulate me, Richard.'

Richard felt the blaze of the fire on his back; it coloured Anne's face as he took one more step towards her.

'I don't think I could even if I tried. I barely succeeded in fooling myself,' he added.

She looked up at him with a sympathetic smile. 'You didn't fool me.'

Was he really that transparent? His powers of self-awareness left much to be desired.

'Ah. That's why the distance?' he asked.

'That's why the distance,' she affirmed.

'I see.'

It took him some effort to step back. 'Well. I said what had to be said. And you've been quite clear.'

'You'll let us know?'

'What?' he asked.

'What's happening with the mosque?'

Richard smiled. He wished it didn't come across as a sad one, but he was too tired to hide his feelings.

'You care about it?' he asked.

'After everything that's happened . . . be hard not to.'

He wanted to say that perhaps she'd begin to care about other things in the same way, but it didn't seem proper. Richard had his faith – if this was a difficulty he had to bear, he would bear it with dignity and without reproach.

'I'm glad,' he said. 'I suppose we both have that in common. And the grave business?'

She shook her head and so he didn't press her further.

'I'm going to go and see Mariam and Bilal today,' said Anne. 'Offer my condolences. Even Dad thought Khala "wasn't the worst thing in the world".'

'Right, I'd better leave you to it then,' he said.

Anne hesitated. 'You can come with me. If you want.'

There was a time to think and a time to feel, and perhaps now it was his turn to allow the latter.

'You wouldn't mind?' he asked.

'You know . . . ' She smiled.

'What?'

'Don't take this as me giving you hope, okay?'

He gave a short nod.

'People do give you a hard time, don't they?'

'It's what I signed up for.'

'Well, you did your job well,' she said. 'With me and Dad.'

'Anne—'

'You should know that. Because whatever else might happen, we'll always be friends, won't we?'

He nodded again. 'Yes. Always.'

Mariam and Bilal had more than a few questions for Shelley. She sat, hands folded over her knees, refusing to take her coat off as she explained her walks with Khala.

'Right,' said Mariam. 'Khala did mention seeing you once, but that was it.'

To Mariam, it added another layer to the mystery of Khala. It increased her fondness for her – a fondness that she wished she'd shown more of. The real surprise came, though, when Shelley said she wanted to organise a memorial for Khala.

'We don't really have memorials,' explained Mariam.

She felt Bilal stiffen.

'I see,' replied Shelley.

'That's not to say we can't have one,' added Bilal, looking at Mariam. 'I think Khala would've liked it.'

'Well, I wouldn't want to do anything to offend your . . . beliefs.'

'It means a lot,' said Bilal. 'That you'd like to do this.'

'I might not have known her very long but there are certain people who, well, you know . . . '

It was odd for Mariam and Bilal to hear words come out of Shelley's mouth so contrary to her usual rigid manners.

'What?' asked Mariam.

Shelley looked put out.

'We know,' interjected Bilal. 'Thank you.'

Just as Shelley got up to leave, the doorbell rang and Bilal returned with Richard and Anne. Shelley looked at both of them.

'Sorry, we . . . I should've called before popping over,' said Anne.

'No. Sit,' said Mariam.

'I was just about to leave,' added Shelley, but no-one moved.

A stillness filled the air, coats rustled, throats cleared.

'Still cold out, isn't it?' said Bilal.

'Windy, too,' added Richard.

Shelley looked like she might move but then thought better of it. 'Tom feeling better?'

'Yes,' said Anne.

'Good.'

Bilal took Richard's and Anne's coats as they all sat down, and for a moment they felt the lack of Khala in the room. The clock ticked in the background. Haaris's footsteps came from upstairs as Mariam caught Bilal's eye.

'Tea?' said Mariam.

'Yes,' added Bilal, shooting up and following her to the kitchen.

'Could you have agreed with Shelley any more about the memorial?' said Mariam.

'Someone had to,' he said.

'It's typical. She completely ignored Khala in public and now thinks she has the right to put on a show.'

'Shh. I don't think it is a show. And keep your voice down. You know, I wish you could be more gracious about it.'

'*Me?*' said Mariam. 'Is that one of my flaws?'

'I'd say it's in the top three, at least.'

She nudged him away, trying not to laugh, as she took some biscuits out. 'And yours is your eternal optimism.'

She would tell him one day, maybe even tonight, that she was grateful for his optimism.

'Don't you think Khala would've loved the idea of a memorial?'

This, Mariam couldn't disagree with.

'Need any help?' Anne appeared in the doorway. 'It's a little quiet in there.'

They carried the tea back in, putting the biscuits on the table. Richard was looking pensive and Shelley remote. Biscuits crunched, teacups clinked.

'I mean the—'

'That Turnpike Constructions—'

'Can you believe—'

Everyone spoke at once and then paused.

'Don't you worry,' said Shelley. 'This is just the beginning.'

'Yes, well done for gathering all those signatures and sending off that letter,' said Richard.

'Big companies do this,' said Mariam. 'They'll tell us things they think we want to hear: economic boost.'

'Less traffic,' said Anne.

'Convenience,' added Bilal.

Richard sighed and looked at the ground. It only just occurred to Mariam how he must be feeling – that he might lose a church in this way.

'What we need to do is show that it's actually used,' he said, looking around the room. 'We can argue that it has cultural significance, but remember we have two churches in Babbel's End. St Swithun's is so close to the main road that there probably wouldn't be much damage to the nature reserves either.'

'But it *is* used,' said Shelley.

Richard looked at her. 'No, Shelley. You know as well as I do that it's not.'

There was a protracted silence.

'I see,' said Shelley.

The four of them stared at her, willing her to say something. If she could come out with it, if they could just get her on side, then they had a shot.

'The archdeacon might change his mind, I suppose, about recommending the deconsecration to the bishop?' she said.

'Given what's happening, I'd say yes. Absolutely,' replied Richard.

Shelley looked at Bilal, her chest rising and falling, as if ready to burst with all the feelings bundled up inside.

'But I was thinking,' said Mariam. 'What if we made it into something that would get even more use?'

Anne looked at Mariam. 'Like a Buddhist centre?'

They both laughed, remembering Gavin standing in his black vest and silver chain, talking about his Buddhist girlfriend.

'Why not just turn it into a contemplation room?' joked Bilal.

Richard nodded. 'A multi-faith centre.'

'I was joking,' said Bilal, now alarmed at the notion. 'It's not quite what we had in mind.'

Mariam held his gaze. 'No. I know.'

'A *multi-faith centre*?' said Bilal, unsure, though not unwilling.

'Oh, heavens above,' interrupted Shelley. 'Is Babbel's End going to become a sanctuary for *hippies*?'

'It's a very good plan,' said Richard, looking at Shelley. 'More viable for the bishop and, I imagine, useful for our petition.'

They all looked at Shelley again.

'I see,' she said after a few moments.

She struggled. It was an ideal she was giving up, after all.

Bilal took a deep breath. 'I suppose this way we might really be able to keep it, if we can prove it's used and necessary.'

Shelley nodded. 'Well. I can't argue with that.' She looked at the ground, visibly pained at the choice before her. 'But I suppose a person should know when they've lost a battle.'

Mariam watched Bilal, waiting for a look of triumph to emerge, as she was sure it had done for her. Instead, he just leaned forward.

'Only because there's a war to be won.'

Even Shelley showed the hint of a smile.

They drank their tea and discussed a collective meeting to let everyone know about the new direction. When their guests had left, Bilal decided to pick up the phone and make the call he knew he should make.

'Hello, Bruce?'

'Yes.'

'It's Bilal.'

There was a pause. 'What can I do for you?'

Bilal sat on the edge of the sofa and thought about it. 'I'm sorry. For the graffiti accusation. I knew that you'd taken the blame for Dan. But you know I had to call the police, what with me thinking you wrote the note.'

Pause.

'But I was wrong. And I'm sorry.'

'Yes, well . . . I'd never consider writing such a thing,' said Bruce.

'Have you found a new job?'

'They're not that easy to come by around here.'

'No. I know.' Bilal paused again. 'Bruce . . . I'd like to offer your old job back.'

Mariam had come into the room and raised her eyebrows.

'Why?'

'Because you're good at it.'

Bruce sighed. 'Well, I appreciate that, but I have to be honest and tell you – I never liked the idea of your mosque and I can't pretend to change my views on it just because there's a job at stake.'

Bilal almost laughed at Bruce's honesty. 'Is that a no, then?'

'I'm just telling you how I feel. But I've always worked hard and that's how I'd continue. You'll have no trouble from me. Or my son,' he added.

'And if the church does get turned into a mosque or multi-faith centre or whatever it's meant to be?' asked Bilal.

'Well, that's the way of the world.'

It wasn't quite what Bilal wanted to hear, but it was a start. 'Then the offer still stands. If you'll take it.'

For a moment Bilal thought Bruce had hung up on him. 'Well, I'm very grateful to you. Yes, I'll take it.'

'Great. Good. Come in on Monday and we'll take it from there.'

'Okay. Thank you.'

Bilal was about to put the phone down when Bruce added: 'Also . . . I'm sorry for all you've been through.'

Bilal breathed a sigh of relief. Why couldn't he have just said that earlier? He finally put the phone down and looked at Mariam.

'Do you want to get Gerald to do his artwork on your door again too?' said Mariam.

Bilal laughed. 'Don't be dramatic. You know it was the right thing to do.'

Mariam smiled. 'Yes, I suppose so.'

'And a multi-faith centre instead of a mosque?' said Bilal. 'I thought you hated being apologetic about anything.'

'If we're going to start seeing compromise as apologetic then we might as well give up now,' she added in her matter-of-fact tone.

He shook his head and put his arms around her waist. At first, Mariam was taken aback, but she liked the feeling of him close to her and it rather surprised her. It made her think: *yes, I am letting go of something. It's finally happening.*

'Get a room, guys,' said Haaris, coming into the room as Mariam and Bilal laughed. Life might be an endless

seam of worries coming apart and gathering themselves
into a knot, but as Khala would say, quoting the Qur'an,
'Allah never burdens a soul beyond that which it can bear.'

chapter thirty-two

SHELLEY WASN'T PRONE TO nerves, but today was different.

The prospect had come to her as if by divine intervention. It was impossible to shake the idea, no matter how hard she'd tried. As promised, a meeting had been set up in The Pig and the Ox to talk about the steps in fighting this A-road disaster. It was a welcome distraction from her now lonely walks.

'We have to pick our battles wisely,' said Shelley, sipping her sherry.

'Damn shame,' replied Copperthwaite. 'But a mosque *is* the lesser of the two evils.'

'Multi-faith centre,' corrected Richard, putting down his pint and joining the group. 'The archdeacon has agreed.'

He explained the new direction the deconsecration of

the church was going to take to an audience of unchanging facial expressions. To most, it seemed one and the same thing.

'So, will there still be calls to prayer?' asked Jenny, James nodding along.

'Dear girl, there never *were* going to be calls to prayer,' said Margaret, quite exasperated.

'Hmph. Multi-faith centre,' said Copperthwaite. 'What're we going to think of next, eh?'

He lifted his red wine as Margaret picked up a peanut from a bowl and threw it at him. Shelley rubbed her fingers together. If the church would no longer be consecrated, then of course her idea made sense.

Mariam and Bilal entered and took their seats as more people gathered. Curt nods ensued, accompanied by a general unease about former ideas and words now that alliances had shifted and a new collective had been formed.

'May I just say . . . ' interjected Mrs Pankhurst, looking grave as she stood up.

Everyone looked at her. Margaret rolled her eyes at Mariam and Bilal.

' . . . I rather like having just the one table,' she added, looking pointedly at her husband, Shelley, Jenny, James and Copperthwaite.

Shelley noticed Anne coming through the doors. She pulled up a seat next to Richard.

'Dad said that if anyone spoke sense at this meeting I should give you all a solid "hear, hear".'

Very soon the awkward nods and addresses were

forgotten by the A-road induced passions: it would change the village for ever. What about the greenery? The extra pedestrian crossings? The noise pollution? Even if they thought it, no-one mentioned the positive things it would mean for the surrounding towns, the jobs it would create and the families it would feed. How could they think of the things that didn't directly affect them?

Everyone's spirits had been roused, but Shelley remained distracted by her idea, which had now practically grown tentacles in her mind. She'd email a plan of action, delegate jobs and arrange another meeting in the next month. A few people left, but most stayed, chatting with one another, basking in the glory of mutual discontent.

'Reverend,' said Shelley, walking over. 'May I have a word?'

He followed her to a table at the back of the room as Shelley looked at him.

'I'd like to do Khala's memorial in the church.'

At first he seemed confused.

'Well, the *multi-faith* centre,' she sighed.

'Oh,' replied Richard.

'Since it's being deconsecrated I thought it'd make sense,' she added.

She wished the reverend wouldn't look at her like that: as if she had *changed*; as if this whole thing made her a *better person*, because Shelley was not in favour of condescension.

'You have a point there, Shelley.'

'Yes, well. I wanted to know when the deconsecration might happen – so I could plan it accordingly.'

'There's no official prayer or ritual required,' he said. 'Let's do it this week.'

Shelley seemed to start at how soon that was, but the world moved at a speed to which she supposed she would have to become accustomed.

❦

Mariam and Bilal sat in the back row. Shelley looked around the church with its stained glass and plaques on the walls, the huge King James bible at the front, the writing in Latin next to it, and she felt a sense of the past slip away.

'We have celebrated the Lord's Supper here and been nurtured by it through our journey in faith,' began Richard, with his litany of thanksgiving. 'From within these walls many have gone out to serve you in the world. As we go now from this house into a further journey of faith.'

The litany was followed by the hymn: 'For the Beauty of the Earth', as Mr and Mrs Pankhurst removed the altar stone, James and Jenny took the host in the tabernacle, while Guppy, along with Harry and others, picked up the statues and sacred vessels. Item by item, the church was emptied of its defining features. Shelley turned around to see Mariam and Bilal's impassive faces, and with the taking away of each item, a new heaviness weighed on her. She was witnessing the loss of something dear and it brought a tear to her usually dry eyes. One look at the reverend told her that for all his liberal airs and graces, he felt the same.

Richard spoke again: 'This building, having been consecrated with the land on which it stands and all objects remaining in it, we now deconsecrate and declare that it is no longer the meeting place of a Christian congregation.' He took a moment as his eyes rested on Bilal. The reverend ended the closing prayer: 'May we be channels at all times of your steadfast love, through the same Jesus Christ, our Lord. Amen.'

Everyone left the building, shaking the reverend's hand, as Shelley heard Margaret say: 'Well, I don't see what the fuss is. First time the church has been used in years!'

⁓

'What do you mean, no alcohol?' exclaimed Copperthwaite.

'If a person's honouring someone,' whispered Shelley, loud enough for Richard to hear, 'then they should at least get the details right.'

They had returned a week later to the church that was now a multi-faith centre in name, if not yet entirely in appearance.

Shelley hadn't been sure whether Copperthwaite would even turn up – but there he was, just like he always had been. She felt a rush of affection for her longstanding friend, who bore everyone's scrutinising looks with a mix of fortitude and humility. He even tried to smile at one or two people – particularly Bilal, though it may have been mistaken for Copperthwaite needing the bathroom. He'd done the right thing and apologised, in his own way. Shelley was grateful to Bilal for accepting it. It occurred to her how much he and Mariam had forgiven just in order to move on. Would she have shown the same grace under the circumstances? Would it have been expected of her?

The church – *multi-faith centre* – (it would take a while before Shelley could say that without letting out an agitated sigh) was again filling with people, an even bigger group, for Khala's memorial. Shelley had ordered halal meat for the patties she made herself. She thought it best not to tell anyone, because she'd heard rather unsavoury things about halal meat, though this was organic and produced by a lovely Muslim couple in Oxford. Oxford was surely a civilised place.

Khala's friends from Birmingham had come, along with the man with a van, who really looked much more charming in a suit. She supposed nothing could be done about the beard. A journalist had asked if she could be present. Shelley wanted to check what the lady's angle would be, whether she'd disrespect her friend's memory, but upon interrogation Shelley was satisfied. The country *should* know about Khala. Haaris was going to video the ceremony and put it up on YouTube – not because they wanted to be exhibitionists, but because it was time the nation saw everyone in the village together. She saw Tom take a seat. He would always be an oppressive presence to her but she would have to let him stay for the memorial. Taking her stand at what used to be the pulpit, Shelley thanked everyone for coming. She cleared her throat and took her notes in her trembling hands.

'I'll keep this brief, rather like Khala's time in Babbel's End. I know she wasn't particularly social, and so many of you won't have met her, but I can tell you that she was a very kind soul indeed.'

Shelley looked around and surprisingly saw nods of assent. Her heart lifted, her hands trembled a little less.

'In the short time I knew her, and even shorter time in which I understood her on account of my poor Punjabi –' a few chuckles came from the crowd – 'she made me realise that it never was too late to change one's life. Her faith in . . . Allah . . . ' It took Shelley some courage to say *Allah*, but she would be resolute. And only three people flinched, which seemed to her rather positive. '. . . was consistent – a virtue which seems to have lost all meaning in modern life.' Many murmurs of agreement. 'She was a woman who had known love with her husband and I pray today that she is reunited with him in the afterlife.'

'Amen,' she heard a few voices say.

'"Now I wear wellies and aronaks," Khala would say,' added Shelley, deciding against mimicking her accent, but not her pronunciation of anoraks. 'In the last six months of her life, Khala had become the person who walked amongst nature, tried to learn English, listened to me and my . . . well, worries – we all have them, don't we? – because I thought she didn't understand, but she did – even with her limited English. She observed people and seemed to just *get* them.' Shelley looked up from her notes, and wished there weren't tears in her eyes, but it couldn't be helped. 'Perhaps language isn't as big a barrier as we think.' Shelley paused to catch the breath that had caught in her throat, pushed down the lump that had formed. 'There are many more things I'd liked to have known about Khala, but I do know that she wrote Urdu poetry. Mariam, would you like to come up and recite one?'

Shelley stepped away as Mariam rested a piece of paper on the lectern:

Apnay des ko chor diya tha
Waqt ka dharra mor diya tha

Ek bhein ke ujhrewe ghar mein
Apni bhi duniya banadia tha

England ka bheegawa Mausam
Apni ankhon se jorra liya tha

Jaisi teri guzri
Apni kismet mein yehi likha tha

Tumhein milay zindagi mein sahara
Mere umeed se khilaywe dil ne, bas yehi kaha tha.

Mariam's voice cracked at one point, but she carried on. Shelley looked at everyone through her blurred vision, some reaching for their tissues, and wondered how many were affected by the poetry and cadence of speech. Were the tears for Khala or for the certainty of loss? Did the older ones, like her, think about the creaking of their knees and see it as another sign of their impending mortality, or did they cry because of the inevitability of change? The younger ones fidgeted and shuffled, not yet realising that their time would also come one day. She hoped and prayed, anyway, that theirs would not be cut short like Teddy's had. Anne rested her head on Tom's shoulder, Bilal held on to Haaris's hand, Bruce sat with his wife, Mr and Mrs Pankhurst sat comfortably next to one another, and Copperthwaite seemed to have ironed out his frown. Arthur never would be by her side, but she knew that if Khala could make a change so late in life, then there was no excuse for Shelley to hold on to consistency as if it were gospel.

She would have to break things before putting them back together. Her marriage was going to be one of them.

Then something quite surprising happened. Margaret got up from the third row because she had a few words to say, and went on to explain the time and effort Khala had put in to sew the shalwar kameez for her.

'And of course I loved it,' said Margaret. 'Who wouldn't!'

Then Mrs Pankhurst got up. Apparently Khala had put her hand on Mrs Pankhurst's arm when she realised that Mr Pankhurst and she were arguing about the mosque and said four simple words: 'It will be okay.'

This was followed by James, who said he lost his beard

in the barn at the Nativity, when Khala turned up and gave it to him. Shelley smiled to herself. Khala really did see everything. And who could forget that they got the church bell back because Khala exchanged her Allah necklace for it. But perhaps most surprising of all was when Tom stood up. Everyone watched as he hobbled up to the lectern with his stick. Shelley stiffened.

If that man spoils today, I will take his walking stick and shall seriously consider putting it in a place where the sun doesn't venture.

'I'm sure you all wish it was my memorial instead,' he said. 'But the good ones always go first. Well, I didn't know Khala very well. Quiet woman. Think I scared her. But she was taking one of her walks when I was walking the dogs and she said to me: "Margaret is very nice woman".'

Shelley looked at Margaret, confused.

'I said, "Well, that's jolly good for her but what am I to do with it?!"' He cleared his throat. 'Don't think she understood me. But you know what that sly, old woman said?' Now Tom fixed his gaze on Margaret. 'She damn well said, "Marry her".'

There followed quite a kerfuffle: outbreaks of whispers and murmurings, people saying things in each other's ears, while Margaret turned a shade of beetroot for the first time in her unashamed life.

'And, I mean, let's not get carried away here,' added Tom. 'But, well, Mags, what do you say? Would you go on a date with a poor man like me?'

Margaret stood up and put her hands on her hips. 'Tom

Lark, I am a hundred-and-fifty-two. Marry me and we can think about that date.'

Tom went red. He'd remembered the note his wife had left him, still in his drawer, and decided he'd finally throw that letter in the fire. It was long overdue.

'Yes, yes, all right, but you'll have to get rid of those bloody begonias. Can't stand the things.'

The room burst into applause as Tom made his way to sit next to Margaret and they both looked ahead as if they hadn't just bound themselves to one another for the rest of their days. However short they might be.

'And on that note,' said Shelley, feeling somewhat perplexed by it all, 'please feel free to take some non-alcoholic drinks and refreshments. Khala's friends were very kind to bring traditional Pakistani food, so do try some, although you stay away from them, Copsy – you can't handle spices.'

The crowd broke out, gathering in groups and taking their food and drink out into the cold winter air. It was an unaccountably sunny day, the chirping of birds filling the air.

'There are troubles ahead,' said Shelley as she and Bilal walked out of the centre.

The truth was Shelley knew – today it was the A-road, tomorrow it would be something else, and she might not have the power to stop it. May not even be around to stop it. (Who knew how long we were all of this earth?) Whatever *it* might be.

'I know,' replied Bilal.

She looked at him, his downcast face, hands in his pocket, before he turned to her. 'It was very moving.'

'I didn't understand a word of the poem. But for some inexplicable reason, yes. It was.'

Shelley realised that it was so often what she wished to do: to move people. Perhaps she had gone about it the wrong way. Although she was never any good at poetry, so she'd have to consider her options.

'I meant the memorial,' Bilal said.

'Oh, well. That's quite okay. She'll be missed,' she added. They stopped under a big oak tree, the sun filtering through the bare branches.

Just then Tom came charging towards them. 'Those damned people.' He was waving a piece of paper that Margaret had handed to him. It was a letter being sent to residents informing them of the construction plans.

Shelley took it from him and read it. So, it had begun. 'Well,' she said. 'This isn't the time. Not today.'

He looked wildly between Bilal and Shelley. 'When will be the time?'

'Tomorrow,' said Shelley. 'We start again.'

Tom grunted.

'Mariam will start a social media campaign,' said Bilal.

'Very good idea. Haaris said something about clogging?' suggested Shelley.

'Vlogging,' corrected Bilal.

'Ah, there's Richard. Reverend!' Shelley called out.

He turned around. Standing opposite him, hidden from view until then, was Anne. She was smiling.

'How do you feel about . . . what was it?'

'Vlogging.'

'Yes, *vlogging*,' Shelley asked a confused-looking Richard. 'Preoccupied, I see,' she added, raising her eyebrows.

'Haaris wants to go to Sam's,' said Mariam, sidling up next to Bilal. 'Harry offered to drop him home afterwards.'

'You know I've always thought that boy is trouble,' said Shelley. 'Now, we'll need money for all these campaigns, and of course to properly convert the church,' she added.

'I'm going to use the money from the sale of Mum's house,' said Bilal. 'I'm giving your donation back, Tom. Especially now, since you're going to have to pay for a wedding,' he added with a smile.

Tom frowned as Shelley took a bite of a samosa and instantly wished she hadn't.

'What if it doesn't work? What if the building *is* destroyed?' She knew how these things often went; a few people couldn't change things really. Not in any significant way.

'We'll start a crowdfund to keep the fat cats out,' said Bilal. 'Anything we can do, we'll do it. There has to be some benefit to becoming a famous village.'

Tom slapped Bilal's back. 'That's the ticket. Crowdfunding. You're brighter than you look.'

'We'd better get back home,' said Mariam. 'Let me just say bye to Anne.'

Tom was already striding towards Richard and Anne, calling the reverend a sly old bastard who should leave his daughter alone. Shelley shook her head.

'Things will still change,' said Shelley. 'No matter what we do.'

'Yes,' said Bilal. 'They never do stay the same.'

Everyone's voices quietened then as the church bell tolled, each person taking a moment to appreciate what they had today.

Shelley sighed and smiled. 'Well, if I've at least done one good thing in my life, it's trimming Tom's unsightly bush.'

⟋⟍

Bilal got home and went out into the garden. He stared at the grave. How much had his mum understood when she'd asked him to build that mosque? Surely she'd have anticipated the breakdown that had ensued. Or perhaps she understood that doing things as you have always done them isn't living; that to live is to change, however hard it might be. Bilal smiled and said a prayer for her. He made a promise to speak more Punjabi in the house. To hold on to things as long as you can before they vanish and become myths. Muttering the opening lines from Khala's poem, he took a fistful of cold, damp earth and scattered it in the grave. Mariam came out and grabbed another shovel.

'I thought you could do with some help,' she said.

After a few minutes they heard the familiar sound of Margaret's quad bike, her faint voice getting closer. 'Now, before you do all that, tell me. How does this look?'

She came into view, wearing a fleece over the shalwar kameez that Khala had made her, farm boots on her feet, pearls still dangling around her neck.

'Perfect for my wedding, no?'

Bilal and Mariam paused.

'Do I look monstrous?' asked Margaret.

'No,' Mariam exclaimed. 'I mean, you'll need other shoes.'

Margaret looked at her feet, as if this was an unfortunate but necessary notion.

'I do like the pearls though,' added Mariam.

'Yes, they . . . go very well,' was all Bilal could manage.

'Excellent,' replied Margaret. 'Don't know how Tom will feel about it, but what does that grumpy old fool know?' With which Margaret drove back to where she'd come from.

'Bloody hell,' said Mariam. 'I kind of wish your mum and Khala could see Margaret wear that on her wedding.'

They both laughed.

'Plenty of other people will,' he replied.

'Yes,' said Mariam. 'I suppose that's something.' She looked at him and added: 'You do know that includes me, don't you? I plan to be there on the wedding day. With you. And, you know, all the days after that. I hope.'

Bilal kissed Mariam on the lips without feeling a flicker of doubt. They both picked up their shovels. This time, neither of them stopped until the ground was even. It would take a while and some care, but once the grass grew over it, the patch would blend with the rest of the garden, as if it had always been that way.

ACKNOWLEDGEMENTS

Thank you to my brilliant agent, Nelle Andrew, for your guidance, unerring support and confidence in this book. I am bloody lucky to have you on my side. To my wonderful editor, Eleanor Dryden; your belief (in me) and excitement about this book made writing it a little less of a pain in the arse. I almost feel ashamed for taking all the credit when the book is what it is because of you. I owe you a title too. Thank you to Sarah Bauer for your meticulous desk-editing, my copyeditor Genevieve Pegg, proof-reader Natalie Braine, marketing whizz Sahina Bibi, publicist Clare Kelly, Katie Lumsden, and everyone at Bonnier. I am eternally grateful for your confidence and everything you've done to make a home for my books. I don't think an author could ask for more.

Thanks to Helen Bryant for being my chauffeur in Dorset, arranging my accommodation, brainstorming plot and character, and always being there for an emergency Skype. And to Mace Bryant for keeping me company when Helen couldn't. You are both wonderful. Alex Hammond, thank you for keeping the screenwriting dream alive, and for the genius idea of the construction threatening the church. Thank you to Anthony and Harriet Sykes for the most incredible month staying in the west wing of Bellamont House. My time in Dorset wouldn't have been the same without your warmth and kindness. And, of course, thank you for Anthony's excellent idea of converting a church into a mosque. I think that plot twist made this novel. (Come to think of it, I owe both major plot twists to other people, which tells you something about my imagination). Thank you to Gwen Kinghorn for speaking to me about being a member of the parish council and bringing me lamb chops; to Reverend Sue Lingford for talking to me at length about the life of a parish vicar; John Thorpe for welcoming me to Sunninghill Preparatory School, taking me to a fisherman's meeting and forgiving me for calling him Julian at least eleven times; and thank you to Litton Cheney parish council for letting me sit in on their meeting, giving me a glimpse into village life.

Thank you to Shaista Chishty for making that first week in Dorset (and my life) so romantic, and between your nikaab, my hat, your hair and my hijab, helping to confuse the maintenance man into thinking there were four of us living in the west wing. There's no one else I'd rather be chased by sheep with. Thank you, Nafeesa Yousuf, for being the constant (and, quite frankly, impossibly fast) reader. You helped lift my doubts with every real-time WhatsApp message. Clara Nelson, thank you for always putting things into perspective, being on hotline, and for giving me a god-daughter. I also couldn't quite get through life without Sadaf Sethi, *the* most interfering and brilliant friend. I wouldn't have it any other way. Jas Kundi, I always have and always will be thankful to and for you. Kristel Pous and Amber Ahmed, you have both provided shelter when I've needed it most – thank you for giving me supplementary homes.

I was determined not to make any new friends in my 30s but then Remona Aly and Onjali Rauf wormed their way into my life; the most formidable duo I know – one day my work ethic might improve because of you two. (Also, thanks for the chicken that travelled from East London to Dorset.) Ailah Ahmed, I never walk past an alleyway without thinking of you. Thank you for all the wisdom, inevitable laughter and romantic days out. And thank you to Sameer Sheikh, whose pessimism brings out the optimist in me.

A writer's life wouldn't be the same without a group to share the ups and downs with – and it's usually more down than up. So, thank you to Vaseem Khan, Abir Mukherjee, Imran Mahmood, Alex Khan and Amit Dhand for filling each and every day with (top ten); bakwaas, unstinting advice and support, a healthy dose of tough love, some therapy (usually needed after the tough love), reality checks peppered with bouts of unreasonable optimism, Bitmojis and Gifs, but most importantly, ladoos. I am most grateful for the belief in ladoos. (Next ones are on Alex.) A special thanks to Abir and Vaseem for getting roped into reading early proofs. Caroline O'Donoghue – fellow cultural antagonist – thank you also for that early read and your flurry of positivity. You only cement my idea that the Irish are great craic. Thank you also to Sarah Shaffi who's been a beacon of positivity about the book. And thanks to Nikesh Shukla.

To the entire Zaffre writing gang, thank you for always being on hand when needed, especially Rebecca Thornton without whom random writerly rants just wouldn't be the same.

Thank you to my khala, Tahseen Sadiq, for listening to me go on about the book in order to write the Urdu poem for me. I am also forever thankful for my niece and nephew, Zayyan and Saffah Adam, who test the limits of my patience and yet somehow manage to surpass the limits of joy. And of course, thank you to my mum and my sister – the women who have raised me and without whom I might have been very thin, but not nearly as blessed. Everything I know about grit and tenacity began with you.

I also want to thank readers around the world who support authors by buying, reviewing, shouting (positive things) about the books we write. It keeps us going.

Finally, thanks to God for each and every one of the above. They are a testament to the fact that it takes a village to raise a writer.

TRANSLATION OF PAGE 439

I left my country
And shifted the direction of time

In the crumbling of my sister's home
I stitched together a world of my own

I fixed my gaze
On the English rain

However your life passed
My kismet was much the same

That you find something of which you wish to be a part
Is the flowering hope of my heart.

QUESTIONS FOR YOUR READING GROUP

1. What do you think are the main themes of this novel?

2. Who was your favourite character and why?

3. At what point in the novel did you most sympathise with Bilal?

4. How do you see Bilal – hapless hero or man of action?

5. Khala Rukhsana thinks that 'home must be where you feel most alive'. How is the concept of home explored in this novel?

6. Do you think Mariam is always in love with Bilal but takes a while to realise it, or do you think she falls in love with him over the course of the book? In what way does the idea of 'letting go' underpin the novel?

7. Bilal's sense of national and cultural identity differs from his mother's. How does your sense of identity differ from your parents'?

8. Bilal's grief for his mother and Anne's for her son are both explored in this novel. In what different ways does grief – or loss – affect all the characters' actions?

9. Rukhsana and Shelley share a strong friendship, even though they struggle to understand one another. In what

ways do the friendships in this novel bridge divides and transcend difference?

10. What can the friendship between Bilal and Richard tell us about faith?

11. Can you truly be friends with someone wholly different to you?

12. Why do you think Gerald and Dan act up in the way they do?

13. Shelley declares 'A place is it people'. In what ways is Babbel's End defined by its inhabitants? How is your local community defined by the people who live there?

14. How representative do you think Babbel's End is of the UK as a whole? How do you feel this story would be different if it took place in a large town or city instead of a village?

15. How do you think you would act if you were in Bilal's situation? What about if you were in Shelley's?

16. At the end of the novel, Bilal realises that 'to live is to change, however hard it might be'. How do you think the characters change over the course of this novel?